HEIST of the OLYMPIANS

A novel

A. Young-Irving

WisdomWing Books

ISBN: 979-8-9897184-0-5 (Paperback)

ISBN: 979-8-9897184-1-2 (E-book)

Library of Congress Registration Number: TXu-2-396-516

Book Cover design by A. Young-Irving

Illustrations by Canva Pro

Back cover profile photo by Helette van Rensburg, Gqeberha, South Africa

First edition 2024

Published by WisdomWing Books

https://www.ayoungirvingauthor.com/

"What men or gods are these? What maidens loth?
What mad pursuit? What struggle to escape?"

Ode on a Grecian Urn, by John Keats

PROLOGUE

E ven the brightest Californian day can play host to the darkest of plans—the kind that starts with a shiver of soil, a whispered promise of an earthquake brooding underfoot. An imperceptible quiver that nudges a blade of grass, forcing it to bend in blind allegiance and disturb the Monarch butterfly clinging to it. Such was the domino effect set into motion when Shivonne O'Roydon left the cool reprieve of the Pallas Museum cafeteria and stepped into the sun-drenched botanical gardens outside.

She made her way along the winding stone path to the crystalline pond teeming with pale-pink lotus lilies straining up out of the water on graceful, long ballerina necks. On any other day, she was like one of those lilies, struggling to keep her slender neck above the fray while rooted to the bottom of life's murky waters.

But not today. Today had been a *good* day.

She took a large bite from the glossy red apple clutched in her hand. They were waiting for her on the manicured lawn in a semicircle, her best friends and confidantes. Bookish museum educators to the world, but the world to her. Angel had her shoes off, her feet resting in Luke's lap. Lorelei sat like a sphinx; her face angled to the sun. They exuded the serenity of a famous pointillist painting: George Seurat's bathers at leisure on *La Grande Jatte*, an intricate map of individual dots that formed a luminous whole when viewed from afar. A quilt of false serenity, she knew, each spiderweb-thin patch of human quandary stitched together with thin, dissolvable threads of hope and resilience.

When Shivonne approached, graceful and silent as a lynx on the pads of her dancer's feet, their heads turned in unison—like satellites—as if they had sensed her presence even before they saw her.

1

"Hi, everyone," she said and sat down, her long legs crossed at the ankles. The smell of freshly cut grass and early-summer blooms swirled around them; a gaggle of ducks were quarreling at the edge of the pond. Yet, overhead, an invisible dark cloud was hovering, threatening an epic storm. Shivonne sensed its electrical current buzzing through her bones ... and shivered.

"Olympians, I called you here today," Angel started, bypassing any pleasantries. Luke snorted a giggle at the preposterous suggestion of the four of them as Olympian gods. But Angel cut him off with one of her steely glares. "I called you here today," she repeated, "to propose something that will shock you at first ..." She waited for their chins to lift, for their eyebrows to drop again. "Hear me out and consider all the facts before interrupting. Okay?"

They regarded each other, then nodded.

Angel pulled her feet in from Luke's lap and curled them under her, rotating her head, owl-like, to scan the perimeter. There were no cameras or security guards outside, just a scattering of visitors milling about and an elderly couple strolling hand in hand by the lily pond. On the far end of the lawn, a young couple was passionately kissing on a picnic blanket.

"Do you remember the discussion we had last Sunday evening after the book group?" Angel asked in a barely audible whisper.

"About art crime, you mean?" Luke asked loudly, plucking a blade of grass and pinching it between his lips, utterly oblivious to the aura of secrecy permeating their circle. When Angel cast him another death stare, he cringed and mouthed, '*Sorry.*'

"Yes, and how uncomplicated it seemed to steal art from a museum," she said.

Luke nodded, still blissfully unaware of the low growl of tension building in the ether around them. Shivonne, however, felt its familiar, icy grip creeping up her spine. She took a tentative bite of her apple, her eyes locked on Angel.

"Um, okay ...?" Lorelei furrowed her brow. The most intuitive of the group, she was the first to sense impending doom.

Angel inhaled deeply and the ducks at the pond abruptly fell silent, as if on cue. A stillness settled around them as if the Fates had held their hands aloft—nature's spiteful conductors—to pause the earth's rotation for a second.

"I have a plan for our team of Olympians ... to make things right," she said, letting the words sink in.

A team. Of mere mortals with Greek-hero alter egos. *A plan.*

The others shifted uncomfortably on the grass; the earth seemed to wobble on its axis, its tempo off. Something was amiss. The Monarch butterfly nearby fluttered its wings—once, twice, three times—triggering a storm of epic proportions, thousands of miles away. At the pond, even the ducks resumed their high-pitched squabble. They, too, had sensed the shift in the atmosphere.

A single drop of apple juice teased its way down Shivonne's bottom lip and hung there in suspense, teasing gravity, before it slipped from her chin just as Angel dropped her bombshell:

"We are going to steal a painting from the museum."

PART ONE

THE OLYMPIANS

CHAPTER 1

THE SECURITY GUARD'S SECRET

To wo weeks earlier ...

"Remember, every painting tells a story."

One could hear a pin drop in the hallowed inner sanctum of the Rococo gallery. Even the oil-painted ladies of So-and-So and the pompous lords of Such-and-Such gazed down from their gilt-framed perches against the damask walls to eavesdrop on the group of first-grade students seated, crisscross-apple-sauce, on the parquet floor.

Angel Hendridge's task as a docent was to engage students, whether it be wide-eyed kindergartners or zoned-out high school seniors, in meaningful conversations about—and *with*—art. If she could coax a single "Wow!" out of an excitable elementary student or a simple, non-committal "Cool" out of a teenager, she considered it a successful day.

"See ... think ... and wonder, everyone," she reminded the group of the three core principles of critical viewing. They had arrived an hour earlier at the Pallas Museum—an acronym for the Palladium of Art and Literature, Los Angeles Society. The six-year-old, private museum perched like Mount Olympus, home of the mythical Greek gods, on a knoll nestled between the desiccated breasts of the Hollywood Hills not far from where the iconic Hollywood sign cast its shadow and the Pacific Ocean glimmered seductively behind a cloud of fog in the distance.

Inside the gallery, the school group's raccoon-eyed teacher stifled a yawn with her fist, unaware that she was in the presence of greatness. In the opposite corner, the security guard on duty, Walter Friedlander, rocked forward on his ortho-pedic sneakers, his hands clasped behind his back. When he sensed her eyes on him, he looked up and winked at Angel. They shared a casual friendship at the museum; he reminded her of her father, a retired history professor, with his silver hair, wire-rimmed glasses, and old-school chivalry. He often held a door open for her when she had her arms full, trailed by a group of youngsters, or practiced a few lines with her in his native German when they passed in the hallways.

Angel smiled at Walter and turned her attention back to the six- and seven-year-olds, still young enough to be dazzled by classical art's fairy-tale splendor. Earlier, they had posed like Neoclassical marble sculptures and anthropomorphized a Rococo chair, imagining it to be a character from *Beauty and the Beast*—an octogenarian grande dame who spoke with a posh French accent and waddled with a bow-legged gait.

Now, they were engrossed in an 18th-century oil painting, *Still Life with Silver Teapot and Narcissus,* one of the dozens of exquisite art objects that a conglomerate of international museums and private collectors loaned to the neophyte Pallas Museum for their curated exhibition, *European Masters of the 17th to 19th Centuries.*

The still life featured a spectacular silver Empire teapot as its focal point, its spout curved into an elegant 'S' with a swan's head at the tip, and its ebony handle strangled with filigreed silver feathers at the base. Next to it, on a re-flective silver tray, five powder-blue porcelain teacups stood on their saucers, each with a petite silver spoon balanced on the rim. The sixth teacup—an outlier—was lying on its side, ear-up, a remnant of golden liquid spilling over the lip and pooling onto the pristine silver tray. Its spoon lay belly-up in the wet spot, reflecting light from a mullion-paneled window somewhere to the painter's left. Right of center, a long-necked crystal vase proffered a single white Narcissus flower, drooping down to regard its reflection in the mirrored surface below. It symbolized the myth of the beautiful mortal, Narcissus, who had fallen in love with his reflection in a pool of water ... and drowned because of it. A beautiful life spilled like tea.

"Okay, everyone," Angel interrupted their quiet observation while fanning herself with her button-down shirt flap—menopause was a bitch. "What does this painting make you wonder about?"

Provide the spark, fan the flames, and stand back to watch the fire grow.

The students' bombardment of questions would have given the stodgy, oil-painted portrait subjects whiplash had they been alive:

"Why does the teapot look like a bird?"

"What kinda flower is that, miss? Is it broken?"

Angel answered and elaborated, delighting in *their* delight.

"I wonder what the tea tastes like?" an apple-cheeked cutie pondered.

Yes! Angel thought. *Engage all five senses in the galleries.*

"Shall we have a tea party and find out?" she asked in her best high-brow British accent. The first graders bounced with excitement. "Let's pretend we can reach into this painting and pick up one of the teacups."

Miming, she pinched the ear of an invisible "teacup," her little finger flexed outward as it would when noble continental ladies with fascinators and elbow gloves met for High Tea. The little ones copied her, cross-eyed with little tongues protruding. A boy in a Darth Vader T-shirt thrust his hand forward, the fingers clenched into a vice-like claw around his imaginary cup as if it were a pewter tankard. Angel imagined the delicate porcelain shattering between his clumsy moppet fingers.

"Perfect," she praised. "Who wants to share what their tea smells or tastes like?"

A dozen tiny hands shot up and when she pointed to one, the others dropped with audible disappointment into little laps. A few die-hards kept waving as if drowning; *Pick me, pick me!* they beamed with their eyes. Angel understood their craving for validation; she struggled with it, too. An acute fear of becoming invisible, like the teacup in her hand—a woman of a certain age, no longer valued by society, no longer relevant to her grown children, and no longer desired by her husband. At the museum, at least, she was appreciated. *Seen. Wondered about.*

She turned to the chosen student, squinting to read her name from the label stuck upside-down on her T-shirt. "What does your tea taste like, Poppy?"

9

Poppy extracted her pointer finger from her nostril. "My mommy is from London, Ing-ga-land, and they drink lots of tea. I don't like tea, yuck! Gampy doesn't either—Gampy says it tastes like hoss piss."

A volley of giggles ensued; the dispassionate teacher lifted her nose from her phone screen just long enough to register the mirth. She had expressed no interest so far other than a brief yelp of excitement when she and *Ponyboy69* had both swiped right on each other's Tinder profiles.

"Thank you for sharing, Poppy," Angel said, suppressing laughter lest she spill a little golden liquid of her own.

From the mouths of babes.

She would bank it for later, to sip from like an urban vampire taking swigs of banked O-positive from a PVC bag. To feed upon happiness in moments of black-dog darkness.

"Anyone else?" she asked.

"Mine is Early-Grey," another student volunteered. A few class clowns declared theirs to be 'hoss piss.' She did not mind the pivot; they would *not* forget the painting. Of that, she was sure.

With a deep sniff, Angel dipped her nose to her own "cup," "Mmm, my tea is Chamomi—"

But just then, a swoosh of sharp motion shattered the blissful moment and trapped her breath in her throat. Her scalp tingled and the four-inch-wide skunk strip that swooped back over her honey-brown hair spiked up like the fur of a threatened cat. Peripheral movement never failed to startle her, ever since the night in Memphis—the incident that had caused a swath of her hair to turn snow white, overnight.

Ergo, in the Rococo gallery, instead of calming chamomile tea, Angelique Hendridge smelled the pungent stench of fear mixed with fetid body odor and barbecue grease.

While seventeen youngsters were engrossed in their dip-and-sniff with flexed pinky fingers and pursed lips, she turned to confront the trigger, her hand over her heart to steady its gallop, relieved to find that it was just her favorite security guard, Walter. He was standing so still—like a marble statue—she had forgotten he was there until he moved his hand in a sharp upward arc. .

Like the swoosh of a knife stab.

Oblivious that he was being watched, Walter's hand was suspended mid-air, his little finger flexed, his nose dipped over an invisible teacup in his wrinkled right hand; the left one flattened into a pretend saucer underneath. His eyes were locked on the painted tea set. She would have thought it endearing had it not been for the single tear dribbling down the old man's cheek.

Goosebumps skittered across her arms; never had she witnessed such raw emotion in front of the painting. Angel Hendridge knew distress when she saw it, and she *never* walked away from it. It was a promise she had made to herself years earlier, in that dark alley in Memphis with the putrid stink of grease traps in her nose.

She rushed through the rest of the tea party before finger-snapping the teacher from her dating apps to conclude the lesson, her mind consumed by the security guard.

"Miss," a little girl lisped right before she herded them through the doorway of the gallery stacked with still lifes and austere oil portraits, "do you live here?"

"No, pumpkin, *these* people live here," she said, sweeping her arm across the gallery walls. The oil portraits stared out at them as if from framed windows of an exclusive apartment complex, among them stern old men draped in billowing, crimson-red cardinal cloaks clutching scholarly tomes and distinguished dames with powdered wigs and the ashen-faced countenance of long-dead ghosts. It would be her worst nightmare to walk these hallowed, haunted hallways late at night with the gilt frames glowing mysteriously in the dim light, and the yellowed portrait eyes moving, tracking her ... waiting for a chance to pounce. "I wonder if they have tea parties, too, when the museum is closed at night," she said with a shiver and a wink.

A hush fell over the first graders; bar none, their heads swiveled back to check whether ghostly eyes were following as they tiptoed past.

Ghosts at the museum.

"Wow," a timid voice gushed.

"Cool," a braver one announced.

Bingo, Angel thought. There they were: those two magic words that thrilled any educator of art or otherwise.

After dropping them at their rendezvous point, she rushed back to the Rococo gallery, her loafers squeaking on the polished floors. The gallery was deserted, except for Walter and the echoes of phantom giggles and exaggerated tea-slurping from moments earlier. His hands were clutched behind his back again, his eyes downcast.

"Walter, hi."

It startled him; a prolonged shiver ran through his body, like the tremors of an old dog running in its dreams. Upon seeing her, he relaxed, his eyes crinkling at the corners. "*Guten Tag*, Angel. Your lesson today, with the children ..." he clutched his heart, "I have never seen anyone else do that." He pronounced his "th"-sounds with a fricative accent: "*ze* children ... do *zat* ..."

A shadow tumbled across one wall as if the sun was dipping down for its lunchtime siesta. As it passed over Walter's face, Angel noticed a glint of moisture in his eyes, but he wiped them with the back of his hand and when she looked again, they were dry.

"Walter, I couldn't help noticing earlier," she probed gently, "when we were drinking our tea ..."

"You saw that?" He wrestled his hands together in line with his chest, "*Es tut mir leid.*"

"No need to apologize," she assured him. "Did something upset you during my lesson? These beautiful art objects evoke so much emotion sometimes."

He ran his fingers through his silver hair; her father did that, too, when he was deep in thought. Or anguished.

"*Nein*, not upset, just a little sad. Because this painting ..." He gestured toward it, a lump bobbing up and down in his throat.

She glanced at the gorgeous tea set, as if expecting the painting itself to reveal the answer. It looked as cheery as before, evoking happy sighs and the tinkle of tiny spoons against porcelain. "You can tell me anything, Walter," she offered with a light touch to his arm. "Anything."

He nodded. Patted her hand. Cleared his throat. Patted her hand again. "You see," he finally said, "this painting should be mine."

"I understand," she nodded, "sometimes, we all feel a familiarity—"

"*Nein, nein,* you don't understand ..." He gazed up at the skylight. "My grand-parents were from a prominent Jewish family in Germany, right before World War II." He clenched and unclenched his fists. "Opa was a celebrated clockmaker and jeweler with prominent clientele. He also collected art over his lifetime—a small, but valuable collection ... including *dieses hier.*"

She cocked her head.

"*This* one," he repeated, pointing to the *Still Life with Silver Teapot and Narcissus* in front of them. "It used to hang over the fireplace in their salon. It was my Oma's favorite painting; my father told me she would sit in front of it and do her needlepoint by the fire."

"I don't understand ..." Baffled, Angel stared at the large painting against the gallery wall. It was a newly discovered masterpiece from a famous Swiss painter known for his photo-real technique, and worth a small fortune.

"I show you ..." Walter pulled a tattered leather wallet from his rear pock-et and withdrew two items. He handed her the first: a vintage, monochrome photo, yellowed and scalloped by time. A family portrait featuring a dapper, middle-aged gentleman with an impressive Kaiser Wilhelm II mustache, dressed in a three-piece suit with an ornate gold pocket-watch dangling from a slit in his waistcoat. Next to him stood a striking woman, her dark hair forming a braided halo around her head, a floral-print dress buttoned up to her throat. Each had one hand on the shoulder of an adolescent boy wedged between them, his eyes piercing the camera—and the decades since—straight into Angel's soul.

"My father, Franck, before the war," Walter said, stroking the face of the boy. Behind the family, above the mantlepiece of an imposing stone fireplace, hung their prized painting—the same one on display in the Rococo gallery of the Pallas Museum.

"How—?" Angel asked. She leaned forward to read the tombstone plaque next to the painting on the wall in front of them: *"On loan to the Pallas Museum by the Trust of the Count and Countess Wolfgang Otto von Sturm-und-Salzenbruck,"* it read. There was no mention of the Friedlander family anywhere on the provenance label, only that it was "lost" during the war and bought at an "undisclosed sale"—glaring red flags.

Walter harrumphed. She sensed a tragic story unfolding even before he confirmed her suspicion. "This painting ... and everything else, was stolen from my grandparents by the Nazis during the Holocaust." His face contorted around the despised words.

"Oh, Walter," she cringed, "I had no idea."

"My grandparents planned to escape right after the destruction of Opa's atelier on November 9, 1938—*Kristallnacht*. Remember?"

Angel nodded. Her father had told his wide-eyed young daughter many heart-wrenching stories of the Night of the Broken Glass.

"Opa had contacts in Switzerland and Holland; his clocks and pocket watches were sought-after there, even by the royal House of Orange. Shortly after the pogrom, when the Nazis started rounding up Jewish men, they sent my fifteen-year-old father to live with a distant cousin on Lake Como in Italy, *Gott sei dank*. They were planning to follow, but they needed money first, so they waited," he took a belabored breath, "too long."

Her heart was racing. "Please, go on."

"One of Göring's art buyers made a 'deal' with Opa," he continued, making air quotation marks around the word "deal," to signal its laughable lack of legitimacy, "to purchase a few pieces of art. Opa thought he was buying their ticket to freedom, but it was a lie, *natürlich*. The Krauts took everything: paintings, furniture, silverware, and, of course, the clocks and jewelry. And then they took my grandparents, too ... on a cattle train, like animals. Oma died of typhus at Ravensbrück women's camp, ten months later. Opa was sent to Auschwitz, where he—" His hands grappled at his throat. "You know."

"Oh, Walter ..." she said, hanging her head, "I'm so sorry." When he gently lifted her chin, his hand smelled faintly of tobacco, with a hint of musky cologne. "Is there a way to fight? To get it back as the legal descendant?" she asked.

"I tried," he said with a shrug. "I have the photo, Opa's ledgers, even Nazi inventory cards—they were obsessive record keepers."

"So, you have a strong case, then?" Angel asked.

"You would think, no? But it is too expensive and time-consuming. The lawyers, *die Bürokratie* ... how do you Americans say? Red tape. My son, Jean-François, helped me get a few items restituted over the years," he said, "mostly furniture, ancestor portraits, a few of Oma's silver candelabra ... They are at Jean's country house in France. We only located this painting recently, by chance."

"How?" she asked. "Where?" Spoliated art had a way of disappearing into thin air.

Walter unfolded the second piece of paper he had pulled from his wallet and handed it to her. It was a newspaper clipping of a wedding announcement from the June 2022 society pages of *Le Monde Parisien*. A photograph of an older couple posing with the bride and groom. The father of the bride's barrel belly strained at the buttons of his tuxedo; his scrawny wife was draped in mink with a choker of grape-sized pearls around her neck. They were posing in front of a dining table set with crystal chandeliers, sparkling stemware, and the requisite stuffed piglet on an ornate, silver platter—an apple shoved into its crisped snout.

Angel translated the French caption below the photograph: "The Count and Countess Wolfgang Otto von Sturm-und-Salzenbruck played host this weekend to the Parisian elite at the wedding reception of their daughter, Gisela, to Monegasque race-car driver, Pierre-Henri LeSallet." She turned to Walter, "I'm not sure I understand ..."

"Look behind the people," he said.

She scrutinized the clipping again and then she saw it, on one of the molded-panel walls behind the table, amid a cluster of still lifes depicting flowers and a variety of *nature morte*—Walter's grandmother's beloved painting.

"Oh."

"It was pure luck that Jean-François saw it in the newspaper that day. We made inquiries. The count's lawyer told my lawyer he had inherited it from his father, who had bought it from a 'private dealer' after the war. But they cannot show clean provenance. He's a billionaire salt baron from an old Austrian family. With a team of Rottweiler lawyers." He pronounced the formidable dog breed in a heavy German accent with his lips drawn back, his teeth exposed.

"This is devastating. And now the painting is here …"

"*Ja*, a strategic move on the count's part. I overheard a curator saying that an exhibition greatly increases an object's value and authenticates it for future sale." Walter smiled, but his eyes did not crinkle. "But the painting is not the only thing the count has that belonged to my Opa," he said, pointing to the photo. "Look."

See. Think. And wonder.

Peeking out from under the count's impeccable tuxedo jacket was a gold *cartouche*-case pocket watch suspended from a thick gold chain that looped through a buttonhole and ended in a ruby-encrusted T-bar—the same one worn by Walter's grandfather decades earlier, in the faded photograph.

"What's that?" she asked, tilting the photo to inspect something dangling from the loop of the watch chain.

"It's a miniature enamel monkey," Walter said, beaming. "It was Opa's signature—adding a menagerie of tiny figurines to his clocks and pocket watches. The monkey moves up and down the gold chain. My father remembered playing with it as a child on Opa Joachim's lap. But now," he gestured to the much more recent newspaper clipping, "the count has Opa's pocket watch as well."

"This is not right, Walter," Angel huffed, handing him the newspaper cutting. "Is there anything I can do to help you get it back? I'm an excellent researcher." She did not tell him she was applying for a position on the FBI's Art Crime unit; it was too premature to announce.

He shrugged with his palms turned up. For a moment, he resembled the polychromed sculpture of a Renaissance saint in the museum's East wing: eyes heaven-cast, palms supplicated. The weight of it all was written in the concertina folds of his brow.

"Sadly, we are no match for the Rottweilers. I'm just a retired German teacher who works as a museum guard. I'm not young anymore," he said, "and I don't want to be angry the rest of my life." His hands lifted like a boxer's before dropping again, dejected. "For now, I'm happy here."

Angel had often wondered why an older man with questionable health would choose a job that kept him on his feet for hours. Now she knew.

"You work at the Pallas so you can be close to your family's painting."

16

"*Genau*. I pretend it belongs to me," he winked. "I stand here," he gestured to the spot of parquet at his feet, drawing a tight pie wedge with his hands, his back pressed into the corner, "because it is the only place where the camera cannot see me cry."

Angel looked up at the conspicuous security camera propped above their heads and then back at Walter—a man literally and figuratively squeezed into a corner by the injustice of a system *still* persecuting his family, almost eighty years later. Another hot flush crept up her neck. This time, it was not hormonal; it was pure anger. She could never look at the oil painting the same way again.

Every painting tells a story.

If this one could talk, oh, the tales it would tell—of being ripped off a wall, loaded by rough hands onto dirty open-bed trucks, driven across bumpy roads with artillery fire zooming overhead, and propped in an underground salt mine alongside thousands of other spoliated pieces, wrapped in oilcloth. Plundered, hidden, transported, sold, and hidden again. Across oceans; across time.

"It's a secret, though," Walter said, looking into her eyes. "The museum cannot know about it; they will think me crazy ... fire me."

"Of course, Walter. I don't want that," she said, dejected.

Walter smiled, dropped his hand to his chest, resting it there for a while as if soothing a burn underneath, then fiddled with something pinned under his navy uniform blazer. When he extended his hand to her, it held a miniature, oval canvas: a tiny replica of the Narcissus flower drooping down from its cut-crystal vase to gaze at its reflection. Attached to the back was an antique brooch pin with the initials 'JFF,' written in calligraphy.

"Exquisite," she declared.

"My son, Jean-François, is an artist like his namesake great-grandfather, Joachim-Franck. He owns an art restoration atelier in Paris," Walter said. "He painted this for me as a reminder of our heritage. Now I want *you* to have it."

Shaking her head, she took a step back. "Walter, I can't."

"*Bitte,*" he insisted, "I have carried this burden alone for so long ... until you showed me compassion. Now my secret is yours, too."

She hesitated, then—understanding the gravity of the gesture—cupped her hand and allowed him to place the sentimental treasure in her palm.

"*Das freut mich,*" he said, folding her fingers around its curves.

"*Danke schön.*" She hugged him and bent down to fasten the pin on the outside of her docent bag, near where the leather handles attached to the canvas. "I will always carry it with me. At the museum," she promised, "and here." Her hand over her heart.

As if summoned by Walter's solace, the sunlight reappeared through the louvered skylight, casting a jagged pattern on the parquetry at their feet.

"Will you join us for a cup of tea next time and tell the students your story?" she asked. The kids, especially teens who possessed the power of critical thinking, could benefit from a personal history lesson about the Holocaust and the ricochet effect of a regime based on intolerance and oppression. The current socio-political crisis in the divided United States demanded such a poignant lesson to avoid repeating horrific past mistakes.

His eyes lit up. "Of course, yes."

Side by side, they stood, dazzled by the devastating beauty ... and the beautiful devastation of human nature reflected by the *Still Life with Silver Teapot and Narcissus*. The painting was talking to them with the sound of delicate spoons in porcelain cups.

Tinkle, tinkle, tinkle!

Angel looked at Walter and raised her hand in an upward arc, her index and middle fingers curled to meet the thumb, her pinky flexed.

"To life," she said.

The older man, who hailed from a different era—a haunted dynasty—raised his hand and clinked pretend cups with her.

"*L'chaim,*" he toasted in the language of his persecuted ancestors.

They stood thus—frozen in time—their hands touching mid-air. Around them, the museum was buzzing back to life with fresh-faced visitors filing back into the coolness from the sunbaked courtyard. An elderly lady shuffled into the gallery and interrupted the solemn moment in a high-pitched voice.

"You there," she squealed, prodding Walter in the chest with the rubber stopper of her walking cane, "where is the powder room? *Pronto!*"

Angel saw the glow drain from Walter's eyes. The gentleman heir of a priceless, Nazi-looted art fortune gave her a parting look of resignation, and shuffled away, guiding the feisty old lady with a stabilizing hand under her elbow.

His "teacup" lingered for a moment in mid-air and then it dropped to the floor, where she imagined it shattering into dozens of shards at her feet.

CHAPTER 2
THE DYING SWAN

*C*rash!

Bisque porcelain didn't fare well when swiped by an angry hand onto a marble floor. The figurine of a delicate swan had been a gift from her best friend, Angel, but now it lay shattered into dozens of shards next to Shivonne where she cowered on the bathroom floor, naked and curled into a fetal ball. A newly hatched cygnet not yet unfurled to the world, its vulnerable neck ducked down between fragile wing nubs. One hand still white-knuckling the edge of the clawfoot tub where she had languished moments earlier, without a trace of fear.

Outside the bathroom door, Fitzi, her six-pound Pomeranian, was scratching frantically, alarmed by the scent of his mistress's distress. Right behind her, Joe breathed deep bison breaths, the kind that siphoned the energy from a room, leaving behind no oxygen for her. She waited—counting the silence in ballet 8-counts—too afraid to look up into the ugly mask of rage on her husband's face. The *drip-drip-drip* from the faucet left tiny concentric circles on the frothy bathwater.

Is it over?

She arched her back ever so slightly, but it buckled under the weight of his Oxford brogue pressing down on her spine.

It's not over yet.

As if to confirm, Joe cleared his throat and lowered his lips next to her ear.

"Ungrateful bitch."

Cradling her head in her arms, she waited for his next move, the copper-penny smell of fear in her nostrils.

"Joey, I—"

"Don't you 'Joey' me, Shiv," he growled, "I ... am ... not ... a ... little ... boy." He stressed each word with a dig of his chiseled shoe into the soft flesh between her ribs like an alpinist's icepick searching for purchase. Her diaphragm clenched, and she threw up a little into her mouth but swallowed it back down. Joseph Cillian O'Roydon did not tolerate a mess.

"Sorry, Joe."

She did not know what she was supposed to apologize for this time; she had risen from bed at six, let Fitzi outside, and prepared her daughter's lunch before running her bath, as she always did before heading to the museum. Stolen moments of peace before the raging storm awoke on the other side of the bed.

"I'm *so* sorry," she repeated, for good measure. But it was not good enough.

He grabbed her by her damp coppery hair, taking strands of rose-gold silk with him, wrapped around his huge middle finger like stacked promise rings—broken-promise rings. Her arms shot up to grab his wrists; the pain was searing, but she didn't cry. Instead, she allowed her mind to dislodge from its physical confines and dart away to a safe space where she could float above herself—a battered Princess Jasmine on her magic carpet, gazing down on the hypnotic city lights of Agrabah below.

A whole new world ...

From that vantage point, she was out of harm's way. And she was young again and at the peak of her ballet career, protected in the arms of her *pas de deux* partner, the charming prince. He would hoist her up in a double-handed lift under the shoulders and hold her there, her taut body an arrow aimed at the moon, suspended long enough to draw sharp breaths from the audience before tumbling her down, and back up again, her ballet slippers skimming the floor—*adagio, adagio*—her back arched, her wings flexed behind her. Every feather shivering with anticipation.

The crowd would roar and applaud, *"Bravo! Bravo!"*

But Joe's voice yanked her back to reality on the cold bathroom floor, her face pressed into the rolled lip of the clawfoot tub, the water within it dark as the sorcerer's cursed lake, threatening to pull her under. "I asked you a goddamn question, Shiv."

"I, I—" She could not recall his question. The orchestral tremolos of the cellos resonated in her bones.

Plié. Arabesque. Plié. Arabesque.

An unnerving vibrato swelled from the imaginary orchestra pit of her mind.

One, two, chassé-chassé. Five, six, grand jeté.

It would leave a bruise, like a ring around Saturn.

"What did I do wrong, Joe?" A single tear rolled from the assaulted eye; she stopped it at the edge of her lip with her tongue. It tasted salty, like regret.

Snorting, he pulled her head back from the edge of the tub, stupefied at the audacity of her ignorance.

Here it comes ... She flinched.

But before he could enlighten her on her offense, the bathroom door edged open, and Riley's tiny face peered through the crack.

"M-m-mummy?" Her green eyes—carbon copies of Shivonne's—were ablaze with raw terror. "Are you okay, Mummy?" She was still wearing her pajama bottoms, her cardigan buttoned up skew, and her unicorn backpack clutched in her hand. The noise from the bathroom must have woken her.

How long have I been lying on the bathroom floor? What time is it?

Fitzi darted through the gap in the door and skidded on the sudsy floor before flopping into Shivonne's lap. A faint melody wafted in from downstairs; for a moment, she thought it was the orchestra's interlude from her mind's stage.

"Mummy?" Riley took a tentative step toward her.

Wiping her face with the back of one hand, Shivonne extended the other, palm up, toward the little girl. *Stop right there, Riley.*

"Mummy's fine, love. I slipped on the floor, silly me." She forced a goofy smile and hoped she did not have blood on her teeth. "Daddy's helping me."

Lies and more lies.

A cloud of doubt passed over Riley's face, her wide-set eyes burning with a maturity far beyond her tender age. She took another timid step forward. Joe whipped around toward his daughter; the tension radiating from his back chilled Shivonne to the bone. It reminded her of a shape-shifting monster at that moment right before it burst from the seams of its human constraints. Joe did not suffer interruption or disrespect. She needed to get her daughter out of the bathroom booby-trapped with emotional landmines a careless person could trigger with the slightest transgression.

"Riley, hun, we are going to be a wee bit late for preschool today. Do yer ma a favor and get yer cereal downstairs. Be a love ..."

The word "love" was double-dipped in Gaelic flavoring, the entire sentence curving upward in a sing-song cadence. Shivonne's Irish accent was always more pronounced under duress. It was an automatic defensive mechanism of sorts; pitiful at that. The Irish lass coming to the rescue.

Riley looked from her mother to her father, and back again, confusion flickering in the shallow pools of her damp, green irises.

"But— but Mummy?" she questioned, her chin wobbling.

"Go on, pet, Mummy's fine." Shivonne flashed a thumbs-up sign, her thumb quivering like a hummingbird, her eyes beaming urgency.

Now, Riley!

But the five-year-old stalled, lingering a tad too long.

Oh no.

Shivonne smelled the subtle charge of static electricity in the air even before it happened. The tightening of tendons in his neck. The flaring of his nostrils. Joe lunged at his daughter, grabbed her by her puppy-soft upper arms, and shoved her backward into the hallway, grunting like a wounded animal. When he slammed the door shut, Shivonne winced to see Riley's tiny fingers pull away from the doorjamb just in time.

Bastard!

They were alone again in the cursed bathroom, its peony-wallpapered walls threatening to close in on her. Black and white flowers, drained of color, of life. She could not remember if they had always been black and white and whether humans saw objects in monochrome before death, as newborn babies did right after birth.

Joe cracked his knuckles, and their gunshot pops wiped the thought of innocent babies from her mind.

"Can't you hear it, Shiv?" Squatting down to his haunches, he twisted her head as a ventriloquist did with his puppet so that her left ear faced the door leading out into the hallway. She strained for sound and heard it again—that faint, electronic jingle emanating from downstairs.

What is that sou—? His sharpened nail at the back of her neck refreshed her memory. *The egg boiler.* She had switched on the red egg boiler before running her bathwater. Six raw eggs, pierced and propped, slowly steaming to boiling point. Just like her.

"*Shite*, I forgot to—"

"*Shite*, Shiv? *Shite?* Your fucking little Irish dribble is all you can manage? Not an ounce of consideration for me while I'm still in bed, trying to sleep after a horrendous night shift, when ... *Bam!*" He clapped his hands together like cymbals, right next to her ear. "Your stupid gadget goes off with its annoying, ice-cream truck tune. And ...it ... won't ... fucking ...stop." This time, he punctuated each word with an index finger jab to her breastbone. "And where were *you* during all the commotion? Lady-fucking-hoo-ha-Godiva in the baaawth." His eyeballs glistened like Vaseline-coated marbles; his hand twitched in her hair.

"S-s-sorry, Joe. I got distracted." Hoisted in the arms of the savior prince, she soared—*arabesque, arabesque*—she could almost feel the breeze waft through her hair. The cellos wept, and the audience sighed. The convenience of a perfect, ten-minute hard-boiled egg felt preposterous at that moment. She did not even like boiled eggs; they were for *him*. Her late mother's famous Irish deviled eggs. The irony was not lost on her.

She shifted on the floor, one arm shielding her breasts, keenly aware of her wet nakedness. In true Pavlovian style, he released her hair and reached down to tweak a nipple peeking through her fingers.

"Shiv."

Her name did not sound safe in his mouth. It was the way he spat out the single syllable, as if the taste of it curdled on his tongue. Americans often stumbled over her Gaelic name, "Siobhán," so she had informally changed it to a more palatable

'Shivonne.' Her three best friends called her Shivvy. It sounded soft and sweet coming from them but her husband, as he did with every other aspect of their lives, butchered it down to the bone, cutting away the fatty trimmings to lay bare a much harsher version: "Shiv." She hated it. She had seen enough American prison movies to know that a shiv was a rudimentary, deadly weapon fashioned out of a sharpened toothbrush handle, its brush head wrapped in layers of duct tape for grip. Joe wielded her name like that—as if it were a shank with which he intended to inflict great harm. Not with a single, clean stab but with multiple frenzied strikes to the soft belly or kidneys, where it would do the most damage.

"Shiv?"

This time, the poison had drained out of it. The shapeshifter had switched back to its human form. Bewildered, his eyes darted across the mayhem he had caused—the shards of porcelain, her tear-streaked cheeks, the flesh rising like pie dough around her eye. "Shiv baby, it's okay. Look at me." The ventriloquist's hand manipulated her chin to face him.

She averted her eyes; any fool knew never to look an angry dog in the eyes. Oh, those puppy dog eyes she used to stare into for hours when they were younger and she more naïve, excusing his fits of jealousy and rage as gestures of undying love and devotion.

"I didn't mean to hurt you, baby ... I snapped, ok? It won't happen again." His brown eyes were pleading. Pleading as they did on those cold New York nights in the courting years, when he would wait for her outside the stage door—post-performance—with a posy of roses in his fist, his breath forming ice-cold vapor clouds of promise and desire between them.

Liar.

She allowed his hand to trace the smattering of freckles across the bridge of her nose. The slightest rejection of his affection at that delicate moment would be catastrophic, so she measured each breath, fighting her body's urge to leap.

Sauté. Sauté. Grand jeté.

Her sympathetic nervous system was on perpetual standby: Fight or Flight. At night, she was tormented by a recurring nightmare: a dragon chasing the fragile dancer up a twisted staircase, clawing at her heels and drooling hot saliva that decimated each stone step behind her, causing it to crumble like bone ash into the ether below. Every time she thought of leaving Joe, the bungee cord of freedom would stretch just so far ... before it would whip back and reel her back in. He had not always been this way, she would argue. He needed help and was it not her sworn vow to stick with him through thick and thin? Besides, she could not report him to the police because he was one of them. A Boy in Blue. A 'copper.'

How proud she used to be of that fact. How safe she used to feel with her police officer boyfriend walking her home in Washington Heights after performances, or through Central Park after a night out, unafraid of what was lurking in the shadows. But that was then; nowadays, she worried about the shadows lurking within *him*. When exactly did her handsome prince turn into the evil sorcerer?

Joe was a plain-clothes LAPD detective on the Gang and Narcotics beat, occasionally working undercover. He often bragged to her about the powerful drug cartel honchos he associated with and his intimate knowledge of "disappearing a body" into the Los Angeles National Forest. How an acid bath would "flush all the evidence down the drain, ha-ha!" He had slapped his knees in gales of laughter, but the message was chilling and unequivocal: "I can kill anyone, Shiv, and get away with it," he would gloat with a crooked, boozy smile, his eyes zippered into slits like a mamba about to strike. "Like this." A snap of his fingers.

Poof!

In those frightening moments—when he seemed to slither out of his skin like a changeling leaving behind the distorted human shell—she thought of him as Hades, the Greek god of the Underworld, sporting his invisible cap, or cloak, of psychopathy. A cloak Joe could deftly twist out of and drape over his arm, ready to dazzle and deceive with his good looks and East Coast prep-school charm.

"Why do you make me do this to you?" he asked the broken swan on the bathroom floor while blurring the fine line between stroking and pulling her hair. "You always bring out the worst in me, Shiv."

"Yes, Joe," she nodded, hugging Fitzi to her chest. "I'm sorry, Joe." Those three simple words—the combination code needed to exit the bathroom in one piece.

"It was the edge of the tub, by the way," he said, gesturing to her battered eye with a dismissive flick of his wrist. He ran his fingers through his dark hair, then wiped his palms on his jeans in a subconscious gesture, washing his hands of the morning's events.

Out, damned spot, she was tempted to say. Instead, she tracked him as he opened the bathroom door and stepped out, leaving a final admonishment in his wake. "Pull yourself together, Shiv. You look like shit."

Once he was gone, and she was alone but for Fitzi, she tried to stand up. Her knees wobbled and scissored underneath her petite frame. *Nope,* they said. Shivonne closed her eyes. Once again, from deep within her subconscious, the heartrending *andantino grazioso* of Camille Saint-Saëns's *Le Cygne* filtered in on gentle strings—the dying swan's final performance. Slowly, gingerly, she rose from the floor, flexing her quads and gripping the edge of the clawfoot tub with one hand. Shards of battered porcelain swan pierced the soft pads of her bare feet and left bloody smears on the floor, but she no longer felt the pain.

Grand Plié and ... Relevé.

In a few wobbly moves, her legs vibrating like plucked cello strings, she pulled herself up in sync with the instrumental crescendo in her ears, her broken wings fluttering upward and scooping air, scattering feathers and powdery down into the fragile daylight.

CHAPTER 3
THE SUN KING

L uke Lorenson flung his arm out toward the larger-than-life painting, *Portrait of Louis XIV*—one of several versions by Hyacinth
Rigaud—and bowed to the ruler, his wrist fluttering down to the floor like
a soft autumn leaf. "My Lords and Ladies of the court, I present to you his
Majesty, King Louis XIV of France. All hail the Sun King."

King Louis gazed back from his elevated pitch, stoic and proud, right into
the eyes of the disheveled group of 11th graders crowded at his feet.

"Ha," a teen boy grumbled, "dude looks more like a *queen* to me."

The observation drew fist bumps from his elbow-buddies in the Ver-
sailles-inspired Decorative Arts gallery, where King Louis XIV reigned
supreme from his perch against the royal-blue flocked velvet. The replicated
Palace de Versailles was one of Luke's favorite stops in the Pallas Museum,
which was also lovingly—and sometimes ignorantly—referred to as "The
Palace." King Louis, the fourteenth ruler of that name from the house of
Bourbon, had built his flashy Versailles to show off his power and style. Like
Luke, the king was a fashionable dandy who had championed the Arts in
17th-century France.

Any grown-ass man who dared to dress like a diva in red-heeled shoes, his feet
turned out to show off muscular thighs, was his idol and a pure joy to introduce
to his students. Teenagers were not always wide awake in the galleries, but they
were usually "woke"—here, in Los Angeles, at least. Always ready to discuss the
injustices of society and its limitations on race and gender. Luke aimed to inspire
thought-provoking topics in the sanctity of the museum, where being "The Other" was not just the norm; it was celebrated. Fashion—the scrumptious outfits,

shoes, jewelry, and wigs—was his ultimate weapon of choice, and he wielded it with gusto.

It was an excellent segue into the discrepancy between the luxury of the royal courts versus the immense poverty of the commoners. And how the royal "let-them-eat-cake" mentality had caused the French Revolution of 1789, which culminated with the heads of those haute-couture-outfitted aristocrats rolling into baskets at the foot of *La Guillotine.*

"Before we take a closer look, let's ponder the observation offered by your friend. What makes this king look like a queen?" He raised his eyebrows, making his eyeglasses slip down the bridge of his nose; it gave him the air of a trendy professor.

"Dude, that hair!" someone exclaimed, and the rest of the group bobbed their heads. King Louis XIV sported an impressive wig that rose about a foot high on top and draped down his shoulders in lush, dark curls. The effect was that of a pampered, elaborately coiffed show poodle.

"That is not his hair," Luke said. "It's an elaborate wig called a *peruke.* It used to be a status symbol for the elite—the higher, the better." He gestured with his hand hovering high above his own dark hair, which he lovingly crafted into a pompadour, every morning, with a comb and pomade.

"So, he wore it to make himself look taller, then?" someone asked.

"Exactly, and perhaps to cover a bald head underneath."

"Were they made of real or fake hair?" a girl asked while stroking her extensions in an unconscious gesture.

Luke relished the detailed questions; they allowed him to dive deep into his extensive art knowledge without boring the students. "Most of the fancier ones, like this one, were made from human hair sold by poor, starving peasants," he explained, recalling a scene from his favorite musical, *Les Misérables,* where the desperate Fantine allows her gorgeous locks to be lobbed off so she could afford to feed her young daughter. "However, if you did not have the gold coins to buy the real stuff, you would have worn a wig made of horse or goat hair."

"Gross," came their anticipated response, and Luke served his next volley.

"Yup, and those farm-animal wigs often came with lice ... or worse." A few students scratched their scalps, which made Luke's head feel itchy too.

Ah, the sweet power of suggestion.

"Dude, what could be worse than lice?" a shaggy-haired boy asked with a look that confirmed he had been at the receiving end of a lice comb on more than one occasion.

"Well, that would be rats," Luke said, grinning while a communal shiver ran through the group. "Because the only way to sculpt those wigs so high and rigid was to apply layers of lard—animal fat—over them, which would attract rodents at night, while the Lords and Ladies were sleeping."

"Dude, you're shitting us," one of the high-school juniors smirked.

Luke put a hand on his heart and pushed his trendy glasses back up his nose with the middle finger of the other—an unconscious gesture that conveyed sincerity ... or stress.

I shit you not.

Here, in front of King Louis XIV of France, he commanded the stage, and his audience was rapt, except for a young, lovesick couple leaning into each other against the back wall, their lips mere millimeters apart. Luke set a mental goal to evoke a filament of interest from Romeo and Juliet by the end of the session. There was much more to discover.

"I'm going to give you five minutes or so to look closer and then we'll discuss," he said. "Your time starts ... now." When he pulled up his sleeve to expose his wristwatch, he noticed a few curious eyes locking onto the totem pole of parallel cutting scars that stretched like a macabre barcode from his lily-pale wrist to his inner elbow. Blushing, he shimmied his sleeve back down and pretended he had not noticed the empathetic looks.

The scars on his inner arm, however, would not be so easily ignored by the person who created them. They triggered a flood of bitter memories that propelled thirty-two-year-old Luke backward in time on a close-look journey of his own: his traumatic childhood. His brow furrowed and his eyes squeezed shut. And when he opened them again, he was no longer in front of the royal portrait in the Pallas Museum; he was back home on his father's dairy farm in the woods of ultra-conservative, small-town Wisconsin.

Toto, we are not in Kansas anymore.

No shit, Dorothy.

He was Luke Andreas Lorenson, son of a preacher man who milked cows in the pre-dawn hours, tilled fields in the afternoons, and sowed the gospel from an evangelical pulpit, twice on Sundays. Though their farm was not geographically in the Bible belt, it was, nevertheless, the land of the Bible ... and of the belt, with which the father ruled as the uncontested head of the household while the mother's task was to raise the children and serve/service her man. "Marriage = One Man + One Woman." *That* kind of back-country community where holier-than-thou hypocrites considered feminism an "F-word" and equated homosexuality to bestiality.

His mama had been shy and soft-spoken, and content in her entrapment, humming hymns while ironing his pa's white Y-fronts and armpit-stained undershirts. Whenever Mama was not singing, she was praising the Lord for every blessing ... and every curse. The Lord was never wrong. Amen. If He smote your farm with tornadoes and killed your livestock or the unborn babies in your womb, He was doing so for a reason. Amen.

Praise the Lord!

He could hear his Mama's voice recounting how she had named her only living son—born nine years after his older sister and the only male Lorenson to survive her hostile womb—after a Bible verse that had ascended upon her the day she went into labor. Mama had been sitting outside the Co-op while Pa was ordering soybean meal for the milking cows, feeding crumbs of Juneberry Pie to the pigeons pecking at her feet, when one of the birds landed on her bulging belly. She had raised her hand to scoot it from her lap when—according to Mama—the sky had rumbled and a voice from the heavens called out the words from Luke 3, verse 22: *"And the Holy Spirit descended on him in bodily form like a dove. And a voice came from heaven: 'You are my son, whom I love; with you, I am well pleased.'"*

"Well-pleased? Ha!" Back in the art gallery, dreamy-eyed Luke harrumphed with such animosity it startled his students. But they turned back to the painting and left him to simmer in the vitriol of the 1990s.

Little did his mama know they would *not* be "well-pleased" with their only son. Ignoring the dark skies overhead and the mangled, clubbed feet of that pigeon, his mama had taken the bird landing on her belly as a sign from God. The irony—it being a filthy rat-with-wings and *not* the snow-white dove representative of the Holy Ghost—had escaped her in its entirety. *Poor Mama!* When her water had broken mere minutes later, accompanied by a sudden downpour from the Lord's grim skies overhead, she had clutched her belly and called out that name, "Luke, blessed Luke," as her husband rushed her home in his Chevy jalopy. Luke wondered if his mama ever regretted pulling him out of the galvanized tub of warm water where she had delivered him that day.

Luke, cursed Luke.

Yes, Mama—bless her stone-cold heart—had tried her best to raise him into a well-pleasing kind of kid: no to pop music and TV, no to comic books and *Super Mario*, no to school dances and sleepovers. And no to martial arts during PE because "one bows to nobody but God." The name of the Lorenson family game was Guilt, and Luke had been steeped in it and left to pickle on a darkened shelf, like a jar of his mother's homemade relish. A man like his father deserved a son who knew how to throw a punch, how to pass the pigskin around on a football field, or how to slaughter Daisy the dried-up milk cow—the same one he had bottle-fed as an orphaned calf—without so much as a sniffle, then flip those treacherous burgers on the barbeque. A son who could honor the Lorenson family's fierce Viking ancestry by growing thick facial hair and balls big enough to propose to the neighbor's pasty daughter, so the two farms could be combined. A dutiful son. A manly son.

Back in the gallery, the tornado of memories made Luke wobble on his feet. When his vertigo subsided, he scanned his watch and notified the students in a gravelly voice, "One minute to go." The concept of time passing reminded him of an old, distressed mantle clock that used to wave its accusing dials at him from its perch on Mama's dining buffet.

Tick-tock, tick-tock.

The deafening sound of disappointment in the scrawny little boy with his knock-knees and weak wrists, unable to lift a half-full grain bucket. His father's disappointed looks and sighs, those eyes boring into him, willing him to "Grow a pair!" The gasps of shame and grunts of disgust that fateful Sunday when twelve-year-old Luke—deep in thought—had sashayed down the church aisle, swaying his hips to the rhythm of "Onward Christian Soldiers" booming from the organ while the congregation looked on, slack-jawed.

Ooh, the scandal. The pastor's son is a pansy.

Everybody had known, even before he did, making it their God-given duty to call his parents out on it. His adolescent years were a blur of conflict and conversion therapy—the pray-the-gay-away kind administered by an itinerant evangelical pastor who also performed the occasional exorcism when called upon. Oh, how Luke had prayed. And prayed and prayed ... till his knees wore the imprint of the polyester Quaker rug by his bed.

Lord, please make me fit in. Please make me normal. Ay-men!

His pa had tried hard to help him with beatings designed to drive Satan out of his effeminate son. His mama, bless her departed soul, had stayed mum, a hand on the Bible and a forbidding silence on her lips, unless quoting the Holy Scripture in defense of his father: "'He that spareth his rod hateth his son,' Proverbs 13:24."

"Yes, Mama. Thank you, Mama. Praise the Lord, ay-men."

It was at Bible camp—*oh, the irony*—the summer of his fifteenth year, where Luke had experienced a pivotal moment. Patrick was three years older, a college freshman who had escaped the farm fields of Wisconsin to study sociology in Chicago and who was home for the summer to earn service hours as a camp counselor. Their interaction had been sweet and innocent, a deep friendship based on shared trauma and mutual trust. Patrick's soft kiss on his lips, behind a thicket of night-cloaked trees after a bonfire Bible study session one night, was the fuse that lit the rocket of Luke's rebellion.

Following the kiss, he remembered looking up at the starry sky, expecting it to cleave open with the Lord's wrath. But nothing of the kind had happened; only the joy of Patrick's soft fingertips as they caressed the most recent scar on his left wrist, soothing the fresh welt where Luke's skin had knitted together their sliced edges into a ragged line.

"You've got to stay strong," Pat had said, reading between the lines. "It's tough out here for people like us."

"Us?" *There were others out there?*

"Yes, but there's always hope. Just look at me."

"Hope?"

"It's an acronym: 'Hang On, Pain Ends,'" Pat had explained. "The next time you feel ... hopeless," a finger stroking his scars, "just remember this."

"You mean, like the quote, 'When you're going through hell, just keep going?'" Luke had asked.

"Hell no," Patrick had scoffed, "If you're going through hell ... turn the fuck around."

Luke's eyes had widened at the use of the vulgar cuss word; its forbidden impact hit him like a sledgehammer.

"What's the point of plodding through the shitstorm you are drowning in?" Patrick had said, exasperated. "No, Luke, you turn around ... you go back, ... and you take a different exit." A prod on his shoulder accentuated each instruction.

The memory of that night, and Patrick's words, made him smile in front of the diva King—those unexpected words of wisdom sealed by a single, forbidden kiss. It had happened fifteen years ago, but the memories were still fresh. Luke had recently searched for his first crush on social media platforms and was delighted to find out that Pat had followed that sound advice himself—to turn the fuck around and carve out a different destination. "Patrick" was now "Patrice" and she worked as a therapist at a halfway home dedicated to LGBTQ+ youth in the Bay area. It was no surprise to Luke that they were both drawn to the same line of work: the rescuing and recalibrating of compasses for lost souls. He, himself, was knee-deep in graduate school applications for a Master of Psychology and Art Therapy.

His watch vibrated against his wrist and snapped him back from his troubled youth to the group of teens huddled in front of the portrait.

"Time's up, folks," he said. "Observations, anyone? What else stands out besides the king's fabulous wig?" He emphasized 'fabulous' with jazz hands, scanned the crowd, and waited. Teenagers never raised their hands. It was best to sit back and wait for someone to fill the awkward silence with sound. One of the girls, sporting a ring through her eyebrow and another through her septum, did the honors.

"Those heels are sick," she remarked.

King Louis's couture shoes never failed to impress. They were the epitome of elegance, cobbled in creamy satin with a spiffy brass buckle and—most strikingly—lipstick-red lacquered, two-inch heels. Five hundred years *pre*-Louboutin.

"Why would a powerful dude wear girly shoes like those?" asked a boy in a Tupac T-shirt, proclaiming that California knew how to party.

"Hmm, good question. What do *you* all think?" Luke pivoted it back to the group.

"He's a drag queen, man ... a fairy," an athlete-type with buzzed hair blurted out, before addressing Luke with a cursory "No offense, dude."

"None taken, dude," Luke said with a shrug. He had been called worse than a "fairy," and he knew that teens—especially those in larger, more liberal cities—were more fluid and tolerant about "The Other" than when he was younger. Talking about art facilitated the conversation around inclusion.

"*Mira*," another student said, "look at how he's standing."

Luke had expected this. "Let's mimic his pose. C'mon, you in the back, too."

The lovey-dovey couple pulled away from each other with reluctance, a hanging bridge of spittle dangling between their lips. Luke shuffled his feet to mimic the king's stance; his left leg slid forward about a foot, its toe pointed outward, and the calf flexed. He adjusted the back foot to point the other way and balanced the pose with his left hand on his hip and his right arm stretched out sideways. In front of him, the students giggled and settled into the pose. Teens usually loved this kind of play-acting—it provided a little comic relief, a break from the stress of exams and college applications.

The ballet pose made Luke think of Shivonne; she had not shown up for her shift that morning. He frowned briefly amid the students' giggling, then shook off the unease.

"Does this pose remind anyone of anything?" he asked, jutting his chin forward and tightening his buttocks as if waiting for bouquets to be flung at his feet.

"It's a ballet pose," a soft-spoken girl volunteered.

"Correct." He graced her with fluttering theater applause. "King Louis XIV was a ballet dancer himself. He's posing in fourth position here." He reveled in the looks of surprise. A French king doing ballet?

Yes, friends, museums are freakin' fonts of cool facts.

"When Louis was around your age, he danced the lead role in a ballet production as the Greek god, Apollo." A handful of boys nodded—Greek mythology was fodder for their Marvel superheroes and fantasy card leagues. Luke *loved* Apollo. The Greek god of the Sun embodied everything he aspired to be—revered, adored, and carelessly happy.

A well-pleasing kind of god.

The group discussion continued to flow, and laughter ricocheted in the small hallway where the Rigaud portrait hung, welcoming visitors to the Royal court before they stepped into the galleries decked out with Baroque and Rococo furniture. One student pointed out King Louis's "dope" coat, and Luke shivered with delight. Galliano and McQueen: famous designers who took inspiration from the "dope" fashion trends of the 18th-century French court. The group discussed lace collars, ermine furs, and gold-threaded *fleurs de lis* that symbolized French royalty.

"What's that?" someone asked, pointing to a staff with a disembodied hand attached to the tip, lying on a bench next to the king. "It looks like a back scratcher." The thought of it scratching a royal itch under layers of embroidered fabric and regalia elicited laughter.

"Quite the contrary, *mon ami*," Luke chortled. "That is his scepter, *La Main de la Justice.* The Hand of Justice."

"Woah, like the one in World of Warcraft?" a boy asked.

Luke shrugged; he had no clue. "Let's just say that if the king pointed that scepter at you ... or you—" he did a slow spin on his heels, pointing at participants in the group at random, "it would mean 'Heads off.'" He sliced his hand across his throat for dramatic effect.

Soon, a chorus of "Off with his head! Off with his head!" rang through the hallways. It was reminiscent of the *tricoteuses,* the infamous knitting ladies who had sat at the foot of the guillotine during the French Revolution, calmly knitting the names of its victims into the wool scarves in their laps, while chanting *"Enlevez leur têtes!"* Off with their heads.

A middle-aged couple sauntered by the gallery and cast a dirty look at the rowdy group. Luke spread his hands out and motioned the students to pipe down, but he had a broad smile plastered across his face—he loved their passion and raw exuberance.

"What was the king's Hand of Justice made of?" a student asked.

"Great question. It was carved from the tooth of a narwhal, a rare and legendary whale that lives in Arctic waters. A bizarre, elongated tooth twirled like soft-serve ice cream," Luke explained, demonstrating its spiral shape with his fingers. "The narwhal's tusk is what ancient explorers and scientists in the Middle Ages often misidentified as the horn of a mystical creature they called ... wait for it ... a unicorn."

"You mean unicorns aren't real?" a teen with long, pink nails asked in a baby voice.

"Sorry to disappoint," Luke laughed, "but unicorns, griffins, and nine-headed Hydras are mythical creatures, the stuff of fairy tales and Disney movies."

"Yeah, like fairy godmothers," the same teen snorted; Luke's smile dissolved.

"Nope, fairy godmothers are very real," he said in a gruff tone. He knew this first-hand; he had been blessed with his own fairy godmothers to fill in the void left behind in his scarred heart. The students looked at him oddly.

"Great discussion, everyone," he deflected. "It's time to wrap up our royal visit with an appropriate farewell to the king in all his splendor."

Summoning the group closer, he started a countdown, and, on the final count, they all bowed in mock supplication to the portrait—even the lip-locked lovers, Romeo and Juliet.

Gotcha, Luke smirked.

Upon their exit, he glanced back at King Louis, and an eerie premonition struck him like a lightning bolt. He sucked in his breath sharply.

Shivonne.

His friend—and fairy godmother—had not shown up for her shift that morning, with no forewarning or reassuring phone call since. Where was she? And why did he feel such awful dread looking at King Louis?

It was the ballet pose, he figured. Or maybe it was the king's shoes.

Those blood-red soles.

CHAPTER 4
AMONG SAINTS and MARTYRS

L orelei McAllister was on her knees in the cave-like interior of the Illuminated Manuscripts gallery, on the museum's subterranean level. Praying to
a different king before joining her friends for lunch.

It was quiet here. Most visitors usually made a beeline for the more com-
mercially famous paintings in the upper-floor galleries—the Rembrandts, the
Rubens, the Renoirs—masterpieces that drew the crowds like moths to a flame,
where they jostled for a chance to turn their backs to it for a selfie. In contrast,
the solemnity of the religious manuscripts scared away the least devout, and a
seeker like Lorelei could find a quiet spot to genuflect in the glow of the medieval
illuminated tomes propped against chocolate brown walls, which made their gilt
surfaces and jeweled colors sparkle like a hundred candles on a stormy night.

Here, a humble human could repose for a while in the company of kings
and queens, saints and their dragons, and beasts of indeterminate origin. She
found the oversized, hand-crafted Missals, Gospels, and Epistles reassuring and
comforting. Here, she was less alone; at times, she even imagined she could hear
voices slipping from between the vellum pages—Eve whispering tempting words
in Adam's ear, offering him a bite of forbidden fruit. Or the knight, Saint George,
sheltering from a fierce dragon under the protective canopy of a magic orange tree;
a princess's life depended on it. Sometimes Lorelei imagined she could hear the
soft sighs of the princess, only to realize it was her own trembling breath instead.

From her humble position on the floor of the gallery, she looked up at the
formidable stained-glass window towering above her, its vitreous-painted glass
panels diffusing a stream of light from the louvered skylight and deflecting it into
a rainbow prism on the floor. The leaded-glass panel, most certainly pried from

the window frame of a long-crumbled cathedral, depicted Saint Margaret and the myth of her escape from the mouth of Satan, portrayed as a dragon. Lorelei understood the plight and martyrdom of poor Saint Margaret all too well. She, too, battled Satan daily, enduring his ire for not conceding.

The word "warrior" did not describe Lorelei in the traditional sense. She was soft in the eye of the beholder, beatific like the stained-glass saint in an ethereal sort of way thanks to her Canadian roots: the porcelain-white skin and baby-soft, platinum-blonde hair framing her face like a mohair scarf. Her eyes, especially, enforced her angelic semblance, being the intense blue color of the inner crystalline layer of Nordic ice, exposed when an iceberg calves. When she looked at someone, those startling eyes pierced deep into their soul, melting any frost, and making a cozy nest in its stead. Everyone loved Lorelei.

Her given name had been Lauren-Anne, but it did not suit the free spirit of a nymph growing up in the enchanted forests of Mahone Bay, Nova Scotia, with soft moss between her toes in the summer and snowflakes on her eyelids in the winter. The earth coddled her there like a native herb and serenaded her with powerful vibrations on the lands where First Nations had roamed for centuries. There, despite her Catholic upbringing, she had learned to straddle religion and spirituality, barefoot and openhearted. *That* was who she was—not a generic "Lauren-Anne." That name was too constricting, so she had cut it loose at the seams and given it room to breathe. The more fitting "Lorelei" had come to her in a series of inspirited dreams.

Only much later did she learn about the folkloric tale of the young woman who, betrayed by her sweetheart, had flung herself to her death from the Lorelei rock on the Rhine River in Germany. A devastating story with a haunting trajectory which, in retrospect, felt very much like ironic precognition as it applied to her present dilemma.

On the gallery floor, she clutched her hands together and lifted her face to allow the prism of light streaming through the gorgeous stained-glass panel to dance across her cheeks. People passing by that gallery would have sworn they saw the martyr, Saint Margaret, step out of the window panel to grace the earth.

"Dear Lord," Lorelei prayed, "please surround my child in your white light of protection. Please bless my Grace with *Your* grace and keep her safe. In the name of the Father, the Son, and the Holy Spirit." She made the sign of the cross and kissed her fingertips to seal it. "Amen."

Her twelve-year-old daughter, Grace, the younger of a fraternal twin set, had been chronically ill since infancy. It was as if she—the frailer twin—had experienced a premonition of the pain and suffering awaiting her on the outside and needed those extra minutes in the womb to stall the inevitable. When the twins were five years old, a team of far-flung experts had diagnosed Grace with a rare genetic blood disorder—an incurable disease so devastating that Lorelei refused to name it, to give it credence. It cursed her child with frequent infections, debilitating bleeds, and bone marrow failure. Lorelei fought valiantly to ensure there were sunny days to celebrate, but the truth was there were more hurricane days that threatened to lift the roof off the McAllister home.

The previous day had been one of those, starting with an innocuous nosebleed and culminating in a midnight rush to the emergency room for a blood transfusion. Grace was a regular there, the way Lorelei was at Tortoni, the local Argentinian coffee shop she and Angel frequented. When they had pulled up with their sick daughter at the triage counter, a nurse greeted the young patient by her name, and read her 'order' from the chart in a mock-barista tone, "One order of delicious Leuko-depleted Packed Red Blood Cells for the customer in exam room three, STAT."

It was an old joke that used to elicit gales of laughter from Grace and her sister, Ivy, who always accompanied her shadow to the emergency room. But the girls no longer found it amusing, as was evident the night before. Pre-teens—especially those cursed with incurable illness—soured quickly on childish adult attempts at humor. Lorelei pitied the nurse at the receiving end of a bone-chilling glower, and her heart had broken for her broken child.

After dropping both girls off at school that morning—Grace looking hollow-eyed and pale next to her rosy-cheeked twin—Lorelei had allowed herself a good sob in her car, deep within the bowels of the museum parking lot. Here, in the gallery where she counted herself one of the illuminated, she could reset and be infused with good vibes. Dealing with *other* people's pre-teens in the galleries was a breeze by comparison. After the tour, she could simply walk away.

God help me, she thought with a little eye roll. And then, to the ceiling, "No offense."

She stood up from the stone floor and reached her arms overhead for a power stretch; her back cracked in grateful response. The museum was a remote island for her—an escape from the mainland reality of parenting a critically ill child. At home, her only reprieve was to retreat to the bespoke backyard studio, where she concocted herbal remedies and tinctures from the medicinal plants she cultivated in her garden. It was therapeutic to dig her fingers deep into the soft dirt and pull a burdock root at the height of its potency or harvest a patch of nettles for a healing tea. It brought her a modicum of therapy in those dark moments of hankering for her hometown and those happier, healthier times in their large old Victorian home on the shore of Mahone Bay. She pined for its quarter-sawn oak staircase and the enclosed porch where the girls would swing on the suspended daybed, sipping homemade lavender tea while their mom puttered around in the red barn outside.

Here, in Los Angeles, her soul ached for the serenity of the woods, the crunch of fall foliage underfoot, the clam bakes and lobster boils. *That* was her home—not the land of fake front lawns, fake suntans, and fake smiles. But Fate had driven them to Los Angeles, with its proximity to the medical experts who specialized in rare blood disorders, and the chance for Benjamin to better support the family with freelance camera-operator work. In Canada, he was known for his poignant documentaries on climate change; here, his brilliance was dimmed by the glare of a thousand brighter sparks, his mind lobotomized behind the camera. Lorelei was the multi-hyphenate nurse, taxi driver, tutor, therapist, and exorcist of all things evil. Someone had to stay home to battle Satan and save the princess. Working as a museum docent was her magic orange tree, a place to catch her breath before picking up her sword again to face the dragon.

She rifled through her Mary Poppins-like bag—equal in both size and wizardry—and pulled out her Manuscripts folder from among the trove of teaching tools: charcoal pencils, sketching paper, and small manipulatives like a piece of marble or a swath of velvet for the students to touch. She loved educating them on how tissue-paper thin gold leaf was applied, piece by piece, and polished to a mirror-like gleam with a wolf's tooth.

Gasp!

Or how the color Carmine Red was created by mixing ground-up Cochineal bugs harvested from cacti growing in Mexico and mixed with egg yolk or horse urine to make paint.

Squeal!

Religious or not, it was about instilling respect. Bare hands had created these ancient tomes, velum by velum, line by line. And despite being hundreds of years old, they continued to shine like bright torches into the hearts and minds of modern society. Assuming the gallery was not too crowded, she would play music from her cell phone to provide the ideal background ambiance for viewing the Illuminated Manuscripts: Gregorian Monks chanting their ethereal morning prayer, the velvety sound reverberating through the cavernous space and thrumming its gentle drone deep into the chest of the listener. The music would evoke monks with tonsured bowl cuts and roped cassocks, scribing oversized calligraphy initials with quills dipped in tree sap and oak galls. She would pass around a feather quill for the wide-eyed students to palpate, to see how its hollow shaft would have funneled the ink down to the sharp point.

Seeing is believing. But touching is gospel.

Satisfied, Lorelei snapped the folder shut and dropped it back into the spacious bag with a sigh. Her eyelids always felt heavy in the Manuscripts gallery—the dark interior soothed and hypnotized the visitor, especially if the visitor had spent a restless night beside a sick child's bed, gripping a clammy hand until it gave in to blessed sleep and slid out of her grasp.

She turned to exit the dark Middle Ages, squinting to counter the onslaught of contemporary light spilling in from the hallway, and almost tripped over the outstretched legs of a figure seated against the wall in the shadows behind her.

"Sorry," a familiar voice mumbled.

"Shivvy?" She would have recognized the mellifluous Irish accent in a crowded room. "What are you doing on the floor? I almost face-planted over you, silly goose."

The shadow that was Shivonne scooched higher against the wall. Lorelei extended her hand to pull her up from the floor. It required no effort; she was scrawny like a day-old foal. Ogling the oversized sunglasses on Shivonne's face, Lorelei pivoted them up onto her friend's forehead, joking, "God's light too bright for you in here?"

But her breath caught in her throat when she saw the burgeoning bruise around the curve of one of Shivonne's beautiful green eyes. She had tried to conceal it under a thick layer of makeup … but to little avail.

"What happened to your eye?" Lorelei asked, licking her thumb to wipe at the bruise. Shivonne flinched and whipped her head to the side. And that was when Lorelei sensed something was wrong. The age-old adage about blood being thicker than water did not apply when your friend's bone marrow ran through the spine of your ailing child. And when your friend donated hers—extracted in a painful procedure from her pelvic bone—to help keep your child alive, there was nothing you would not do for her. She owed Shivonne a debt she could never repay.

Scanning over her shoulder to ensure that they were alone, she pulled Shivonne onto the padded bench facing the back wall. "Talk to me," she soothed, stroking her friend's hair as she often did for Grace. *Touching is gospel.* "What happened?"

A bruise of that caliber demanded an explanation, and Lorelei braced for the answer. Something about the way Shivonne had cowered in the dim sanctity of the gallery alerted her to expect the worst.

Shivonne averted her eyes to the wall opposite them; Lorelei followed her gaze to a single painting framed on either side by gilded bestiaries in shadow boxes. Shivonne's hand gripped hers in silent affirmation.

See? that grip demanded. *Think … and wonder.*

Lorelei had been so focused on Saint Margaret and the dragon that she had neglected the other martyr in the room: the legendary Roman heroine, Lucretia. The 17th-century painting, *Lucretia,* by one of the few female master painters

46

revered by the art world, Artemisia Gentileschi, was breathtaking—bone-chill-ing—in its relevance at that moment. The Roman maiden, Lucretia, was nude from the chest up, her tormented gaze cast heavenward, her auburn hair tumbling down her back. In her left hand, she clutched a dagger, its sharp, steel point angled upward on a tilted trajectory toward her breast, destined to pierce the plumpness. Most disquieting, her right hand gripped her exposed left breast with such brute force, it evoked the very violence that predated her desperate act: her brutal rape by a royal acquaintance of her husband's. To avoid the dishonor that her rape would cast upon her husband and his noble family, Lucretia had taken her own life by plunging a dagger deep into her heart.

The "Me Too" theme of the victimized woman was omnipresent in Artemisia Gentileschi's work because a fellow apprentice had raped her, too, and humiliated her in a public trial where she, the victim, was blamed. Her *Lucretia*, displayed on the wall in the Pallas Museum hundreds of years later, was a study of her private pain. Her revenge turned inwards. An act of ultimate self-harm.

That hand. That dagger. That look of despair and determination.

"She's me, Lore," Shivonne said. "I *am* Lucretia."

The significance of the sharp-pointed dagger gripped Lorelei by the throat. She looked at Shivonne, her eyes wide with fear. "Shivonne," she said breathlessly, "you're not thinking of ...?" She angled her chin toward the dagger, too afraid to say the words aloud as if vocalizing it would plant the thought. In the dim light, Shivonne seemed to be smiling, but Lorelei knew better. Her despair involved injustice, she thought, at the hands of a man.

"Is it Joe? The bruise?"

Their tight little group of friends knew of Joe's controlling personality, his anti-social stance, and the fits of jealousy. But Shivonne would always justify his behavior, citing his occupation as a cop. "That's just how they are," she would say. Opposites attracted but, in their case, the discrepancy was striking: the gentle ballerina ... and the gruff bully.

"Is it Joe, Shivvy?" Lorelei asked again, squeezing her hand.

"No," Shivonne said a little too quickly, but then added, "Sometimes ..." Cradling her face in her hands, she whispered through her fingers, "I'm afraid he

might lose control one of these days ... and k-kill us. I look at her and I wonder ..."
She hinted at Lucretia's dagger with her eyes. "But I have to stay strong for Riley."

Try as she might, Lorelei could not speak; all her words had piled up on top of each other, stuck behind the large lump in her throat. She opened her arms and folded Shivonne in an embrace that spoke volumes of wisdom in ancient tongues. From the stained-glass saint in the hallway behind them, an errant ray of sunlight deflected and illuminated Lucretia's face, donning a distorted halo over the martyr. Lorelei thought of her own husband, salt-of-the-earth Benjamin, and how lucky she was to feel protected and cherished by him. She could not imagine the horror of having to fear for her safety, or for that of her children.

"Come," she said, hooking her arm through Shivonne's and pulling her up from the bench. "Let's go meet the others in the Pallas cafeteria. Angel will know what to do. She always does."

"It's a shiv," Shivonne said, looking back at Lucretia.

"Pardon?"

"That dagger ... it's a shiv, don't you see? I'm it and it is me."

From her perch on the wall in a gallery filled with martyrs and saints, the doomed Lucretia seemed oblivious to the resemblance. She simply looked to the heavens, praying for strength and forgiveness for what she was about to do, and intensified her grip on the cold steel dagger on its arc toward her breast.

CHAPTER 5
THE NAMING of the GODS

A ngel could not stop thinking of Walter's story as she crossed the
sun-drenched courtyard toward the museum cafeteria. She felt as if she had
checked out a spine-chilling book from the Library of Life and become engrossed
in its pages—an epic tale ripped from one of history's worst chapters.

Outside the cafeteria doors, she inhaled the intoxicating scent of the jasmine
drooping in waterfalls across the roughhewn stone walls ... and thought of death.
A museum like the Pallas was a tomb of sorts—a beautiful ark of historic treasures
dipped in gold leaf, imbedded with lapis lazuli, and splattered with dazzling oil
paints. Even so, a tomb, encasing death with its tales of slavery, sacrifice, martyrdom, and violence. So much pain and so much beauty, together under one roof.

Inside the Palladian Cafeteria, the smell of the day's lunch offerings flushed out
any trace of jasmine—grilled cheese sandwiches oozing monterey jack, bowls of
pho rice noodles slithering in *hoisin*, and overstuffed burritos. She gravitated to
the salad bar and flagged down a server behind the glass partition.

"The chef's salad of the day, please, but without the nuts. Please make sure
of that, thanks," she said. She swiped her docent badge to pay, eager to join her
friends and tell them about Walter and the looted painting. They were already
there—Lorelei, Shivonne, and Luke—in the far corner where floor-to-ceiling
glass walls offered a panoramic look-out over the bougainvillea-strangled hillside
outside.

Seeing them huddled so close transported her back to the day when they had
first met—six years earlier—shortly after the Pallas's grand opening. It was the
first day of new docent training and the four of them were sharing an elevator car
from the parking structure below, an hour before the museum opened to visitors.

Strangers to each other, except for Shivonne and Luke, who had met years earlier in New York. In retrospect, it had the ironic ring of an age-old joke: "A stoic Angeleno, a free-spirited Canadian, a beautiful Irish ballerina, and a flamboyant, younger man from the Midwest walked into a bar ..." Or rather, stepped into an elevator car expecting nothing but a quick ride to the top floor.

Meanwhile, a spark from a car tire on the freeway nearby had lighted a brush fire in the surrounding hills, triggering the museum's emergency evacuation protocol with sirens blaring, staff evacuated, heavy exit doors sealed ... and all elevators suspended. All according to plan, except for the four docent-trainees trapped inside an elevator because of a control system malfunction caused by the fire.

Or was it Fate that had assembled them inside the dark, sweltering box?

For almost eight harrowing hours—even after the threat of fire had dissipated on the outside—they were stuck. Without food or water, without air conditioning, and with no communication with the outside. An elevator was a large Faraday cage, absorbing and reflecting cellular frequency waves. Who knew? Though they were never in any grave peril—the fire outside had been tamed with an expedient airdrop of flame retardant while a team of engineers worked frantically to free them—the four docents were trapped in the dark for what seemed like an eternity, imagining the worst-case scenario: that they would die there, consumed by fire or smoke.

And so, as mortals did when confronted with disaster, they had strategized ways to free themselves at first, taking turns to scream for help and bang on the metal walls until their voices were hoarse, hoisting the lightest one—Shivonne—up on a pyramid of shoulders to push against the ceiling panels as they had seen in movies. And peeing into Luke's empty XL soda cup when their bladders could no longer pinch. When all else had failed, they settled down, kneecaps to kneecaps, and bonded the way humans did when they thought they were about to die.

As the eldest—and the calmest—of the four, Angel had emerged as the unspoken leader, guiding them through deep breathing and grounding techniques. Through laughter and tears, they shared their deepest desires and insecurities, as if doing so would immortalize their souls. About six hours into their ordeal, they had vowed to remain best friends ... on the condition they survived.

Hope. Fate. Luck?

Hours later, dehydrated and mentally drained, they emerged into the fading daylight, looking dazed and clinging to each other like a single, symbiotic organism. An unbreakable bond had been forged—a phenomenon called trauma bonding, as Angel found out later from her therapist. For her, however, it meant so much more; it was the revelation of a brilliant, multi-faceted diamond, formed by the intense heat and immense pressure of trauma. These were her diamonds, her closest confidantes. Her life buoys in the stormy seas of life.

And that was why, upon approaching their table, she sensed immediately that something was amiss, even before anyone spoke a single word.

"Hi, all." She set her tray down on the table; the clatter of plastic on plastic made Shivonne jump in her seat, prompting Luke to touch her shoulder in a comforting gesture. The tension was tangible. Inside Angel, the black dog stirred in restless sleep. "What's going on?" she asked, glancing sideways at Lorelei for clues.

"It's Shivvy," Lorelei obliged her, "I don't know how to explain ..."

"None of us knew," Luke interjected.

"Knew *what*?" Angel asked, sitting down opposite Shivonne. Didn't they know everything about each other since that day in the elevator?

"Do you want to tell her, Shivonne?" Lorelei prompted. But it was Luke, wound tightly like a jack-in-the-box waiting for its big reveal, who blurted it out without a filter.

"He hurts her, Angel. He abuses our Shivvy."

Angel cocked her head. "Who?" She was still reeling from Walter's revelation and subconsciously pushed back against the latest information. Besides, nobody hurts Shivonne; it was an absurd notion. Who would hurt a gentle soul like her?

"Luke, behave yourself. Look around you," Lorelei said, scanning the rest of the lunch crowd. Shivonne shrugged inward like a turtle retracting deeper into its protective shell, which pushed her sunglasses askew and revealed the contusion around her eye.

51

"Oh!" Angel's hand flew to her mouth; suddenly, she was overcome by the cloying smell of bleach wafting up from the tabletop. The Irish-bred pallor of Shivonne's skin projected the bruise to resemble one of Monet's foreshortened purple lilies against a backdrop of misty waters. "What the hell?" Angel blinked rapidly. A morbid Rolodex of images was spinning through her memory, flagging previous injuries she had noticed on Shivonne, which her friend had always explained away so seamlessly.

The bruised knees? "A tumble down the stairs, holding the laundry basket."

The swollen bottom lip? "Bumped it on the bathroom faucet while brushing my teeth."

The scratches on her face? "Fitzi's sharp little claws, little bugger."

It was clear now, hindsight being 20/20. Angel could kick herself for missing the signs.

"Shivvy, my God, I had no idea. You said ..." She caught herself in time, her hands gripping the edges of her plastic lunch tray so hard that one of her nails split and tore into the nail bed.

You're a terrible friend, Angel. You should have known.

Perhaps she did—a niggling intuition—but she was too ...

Too what, Angel?

Too wrapped up in melancholy, the trauma lurking in the undertow of her mind. She wanted to ask: *Why did you not tell me?* But she knew never to use an accusatory tone with a victim of abuse; never to ask a "Why-question". She remembered how it felt to be on the receiving end of such a "Why?"

"Why were you out so late, alone? Why were you not more careful, Angel?"

A heaviness settled low down in her belly. She should have recognized those familiar signs of post-traumatic stress; she knew it first-hand. Was that why she had been blind to it? The pain in her fingernail was stabbing, punishing her. "Your bruises, these past few months," she said, "I believed you when you said you were just clumsy. What a fool I've been."

"Shivonne, clumsy? Gimme a break," Luke huffed. "She's the *least* clumsy person we know. Have any of you seen her dance on a stage?" He knew they had not; he was the only one who had known Shivonne during her heyday as a prima

52

ballerina in New York. "She's freaking Margot Fonteyn. Clumsy? My small-town ass."

"Please calm your small-town ass down," Lorelei implored.

But his words hit a nerve. It was the truth—Shivonne was shy and soft-spoken, but when she moved, all bets were off. Shivonne O'Roydon did not walk as much as she *glided*, rolling through each step, starting with the toe, through the ball of the foot, and followed by the heel's gentle rock. A muscle memory and grace that never faded.

"Everyone, please ..." Shivonne spoke, her voice a whisper. "You did not see the signs because I tried very hard to hide it from you." With her secret revealed, she removed the sunglasses and fiddled with the plastic temples.

"But why, Shivonne?" And just like that, Angel had let an accusatory "Why?" slip from her tongue. She regretted it immediately.

"Because ..." Shivonne grimaced, "because it is not as bad as it looks. It was the bathtub ... My skin is very pale. I bruise easily." She was clutching at straws. "He loves me so passionately, he just sometimes ..." She stirred her spring pea soup, keeping her eyes downcast to avoid the questioning looks. "Sometimes he just snaps." Her soup spoon was twirling, twirling, twirling. An eternity-8 symbol—over and over.

None of them knew Joe very well, other than around the fringes of Shivonne's life: a birthday celebration for Riley, or the odd evening *soiree* at the museum. On those occasions, he always seemed charming enough—handsome, and stoic—his hand perpetually at his wife's back. Angel had always been envious, interpreting Joe's protectiveness as a gesture of affection and pride. Every woman wants to feel wanted. The truth was, it had been something much more sinister—a measure of ownership and control—prancing his trophy wife around the room like a show horse. She grimaced at the thought.

"Has it always been like this? Has he always done this?" she asked, gesturing toward Shivonne's eye, no longer concealed behind the safety of darkened, polarized lenses.

"No," Shivonne answered unflinchingly. "He's always been controlling, yes, but the uh, aggression has been gradual. The lockdown isolation during the pandemic triggered something in him and then the whole George Floyd thing happened ... He started locking himself in his office, drinking, binge-watching Fox News, and talking to himself. From there, it escalated." She mimed an atomic explosion with both her hands, soup flying from her spoon. "But it's okay, I can manage it ... him." Shivonne was desperate to de-escalate the situation. The spoon went back into the bowl. Stirring, stirring, stirring. Carving a figure-8 into her soup.

Eternity sucked sometimes.

"Shivvy, in the Manuscripts gallery, earlier, you told me you were afraid he'd kill you and Riley one day," Lorelei reminded her gently.

Shivonne flinched. Luke rose from his seat and leaned toward her, his voice cracking. "Shivonne ..." His use of her full name made her look up at him, wide-eyed, like a child chastised by a parent. "It's *not* okay, you hear me. Never."

Lorelei pulled him back down into his seat. Luke always wore his emotions on his sleeve; it was part of his charm. But the situation demanded calm, not drama.

"We need to report this to the police," Angel said, pulling her phone from her docent bag. It seemed the right thing to do. But before she could dial all three numbers, Shivonne grabbed her by the wrist.

"No, Angel, don't!" A few heads from neighboring tables whipped around this time, so she lowered her voice. "I can't call the police. I did it once ... called 911 after he had locked me out on the balcony for hours with nothing but the baby in my arms. They spoke to him outside the house; he must have fed them a lie about his hysterical wife because they left. Without him. Turns out he knew both officers; they were drinking buddies from the precinct. Joe was livid. Threatened to kill me and Riley if I *ever* called the authorities again. I believed him then. I still do."

The four friends sat in stunned silence around the table, their lunches untouched in front of them. Outside the glass wall, a group of students galloped by, bubbling with effervescent laughter. Their unbridled exuberance seemed cruel—almost spiteful—in that austere moment. Angel set her phone down and wrapped her hand over Shivonne's. A few seconds later, Lorelei added hers from across the table, and then Luke followed suit. A motley crew they were: three middle-aged women and one queer Millennial facing down a mortal dilemma and its complicated web of intrigue. It was evident, even before Luke said as much.

"You are like Persephone," he said to Shivonne, "the beautiful Greek goddess abducted by Hades and held hostage in the Underworld. You even look like her."

In a gallery not far from the cafeteria hung a large-scale painting depicting a haunting scene: the maiden Persephone flung over Hades' shoulder, petrified, as he hauled her off to his hellhole. The resemblance was uncanny: Joe was Shivonne's Hades—a brute, like that devil himself—charming on the outside, but evil to the core. And his wife? She was like the beautiful daughter of Demeter, held against her will, guarded by the three-headed dog-beast, Cerberus, loving her brutish husband despite his malfeasance—a classic case of Stockholm syndrome. It was an appropriate fit for Shivonne. Ironically so.

Even Shivonne nodded in acceptance of the moniker. "I guess I can see the resemblance. He likes to keep me home. The only reason he allows me to work here at the museum is because he considers it a 'safe zone.'" She formed air quotes around those two words. "He doesn't view any men here as a threat. He thinks all male museum workers are gay." She turned to face Luke. "That's the only reason he's allowed you to be in my life for so long, Lukey, so don't you go switching sides on me, okay?"

"Honey," Luke said, flipping his dark fringe back, "I'd rather stab myself in the eye with a blunt pencil. Loud and proud, thank you very much. Like Apollo, the golden god of sunlight and music."

"Nice try, Luke, but you're no Apollo," Lorelei snorted. "Apollo is sunny and musical. You're a little glum. Plus, you couldn't carry a tune if it saved your life."

Luke's face fell like a souffle hot out of the oven. He had always idolized the god of the sun, just like his favorite, well-heeled king.

"She's right, Luke, you are much quirkier, a touch darker," Angel said. "Your personality reminds me of Hermes, the mischievous messenger of the gods. You even wear the mark of Hermes." She gestured toward his waist, where he kept his beloved Danish grandfather's vintage Hermes scarf threaded through one of the belt loops of his jeans.

Her explanation went a long way to assuage his letdown. While fingering the silky equestrian-motif kerchief under the table, he acquiesced, "You're right, I am more of a Hermes, the psychopomp. Wings at my feet; a twinkle in my eye." He winked. The moniker suited him well—the Peter Pan kind of naivete steeped in decades of hardship.

The four friends simmered in the moment of comic relief before Lorelei steered the conversation back to the harsh reality. "Shivvy, we are going to help you figure this out." She twisted sideways in her seat to dig through her docent bag. Everyone waited with bated breath to see what she would pull from it. In the past, they had joked about the "bottomless Mary Poppins bag of remedies" Lorelei carried by her side—ready for any emergency, be it a bee sting, a bloody nose, or a broken heart.

A spoonful of sugar ...

She straightened up and held out her hand toward Shivonne. In her palm lay a beautiful crystal, cut, and honed into a multi-faceted prism. The stone shimmered a rosy pink when she folded it into her friend's hand. "It's Rose Quartz," she said, "known as the Master Healer. It will help you manifest a higher state of consciousness. And draw love into your life. Keep it close to your heart."

Shivonne lifted the crystal to let the afternoon sun filter through it and clutched it to her breast—the same breast so savagely gripped by Lucretia in the Gentileschi painting. "Thank you," she whispered.

Angel was not a believer in the healing power of rocks, chants, or tarot cards, but the gesture came front-loaded with Lorelei's deep conviction and optimism. Did David not conquer the giant, Goliath, with nothing but a single stone?

Luke, who had been watching Lorelei's ceremonial gift offering, pointed at her and wagged his finger as if he had just made a discovery. "You, Lorelei, you are like Demeter, the nurturing goddess of nature. Always mothering us and healing our ailments with your potions and spells."

"And, not to forget, fierce protector of her daughter, Persephone," Angel said.

Lorelei blushed; she had always admired Demeter's attributes—her vast knowledge of healing plants and her tendency to nurture. Like Demeter, she had her feet planted firmly in the soil and her head in the clouds. And, like the goddess, Lorelei appeared serene and harmless, even if it was not always the case underneath that soft, innocent exterior.

"Nobody messes with my Persephone," she said, her eyes locked on Shivonne.

Angel centered her gaze back on Shivonne; it was hard to ignore the ugly bruise. "Shivvy, domestic abuse is a criminal offense," she said. "You're not safe there. We need a safety plan. For starters, you and Riley can move in with me. We have the room now that Clio has moved out."

Shivonne shook her head slowly. "That won't work, Angel. If Joe were to come looking for us, he would start with you, Lorelei, and Luke. He can't know that I told you about this. It's too risky. For us *and* you. When he goes into one of his rages, he ... I would never put any of you in harm's way."

Angel nodded, understanding the potential threat. Her eyes fluttered to keep up with the barrage of thoughts swirling inside her head: solutions, strategies, emergency plans. "There are special organizations for battered women in Los Angeles, walk-in shelters, and safe houses. Deacon and I have a lawyer friend who might have advice. I will ask him about a restraining ord—"

Shivonne interrupted her with a soft but insistent touch to the arm and included Luke and Lorelei in her gaze. "I appreciate all your concern, I do, but we'll be okay. He's just been in a foul mood lately and drinking too much. He's not always—" she gingerly palpated her swollen eye, "this forceful. He mostly leaves me alone ... unless I provoke him."

"You? Provoke someone?" Luke's eyebrows shot up. "That's like saying Little Red Riding Hood provoked the wolf."

Angel frowned; it was not unusual for a victim of abuse to stay with the abusive partner and make excuses for him or her, fooled into believing that *they,* themselves, had instigated the beatings. Especially when the abuser followed those incidents with periods of remorse and repentance, as was part of their *modus operandi.*

"It makes sense that you would defend his actions," she said in as soothing a tone as she could manage. "He's the father of your child and you ... well, you are a forgiving person. An abuser manipulates by blaming *you* for the assault and making you doubt your thoughts. To create confusion and lack of confidence.

Then he'll shower you with love bombs the next day to keep you trapped in the vicious cycle. There's a name for it: 'gaslighting'. Whatever he wants you to believe, it is *never* your fault. The important thing is that you listen to the inner voice that has been telling you it will get worse." She leaned forward to stress the point. "And allow us to help you break that vicious cycle. Right, Olympians?"

She stared them down—the newly minted Persephone, Demeter, and Hermes. From somewhere inside the bustling cafeteria, someone shouted "Whoo-hoo!" and that cheer seemed perfectly timed to seal their vow.

"Right," Lorelei and Luke chimed in.

"This is how it's going to work," Angel said. She spoke with the conviction of someone who had endured years of cognitive-behavioral therapy and EMDR sessions in the wake of one traumatic night in Memphis. "You'll keep a journal to record every threat he makes, every time he lifts his hand at you. Every single, critical word out of his mouth, okay, Shivvy? There's a website you should use ... don't worry, it's password-protected for confidentiality. Write down everything you remember, going back as far as you can. Can you do that?"

Shivonne stared at her soup. "He does not let me use my phone or his computer at home, but I can try when I'm here, at the museum."

Angel nodded. The Pallas had a well-equipped library with computer terminals available for staff use. "Did you ever need medical treatment for any injuries?" she asked. "There will be records to attest to ongoing abuse."

"Um, just the one time ... for the miscarriage," Shivonne said, so softly, they had lean forward and to strain to hear her.

"I don't understand," Angel said.

"The miscarriage," Shivonne repeated, a little louder, and then seemed to flinch from the very word, "a year or so after Riley was born. But I didn't tell the doctor *how* it happened." She stared into the distance. "He would have turned four this winter."

Lorelei made the sign of the cross and cast her crystal eyes to the coffered ceiling. "Bastard," she said under her breath.

"It could also have been because I was considered an older mother then, over forty," Shivonne said. "A risky pregnan—"

"Shivvy, I'm so sorry," Angel interrupted Shivonne with a sharp squeeze of her hand. "But this has to *stop*." She meant the abuse but also Shivonne's tendency to blame herself. "Lorelei," she said, back in strategy mode, "please take photos of Shivvy's bruise once we finish here, in a restroom stall, perhaps. Save them in a file on your phone and send me copies." She was on high alert, her mind in solution mode, strategizing.

Next, she pivoted to Luke, who had been sitting in pensive silence, his dark hair wrenched in both fists. "Luke, hello?" She snapped her fingers in front of him and he shrugged out of his stupor. "Please help Shivvy on the library computers. Teach her how to do online banking and use the journaling app, and how to cover her tracks ... that kind of thing. She needs to be computer savvy to move forward and out of Joe's clutches."

"Aye-aye, Captain." He gave her a little sailor's salute and smiled at Shivonne.

"Make sure you clear your search history and exit out of any websites you navigate on your phone. Every single time, Shivonne, okay?" she added. "It's crucial for your safety. Promise me."

Shivonne bit her lip and nodded. Angel was not done; she was on autopilot. Her *See, Think, and Wonder* had morphed into *Plan, Prevent, and Protect*. "When you get home, pack a few essentials for you and Riley, a getaway bag of sorts, in case you need to run on short notice. Just a few necessities like a change of clothing, essential medications, passports ... and cash. Withdraw insignificant amounts of cash over the next few weeks and hide it where he won't look." She stood up and pushed her chair in; the sharp squeal of it scraping the floor echoed through the dining hall. She was livid, fuming at men who could not keep their hands off women. "This is going to stop," she proclaimed again as if it were a done deal.

As she stood thus, gripping the back of the chair with three pairs of eyes locked on her, Lorelei stated the obvious: "You, Angel," she pointed at her, "you are our Athena, our goddess of wisdom and strategy."

"And war," Luke said with a fist-pound on the table. "This is war."

"You even have Athena's war helmet on already," Lorelei winked, shifting her pointed finger higher to Angel's strip of white hair.

The room spun around her like the Tornado carnival ride at an amusement park. *It's come to this,* she thought, *a pitiful group of wanna-be Olympian heroes*: one Persephone in distress, one Demeter with ineffective healing powers, one Hermes twitching to fly, and one Athena with a major case of imposter syndrome. Museum nerds playing pretend. But as ironic as it seemed, they needed those Greek alter egos to put a buffer between them and the harsh realities of life.

Her eyes darted to and from each of her friends' faces, taking stock of the despair. Even though she struggled with it, too, they did not need to see their Athena showing weakness amid a crisis. So, she leaned forward and placed her right hand over Shivonne's on the table. One by one, their hands slapped down until there was a mushed-up pile on the table—an abstract sculpture of flesh, blood, and bones, symbolizing unity, strength, and love. Like a twisted game of Jenga, risking all if one faltered.

"Olympians," Angel said, deputizing them with superficial courage.

"Olympians," they echoed.

It was a done deal: the naming of the gods. When they pulled their hands back, Luke pushed his glasses higher up the bridge of his nose, Lorelei made the sign of the cross, and Shivonne tucked an errant curl behind her ear. Their lunch plates stood untouched on the table—a deflated burger with shriveled fries, a rubbery tofu rice bowl, a limp salad without almonds, and a sickly green pea soup, the eternity symbol embossed into the congealed pottage resting on top.

Nothing but ambrosia for hungry gods and goddesses.

CHAPTER 6
THE PADLOCK with no KEY

S hivonne's mind was stuck on the image of a horror-stricken Persephone, hoisted over the shoulder of the brute. That look of terror mixed with resignation, that hand pushing away from the bulging biceps entrapping her, those eyes heaven-cast.

Me too, Persephone. Me too.

She was the last of the group still seated at their table when the cafeteria crowd dissipated. The conversation with her best friends had been draining. Having kept them—Angel, in particular—in the dark, had been so hard. But now that her secret was out, she could breathe more freely, even though each breath felt like the desperate gulp of a drowning victim; a last-ditch pull of air before the riptide sucked her under again.

Although her confession did not solve her immediate problem, she was no longer adrift without a raft. But she needed to remember that even those marooned, who had a raft to cling to, still drowned if they were too weak to hold on. And that was how she felt: weak and insignificant against Joe and the knowledge that there would be hell to pay if she and Riley ever ran from him.

A chill crept up her arms and settled in the hollows above her shoulders. Her wristwatch buzzed, reminding her to pick Riley up from preschool, and she stood up—a little too fast. A wave of dizziness overcame her, and all sensation drained from her hands. Something dropped from her left hand and rolled over the floor underneath the table.

My quartz crystal!

Tucking her gray pencil skirt under her thighs, she bent at the knees to fumble around under the table. Her fingers brushed across stale breadcrumbs and wilted lettuce, and she sighed with relief when she located the cool stone and coaxed it into her palm. She was about to surface when a pair of men's legs—dressed in flat-front khakis—materialized about a foot away from her crouched position. Instinctively recalling the incident on her bathroom floor, she recoiled and bumped her head hard on the underside of the table.

"Oof!"

But then she heard the ambient cafeteria sounds and remembered where she was. Safe. Far from home. She rose gracefully like the ballerina she used to be, straightening the creases in her skirt as she stood upright. In front of her was an attractive man—in his late thirties or early forties, she guessed—a bemused look on his face, both hands extended out to help her up.

"Are you okay, ma'am?" he asked. His glossy dark hair was swept back into a man-bun, his skin the color of milk coffee. She blew an errant lock of strawberry-blond hair from her face and locked eyes with him. His were a deep brown with honey-colored flecks; she fantasized about diving into those amber pools of molten gold.

Shivonne, what is wrong with you?

A pinkish flush crept over her porcelain-pale skin; she took a half-step back to create distance between them.

"I did not mean to startle you like that," the man said, his hands still outstretched, "but you look like you could use a hand."

"I, I—" she tried, but her tongue resisted formal structure. "I dropped something."

She held out her hand to show him the crystal—as if he had demanded proof—like a child rushing ashore from the water's edge to show a parent the shimmery shell in her hand. He took it from her upturned palm, his forefinger grazing her skin, and palpated it with his long, tan fingers.

"Ah, quartz," he said, flashing perfect white teeth and a solitary dimple in one cheek. "For a spell of love, perhaps?"

The color deepened on her cheeks, and when he handed the cool stone back to her, it seemed to sizzle in her palm.

"Uh, I'm not sure. I guess the clear one is for healing. My friend ..." Her voice trailed off. The man was still smiling; she noticed he was wearing a double-breasted chef's jacket with his name embroidered in blue on the starched, white cotton, right over his heart. "Chef Cristian Alexander," it read. She played the sound of it in her head; it rang with the essence of cello and clarinet. "Cristian."

Oops, did I just say that aloud?

"That's me. Pleased to meet you." One of those velvety hands reached out again, and this time she met it with her own, her hand disappearing in his large paw. It felt safe and warm there.

"Alexander," she asked, "like the Roman emperor?"

"Nope, I'm of Costa Rican royalty," he winked, "but my last name is Greek. It means 'guardian' or 'protector.' And you are ...?"

Her breath caught in her throat. *Protector.*

"Uh, Shivonne ... O'Roydon," she said, hesitating before her last name as if distancing herself from Joe. "Shivvy to my friends."

Oh, so he's a friend already?

"Shivvy." He seemed to taste her name with his lips and tongue, the way a chef did with a special sauce or a decadent pudding. "Like a shiver?" He mimicked a shiver running through his body.

For the first time that day, Shivonne smiled and all preoccupation with Joe and his abuse disintegrated around her and dropped to the floor, settling into the cracks among the wilted lettuce. It was as if she had known this man in a past life ... and the Fates had destined for them to meet again. She briefly closed her eyes to savor the sweetness of tender harp strings performing "Rose Adage" from Tchaikovsky's *The Sleeping Beauty,* reflexively cupping her hands, Vaganova-style, preparing to turn on both toes and swoop the air with delicate ballet arms, ending in a crown—*en couronne*—over her head.

But she quickly realized that the music was only in *her* ear and that her hand was still wrapped in Cristian's handshake. Embarrassed, she pulled it back, the heat from his fingertips lingering for a tenuous second or two. In her left fist, the quartz crystal had taken on a life of its own, buzzing a frantic message in sensory Morse code against her palm. She noticed him glancing down at her hand and felt relieved that she had not worn her wedding band that day. The relief lasted an instant before a frisson of guilt took over. The familiar teeter-totter of paradoxical emotions.

I am a married woman.

A married woman whose jealous, vindictive husband kept her locked away in a tower, suspicious of any man who dared to cast appreciative glances at her. "Most of those museum guys are fags anyway," she had overheard him telling a colleague once during one of his precinct parties at a dive bar, where the wives and girlfriends sipped cheap dirty martinis at the greasy bar counter while the "boys" shot pool and tequila. "No threat there, ha-ha!" Guffaws of laughter and backslaps had encouraged his drunken bravado. Later that same evening, she saw Joe drunkenly scribble his phone number on a napkin and slide it over the bar counter to the busty bartender who had over-served them all night, teasing the "boys" with body shots—a lemon slice propped in her cleavage.

Boys will be boys, right?

"Right," Cristian said as if he had read her thoughts.

"Excuse me?"

"I asked if everything was all right."

"Oh, sure," she said, blushing. "Yes, sorry." She smoothed her skirt with her palm and reached under the table for her bag. "It was nice to meet you, Cristian. I must get going." She turned to leave.

"Wait." He grasped her by the wrist—his touch light but insistent—and she flinched; right under his gentle grip was a cluster of tiny, crescent-shaped punctures left by Joe's sharpened nail—he kept the little finger ones filed to a point. Cristian withdrew his hand. "Apologies. Just wanted to say, I hope to see you again. I'm here," he swept his arm over the stainless-steel hull of the kitchens behind the serving counters, "on duty every day except Mondays and Saturdays."

"I'm a school docent, Tuesdays and Thursdays only," she said, her mind executing a synchronized dive into those pools of molten gold. "We always meet here for lunch."

"We?"

"My fellow Olympians and I." She had no idea why she said that.

He grinned, and that deep dimple dipped into his cheek. It was contagious; Shivonne returned his smile and walked away, hesitant to look back for fear there would be no one standing there but a figment of her wildest imagination. A mirage of wishful thinking.

Is he real? Did I imagine the whole thing—the spark?

At the exit doors, she broke the spell and looked back. He was still there, frozen in a pensive stance next to their table, his right hand tucked into the overlay of his jacket, resting over his heart. When he noticed her looking back, he pulled his hand out and raised it in a silent salute. The pose reminded her of something—of someone—a handsome man in a heroic pose, his hand raised to the skies.

But what? Who?

Outside, on the fragrant patio, it came to her; he had resembled the young Emperor Napoleon as depicted by Jacques-Louis David in his masterwork, *Napoleon Crossing the Alps.* The knight—*the protector*—on the back of a white Arabian stallion, rearing up and exalting his rider to the sky, the young man's hand pointing to the summit of the mountain range he aimed to cross. The intensity of this vision lingered as Shivonne ran to the parking lot, rushing against the clock ... and away from the mysterious man with the amber eyes.

On the freeway leading away from the museum, she realized she was shaking despite the thermometer showing 85 degrees.

Like a shiver? he had asked.

Yes, she thought while one rolled through her body. Not a cold shiver, but rather a tsunami of emotions—a seesaw of fear and joy—and their potential repercussions. She was so distracted that she narrowly avoided sideswiping a pickup truck during an abrupt lane change to make the off-ramp in time. The screeching of tires and ugly cuss words flung at her from an open window was a rude wake-up call.

That is what you get for swimming in another man's eyes, Shivonne.

She was fifteen minutes late when she pulled up to the curb in front of Riley's preschool. With the engine running, she bolted to the office door, but before she could touch the handle, it pushed open from the inside and the principal stepped out to greet her.

"Good afternoon, Ms. O'Roydon. You just missed your husband. He took Riley home a few minutes ago."

Oh no.

She froze mid-step and frowned at the principal. It was never good when Joe had to come to school. That was women's work.

"I'm only a few minutes late, Ms. Shapiro. I don't understand why she didn't just wait for me here." Her voice sounded anxious and accusing, so she made a mental note to sound calmer. But any sense of calm dissipated when Ms. Shapiro delivered a shocking revelation.

"I'm afraid we had a little situation today, and we needed to call a parent to come to school for a chat," she said. "We tried to reach you first, but it went straight to voicemail, so we called Mr. O'Roydon instead."

Shite.

"Oh?" Shivonne fought to control the tone of her voice, but on her mind's stage, she was performing a *Danse Macabre*, sweat flung from her body as she pirouetted, her head whipping around with dizzying speed, her arms pinwheeling. "I'm sorry you couldn't reach me. Wh-what was the issue?"

"Well, today, during recess, one of our teachers, Ms. Danielson, noticed bruises on Riley's upper arms. Here ... and here," the principal indicated on her jiggly upper arms. "When we questioned her about them, she told us her father had grabbed her by the arms and shoved her out of the way."

A sharp pang shot across Shivonne's chest; Halley's Comet with an acid tail reaching deep into her belly. "Sh-shoved her out of the way?"

Stay calm, Shivonne. She pressed her sunglasses tighter to her face.

"Yes, that's all Riley would say before she slammed shut like a clamshell. Shy little darling, she is," the principal cooed. "As educators, we are mandatory reporters of any suspected abuse, but luckily, Mr. O'Roydon arrived to clear up the mystery. He explained about the scary dog incident—"

"Um, yes, the scary dog incident," Shivonne mirrored, waiting for Ms. Shapiro to fill in the rest. Her heart was racing; if child protective services had been called, the aftershock would have been disastrous for her and Riley.

"It was fortuitous that your husband was close by when the neighbor's dog charged at Riley," Ms. Shapiro said.

"Uh-huh," Shivonne replied with a series of vigorous nods. There was no dog. The neighbors had an obese, diabetic cat named Chubby.

"Indeed," Ms. Shapiro said, "if he had not grabbed Riley by the arms to yank her out of the way and up onto that dividing wall ..." She tsk-tsked through her mind's worst-case scenario, "who knows what would have happened? A vicious dog like that needs to be put down, I'm telling you, Ms. O'Roydon."

"Uh-huh," she lied, "and what did Riley say about all this? The dog situation?"

"Oh, she agreed she was a lucky girl that her daddy was nearby to prevent an attack. Poor little thing was terrified, bawling while Mr. O'Roydon recounted the horrific incident. She's obviously still traumatized by the whole thing, *tsk-tsk*."

"Yes." *Obviously.*

Shivonne could not bear hearing another word of Joe's intricate web of lies, so she mumbled a quick excuse and climbed back into her car. The principal continued to ramble on about the dangers of large dogs, even as the window was winding up in her face. With a dismissive wave, Shivonne pulled out of the drop-off lane. She had to get home as fast as she could for damage control. The ten-minute drive home felt much longer than it was. Along the way, a swarm of questions rushed at her like rotten tomatoes flung at the dancer on the stage.

Why did Riley lie for her father? Had he threatened her to keep her mouth shut about that morning in the bathroom?

Ignoring the speed limit's *ding-ding-ding* from the dashboard, she drove as fast as she could. In the rear-view mirror, she saw she was chewing her bottom lip and that her mascara had smudged into a raccoon mask under her eyes. The last thing she needed was another provocation at home, so she licked her thumb and rubbed frantically at the smudges.

At home, she parked her car askew in the driveway and hurried up the brick stairs, hiking up her skirt. At the front door, she took several composing breaths, then stuck her key into the lock.

Click.

The sound startled her, as did the rush of chilled air from the resident evil entity's breath, greeting her the second she stepped through its portal to hell.

Welcome home, Shiv, the house ghoul jeered in the voice of an evil clown luring children into his rain gutter. *Why don't you come inside?*

She dropped her bag on the antique demi-lune table by the door and bent down to greet Fitzi, who always waited for her there, tail wagging—the very antithesis of the evil that blew through the house. She lifted the tiny ball of fluff to her face, burying her nose in his fur, and carried him—wielded in front of her body like an evil-averting amulet—into the kitchen. Riley was sitting on a barstool at the marble counter, a half-eaten burger with a cone of fries in front of her.

"Hi, Mummy," the young girl greeted with a wave.

"Hello, my pet." *Thank God she's okay.*

Joe was standing behind his daughter with his gigantic hands resting on her tiny shoulders, his fingers so large that the young girl resembled a hapless little fly inside a Venus flytrap. It was a message to Shivonne, and she interpreted it loud and clear.

"You're late," he said through his teeth.

She lowered Fitzi to the floor and pulled her cashmere sweater tighter across her breasts against the chill.

"I'm sorry, Joe." *Those three words.* "I was running a few minutes late today. I arrived right after you two had left." She stepped forward to hug her daughter, but Joe's fingers intensified their grip on those little shoulders; Shivonne rocked back on her heels. "Riley usually waits for me in the office if I'm running late. You and I need to discuss the 'incident' at school." She flashed him her "in private" eyes.

Joe smirked; his eyes were glazed over. "Oh, it's all good. Riley and I sorted it out. We took care of that old sourpuss, Miss What's-her-name, didn't we?"

Riley nodded—a slow and deliberate act—her chin ducking down in a turtle maneuver identical to the one her mother had exhibited earlier, in the cafeteria. "And we don't need to talk about it anymore, do we, Ri-Ri?" His hands clenched and unclenched on her shoulders. The little girl shook her head—a puppet in the master's hands. "We had a great daddy-daughter day today; we picked up In-N-Out burgers and talked about leaving that horrible preschool and starting home-schooling in the fall. Didn't we, Ri-Ri?" Riley's head bobbed up and down again in agreement, but her bottom lip was quivering.

"No way, Joe," Shivonne protested, "she needs friends to socialize with, teachers—"

A few hours away from the ticking time bomb at home.

He cut her off with a chilling *did-you-just-say-no-way-to-me?* look. She knew better than to continue pressing him, even though she was certain that pulling their daughter from school would be another nail in their shared coffin.

Over my dead body, Joe.

His eyes agreed with her. *If you say so, Shiv.*

"Look," he said to change the topic, "I'm in a good mood today. Burger and a milkshake for my girl, and a gift for the love of my life." He gestured with his eyebrows to the kitchen counter next to where Shivonne stood, her arms crossed over her chest to fend off the icy breeze wafting from those dead-pool eyes. She followed his gaze to a small black box wrapped in a silver bow. *Other* men's wives would light up and glow at the sight of the silver bow. She shivered.

"For you," he said to his wife, while massaging down hard on Riley's shoulders.

It was his modus operandi, precisely as Angel had mentioned: the gift boxes and floral bouquets he would proffer after a harrowing incident—peace offerings, loaded bribes—shiny, sparkly things designed to buy a woman's forgiveness and absolve the actions of her abuser.

"Love bombing." Is that what Angel had called it?

Any sign of hesitancy would incense the dragon, so Shivonne lifted the lid off the box. Inside was a chunky silver padlock, the size of a nickel, with the word "AMOUR" embossed into the metal. The closed-shackle padlock hung from a heavy-gauge cable chain, the kind of choker a biker chick would wear to accessorize her neck tattoos and spiked leather vest. Shivonne pulled it from its cushioned perch between her forefinger and thumb and assessed its weight in her palm. It was heavy and cold—a far cry from the warmth of Lorelei's quartz crystal earlier that day—its symbolism undeniable: she was locked in and bound to him until death did them part. Light-headed, she swayed on her feet to the opening chords of The Police's "Every Breath You Take" echoing in her ears.

Every breath, Shivonne ... every day.

She held her breath, turned the gift box upside down, and shook it. There was no key for the padlock. Joe was waiting for her response, and she knew it had to sound sincere.

"I love it, Joe, thank you," she lied, pivoting the shackle away from the body of the padlock, and pushing her hair to one side.

"Here, let me ..." He stepped away from Riley and fastened the padlock chain behind her neck by looping the shank through a link and clicking it into the locking mechanism. For the second time that day, the *click*-sound chilled her to the bone. He drew his hands around her neck, both thumbs pressing into the hollow at her throat where the padlock was burning its icy-hot message against her skin. Every time she swallowed, it bumped against her throat.

"*My* Shiv," Joe murmured, emphasizing the possessive pronoun while thumbing the pulsating vein at her neck. "Am I forgiven for being a bad boy?" His breath fluttered vodka fumes under her nose.

"Yes, Joe. But how do I take it off?" she asked. "It's a little too tight around my throat and I didn't see a k—"

"You can't," he chuckled, flashing her a Cheshire Cat grin, and held up a small Allen key that looked to be the male part to fit inside the "O" of "AMOUR." "Only I can unlock it, so you'd better play your cards right and suck up to Daddy Joe." He shoved the key into his back pocket.

She tilted her head back to loosen the pressure around her neck and regretted it immediately. He mistook it for an invitation to slide his hands from the padlock around her neck down her breasts, pinching her nipples hard before resting them on her buttocks. Over his shoulder, Shivonne saw a look of horror on Riley's face. She took her chances with Fate, wriggled out from under his grip, and signaled with her eyebrows to their daughter. With a sigh, he withdrew his hands from her body.

"You are such a tease, my Shiv. Say thank you to Daddy."

"Thank you, Daddy."

He presented his cheek to her, and she obliged it with a peck, the scruff of his stubble assaulting her lips. And then, with a wink, he held his hand out, palm up. Like a good, obedient wife, she walked back to the entrance hall, retrieved her mobile phone from her docent bag, and placed it in his greedy palm. He would unlock it later by keying in the password *he* had programmed into it and scan it for any indiscretions or discrepancies. She worried about the password-protected website with the incriminating details of his most recent assault that Angel had helped her install earlier that day in the Palladian Cafeteria.

Did I remember to delete my history? I'm dead if he finds it.

He was a detective, a master in the art of deceit. She could only hope that, conditioned by years of passivity from her, he would take only a cursory glimpse at her phone activity—especially since he was already three sheets to the wind. In the morning, she would find her phone on the console table by the front door, prodded and pried open—just like her, the night before—his fingerprints smudged all over the surface.

But, until then, Joe slipped her phone into his pocket—as if it were the most normal thing a husband did after a long day—and staggered toward the liquor cabinet at the end of the kitchen counter. A prism of colorful temptations holding intoxicating promises beckoned him through the speckled glass panels. As an afterthought, he turned to her where she stood tugging at the locked padlock pressing against her carotid artery. His voice was as cool as the evil entity blowing its icy breath through the air filters by her shins.

"Remember, Shiv, ... I'll be watching you."

CHAPTER 7
THE OWL and the PEACOCK

A ngel squinted and tracked a majestic golden eagle soaring on a hot air current above the gleaming titanium exoskeleton of the Pallas Museum. The metal cladding intensified the bright California sunlight, bouncing the rays between the buildings. Her head was reeling as she left the cafeteria; a spiteful migraine was building on the horizon. While pulling her sunglasses from her docent bag, she paused for a moment to touch the Narcissus token Walter had given her earlier. It no longer represented vanity to her ... the drooping flower looked bent over in sorrow. As if mourning.

"I pretend it belongs to me."

She ran her fingers through her hair as if to expel the disturbing tale and flopped down on the edge of the marble bench flanking the courtyard's focal fountain. She could see her reflection alongside that of the life-sized marble statue in the center of the fountain: Athena's childhood friend, Pallas. Yet another tragic tale of pain, abuse, and injustice.

It was everywhere.

The Pallas Museum had risen from the dirt thanks to a generous donation from a Greek film tycoon, in memory of his beloved daughter who had accidentally been killed by her best friend in a freak harpoon-diving accident off the coast of Corfu, during their spring break. According to Greek Mythology, Pallas was the mighty Athena's childhood friend, a mortal killed in a freak accident—similarly speared—by Athena during a training maneuver. Devastated by the loss she had caused, Athena often assumed the moniker Pallas, in honor of her friend. And so it was, too, for the Pallas Museum: a place of divine beauty born out of tremendous pain.

A little Greek tragedy in the heart of Los Angeles.

The marble Pallas was on her knees in the shallow water, having been mortally wounded by Athena's spear, her arms extended forward and upward, with water—symbolizing her blood—pouring from her palms into the pool below. Across her marble knees lay Athena's Aegis, the shield that cunning Zeus had used to distract Pallas with, to give his favorite daughter an unfair advantage. In its center, the face of Medusa contorted under the shower of water.

But around Pallas' knees, the fountain settled into a shallow reflecting pool. It was the perfect spot for a pseudo-goddess to sit and reflect on her day. Angel kicked off her loafers and pivoted so both feet hung over the edge, her toes dipping into the pool.

Ahhh, bliss ...

Her stress dissolved into the water. A steady stream of visitors was filing past her in fast motion, but at the edge of the fountain, time stood still. She looked from her feet to the sorrow on Pallas' upturned face.

They think of me as their Athena. Their leader, the goddess of wisdom and strategy.

Outwardly, she knew she projected strength and confidence, even exuberance at times—like a peacock. Inwardly, however, she grappled with insecurity and depression, concealing it from the peacock-lovers in her life. Only her husband and her three closest friends knew the truth of her inner turmoil. Despite this, they still looked to her for guidance.

She shook her head, recalling their last family Thanksgiving dinner when—tipsy from prosecco and laced with turkey tryptophan—her children had surprised her with their inherent impression of their mother. It was a popular parlor game: choosing an animal alter ego that matched the person's personality. Like Harry Potter's *patronus*, the stag—regal and perpetually hunted.

Her husband, Deacon, the strait-laced lawyer, chose an eagle as his symbolic animal: strong, keen-eyed, with a take-no-prisoners attitude; it lined up perfectly with his family's impressions of him. Their daughter, Clio, who worked as an EMT in San Diego, selected a hummingbird: bright, energetic, and industrious. And their son, Roman, chose a koala bear: reserved, introverted, and active mostly at night. But when it was Angel's turn, and she elected an owl as her animal alter ego, they objected.

"An owl? Mom, no effing way," Clio laughed. "Owls are quiet and demure. You? You are more of a peacock."

"Oh, snap!" Roman laughed, slapping his thighs.

"A peacock?" Angel asked, genuinely surprised. Peacocks were flashy but stupid. They danced solo in blues clubs late at night, attracting the wrong kind of attention. "Surely you meant peahen. A peacock is male," she deflected, a touch miffed.

They stared at her in silence before exploding into laughter.

"That just proves my point, Mom," Clio said when she had caught her breath. "Only *you* would insist on the correct term for a female peacock. You're always the one correcting people's grammar or showing off your art knowledge, flashing your tail," she added, fanning her arms out behind her head.

Angel had been tempted to say, *It's called a train, not a tail. Only an owl would know that.* But she stayed mum.

"At least she didn't say 'skunk,' Ma," Roman said, which aroused renewed gales of belly laughter.

Cringing, Angel stroked her landing strip of dead, white follicles. Her children were too young when it had happened; they did not know of the trauma that had turned their mother's hair white overnight. They wouldn't have laughed so uproariously if they did.

"It's called Marie Antoinette syndrome," her therapist had explained during her intake session back then, "*Canities subita*, a condition where hair spontaneously turns white due to injury or stress." It had allegedly happened to the doomed queen the night before her final walk to the guillotine.

At the edge of the fountain, Angel remembered looking at Deacon for support over the picked-clean carcass of the Thanksgiving turkey—which very much looked like a dead peacock to her—but her husband leaned back in his chair, so delighted at the jovial laughter of his children that he missed the deflation of his wife's ego. The triggering of her insecurity about her past peacock actions.

Surely, he sees me as an owl.

She had known it long before that night's silly guessing game; ever since the incident in the back alley behind a barbecue restaurant where her peacock behavior had gotten her into trouble. That night, when she had vowed to change, to be more guarded. Not long after, she had received confirmation of it on a trip to visit Lorelei at her summer home in Nova Scotia. There, in the dense forest on a starlit night, they attended a traditional drum circle, hosted by the Keeper of the Drum of the Indigenous group, which still maintained a presence on their ancestral land. She would never forget the spiritual gravity she had experienced that night; the smell of pine needles and smudged cedar was burnt into her memory. Lying on a soft sheep's fleece, peering through the canopy of trees at a sky dusted with millions of diamonds. The tribal elder was beating a steady rhythm on her large deer-hide drum.

Boom-de-dah, boom-de-dah ...

"Listen to the drum and let it guide you. Slow and steady, like your heartbeat," the drum leader instructed. "Allow your mind to drift to your happy place. Wherever it takes you, your spirit guide will show itself."

Oh-kay then, Angel-the-skeptic thought with an eye roll. She was a realist—not a granola-eating, sage-burning dreamer like Lorelei—with no grand expectations of meeting some guide, never mind an animal one. But she would try anything once, so she allowed the drum to talk to her.

Boom ... Boom ... Boom ... Boom ...

Slowly, surely, it increased its pace, *boom-boom-boom-boom,* until the snare reverberations mimicked the drone of a thousand bees buzzing.

Bzzmbzzmbzzmbzzm ...

On the forest floor, Angel sank deeper and deeper into the cloud of fleece beneath her, listening ... waiting. *This is not working. I'm too much of a reali—*

That's when it happened, as if to chastise the doubting Thomas in her.

Oh, ye of little faith.

Against her closed eyelids, the dark sky yawned above her to reveal the swirling green and violet contortions of the Aurora Borealis. She wondered if the elder had burnt something more hallucinatory than just cedar and sage. Whatever the intoxication—the bone-chilling drone of drums, the mysterious morphing sky,

76

the cedar fumes—she felt drugged. High as a kite, floating so high above herself that the bad memories seemed too distant. Insignificant. The drum was insistent, calling her and demanding focus.

Suddenly, against the backdrop of her heavy eyelids, she saw a sharp object trying to pierce through the star-sprinkled sky—like a demon in a horror film, its face stretching the pliant wall above the sleeping heroine's bed.

Wake up, Angel wanted to shout at the unsuspecting sleeping beauty. *It's right there, above you!*

She sucked her breath through her teeth and stiffened. In the sky above her, something sinister was trying to pierce through her consciousness, grabbing for her with stubby, callused fingers. The Northern Lights were putting on a frantic cabaret show, and the earth was pulling her deeper into the warm sheepskin, as if *something* was trying to suck her body through time and space. Her back arched to resist its pull, but she failed ... and fell, *whoosh,* through the darkness, emerging unharmed on a deserted plane existing in the outback of her mind.

There, she looked around and saw she was no longer supine on the forest floor, but standing in the middle of a prairie, surrounded by a distant, silhouetted mountain range with no visible channel through which to exit. She could smell the smoldering embers of a recent campfire and hear the distant howls of a wolf pack's adulation at the moon. Yet, despite the solitude, she was not afraid. The drumbeat enveloping her body had created an energy field around her, protecting her.

The rhythm slowed then.

Boom-boom-boom ... Boom-boom-boom ...

She tried to cry out, *"No, wait, I'm not ready yet."* But the energy field around her muffled her voice, and the drumbeat continued to slow until it matched her heartbeat.

Ba-boom ... Ba-boom ... Ba-boom.

The sharp object kept pressing down, and the sky stretched under the pressure, like a balloon on the verge of bursting.

Boom ... Pause. *Boom ...* Pause. *Boom ...*

With the drum in its final rhythmic spasms, the object finally pierced through her dream sky to reveal itself; it was the beak of a majestic owl. Sharp and triangular, gleaming like polished ivory. A great-horned owl, with copper-flecked feathers flaring outward from yellow saucer eyes. It looked down at her where she was reclining on the forest floor. And when it blinked those majestic eyes, an incredible calm flooded her body.

The drum came to an abrupt halt, but the owl lingered another second or two before it pulled its head back through the slit it had torn in the dark canopy, leaving ripples in the ink-blotted Northern Skies the way a rock did when skipped across the surface of a lake.

"Your spiritual guide is the owl," the drum leader confirmed later. "Its struggle to break through to you means you have been seeking its wisdom for a long, long time. But ..." she soothed, "now that it has pierced your conscience, the owl will guide you from here on forth with wisdom and grace. Heed its advice, and it will lead you out of the valley of no exit you find yourself in."

How did she know about the valley with no exit I saw in my vision?

Despite the sun beating down on her back where she sat by the Pallas fountain, Angel chilled upon revisiting that night in the forest. The emergence of her animal spirit guide.

A peacock? No way. Not anymore.

A night in the forest under an elastic sky had proven otherwise. She had the spirit of an owl, as the naming of the gods in the cafeteria had confirmed. Athena's wisdom and grace.

She was never like those "peacock" mothers who had standing manicure appointments in between hot yoga sessions and Brazilian waxes at the salon. She had been a travel and entertainment journalist before having Clio—nothing Pulitzer-worthy, but still ... a career full of creative opportunities and occasional "peacock" events like movie premieres and celebrity fundraisers. Trips to exciting locales to report on the sights and the food: Vancouver, Santa Fe, Austin, Hanalei, and ... *Memphis.*

Angel had tasted Robin Leech's "champagne wishes and caviar dreams" for fleeting moments when her plastic "PRESS" pass gave her access to the esteemed citizens of La-La Land—to eat their fancy, bacon-wrapped water chestnuts and sip their chilled flutes of Perignon, sitting in her discount-store taffeta skirt on seats warmed by their overpaid haute couture-clad asses.

It was at one of those hoity-toity fundraisers where she met her future husband, Deacon. He was an associate on track for partnership at a private entertainment-law firm that oversaw wealth management for a cluster of B-list celebs and a washed-up rock star or two. Like her, he stood out like a sore thumb among the glamorous one-percenters, dressed in his department-store suit, his hair clipped short and greying prematurely at the temples. In a sea of expensive cologne and cocaine-dusted noses, he looked real and approachable. And when their eyes locked—the eager lawyer, and the underpaid journalist—it was a done deal: a man from Mars and a woman from Venus.

Angel was still reminiscing when her phone rang in her lap, disrupting thoughts of Deacon and their wilting marriage. "Hello?"

"Good day, may I speak to Miss Angelique Henstridge please?" a saccharine-sweet voice oozed from the other side, mispronouncing her last name—a pet peeve of hers.

"It's Hendridge, with a 'd,'" she corrected the caller politely. "This is she."

"Ah, Ms. Henstridge, this is Rebecca Jones from the Federal Bureau of Investigation Recruitment Office, calling on behalf of Special Agent in Charge Colton Jamisson. How are you doing?"

Angel whipped her posture upright and lifted her feet from the fountain water up onto the ledge. "I'm doing well, thank you. How about you?" Her pulse was doing jumping jacks.

"Ms. Henstridge, I'm calling about your recent application for a position in the FBI's Art Crime unit?"

The world outside the phone glued to her ear went still.

"Yes, yes ... of course."

Breathe, Angel, breathe.

"Well, I'm the recruiter in charge of new hires for the Art Crime unit and I wanted to talk to you about your application. Is now a good time?" Ms. Jones sounded cheery and warm. Angel took it as a positive sign.

"Now is a great time. I am at the museum right now," she said. She crossed the long fingers of both hands for luck and almost lost her grip on the mobile phone.

"Well, Ms. Henstridge, I'm glad I caught you," the recruiter cleared her throat. Angel frowned. "I'll have you know Special Agent Jamisson was incredibly impressed with your resumé: your Art History training, your teaching experience, and your polyglot status. Six languages? Ah-mazing."

Angel could not help thinking the woman had just described a peacock. For the second time that day, something set off her spidey senses.

"Uh, thank you. I believe my skills would be an asset to the Art Crime unit, in terms of global research—"

But Rebecca Jones had run out of the requisite small talk. She coolly interrupted before Angel could continue her hard sell. "I'm afraid I am the bearer of unfortunate news, though, Ms. Henstridge."

"It's Hendridge, with a 'd.'" A hollowness stirred in the pit of Angel's stomach—that instant of zero gravity right before the roller coaster pitched forward into a death-defying drop. The position of Art Crime specialist for the FBI was her dream job. Working on international art crime cases—forgeries, thefts, auction house frauds, and Nazi-era looting cases like Walter's—would provide the stimulation and validation she so desperately craved. Owl-worthy work; way over the head of any peacock.

"Apologies, Ms. Hendridge, I'm calling today to thank you for your impressive application and to inform you that, most regrettably, you have been disqualified based on one of the prerequisites of the application process. And I'm afraid we cannot offer you a—"

Wait ... what!?

"Disqualified? Which prerequisite?" She tried to recall the fine print of the documentation she had filled out. She had stellar references from the museum and from two London auction houses, where she had taken post-graduate classes in Art Crime and Law.

"That would be the Bureau's *age* prerequisite, Ms. Henstridge." The annoying woman was back to using the "s" instead of the "d" and Angel was about to lose every ounce of politeness she had in her.

"'Hen*dridge*,'" she insisted, a tad more forceful than before, "and what age prerequisite are you referring to?"

"You must have missed that section on the paperwork," the recruiting agent said in a cheerful tone. "The FBI has an age cut-off for acceptance of any recruits. That cut-off is thirty-seven, I'm afraid."

Angel almost dropped the phone into the reflecting pool.

What, do the wheels come off at thirty-eight?

"*Excuse* me?" She kept her voice measured and cool, but a storm was raging inside Angel Hendridge-with-a-"d." Zeus was not happy when someone insulted his favorite daughter, Athena.

"Yes, I'm afraid any applicant to the Federal Bureau of Investigation must be younger than age thirty-seven to qualify. I'm afraid you ... you, um, exceed that requirement by quite a few ye—"

"Yes, okay, I get it." No more polite words for the recruitment bitch who seemed so very "afraid," all the time. "The truth is, Ms. Jones, I was hoping to come aboard on a more senior level. I've jumped through all your background-check hoops. I'm almost fifty-three. Someone in the Bureau of *Intelligence* would have noticed the discrepancy, no?" She stressed the word "Intelligence" to hammer her point home.

"Um, I'm afraid we must have overlooked it somehow—an oversight. You're clearly past our ... uh, past your ..."

If she says "prime," I'm going to scream.

"Kindly put me through to Agent Jamisson so I can discuss this with him, in person." Angel no longer felt *kindly*. She was about to lose her shit.

"I'm afraid it is out of the question, Ms. Henstridge. Special Agent Jamisson is a very busy man and—"

"You really should stop being so 'afraid' all the time, Ms. Jones," Angel spat through clenched teeth. "It is *not* a good look for an FBI employee." She no longer feared burning that bridge; the match was lit.

"Well, uh, I—" Rebecca Jones gulped, "I'm afraid—I mean, I'm sorry that our age policy excludes you from our employment despite your very impressive resumé, Miss Henstridge." Despite Angel's insult, the poor recruiter was still trying to appease her. "We appreciate your intere—"

This time it was Angel who did the interrupting. "Never mind, Ms. Jones, I have another call coming in. I'm *afraid* I'll have to let you go."

The devil in you, Ms. Jones.

"I understand, thank you for your ti—"

Angel hung up the call and resisted the urge to hurl the phone into the fountain. Instead, she stared at the screen with a mixture of incredulity and resignation, then slid it back into her docent bag.

Overeducated, underappreciated. Past her prime.

The threat of tears was burning her eyes, but she resisted the compulsion. Crying was for peacocks. She settled for twirling tiny concentric circles in the fountain water with her big toe. Four circles clockwise, then four counterclockwise. The shimmery aqua nail polish on her toes made them look like a school of little fish darting right under the surface. The afternoon sunlight was starting to dip and soon it would tuck itself in for the night under a soft lilac comforter, spread out over the Pacific Ocean. The light was perfect, the golden hour. After a quick perimeter scan, she picked up her mobile phone from her lap and aimed it at her bare feet submerged in Pallas' pool.

Screw them. Screw them all.

The viewfinder wobbled as it tried to focus on her shimmering toes. She zoomed in and pressed the button to capture the shot. *Click.* And then again, *click, click, click, she* spread her toes as wide apart as they would go, zooming in and snapping photos.

Once she was satisfied, she got up from the fountain's edge, picked up her loafers, and headed for the exit, leaving a trail of glistening footprints behind her.

To add insult to injury, the freeway was also a bitch. After wrestling through stop-start traffic, she walked into her living room to find her son lounging on the sofa, his feet on her vintage embroidered throw pillows, his head buried in a pair of bulky headphones. It was a natural habitat for the koala, wiling away his summer on the sofa while counting down the days to his escape for a gap year in Copenhagen. He didn't even glance up from his mobile when his mother walked in, exhausted. Deflated.

"Hi, Roman," she mouthed, motioning him to remove the headphones. He pulled one cup from an ear and regarded her with a raised eyebrow.

"Yup?"

She leaned forward to kiss his cheek, but he ducked out from under her kiss. It hurt her feelings.

"I'm fine, Roman. Thanks for asking. How are you?"

She was desperate for a warm, human connection after the horrible day she had. Roman was her best bet, speculative at that.

"Fine."

"Just fine?" She needed more than that.

He rolled his eyes and flipped the headphone cup back over his ear. She stood for a while, willing him to enquire after her day, to ask for a sandwich or gas money ... *anything*. But he was in a different realm. *In*different.

She admitted defeat—a recurring theme of her day—and retreated to her bedroom, shutting the door behind her. The quiet was oppressive. Deacon was still on one of his international business jaunts—London, Hong Kong, Timbuktu—she had lost track. She was a solitary owl long deserted by her mate, empty-nested by her chicks.

At least peacocks had more fun.

While wriggling out of her bra through her sweater sleeves, she cued the soothing tunes of Debussy's "Clair de Lune." Not soon enough, it filtered through the room, cocooning her in harmonious arpeggios. Her mind drifted to Walter Friedlander's tragedy and Shivonne's horrible plight. The once-distant migraine was fast approaching like a desert sandstorm; it was time to batten the hatches. But she had one more thing to do before then. Those past their prime often resorted to desperate measures to find attention and validation.

She typed *"Feetfinder.com"* in her browser, logged into her account, and scanned the notifications for recent activity. There were thirty-one "likes" on her previous post—a five-second GIF of her weaving a red silk ribbon between her toes. It made her happy to be desired, to have something others were willing to invest in. Her feet, she realized, were still in their prime: lean, smooth, and sexy ... unlike the rest of her.

She uploaded her favorite photo from that afternoon's impromptu shoot at the Pallas fountain: the sun reflecting from her toe polish at just the right angle to create an evanescent shimmer of movement. She added a blurry filter so foot fetishists would have to subscribe for the right to squirm over her seductive toes. *Not* her journalistic qualifications, her art expertise, or her owl-like leadership. No, her feet.

Peacock feet.

She let her phone slip to the floor, dry-chewed two extra-strength Acetaminophen tablets, and lay back against her bed pillows, waiting for the sandstorm to engulf her. Flexing her toes like a peacock's tail, she peered through them at her reflection in the dresser mirror. The face of an owl stared back at her. Why couldn't she be both, she wondered, an owl *and* a peacock? Itching to do something risky, something to make her feel alive again, despite knowing better.

"What do you want from me?" she asked the owl. But before it could answer, she had dozed off, cradled by Debussy's lullaby, and dappled by the afternoon sunlight frolicking on her bed.

CHAPTER 8
THE KICK-ASS MOUSE

"**G**loria! Gloria! *In excélsis Day-ay-oh!*"

Lorelei shut her hymnbook with a loud *thwap*. The last vowels of the hymn echoed in the nave of the church and diffused among the sunlight sifting down from the stained-glass window panels.

For the McAllister family, Sunday morning mass had begun innocently enough with an uplifting sermon about the parable of the Good Samaritan. It was one of Lorelei's favorite stories from the Bible and a poignant, teachable one at that. In a world rife with discrimination and xenophobia, she and Benjamin were raising the girls to look past differences and embrace compassion—like that Good Samaritan, who had helped the injured Jew even though they were supposed to be enemies.

Listening intently, she sat in the pew holding hands with Grace to her left and Ivy to her right, casting content glances at Benjamin, and relishing the peace. Had she not been so engrossed in the Good Samaritan, she would have registered the first few sniffles from Grace much sooner, but it was only after the sixth or seventh one when a hint of unease crept up her spine. By the time the congregation was kneeling in prayer, Grace was in full-blown crisis with one of her epic nosebleeds.

God had ironic and comedic timing, it seemed.

The spontaneous flood burst from Grace's mucous membranes, pooled in her cupped hands, and dribbled through her fingers onto the pine floorboards. When she lifted her chin toward her mother's unsuspecting face, she resembled Carrie—from Stephen King's eponymous novel—crowned prom queen under a shower of pig's blood. Before the priest could say "Amen," her pale blond hair was streaked pink with blood.

"Mom," she pleaded, her eyes hollow.

Lorelei reacted as any mother with a chronically ill child would—with speed and nonchalance. She rose from her seat and cupped her hand under Grace's nose to catch the worst of the flow. "God damn it," she groaned under her breath, loud enough to provoke gasps from the pews closest to them.

Nothing to see here, folks.

She usually carried a first aid kit's worth of supplies in her docent bag, but today she wanted to look carefree and pretty, so she had tempted fate with vanity and brought a much smaller, cross-body purse instead. She rummaged through its pitiful contents with her free hand: a twenty-dollar bill for the collection plate, breath mints, lip balm, and a handful of tissues. But flimsy tissue would not stand a chance against the plague of blood, so she resorted to the next best thing: one of her super-flow Maxi pads. She tore it noisily from its plastic wrapper with her teeth and pushed it under Grace's nose with one hand while pulling her up by the elbow with the blood-stained one. There was nothing graceful about the way they shuffled out past the raised knees of fellow congregants who were recoiling like the sea parting before Moses. It was hard to ignore the stares as they passed the pews—some concerned, a few annoyed by the spectacle—but Lorelei kept her head high. When it concerned her children, sweet, healing Lorelei took after her alter ego, Demeter, who once blighted the earth when her daughter, Persephone, was in peril.

Hell hath no fury …

Father Bernardo—bless his soul—had witnessed the entire ordeal from his pulpit and signaled the organist to play. And so, accompanied by the majestic timbre of the hymn, "Be Not Afraid," mother and daughter shuffled down the aisle toward the back doors, Grace dropping splatters of bright-red blood like a gothic flower girl scattering rose petals at a wedding. Lorelei knew Benjamin would follow suit at the first appropriate moment, mumbling excuses while dabbing at the blood drops with his handkerchief as he and Ivy traced their bloody retreat up the aisle.

Back at home, she dipped a dampened cotton swab in Cayenne pepper and gently swabbed the inside of Grace's nostrils, while pinching the bridge of her nose to staunch the bleeding. If the nosebleed needed cauterization, as it had so many times before, they would have to go to the ER. But the cayenne pepper did the trick this time. As soon as Grace was comfortable on the couch with a cool compress on her forehead, Lorelei escaped out the back door to her happy place: her garden.

Outside, with the perpetual California sun baking down on her, she could shift her focus and count her blessings rather than the curses. Shivonne's gift of bone marrow, for one. And, because she was a perfect match for Grace, Shivvy's commitment to donating a kidney should Grace ever need a transplant—a real possibility down the line. Lorelei had no idea how she could ever repay her friend for offering up a menu of her body parts to save Grace.

Thank God for Shivonne. An authentic angel in a city of fallen ones.

She rose from her dirt patch, where she had been aerating the ground around her lavender bushes and dusted her knees. In the far corner of her sizeable garden, behind a bed of echinacea, stood a small greenhouse. She stooped to avoid hitting her head on the glass A-frame, but once inside, she could stand tall amid six rows of cannabis plants, their buds crowned atop seven-leafed collars unfurled to the sun. She rubbed one between her thumb and middle finger to activate a little of the pungent oil. It smelled good—of nature and of Demeter's healing powers.

She had cultivated cannabis long before they moved to the United States, inside the red barn in her Mahone Bay backyard—a winning crop which had seeded the one in Los Angeles, even before it was legal to grow and use. The Cannabidiol properties she extracted from those darling buds made an excellent therapeutic remedy—however fleeting—for Grace's chronic pain and bouts of nausea. All those years of risking felony possession and distribution charges had been worth it when weighed against the benefits. A mother would risk anything to save her child.

Even jail time.

"Grow, my babies," she told her crop. It was bittersweet that her miracle plants thrived outside, while inside—ensconced in a hospital-grade, HEPA-filtered bubble, and nourished with the finest organic foods and homeopathic supplements—her daughter was slowly shriveling up like a desiccated rose, its pinkish color fading fast, its head too heavy for the wilting stem.

Lorelei hung her gardening tools back on their hooks inside her garden shed, stepped out of her muddy clogs by the kitchen Dutch door, and headed back inside. She had to finish reading the last few chapters of the assigned book for the discussion later that evening. Moms of ailing children had little time for reading, other than stolen moments while waiting in the car, or sitting on the toilet. The monthly event was a highlight—a rare evening away from the stress at home. Otherwise, her days stuck to each other like the disappearing edge of a jumbo roll of packing tape, with no telling where one part ended and the other began. A continuous, frustrating fight—cooling a feverish brow, wiping away frustrated tears—just to retreat to bed late at night and collapse into a pile of mush, screaming "Fuck you, cancer!" into her pillow, followed by an apologetic glance to the ceiling, "Pardon my French, Lord."

It was during moments of weakness like those when she found it particularly ironic that her best friends thought of her as calm, nurturing Demeter when she was so helpless as a mother ... and even more so as a healer. She missed the Lorelei she used to be before motherhood: the skinny-dipping, berry-picking, daydreaming nymph. Wild and fancy-free. Without a care in the world.

She set to task, blending an immune-boosting smoothie for Grace: one cup of kale, two beets, half a cup of frozen blueberries, a little coconut milk, and a dash of turmeric. Turmeric was supposed to heal anything—except for rare blood cancers, of course. When she bent forward to place the smoothie next to Grace's plate on the kitchen counter, a stabbing pain pierced her chest. Bracing herself against the counter, she waited it out with deep breaths. She was no stranger to panic attacks.

"Five things, Lorelei," she recalled Angel coaching her the first time it had felled her, inside the firebox elevator. "Name five things you can see ... four things you can feel or touch ... three things you can hear ... two things you can smell or taste ... and one positive characteristic of yours. One awesome strength you possess, Lorelei."

Words of wisdom: a grounding technique designed to distract the sufferer from crushing panic. So, Lorelei took one more deep breath in her kitchen and started searching for five things she could see on the butcher block island in front of her, where they kept a revolving smorgasbord of clutter.

"Keys ... hair scrunchy ... coins ... a corkscrew ..." she started listing them but got no further; her mind had stuck on the fifth thing she saw on the counter: a stack of bills, their envelopes torn open, their bold, red print accosting her through their thin, paper sleeves.

So much for panic relief.

She pulled one bill from its envelope and scanned the contents even though she knew what it said: *"BALANCE PAST DUE—Pay now to avoid penalties."*

She pulled another from its white mortuary sheath.

"DELINQUENT account. FINAL NOTICE."

She was so engrossed, she did not notice Benjamin sidle up behind her until he wrapped his arms around her, his lips nuzzling her neck. She melted backward into his embrace.

"I know," he said, "it's bad, but we will figure it out. We always do."

"How?" she asked, exasperated, letting the overdue hospital bill slide from her fingers. "When? They keep coming ..." She looked toward the door and lowered her voice to a whisper, "and she's not getting better."

Benjamin spun her around to face him and rubbed her upper arms. "Hey, it will be okay, I promise. What do we always say about the McAllister family?"

She rolled her eyes. It was silly, but she humored him, "We are like the mouse in the bucket of cream, churning away." It was from a scene from one of their favorite films, *Catch Me If You Can.*

"Uh-huh, and what happens to the cream?"

"It stiffens, turns into butter."

"And the mouse?"

She rolled her eyes again.

"Exactamundo," he said, "we've always managed our way out of a sticky situation, somehow. We're a winning team, remember?"

"I haven't been a winner in a long time, Ben," she said against his chest. "Not for the last eleven years."

"Hey, little mouse," he soothed, lifting her chin with his finger, "we will find a way. We have the option to move back to Canada if push comes to shove."

"We can't do that, Ben," Lorelei demurred. "All the specialists are here for Grace, and film work for you." Reality was a cruel tease.

"For now, yes," he said, "but that might change. They're building a brand-new medical center in Halifax. Who knows?"

"We need solutions *now*," she emphasized with a soft punch to his chest. His pectoral muscles tensed under her fist.

"Look, I wasn't going to tell you yet," he said, "but I am short-listed for a job that could help us dig out of this hole."

"Yeah?" she asked, perking up a bit. "What's the job?"

He shifted on his feet. "Oh, it's not ideal. It would take me away from home for a while, but my colleague, Alex—remember him from Reuters? They're filming a documentary and need an on-location DP for the cinematography. He's putting in a good word for me with the producers. I'll find out soon."

"On location? Where?" She fiddled with his shirt buttons.

"Um, Sudan. It's a documentary feature on the lives of child soldiers and the atrocities of war. I figured—"

"Are you *kidding* me, Ben?" she pounded against his chest, "a war zone? No freakin' way! It's too dangerous; all the foreign embassies are evacuating staff as we speak. I won't let you ... We can't risk losing you." She was protesting even as she understood the unequivocal truth; they did not have the luxury of refusing a solid offer of income.

"Lorelei, honey, please don't fret. It's not a done deal, but we must consider it. We will be in a green zone with constant security and interpreters."

90

"It sounds like 'we' have already decided," she pouted, gripping, and releasing his shirt sleeves. He drew her in tighter, and she knew: Sudan, it would be. And just like that, it was back—the searing tightness in her chest.

Damn.

From the living room down the hall, she heard a cough followed by a gagging sound.

"Mom, come quick," Ivy called, sounding more annoyed than alarmed. "Grace just barfed all over the sofa!"

With a deep sigh, Lorelei unwrapped herself from her husband's embrace and pushed back from the butcher-block counter, disturbing the pile of bills on it, and sending them fluttering to the ground. "I'll be right there," she called out, her voice unwavering.

"I've got this, hon'," Benjamin said. "You managed the plague of blood in church this morning. Go, get ready for your book group thing. You deserve a break." He pecked her on the lips and followed it with a playful smack on her bottom.

God, how she loved this man. He maintained calm when she raged at the moon; picked up the bits when she fell to pieces. He was right, of course, she *was* like the anecdotal mouse who fell into a bowl of cream—not the one who gave up and drowned, but the other one who kicked and pedaled, refusing to give up, until it had churned the cream into butter so stiff that it was able to scamper out to safety. She simply needed to pedal like crazy.

Kicking and screaming, like a feisty little kick-ass mouse.

CHAPTER 9

APOLLO and the GODDESS-MOTHER

L uke was saving a life when his doorbell rang.

It was something he did twice a week as a volunteer crisis counselor, manning a suicide hotline for LGBTQ+ adolescents in crisis. It was grueling work he was drawn to and uniquely cut out to do, counseling the depressed, the shunned, and the forsaken. Offering a sympathetic ear and sound, hard-earned advice. And, occasionally, in the case of an imminent suicide risk following a ladder-up assessment, alerting a supervisor for emergency 911 intervention.

"How are you feeling right now, buddy?" he asked the thirteen-year-old boy on the other end of the line, ignoring the shrieking of his door buzzer. The call had gone past his session end time, but he needed reassurance that the anonymous caller would stay safe once he disconnected. He had *been* this boy once; he knew the value of a calm voice to de-escalate and comfort.

"Do you promise not to make any rash, permanent decisions for this temporary situation you find yourself in?" he asked.

"I think so," the boy answered. "I feel much better."

"So, you will lock away the razor blades like we discussed?" Luke prompted.

"Yes, but—" the boy said.

"Yes, *and* ...?" Luke said, reminding him to use the positive affirmation instead of its evil twin.

"Yes, *and* I will try some of the coping tools you mentioned."

"Atta boy," Luke said, relieved. "That takes incredible courage and strength. Next time you feel these overwhelming urges, remember what I told you about HOPE."

"Uhuh," the teen replied. "Hang On, Pain Ends. I will never forget."

Tension released her grip on Luke's shoulders; it was what he had been waiting for—a sign that the boy would stay safe through the night ... until the next time. The next incident. The next bullied kid on the ledge of a bridge, desperately in need of a fairy godmother.

"It *does* get better, buddy. I promise you," Luke said, in closing, before ending the call.

The doorbell buzzed again—a shrill electric zap that fired up every nerve ending in his neck—followed by insistent pounding.

"Okay-okay-okay." When he finally opened his front door, Lorelei stood on the doorstep, glowering, and blowing wisps of blond hair from her face.

"Luke, what the hell?" she said. "I've been standing here ringing your apartment's call button for ages. What were you doing in there?"

"Oh, nothing much," he shrugged, "just life and death stuff, you know?"

"Ugh, you're always so dramatic, Hermes." She stepped into his studio apartment, her cheeks red with exasperation after climbing four flights of stairs to his walk-up; Luke's art deco apartment had no elevator and no air conditioning. She had offered to give him a ride to their monthly book discussion at the museum. Despite being thirty-two, Luke did not own a car; he was a typical Millennial who favored the convenience of Uber, DoorDash, and Venmo, among other disyllabic amenities.

"Let me use the commode quickly and then we can head to the Palace," he said, popping into the bathroom and sliding the pocket door shut. She could hear him tinkle in the porcelain bowl. "Grab yourself something cold from the fridge," he spoke through the door.

"Thanks." She grabbed a bottle of water from his mini fridge and turned around, unsure of where to sit. The all-in-one studio was a study in Luke's peculiar brand of quirk—every surface was jampacked with art books, bolts of fabric, and rolls of ribbons skewered on a pole where there should be a roll of paper towels. She squealed at a piece of faux fur sticking out from between two seat cushions on the sofa, thinking it was a hamster that had escaped its cage. A smile spread across her lips. Luke's studio space was so like him: quirky, disorganized but oh so fascinating.

Taking a sip from the water bottle, her roving eye caught a gorgeous silk dressing gown hanging on a padded coat hanger from a hook behind the front door. She had never noticed it there before; the door was usually flung open to allow a breeze to flow through the cramped studio. Intrigued, she reached out to stroke it and let the silkiness tumble through her fingers like drips of honey.

"Luke," she called out, smiling, "you didn't tell me Rita Hayworth was staying over."

"Hmm?" He was running water in the sink.

She pulled the gown from the hanger and slipped her arms through its cascading bell sleeves. It felt cool, soothing her flushed skin. Swaying, she modeled for the beveled mirror behind the door, letting the kaleidoscope of colors swirl around her. The gown was a lively cerulean blue, embellished with pastel-colored birds perched on pink peonies and blue hibiscus clusters. It was the stuff of Old Hollywood glamor.

"What are you doing?" Luke bellowed from behind her. She froze, but the gown did one last swivel of inertia around her waist before settling, deflated, against her thighs. "Take it off." He stood rigid, his hand extended for the gown, his mouth pulled into a tight line.

"Okay, jeez. I'm taking it off." Blushing, she slipped out of it and held it out to him. "I don't see the harm."

He grabbed it from her hand and hung it back on its hanger behind the door, adjusting the shoulders and smoothing the drape of the silk. His fingers lingered on the hem, picking at nonexistent lint before turning to face her.

"Lore, I'm sorry for my outburst. I'm still tense from the call I was on just now. It's just ... this is no ordinary gown; it means the world to me."

Lorelei bit her lip, baffled by his icy reaction but wanting to give him the benefit of the doubt. It was a very uncharacteristic tantrum from witty, mischievous Luke.

"Come," she said, tucking her arm through his, "let's get going. You can tell me about it in the car."

He nodded, scrambled to find his copy of the discussion book from under a pile on his coffee table, and then they descended the stairs, arm in arm. She cast a nervous glance at him while they walked, scanning the color of his aura. It measured a steady, somber over moody. Of course, she knew all about Luke's oppressive childhood, but she sensed a desperate need for him to unload, so she listened. Mulholland Drive's twists and turns were the perfect pathway to shuttle them back into his youth, to the day of his sixteenth birthday.

Luke was in his high school library, where he found refuge from constant bullying. There, ensconced in the dusty smells of old leather, the comforting sounds of rustling pages, and the deep sighs of fellow escapees, the librarian, Ms. Marybeth Latsky, had taken him under her wing.

"Ms. Latsky was the only person who understood me and accepted me back then—the *real* me," he said. "She guided my path to enlightenment through Art History—from Raphael and Michelangelo to Hirst, Warhol, and Mapplethorpe. From there, the skip to the drama and theatrics of Alexander McQueen and Gaultier was a natural segue."

Lorelei nodded and waited for him to continue.

"She was the fairy godmother who changed the country bumpkin into the current version of Luke you see here." He gestured from his head to his toes.

"I love this version of Luke," Lorelei said.

"She freed my mind, but she also freed me ... literally. Did I ever tell you this story?"

"Can't remember," she said, despite remembering the topic surfacing during those claustrophobic hours stuck in the elevator six years earlier. But he needed to tell it again. *Talk* therapy was called that for a reason.

"A week or so before my sixteenth birthday," he continued, "she walked up to me in the library and, without a single word, slid a form across the table. A document titled 'Legal Emancipation of a Minor.'"

"Ah," Lorelei nodded—it was her favorite part of the story; how Luke had escaped his repressive youth, his persecution for being different.

"I still remember how she motioned me with her finger to her lips. '*Shhh,*' that gesture shouted, '*this is our secret.*' Good old Ms. Latsky," he sniffed, his eyes moist. "My very own fairy godmother."

Lorelei glanced over to see if he was crying.

"Just like that," he said, "she handed me the keys to my restraints—the legal tools I needed to escape from a doomed existence as a neutered farm boy."

"Heaven forbid," Lorelei snorted. The idea of 'Farmer Luke' was preposterous.

"Ms. Latsky even paid me a stipend to work as her library assistant, from her pocketbook, I suspect, knowing I would need cash to fund a fresh start."

"Wow," Lorelei said, "and the gown?"

"It was a gift from her, on the day of my sixteenth birthday. My 'Freedom Day' she called it," Luke said. "It was the most beautiful gift I have ever received: a silk gown. *Her* gown." He sighed. "I didn't know it then, but Ms. Latsky had been diagnosed with pancreatic cancer weeks before her courageous move to give legal advice to a minor. Her prognosis must have given her the 'I-don't-give-a-damn' impetus to shelter the wounded fledgling ejected from his own nest ... and send it soaring into flight."

The bird imagery felt heartbreakingly appropriate to Lorelei.

"The gown—the birds ..."

"Yeah, the gown was supposed to be her convalescent gown ... before she decided to forgo treatment. I did not understand what was happening, but it was fast—her decline."

Lorelei was silent.

"I mean, you saw the gown. Imagine me, a sixteen-year-old closeted gay boy gifted an item that single-handedly validated every ounce of my being. It was just ... *Kapow!*" He mimed fireworks exploding. "That gown, Lore ..."

"Yes?" She glanced at him; he was staring straight ahead, his eyes following the curve of the road as the car snaked along.

"It's what love looks like and what love *feels* like to me."

"It is beautiful," she said, "the silk gown and your story about Ms. Latsky. What happened next?"

"About five months later, the day after Ms. Latsky had earned her permanent angel wings and departed the musty old library for good, I packed a single saddle bag and snuck out of the farmhouse in the dark, hours before my father would wake to milk the cows. Without looking back, without shedding a single tear. With nothing but the money I had saved, the clothes on my back, and Ms. Latsky's silk gown wrapped around a weathered copy of *A Tale of Two Cities*, liberated from the same library that used to be my haven."

"Wow," Lorelei said, imagining the lonely silhouette of a skinny farm boy outlined against a star-scattered sky on a blustery autumn morning.

"Her death was the final shove I needed to get the hell out of Dodge. I took the earliest Greyhound that day to the most glamorous place I could think of—the antithesis of home."

"New York," she remembered.

"New York! New York!" he sang. "The city that never sleeps: the shows, the art, the fashion. Freedom. I found minimum-wage work as a costume designer's assistant at the New York Ballet—fixing hems, sewing in bra pads, and helping dancers change in between performances. That kind of stuff."

"Ha, glamorous," Lorelei smirked.

"It was hard, yes, but at least it was not hell. Coming from hell, I knew the difference. Besides, that is where I learned to sew and where I met Shivvy." He paused, turning to look back at the curves of Mulholland after it spat them out at the base of the hill. "She was one of the principal dancers on the first production I worked on. *Esmeralda,* I believe it was, or *Carmen* ... too many shows, too many years ago. She took me under her wing and looked out for me like an older sister."

"You were so young to live alone in a harsh city like New York," Lorelei said, wondering how he had managed to navigate its dark underbelly.

"Yeah, but I was not alone; I stayed in a youth hostel with a bunch of other lost boys."

"Runaways, like you?"

"*Throw*aways, like me. Cult escapees, young Amish men on Rumspringa, Mormon fundamentalist teens excommunicated to free up the young girls for the polygamist elders ..." Deep parentheses appeared between his brows. "There was a ton of dysfunction, pain ... drugs. But good times, too. During the ballet off-season, I washed cocktail glasses at a gay go-go club in NoHo. I lied about my age to get that job. I saw some crazy shit there ..." He laughed at her mock-shocked expression. "Hey, I was young and suddenly liberated, remember? The world was my oyster and oysters were a delicacy for a farm boy from Wisconsin." Giggling, he pushed his glasses higher along the bridge of his nose. "Eight years later, I followed Shivvy to Los Angeles after she married Joe. She helped me get my GED and later helped pay for my community college classes. She has done *so* much for me. I would do anything for that woman ... *Any*thing! My fairy godmothers, they were—Shivonne and Ms. Latsky."

"I'm so sorry if I disrespected Ms. Latsky's gown," Lorelei said, "I had no idea."

"Oh, stop it," he soothed. "As you said earlier, I'm such a drama queen. The gown is my lucky charm; I touch it before leaving the apartment every morning and imagine transforming into one of those colorful birds—wild, fancy, and free. A phoenix rising from the ashes." He hooked his thumbs together and flew his hands up to the windshield.

"That's so poetic," she said, patting one of his hands after it landed in his lap again, "and now you're our Hermes, wings, and all. You, dearest Luke, were destined to fly."

At the museum, Lorelei pulled into a docent-allocated spot in the near-empty parking lot. They arranged to meet at the book group session at 6:30 p.m. and went their separate ways: Lorelei to the cafeteria to hunt down cookies for the book group participants, and Luke to the Neoclassical sculpture gallery. It was almost closing time and visitors were filing past him toward the museum store for a meaningless souvenir magnet or a T-shirt that showed poor Van Gogh cupping his hand over the stump of his severed ear, proclaiming, *"Say what?"* Luke scoffed at the kind of visitor who speed-walked through the galleries of "boring, old stuff," stopping only to take the requisite selfie in front of the showstoppers while ignoring the genius of Turner or the splendor of Vernet, Pontormo, or Titian.

He sauntered into the empty gallery, circled a collection of bronze figurines and marble goddesses, then positioned himself in front of his favorite of all the immeasurable treasures in the museum: a sculptural masterpiece by the French Napoleonic sculptor, Joseph Chinard. Chinard used to be a wedding-cake decorator before he turned royal court-sculptor, Luke always told his tour groups; he marveled at the nugget of knowledge that so beautifully explained the exquisite attention to detail in the artist's sculptures: the marshmallow clouds that looked soft enough to bite into, the solid marble drapery one could see through when light shone from behind.

The allegorical sculpture depicted a mother dressed in costume as Minerva—Athena's Roman equivalent—symbolizing her strength and courage in the absence of her husband, who was away at war. The most heart-rending feature of the sculpture for Luke was how the mother held her shield, with her cloak draped over it like a protective canopy, over her young son. Asleep, naked, and vulnerable, at his mother's feet, an oversized dagger in his hand.

Ms. Latsky had shielded him like that once, from the inclement elements of society. The Chinard sculpture would have made an appropriate headstone for her grave.

My Goddess Mother.

He felt a sharp pang of anxiety for the young boy, who looked about ten years old and utterly defenseless despite the dagger in his limp hand. Luke subconsciously stroked the ladder of raised scars on his inner arm. The boy's skin—it was easy to forget that it was solid marble—glistened with the perceived damp of night terrors, as if he would wake up any second with beads of cold sweat on his brow. It made every hair on Luke's body stand on end. He had *been* this boy once, growing up in the absence of a father's protection, feeling exposed amid constant threat and persecution. He couldn't help but envy this boy.

Luke pulled a Moleskin notebook and a stubby pencil from the pocket of his seersucker sport coat and started jotting down a few lines of poetry. When he read the lines aloud, his voice echoed through the empty gallery in rhythmic, syllabic haiku:

"The Mother Goddess,
She watches while I slumber,
Her shield my roof ..."

"Ugh, shitballs." Frustrated, he pushed his glasses higher and tried again:

"My Goddess Mother,
She shields my fragile psyche,
I ... I ..."

"I fear no longer," a velvety voice spoke up behind him, completing the poem in five poetic syllables. Startled, Luke spun around to face his interlocutor, a twenty-something Black man wearing an argyle pullover, khakis, and a tentative smile on his lips. He resembled a young Denzel Washington, only edgier with bleached-blond tips in his hair, giving him the effect of wearing a crown of gold.

Like Apollo, the God of the sun. Luke blushed at the thought.

"Didn't mean to startle you," the young man said, flashing clear braces over seemingly perfect teeth. "I didn't expect anyone else to be here at closing time. I'm Jerome Ap—" A high-pitched ringing in Luke's ears drowned out the rest of Jerome's introduction.

Is this love at first sight?

He shook Jerome's outstretched hand, "Luke ... eh, Lorenson. Is this your first visit to the Pallas?"

"No, I work here," Jerome responded in his velveteen voice, "at the museum gift store." He flashed another blinding smile and glanced at the key card hanging from the ball chain around Luke's neck, its purple color indicating his status as an art educator. "Ah, this would explain why we were reciting poetry in here."

"Yes, I'm planning a student activity for next week. Beautiful finish, your haiku," Luke said, gesturing with his thumb toward the Chinard. "You seem to respond to this sculpture the same way I do."

Jerome circled the sculpture, scanning it *a tutto rondo*—in the round—as only an art connoisseur would know how to do. Luke watched with interest.

"Beautiful piece. Dreamy, yet thought-provoking. Your favorite?" Jerome asked with elevated eyebrows. Luke nodded, at a loss for words. Jerome swerved with an agile side-step to the neighboring sculpture, a striking head-and-shoulder bust of a man of African heritage, carved from a gleaming black touchstone. "This here is *my* favorite," he proclaimed. "Francis Harwood. He did several renditions of this particular Black model."

The unnamed model's posture projected a sense of pride and enigma, his head aloft, his eyes intense yet evading the gaze of the viewer. His chest was strong and muscular, and his shoulders pulled back, causing the muscles around the collarbones to flex. The fading daylight bouncing back from the black stone gave it the effect of moist, oiled skin.

Luke held his breath, regarding the sculpture as if it were the first time that he had seen it. The truth was, he had walked by it and stood near it countless times before, hypnotized only by the beauty and mystery of its neighbor, the Chinard.

"He's exquisite," he said. "So strong."

"He is," Jerome agreed. "Proud and regal. Like a king."

Judging from the way the sculpture subject's shoulders angled backward, Luke had always assumed that his wrists were shackled behind his back—that he portrayed an enslaved person torn from his homeland. But Jerome's observation made him regard the sculpture with fresh eyes. Now, he saw pride in its expression rather than defeat.

"Who was he?" he asked.

"The artist, Harwood?" Jerome asked.

"No, our king here," Luke said.

Jerome shrugged. "Little is known about this subject, according to the info here," he gestured to the plaque against the wall, "but, historically, the Black model has always been inconsequential and invisible in art."

"Sad but true," Luke agreed. "I recently read the Musée d'Orsay's 2019 exhibition catalog, spotlighting models of color like Géricault's favorite, Joseph, and many others, throughout the genres. Featuring them. Naming them and giving them a voice. It's about time the art world recognizes their contribution."

Jerome regarded Luke. "How about we give this guy a voice, too? It calls for a different poem. Spoken-word style," he said. "What do you say?"

"I, uh, I—" Luke stammered. Deep down, he was still a small-town boy from a farming community in Wisconsin. He was about as familiar with free verse as Jerome was with cow-dung surfing, he assumed. But then he remembered that not even *he*, the farmer's boy, had ever understood the point of hanging onto a cow's tail and skating across its manure. He thought about saying as much to Jerome but held his tongue. For vanity reasons, he did not want to reveal his backcountry roots to this sophisticated man.

"You go first," he said, with a sweeping arm enveloping the bust.

"Okay," Jerome agreed, "on the condition you continue where I leave off. We can bounce back and forth. Cool?"

The mere idea of bouncing back and forth with Jerome made Luke blush again. He pushed his glasses up their familiar slipway to detract from his reddened cheeks.

"Cool," he said.

Jerome took a moment to gather his thoughts and then the most evocative free rhyme flowed from his lips and bounced through the acoustic space inhabited by frozen figures:

"Your heart is stale, don't blame the blameless.
Too late, you say, it's me—I'm shameless,
I hide my pride for fear it scares you,
I try not to cry, but
my tears dare to break through.
Your clock is my tick-tock,
my shock is your detox,
Ancestral visions of missions in boondocks.
Decision, division, disaster's my master.
Succession, revision, you're fast,
but I'm faster.
Don't revile me, I'm regal.
Regale me the legal,

the lies, the recession,

which make me the relic of

my own oppression."

Jerome paused, then yielded to Luke with both forefingers pointed like a thespian gunslinger. But Luke was speechless, awe-struck by the poignant verse Jerome had created with so much ease and had delivered with so much style. He felt like Saint Sebastian, tied to a tree, judged, and pierced by arrows of truth slung at his sensitive psyche.

"No way," he backpedaled. "There's no way I can follow that. Are you kidding me? How did you do that?"

Jerome flashed his megawatt smile and touched one fingertip to his temple. "It cannot come from here the way haiku poetry does," he said.

"From here?" Luke asked, placing his hand over his own heart.

"No," Jerome said, "from here ..." He pressed his fingertip into the soft *solar plexus* right underneath Luke's sternum, "from your gut."

"Oh," Luke's breath caught in his throat.

"Perhaps you'll come and support me at one of the slam poetry sessions I perform at on Saturday nights?" Jerome asked. It sounded to Luke like an invitation to a date. He had every intention of accepting.

"I might just do that," he said coyly, "on the condition you help me lead a compare-and-contrast activity with a student group here, another time. We can start with more formal haiku in front of the Chinard and then pivot to spoken word or even rap in front of the Harwood bust. Bounce back and forth? It will give students a chance to flex their creative muscles and help them put a contemporary spin on these classical sculptures."

"Cool," Jerome said, "just DM me and I'll try to take my lunch break then."

He pulled a business card from his pocket and slid it in between Luke's notebook and the stubby pencil with teeth marks on the eraser still clutched in his left hand. The card was black with a single, gold-embossed quaver music note in the upper left corner. Centered below, in similarly embossed gold, the card said:

"JEROME APOLLO, MUSICIAN/DJ/SLAM POET."

Luke thought his mind was playing tricks on him, so he read it again and a slow smile spread across his face. "Your last name is Apollo?"

Kismet. Fate.

"My stage name, yep. Coincidence that I'm working in a museum with a name like Apollo, right?"

"Coincidence, absolutely," Luke said. *Serendipity*, he thought, instead.

"This was fun," Jerome said, slinging his backpack over his shoulder. "'Til next time in the gallery, Luke Lorenson."

Yes, this was fun. "Till next time, Jerome Apollo," Luke said, watching with regret as his Apollo dissolved out of view, the last of the day's sun rays bouncing from the golden tips of his hair.

Golden hair, golden music note?

"The girls will never believe me," he giggled, and then he remembered the book group discussion. He was late, as usual. But one could not ignore an impromptu meeting of the gods: Hermes and Apollo.

Luke cast a final glance over his shoulder at the averted eyes of Harwood's stone bust and the steely gaze of the goddess-mother with her owl perched on her helmet, her magical cloak shielding the little lost boy sleeping at her feet.

"I fear no longer," he said.

CHAPTER 10
THE FINE ART of FINE-ART THEFT

W hen the four friends stepped out into the refreshing breeze outside the Pallas Library's conference room, they took a communal deep breath and linked their arms through each other's. Like children on a playground during recess—*Red Rover, Red Rover*—in a show of unity and affection.

The air had been oppressively stuffy inside the conference room where two dozen or so bookish docents had gathered minutes earlier, discussing art theft and forgery around piles of hardcover books and a tray of stale chocolate-chip cookies.

"Oh, lookie how cute you are, the Firebox Four!" a docent colleague called out as she shuffled past them, using the cutesy-cruel name the others sometimes called them, referring to the infamous elevator incident. "Fascinating discussion tonight, don't you think?" She didn't stick around for their feedback. Good thing, too, as she missed Lorelei's spikey glare.

"She's just jealous," Luke grumbled.

They were all aware of the gossip swirling in the undertow of the teaching corps—that the four of them were exclusive and standoffish. It was not entirely untrue; they spent every moment together at the museum, semi-attached at the hips like mythical quadruplets.

A protective shield against the world.

"Anyone want to grab a drink nearby to digest the night's discussion?" Angel asked, pausing at the fountain bench to slip into her jacket while Luke held it by the nape.

Pallas's fountain was dormant at this late hour, the marble mortal on her knees as if in bedtime prayer. The crisp night air was nibbling at their heels. The museum campus was deserted save for the echo of shoes heading for the parking lot, its doors locked, its galleries dark. Void of life but for the painted Lords and Ladies of Such-and-Such watching the gilt bronze dials of a grandfather clock, counting down to a spot of midnight tea.

"I can't, sorry," Shivonne said, checking her watch. "I've got to get home."

"Of course," Angel said, regarding her with concern, "let's walk." They headed to the stairs that descended into the parking lot. A night guard in uniform tipped his non-existent hat in greeting when they walked past him.

"G'night, ladies," he said.

"Good night, sir," Luke replied in his deepest bass timbre.

"You're such a goof, Hermes," Lorelei giggled, glancing over her shoulder to register the guard's reaction.

"What did you think of the discussion?" Angel asked.

"Riveting stuff," Lorelei said. "I can't believe the Isabella Stewart Gardner Museum heist is *still* unsolved. I mean, it's been thirty years and there is a $10 million reward for a viable lead. Surely someone who knows something would want to spill the beans, right?"

"How much art was stolen from the Gardner, again?" Luke asked. He had not paid attention to the conversation; his mind was still fixated on the chance meeting with Apollo.

"A half a billion dollars' worth," Shivonne said.

"Well, *that* would explain why no one has come forward," Luke said. "The thieves are too scared, or they got paid more for the goods than the offered reward."

The Gardner heist was without equal in simplicity ... and audacity. Crooks dressed in fake Boston PD uniforms duped a couple of night guards, tied them up with duct tape, and leisurely proceeded to carry away more than $500 million of precious artwork.

"Just think," Angel remarked, sweeping her arm over the vast night sky, "somewhere out there is a cache of masterpieces—Vermeer, Manet, Degas, and several Rembrandts, including his *only* seascape—crated up in a dungeon or stacked cheek-by-jowl in some crime boss's private, walk-in vault."

"Yeah, or ..." Luke said ominously, "cut up into shreds and floating in a canal."

"Ugh, don't even say that!" Lorelei cringed and crossed herself.

Just that evening the book group participants had discussed the infamous case of a devoted mother who—after discovering a bounty of precious art stolen by her son, Stephane Breitwieser—had cut priceless masterpieces from their frames and dumped precious artifacts, jewelry, and sculpture into the Rhine-Rhone canal near her home in France. To destroy evidence of her son's crime after he had been arrested. A mother will do anything to protect her child. *Anything.*

"So much stolen art disappears forever but, sometimes, like the still life looted from Walter's family by the Nazis, it pops up again decades later," Angel said. "Not all art crime is victimless." They all fell silent, ruminating on Walter's tragic story she had shared with them earlier that evening.

"What gets me is the simplicity of most of these heists," Lorelei remarked. "Take the theft of Edvard Munch's *The Scream* from the National Gallery in Oslo ... when was it, again? 1993?"

"1994, the night of the opening ceremony for the Winter Olympics in Lillehammer," Shivonne remarked. "The perfect distraction for a heist."

"Yeah, I remember following that one on the news," Angel said.

"Not me," Luke said. "I was but a babe in arms back then."

"Show-off!" Angel elbowed him in the ribs while Lorelei hummed the tune of "Rock a Bye Baby," rocking her bag in her arms.

Shivonne cracked a rare smile.

"I agree, Lore, about how uncomplicated art crime can be," Angel said. "The Munch theft required no more than two thieves ..." She held up two fingers. "One long ladder 'borrowed' from a nearby construction site hoisted against the gallery's exterior wall ..." One finger aloft. "And a very convenient, unbarred window. It took them less than a minute to abscond with Norway's national treasure. Wham-bam-thank-you-ma'am!" She made swish-swash motions with her hands.

"A ladder? Duct tape?" Luke shook his head.

"Hell, if it came down to such simple tools, even *I* could pull off an art heist," Angel laughed. "Nobody would suspect a middle-aged art geek like me. A woman past her prime."

It was but a passing, preposterous remark and they all laughed it off, waving away the thought as if it were a gossamer spider web glistening in front of them in the darkness. Even Shivonne tittered softly, her shoulders relaxed, and her arms linked safely between Luke on her left and Angel on her right. When the group reached the stairwell down to the parking lot, Angel pulled her aside while Luke and Lorelei descended together.

"Shivvy," she said, "you seem a little lighter tonight. How are things going at home?"

Shivonne shrugged and graced her friend with one of her pacifying smiles, the kind that heals cracks the way molten gold fills imperfections in Japanese *kintsugi* ceramics.

"It's so much better," she said, while tugging at the padlock necklace around her neck. "He just had a rough time last week. He is under a lot of pressure at work. I feel bad for making such a big deal out of it ..." She smiled. "He's been sweet to us lately. Allowed me out tonight with the Firebox Four ..."

Angel frowned at the word "allowed" but took some comfort from Shivonne's countenance. She did not want to cast unnecessary gloom.

"I'm glad to hear it," she said, "but please, be careful. Stay on your toes, okay?" It was an appropriate metaphor for a trained ballerina.

Shivonne squeezed Angel's hand. "I will, I promise."

"Good," Angel said, gripping back the hand that held hers. "Good."

"*Mo anam cara,* Athena," Shivonne said as they clip-clopped down the stairs into the underground parking. *My soul friend.*

"I love you, too, Persephone," Angel said. The heavy door swung shut behind them, so they were not privy to the shooting star that streaked nakedly across the sky. In response to nature's syncope, a few of the spotlights over the departure patio flickered a frantic morse code through the swaying tree canopies.

The Fates were stirring overhead.

PART TWO

THE PLAN

CHAPTER 11
THE GUARDIAN ANGEL

The fine art of fine-art theft was swirling in the goddess Athena's head as Angel confronted her alter ego in the mirror, brushed her teeth, and slid between the cool sheets to settle down for the night.

A masterpiece, a ladder, a distraction ...

The space next to her in bed was empty, as usual. Deacon was still on assignment in Hong Kong. She glanced at the alarm clock and imagined him dining on *dim sum* and drinking Yuzu gin with his colleagues in a dingy, dimly lit bar—a stark contrast to her quiet evening in the Pallas library's small conference room, discussing art crime.

Duct tape? You've got to be kidding me!

It had stung a little to hear tales of investigators stumped by art theft, so fresh on the heels of her blatant rejection by the FBI's Art Crime unit, but she had sunk her teeth into the topic, devouring every detail of those ingenious forgery cases and heists.

Still ruminating, she leaned over to set her alarm and switch off the bedside lamp, then drifted off into restless slumber, dreaming of the Munch painting's distorted face wound in layers of duct tape, squirming, agonizing against its restraints. Then ... a primal scream tore from that gaping mouth; a piercing sound that jolted her awake.

She sat up with an expulsive breath, relieved to discover that it was the ring of her cell phone and *not* the skull-penetrating scream of the gagged figure from her nightmare. Fumbling for her phone, she knocked the alarm clock to the floor; its radium-green dials flashed '1:54 a.m.' from the rug. Icy cold tentacles clenched her intestines as she brought the phone to her ear. No call at 2:00 a.m. was *ever* good news.

"Hello?" she said.

"Angel ... it's me." The voice sounded muffled, as if reverberating in a Mason jar.

"Shivvy?" The caller ID confirmed it was her, but Angel had to ask because the voice sounded like a young girl's. "Is everything okay?" She fumbled for the lamp switch; she was wide awake now. "Talk to me. Where are you?"

"I'm home," Shivonne whispered. "He's sleeping now, I think. I took my phone from his jacket pocket and I'm in the bathroom, in the tub ... under some towels. I'm cold, but I'm safe here."

Safe?

Angel was confused; a couple of hours earlier, at the museum, Shivonne had reassured her how much better things were at home, with a smile on her face. Now she was hiding in a bathtub, sounding panicked.

"What's going on? Are you hurt?" Angel asked.

"I'm okay now. Just a chipped tooth, I think."

"And Riley?"

"Locked in her bedroom," Shivonne said. "He's got the key under his pillow, right next to his Glock. I was too afraid to take it."

A gun?

The image of that distorted face of her nightmare, wrapped in duct tape, flashed in front of Angel. It must have been her intuition, alerting her of impending doom even before the phone rang.

"He's keeping you from your child?" she asked.

"He knows I won't run without her."

Run?

"What happened?" Angel reached under her bed with her toes, searching for her shoes.

"I got home from book club shortly after nine," Shivonne said, her words deliberate and slow. Too slow for Angel's liking. "I went straight to Riley's bedroom to kiss her goodnight, and I found Joe lying in bed with her." She paused, and the silence rang with an undercurrent of horror.

Cold shivers skittered up and down Angel's arms. "What the—? Did he hurt Riley?"

"No, no, I don't think so. But when I saw him there ... he's been so unpredictable lately. I panicked. Told him to get out ... and he did. Pulled me by the hair into the hallway and locked her room." Shivonne sniffed and her voice wavered. "I can't believe I did that! I stuck my head in a hornet's nest. Dared to raise my voice at my child's father ... in front of her. He—he was furious, Angel. Started questioning me about where I was tonight and why I missed curfew even though I was just a few minutes late ..."

She has a curfew?

"What happened next?" Angel felt like strangling Joe with her own bare hands.

"He dragged me into our bedroom like an animal dragging its prey. Like Hades does with Persephone in the painting. He ..." Her voice trailed off into a muted bell-jar echo.

"He what?" Angel pressed gently.

"He threatened to take Riley from me. Said he had proof that I was a negligent mother ... photos. Then he—" A plaintive squeal escaped from her mouth—the sound of a fox caught in a steel trap. "He threw me on the bed, face down, and forced himself on me with his gun to my head."

Angel's heart somersaulted in her stomach; she felt sick. "Oh God, Shivvy, that's rape." Pinching the phone to her ear, she grabbed the previous day's cardigan from the ottoman at the foot of her bed and wrestled it over her pajama top. "That's it! I'm dialing 911."

"No," Shivonne said in a harsh, whispered tone. She fell silent for a moment; Angel assumed she was waiting to see if her loud protestation had woken Joe. "Don't call them, Angel, I beg you. We've talked about this. He has colleagues on duty every night. They will—"

"Shivvy," Angel rebutted, "I will never forgive myself if something happened to you or Riley and I knew about it but didn't do anything. I *have* to make this call."

"If you do," Shivonne said, "you might never forgive yourself for what Joe will do to *us* after the cops show up on our doorstep and let him go with a slap on the wrist. He won't live down the embarrassment this time. He warned me he would hunt us down ... punish us." She broke down into muffled sobs.

"Shit, okay, okay. I won't call," Angel assured her, sliding her feet into her Birkenstocks, "but I'm coming over to get you and Riley. Okay?" Keys in hand, she was on the front doorstep already when Shivonne replied.

"He'll never let me go with you, and I won't leave Riley with him. Over my dead body," she said.

Angel stopped dead in her tracks. "Don't you *ever* say that, Shivonne." If Lorelei had heard it, she would have crossed herself and spat over her shoulder to banish the devil.

"I'm sorry I woke you," Shivonne deflected, "... the worst is over. He'll be calm by morning. I'm not hurt ... he is my husband, after all."

Angel cringed at her friend's desperate attempt to excuse Joe's assault, but she understood her denial, considering the sword of Damocles that hung—by a horse's hair—over her head. But she had to do *something* despite Shivonne's protestation.

"I'm coming over anyway," she insisted. "I'm already in my car." To corroborate, she turned on the ignition, revved the engine, and backed it out of the driveway, her tires screeching and leaving angry tread marks behind. "I'll text you when I get there. Keep the phone near you. On mute," she added. It would be disastrous if Shivonne's phone rang and woke Joe. "Do you hear me? I'll be there soon."

"Y-yes," Shivonne said, "okay. But don't come to the door." The line disconnected with a disturbing click in Angel's ear.

She sped through the dark, deserted suburban streets, rolling through stop signs, and gunning the accelerator through not-red-enough traffic lights. Her mind was racing too, scrolling through scenarios to help her friend. Without police backup, what could she do? All on her own?

What would Athena do?

Gripping the steering wheel with her left hand, she swept through her glove compartment in search of a makeshift weapon. Its yield was disappointing: a roll of stale mints, an old pair of sunglasses with one lens popped out, and a handful of parking-meter coins spilling out from an unzipped pouch onto the floor mat under her feet. Had Deacon been there, he would have scolded her for not sealing things properly. She never did.

"Shit."

And then, her fingers hit pay dirt: a canister of pepper spray which she had stowed there in the wake of the incident in that back alley behind crowded Beale Street. "Carry it with you at all times," Deacon had ordered. "Be prepared next time." She remembered the sting of his words, not even a day after it had happened when he met her at the airport with just the right amount of concern veiled over his reproach. "Christ, Angel, what were you thinking, walking alone in an unfamiliar city, so late at night?"

What was the alleged victim wearing, your Honor? How many drinks had she consumed before the alleged incident?

"The street was crowded, Deke," she had said, "and my hotel was only a couple hundred yards down that street."

"And, what the hell did you do to your hair?" he had asked then, not validating her reply, her state of shock. She had no inkling of what he was talking about; upon touching her head, nothing had felt out of place except for tenderness and a tingling sensation around the bump from the brick wall.

In the car outside Shivonne's house, Angel looked down into her lap and saw that she was gripping the pepper spray in her hand, her thumb poised over the spray switch.

Would it still work after all these years?

She placed it on the seat next to her; its lipstick-pink casing instilled little confidence, neither did the knowledge that it would not deter a large, incensed abuser for long. But it was all she had. She made a mental note to buy bear spray for future emergencies.

Slowing the car to a crawl, she turned into Shivonne's quiet residential street and continued down the winding drive to where it culminated in a cul-de-sac.

The O'Roydon house sat back from the street just far enough to suggest privacy and privilege, with iceberg roses and purple sage blooming against a whitewashed picket fence. An imposing Cape Cod painted a crisp white, which made it glow in the full moon; its dark, mullion-paned "eyes" glared into the dark. Watching her, warning her to keep her distance.

She cruised past the house, her eyes fixed on the sinister windows, detecting no blink of light from inside. After circling the cul-de-sac, she parked opposite the house with the nose of the car facing toward the escape route—exactly as a cunning goddess of strategy would do. She cut the engine and rolled down her window to listen for sounds. It was quiet, apart from crickets cajoling in the underbrush of the neighbor's ivy-covered fence. She unclipped her seat belt and guided the strap up quietly.

The house was glowering at her from across the street, its prey possessively clutched in its shiplap claws. Angel lifted her phone from between her thighs and changed the setting to dark mode so the glare would not betray her position in the dark. Then she texted Shivonne:

I'm here, parked outside your house. Are you okay?

She pressed "send" and hoped that Shivonne had muted the sound on her end.

I'm ok. Still im Bathtib. Joe askeep.

Shivonne's text was studded with spelling mistakes—evidence of cold, shaky fingers.

Can you come outside and talk to me? Angel typed.

Can't, Riley locked.

Stua here.

Damn. Angel leaned back against the seat for a second before replying:

Okay, but I'll be outside, all night long.

If anything happens, scream or flicker the lights inside.

I'll be there ASAP. I have pepper spray.

Okay.

A safe Shivonne would have insisted Angel go home; *this* Shivonne sounded resigned, clinging to her friend's proximity as if it were a safety net suspended below her, a child's night light that kept the monster under the bed at bay.

Thank u. U R an angel.

Try to get some sleep.

I'll be here, standing guard.

Angel thought of her promise to the old man in the alley and the irony of her name hit home right then: Angel. Standing Guard.

Guardian Angel.

As if it had been her destiny all along, even before that night. She would do anything for Shivonne. Shivvy had been there for *her*—in a reversal of roles—comforting her after that awful incident years earlier. Listening when she needed to talk. Sitting with her in silence when the talk ran dry.

There was no further communication from Shivonne. As an afterthought, Angel typed:

Delete all the texts, ASAP!!!

She stared at her phone screen, willing it to *ding!* one last time. When it finally did, she breathed a long sigh.

Will do, thanx.

Angel closed her eyes and leaned her head back against the headrest. The night's events had scratched at the thin scab over a deep wound still festering inside her—her *own* trauma at the hands of monsters who called themselves men. Three roughnecks, in Memphis on a "boys' trip" to pay homage to the King—*their* king, he of the loose pelvis and not the one assassinated by one of their racist forebears. Two brothers and a cousin, they said upon approaching her on the dance floor. "Hot damn, you can move those hips, Suga' Pie." Dirty fingernails, unkempt beards, and untucked flannel shirts, flashing beer bellies with faded tattoos of naked centerfolds.

"Hollywuud!" they taunted, having detected her So-Cal accent when she declined to give her name and their offer to buy her a drink. "What is a young lady from Hollywuud doin' in this here joint, all by her lonesome?"

She felt flattered, just for a second. They had called her "young lady"; it made her smile—a single, appreciative smile. Was that what did it, what lowered her defenses and spurred them on?

119

On Lavender Lane, Angel scooted higher in her seat; she could not risk falling asleep in the car. A sleeping guardian angel was of no use. She opened the passenger window a crack so cool night air could flow through the interior and bent down to retrieve the roll of mints from the carpet. Peppermint was a stimulant, so she popped two in her mouth and hoped it would keep her from nodding off. She scrolled through her email inbox to kill time. No new messages from friends or favorites; they would all be peacefully asleep in their cozy beds right now, blissful as babies on a belly full of milk. Her junk folder had more interesting offerings at the bewitching hour: a retailer targeting her with a buy-one-get-one-50%-off sale on compression undergarments, a dodgy med spa promoting anti-aging snail mucin skin treatment, and someone named Hunni Barbie tempting her to click on a link to "Slap my buns."

Slim pickings, indeed. She shriveled her nose.

The darkness was oppressive; Father Time was dragging his heels through a swamp of quicksand. She drummed her fingers on the dashboard and blew dust from the instrument panel. Reached for her phone to call Deacon but stopped halfway through the dialing.

What would be the point?

Her legs were cramping in the footwell, so she pushed the seat back as far as it would go and rested her feet on top of the dashboard. In the lilac interior light, her toenails glistened like neon Broadway lights reflected on wet tar. She aimed her phone camera at her feet and thought of a suggestive heading that would entice her foot-fetish clients. But she did not take the photo; how could she, when her best friend was cowering in a bathtub, a mere stone's throw away?

What now, Athena?

For lack of an alternative, she switched on the radio with the volume knob turned down. Music always calmed her when she needed to relax or stimulated her when she needed a boost. When she heard a faint overture, she toggled the volume higher, expecting to hear the mellifluous sounds of Chopin or Debussy. But, instead—as fate would have it—the melody flooding the cabin was Otis Redding's "Try a Little Tenderness." She shuddered.

The song playing inside the stake-out car on a suburban cul-de-sac at 3 a.m. was the same one she had been dancing to in the R&B club that night, when the bayou boys approached. Oh, the irony of the lyrics, in retrospect: the importance of tenderness when dealing with a woman. *Ha!* Scrambling to find the volume control, she killed the music and fell back into her seat, trying to think of anything else. But it was too late.

The song had already triggered painful memories and transported her back to that night in Memphis, home of Elvis, B.B. King, and Jerry Lee Lewis. The heart of rhythm and blues. On a freelance assignment to report on the city's offerings for a travel magazine: the riverboats, the barbecue, and the music. With the teenagers under Deacon's watch, she could escape mundane motherhood for a weekend. Free as a bird. A peacock, as it turned out to be, unaware that it would be unable to fly with such heavy tail feathers.

Things had gone south even before the dark alley behind the blues club. Even before she set foot on the city's pavements, she soured on it thanks to the rideshare driver who proudly showed off his city's bronze equestrian statue of Confederate general Nathan Bedford Forrest, on the drive from the airport.

"One of the founding fathers of the Ku Klux Klan," he told her. She remembered stiffening in the back seat. "The Klan was not always evil," the garrulous driver insisted. "They started as a brotherhood." He accentuated the word by thumping his chest with his forearm. "Besides, they say General Forrest's slaves loved him. They were *proud* to have him as a master."

What the actual fuck!?

That had done it for her. She should have packed it in right then and turned back to the airport, but she had a job to do, one she hoped would lead to more such assignments. And so, she stayed despite the rude introduction, paid her respects to Graceland, and stood in silent homage outside the infamous Lorraine Motel with her head tilted up toward the turquoise balcony railings where Martin Luther King had spoken his final, famous words. Where a single bullet had snuffed out his dream. She ate their molasses-drenched barbecue, drank their beer, and danced her heart out on the dance floor of a famous R&B club—its name since blanked from her memory—dressed in a chambray shirt with its tails tied into a front knot, a denim skirt, and cowboy boots, the way the local girls did. Like a peacock—showing off a midriff not yet muffin-topped by menopause.

Too sexy for a middle-aged mom?

No, just too polite to decline their attention more forcefully, the shot glass of liquor they pushed into her hand, or the door they held open for her after her alarm bells had signaled it was time to leave.

"My friends are waiting for me. I need to go." It was a lie, but it was already too late. They had smelled her inherent politeness—a sign of weakness—like tumor-sniffing dogs locked on, refusing to lift their noses until they got their treats. She should have asked the bartender to watch her back or the bouncer to call her a taxi.

Should have. Could have.

Would have, had it not been for the fact that her hotel was only a few hundred yards down the street, packed shoulder-to-shoulder with crowds of exuberant visitors. Safety in numbers, right?

Wrong, Athena whispered in her head.

In the car outside Shivonne's house, Angel lifted the pepper spray to her nose and inhaled a faint whiff of capsaicin. It was pungent, like the grease traps in that dark alley behind the club where three pairs of rough hands dragged her after following her outside, catcalling to her from behind until they caught up with her.

"Hold up, baby girl. What's the rush?"

Then, a sudden shift. A narrowing of eyes. A flaring of nostrils. A sideways glance as they shoved her up against a brick wall between two large dumpsters with the smell of pork fat and fetid body odor ambushing her. No more sweet "Suga' Pie baby girl."

"Cockteaser!"

Their stubby, callused fingers groped her, hiking up her skirt, tearing away her underwear, and taking pieces of her most sensitive skin with them under their sharp, filthy fingernails.

"No," she tried to scream, "stop!" But only a hoarse cough escaped from behind the giant hand clamped over her mouth like duct tape; the other garroting her by the throat. And then she was slammed, head-first, into the brick wall.

"Shut the fuck up, cunt."

And she did. The shock of that obscene word—and the head trauma—had sucker-punched the last trace of resistance out of her. Her legs betrayed her then; they buckled and jack-knifed her to her knees. One of the bayou boys unzipped his pants, mumbling something about "southern cock," but all she heard was "peacock."

Peacock. Peacock. Peacock.

This is what you get for being a peacock, Angel.

For daring to dance solo on the dance floor of a blues bar, far away from the safety and mediocrity of a bland marriage. For being too polite to decline the compliments. Women were too nice for their own good, she knew; helping the friendly man with the plaster cast on his wrist load items into his car, allowing a stranger to watch their drinks when they went to the restroom, or letting three drunk rednecks hold a door for them. Yes, Angel was sure politeness could kill. It had almost killed her that night.

Was it then when the old man appeared? An unhoused man, by the look of it, blending into the night, had it not been for his grey peppercorn hair and one milky-white eye, his scrawny frame wrapped in a tattered overcoat. A scruffy mongrel on a rope at his side.

"You okay, ma'am?" His baritone-deep voice was unwavering even though they were both vulnerable minorities, trapped in a dark alley between two dumpsters and three roughnecks prancing like cock-fighting roosters primed with cayenne up the anus.

"Well, I'll be," one of them sneered, highly amused, "whatcha gonna do, ol' boy? Sick your dawg on us?"

"Lookit, Darryl," another one guffawed, "if Gramps had one more wrinkle, he might-could screw his hat on."

But the old man stood his ground, glaring them down with his cataract-painted eye, his coat spread open as if to offer her wider coverage behind him.

"Ooh, lookie here, y'all. He's goin' all Matrix and shit on us, ha-ha! Hold my beer, cousin Larry."

The old man might have flashed them a weapon hidden in his waistband; she would never know. But the spread of his threadbare coat had afforded her the chance to pull out her phone and dial 911. And when the three lugs advanced on the old man, she stepped out from behind him, her lit-up phone screen hoisted like a strobe light.

"Hey assholes, the cops are on their way," she remembered saying, a thin trickle of blood running down from her forehead. "Do *all y'all* wanna hang out here and wait with us?"

Her peacock bravado that night still chilled her to the day, but the bayou boys had taken the hint and oozed like the grease they were into the creases of the crowds, leaving her in the alley, alone with her rescuer and his dog. In shock. Bent over to vomit in the gutter. By the time the police arrived with lights flashing at the mouth of the alleyway, the old man, too, had slipped back into the shadows with his dog before she could thank him. Instead, she had vowed, right then, a pledge to always step in front of someone in distress, her coat spread wide open.

And that is exactly what she was doing outside her friend's home in the dark of the night—showing up for Shivonne, the way the messianic man with the cataract eye had done for her.

A guardian angel.

In her car, the pepper spray rolled from her hand onto the seat, and she glanced around, frustrated to see that it was still pitch dark outside. Thoughts of the old man's overcoat triggered a looping memory from their book group discussion the previous night; the theft of Leonardo DaVinci's *Mona Lisa* in August 1911 by a Louvre employee, no less, who had strolled up to the small portrait without fanfare, taken it from the wall, and walked out with it shoved under his overcoat. Such insolence. Such nerve. A sizzle of neurons nibbled at her frontal lobe, teasing for an instant, then dropping back into oblivion.

A museum employee. Under his coat. Duct tape and a ladder.

"What was that?" she asked the fleeting thoughts, as if to summon them back to explain themselves. Subliminal messages mixed with cortisol and adrenaline spun round and round in her mind's tumble dryer. A caustic cocktail.

A docent could do it.

And *there* it was: in the darkness of her car, Angel Hendridge had experienced a lightning-bolt epiphany. The underpinnings of a plan were formulating in her head. A crazy, brilliant, stupid plan.

Angel, that's nuts. It would be the ultimate peacock thing to do, Athena warned.

Think about it, though. It could work.

Don't be a fool. You're exhausted; your mind is tricking you.

Perhaps...

From the open car window, she could hear early-morning tweets from the tree canopies; thousands of birds were stirring in their nests, ready to greet the day. Her phone screen announced it was 5:37 a.m. She composed a group message to her posse of friends, using their Greek monikers for a rudimentary layer of security:

Calling Demeter, Persephone, and Hermes.

Athena has a strategy to share. Meeting of the

Olympians on Tuesday, after tours, on the lawn

by the lily pond. Secrecy is imperative.

To underscore the gravity, she added a cryptic quote from Homer's *The Odyssey*:

"Come, weave us a scheme so I can pay them back!

Stand beside me, Athena.

Fire me with daring, fierce as the day we ripped

Troy's glittering crown of towers down."

Your Athena.

She sent it off on virtual wings and dropped her phone onto the passenger seat next to the pepper spray—weapons of destruction, both.

The predawn air had a nip to it, so she powered the car windows up and rested her head against the glass, letting her mind sway like a wind chime in the breeze. Gently ... slowly. Her eyelids felt heavy, so she allowed them to close just for a second or two, the lashes tickling her cheekbones with fluttery kisses. Adrift, she was bobbing in an unmoored rowboat on a wind-still sea, accompanied by the undulating tunes of Beethoven's "Moonlight Sonata." Lulling her with its simple yet haunting piano melody, rocking her, rolling her, rocking and rolling her ...

Until a curious sound disrupted the calm.

"Tap-tap-tap. Tap ... Tap ... Tap. Tap-tap-tap."

Her eyes fluttered open, and she saw that a giant owl had swooped in from overhead and landed on the side mirror next to her window—a coincidence of epic proportions. It stared at her through the window while tapping a frantic code against the glass with its pointed beak.

"Tap-tap-tap. Tap ... Tap ... Tap. Tap-tap-tap."

Angel cocked her head, the way a dog did upon hearing a high-pitched whistle. If she did not know better, she could have sworn the owl was tapping an S.O.S. in Morse Code.

"Tap-tap-tap. Tap ... Tap ... Tap. Tap-tap-tap."

"What do you want from me?" she asked the impatient owl. It blinked—once, twice, three times—and she blinked in response. After the third one, she opened her eyes to see bright daylight outside on Lavender Lane. The car's clock read 6:48 a.m. and she was still outside Shivonne's house. She had done the *one* thing she had vowed not to do: fallen asleep.

"Shit!"

"Tap-tap-tap-tap-tap-tap—"

"Goddamn you, you insistent owl," she said, turning to face it at the window. But there was no owl.

"Joe!"

All six foot two of Joe O'Roydon was standing next to her car, his face pressed against the windowpane, angrily tapping the glass with the corner of his mobile phone. He motioned for her to wind down the window. With her heart jumping in her chest, she started the engine and did as he commanded.

Think Angel, think! What would Athena do? What would Athena say?

A chill of indeterminate origin blew in through the open window.

"Oh, my gosh," she improvised, hoping that a snippet of truth would explain her discomfort, "I must have fallen asleep."

"What are you doing here?" Joe asked, bile dripping from each syllable.

Safeguarding your family, you piece of shit, she wanted to say. "Oh, long story ... I'm a bit embarrassed, to tell you the truth." She was stalling.

Help me, Athena!

"What ... are ... you ... doing ... here?" he repeated in the same robotic tone, enunciating each word as if she were hearing-impaired. He reeked of evaporated alcohol and uric acid. She fought the compulsion to recoil.

"Well, you know we had our monthly book group meeting last night?"

Not a single muscle moved on his face.

"I went out for a drink with the other night owls after Shivvy left. We did a bit of karaoke, and one drink turned into two ..." She faked a giggle to stall, her mind scrambling to fabricate the rest of the deceit. "By the time I left the bar, I was a little tipsy, so I drove here—slowly, mind you—since your house is halfway to mine. I planned to park here briefly to sober up. Didn't want to wake Shivvy—the house was dark already. I guess I dozed off."

Angel realized she was talking too much, too fast, and that lies often came with lengthy explanations, so she sunk her face into her hands to feign embarrassment and peeked at him through her fingers. The lifeless mask of his face scared her more than an angry face would. She reminded herself that sociopaths showed no emotion, regardless of the horror churning inside their twisted minds.

"Please don't tell Shivvy I was too impaired to drive last night," she said. "She made me *promise* to be careful." She needed to shield her friend from any suspicion.

The zombie who used to be Joe stared at her—*through* her—then motioned with a swoop of his finger down Lavender Lane. "Go home, Angel."

"Yep," she blurted, grappled with the gear shifter, and sped away from the curb so fast that the pepper spray rolled off the seat and landed in the footwell next to her bare foot on the accelerator. In her rearview mirror, Joe stood like a salt pillar in his undershorts, his mobile phone limp by his side.

As soon as he was out of view, she pounded the steering column. "Shit-shit-shit-shit!" She could kick herself for falling asleep. Had her silver-tongued excuse been enough, or would Joe interrogate Shivonne about why her friend was parked outside? God forbid.

Guardian angel? What a joke. "Damn you, Athena," she cursed. "Where the hell were you when I needed you?"

I sent my owl, her goddess replied with a shrug.

But, like that night in Memphis, Angel had been too slow to interpret her inner owl's warning about the approaching threat until it was, quite literally, knocking on her door.

CHAPTER 12

ATHENA'S PLAN

S hivonne tucked a lock of hair behind her ear and waited for her student group to settle down. It was a nervous tick of hers—sometimes there was no loose lock of hair, but she tucked it anyway.

Today she wore her hair gathered under a cheery, floral-print kerchief, tied into a knot above her hairline to hide the bald spot where Joe had ripped a clump of hair from her scalp on Sunday night. Several fellow docents had complimented her earlier that Tuesday morning during the pre-tours huddle.

"You look like an exotic gypsy with your gorgeous red waves under that pretty scarf," a well-meaning—if clueless—colleague remarked.

"Thank you," she answered, cringing while touching the scarf over the tender, scalped spot underneath.

When she had woken Monday morning, Joe was gone. He did that sometimes, disappearing for days after one of his outbursts. She was not sure whether it was because of shame or fear of losing control and inflicting even greater harm. Whatever his reasons, she was relieved to find him gone the next day. It meant she and Riley could run through the hallways and slide on the Turkish carpets instead of tiptoeing on eggshells. They could loudly crunch potato chips on the sofa or leave toothpaste spit in the sink.

A handful of times, when Joe disappeared that way, she considered grabbing Riley and making a run for it, but then the petrifying fear would anchor her in place, remembering his threat to hunt them down "like jackrabbits." *Better the devil you know and still have a roof over your head*, she would convince herself, *than being on the run with the dragon on your trail. Not knowing when or where he would strike.*

Joe would be back, but until then, she would enjoy her brief serenity at home and at the museum. Her student group had traveled from the foothills of the San Bernardino mountains—three hours on the school bus—only to arrive late and miss the first half of their tour. She was quietly relieved to have skipped the first assigned gallery of the day—the one that included the disturbing painting of a nude Hades with Persephone slung over his shoulder like a sack of potatoes. Shivonne could do without that kind of reminder so fresh on the heels of her own assault.

On the last leg of her tour, she led the elementary schoolers past a series of 18th-century Beauvais tapestries, explaining how the woven masterpieces told stories and used to hang against damp castle walls to trap the heat from the hearth inside. How it had taken years for weavers to weave a single panel—thread by thread, inch by inch—their hands raw and stained blue from the indigo dye.

Outside the doorway of their final gallery, she halted them and waited until a communal and expectant hush fell over the group. "My friends," she announced, "did you know I can sometimes predict the future by reading minds?" They met her statement with a chorus of disbelief. "I will prove it to you," she said, "by writing down *one word* I bet you will all think or say when you see what's inside this gallery. Deal?"

Yes, it was a deal.

She pulled a sheet of paper from her docent bag, pretended to scan their thoughts with her crystal-green eyes, and then, in oversized letters with exaggerated pantomime, wrote a single, three-lettered word on the back of it in black Sharpie. Holding it close to her chest to compound the suspense, she instructed the children to close their eyes. Guided by her and their teacher, the group shuffled forward with tentative steps. The suspense was tangible.

"Stop right there, everyone," she instructed. "Are you ready? ... Now, open your eyes."

Sixteen pairs of eyes flicked open, and sixteen little heads swiveled up to gawk at a grouping of sculptural chandeliers suspended from the 30-foot ceiling. At first, the objects resembled the soft, slumbering petals of giant white dahlias, collapsed in for the night, shielding their vulnerable pistils from the elements. But then, with the soft clatter of mechanisms, the chandeliers dropped from overhead, bellowing like giant jellyfish—unexpected and asynchronous—unfurling their giant silk petals like parachutes, scooping up the air with a *whoosh* and stealing the breaths of the awe-struck faces gazing up from below. And then, up they went again to repeat their bloom in a mesmerizing dance of silk and light. The students were dazzled.

"Wow," someone said.

"Wow ... Wow!" more voices joined the chorus.

Speechless, the students had no choice but to settle on the single, repetitive palindrome.

"Wowwww ..."

Shivonne allowed them a moment to simmer in the thrall, then snapped her fingers to summon their attention to the sheet of paper she had been guarding against her chest. With much fanfare, she flipped it around to reveal the single word she had written on it: "*WOW.*"

"How did you do that, miss?" the students marveled.

It was one of her favorite tricks; it worked like a charm in the gallery where the Dutch kinetic light fixture, *Shylight,* by Studio DRIFT, was on loan for the exhibit.

"Magic," she said cheerfully. *If only I could predict real life as easily,* she thought wistfully, instead.

The children's wonderment breathed air into Shivonne, lifting her up, up, and away, like those stunning silk flowers—away from the reality of Joe and the clump of missing hair under her cheery scarf.

When the tour was over, she popped into the Palladium Cafe for a quick snack before the important meeting their Athena had called them to in such a cryptic manner. There was nothing lighthearted about the message she had woken up to, still clutching her phone in the bathtub after the horrific night before. It had mentioned "secrecy," and that it was "imperative." It sounded serious.

Distracted, she almost bumped into him by the refrigerated deli shelf—a dose of serendipity on the menu for Shivonne on that Tuesday afternoon.

"Shivvy." That shiver, once again.

"Oh, hi, Cristian." An instant flush of heat flooded her face—the kind radiating from a cast-iron wood stove on a wintery night, drawing you nearer but scalding you if you dared to get too close.

"Where have you been since last week when you left your glass slipper here, Cinderella?" The dimple in his cheek dipped deep.

"I've been busy," she said, "mopping floors and darning socks for the evil queen."

"Ah, but surely the princess must eat sometimes?" he shrugged.

Shivonne drank in the cadence of his speech; it was music to her ears, the stroking of taut cello strings—Yo-Yo Ma at his best. She blushed. It was no feat for a porcelain-skinned redhead of Irish descent to blush a pinkish hue at the slightest suggestion, but it was prevalent in the presence of this man.

"Um, yes," she tapped her wristwatch, "I just came in to grab a snack. I have a meeting to go to." She looked around for the closest thing to grab—for a quick escape.

Cristian leaned forward to reach into the open refrigerated shelf directly behind her. The move was so quick and unexpected, she briefly thought that he was moving in to hug her. But before she could protest, he stepped back and held his hand out to her. In it was a Red Delicious apple. He rubbed it to a shine against his crisp-white coat, right over his heart, and offered it once more.

"Chef's special of the day. On the house."

Their fingers touched for a split second when the apple passed from his hand to hers.

From Adam to Eve, this time ... the temptation.

There was no snake's whispered warning in her ear, so she gave in to it and pulled the apple to her chest with a sense of déjà vu—his hand passing the crystal quartz into hers. It was a pattern, she realized, like waking up every morning and experiencing the same day over and over, but with a different outcome each time. She was uncertain if it was a good thing, or bad.

"Ta," she said to break the spell, "got to go."

"Wait, Shivonne," he said. This time, he did not grab her arm.

"Shivvy," she insisted, her fingers gripping the waxy apple skin.

"Shivvy," he repeated. "Do you want to meet for coffee sometime? On Thursday, before your next shift, say 8:00 a.m. by the coffee cart on the patio?"

"Only," she said, "*if* my fairy godmother allows me to go."

What are you doing, Shivonne? Playing with fire?

His eyes crinkled at her return. "'Til then, Cinderella."

She turned and walked away; this time she did not look back. She knew he was watching, and she basked in the thought. But she had somewhere more important to be. A meeting of the Olympians.

Outside, she followed the quaint walkway that snaked its way down a gentle incline to a glassy pond overgrown with pale-pink lotus lilies straining up out of the water on graceful, long ballerina necks. Her friends were waiting for her on the manicured lawn.

"Hi, everyone," she said, and sat down, her long legs crossed at the ankles.

"We are going to steal a painting from this museum."

Angel had said it so matter-of-factly that it took Shivonne a few seconds to comprehend the significance. The gleeful screams of merry children chasing each other on the lawn echoed the surreal moment. And then the delicate bubble of peace burst around her. Somewhere, a butterfly was flapping its powdery wings, setting into motion a Rube Goldberg chain reaction of epic proportions.

"Hold up ..." Luke's finger hovered in front of his face, his eyes toggling between Lorelei's and Shivonne's stunned expressions. "You're kidding, right? Ha-ha?"

"Yup, she's joking," Lorelei said, willing it to be so, nodding to the others like the peacemaker she was, always the one to straighten the applecart.

But Angel's face had taken on a rigid pallor, projecting stony resignation like that of the marble Athena in the sculpture gallery a short amble from where they were sitting. For the second time, Shivonne felt an invisible breeze blow its icy breath across her shoulders and settle with a death grip at the base of her skull. She yearned for the flush of heat and the moments of sweet innocence in the cafeteria.

"I'm *dead* serious," Angel said. Athena was not the jesting kind; that much was gospel. If anyone could get a motley group of art nerds to commit to a cause—albeit a crime—it would be her. Their Athena: goddess of wisdom ... and war.

Luke slapped his forehead. "Holy shitballs, Angel. Do we look like thieves to you?" He encircled the group with a swoop of his arm: three mild-mannered, middle-aged women and their younger, queer friend. Hardly a team of hardened criminals.

She leaned forward to pat his hand. "That's kind of the point, Luke. I know it sounds crazy, but the book group discussion the other night gave me an idea. Just hear me out ..." She dipped her head and lowered her voice, forcing them to lean in. And then she told them about her epiphany, her crazy plan for their little team of pseudo-Olympian gods.

Passersby intrigued by the little group huddled on the grass, deep in concentration as if meditating, might have heard snippets of the conversation had they strained their ears to cut through the din: "... three weeks to plan ... Greek Hero Exhibit ... costumes ... chaos and distraction ... the laughing man ... the bag ..."

For the first time in a long while, since the fog of menopause had settled there, an inextinguishable flame was burning in Angel's dove-grey eyes. When she finished laying out the plan, she sat back and waited. Exhilarated.

"No way, it's batshit crazy!" Luke cried out before Lorelei could muzzle him.

"Shush, Luke," she implored, glancing over her shoulder before addressing Angel. "Okay, I'll humor you. In theory, it sounds like a brilliant scheme. Very Athena, I dare say. But with so many moving parts ..." She shrugged her shoulders and eyebrows.

"You call those 'moving parts?'" Luke said. "You mean risky-as-fudge dangerous pitfalls, don't you, Lore?" He harrumphed with gusto.

"Think about it, Luke," Angel said. "No one would *ever* expect museum nerds like us to pull it off—you said so yourself, earlier. We are harmless, pedantic art lovers who lead student tours and discuss painting techniques and mythical beasts. We are the underdogs here. As in *under* the radar."

Shivonne's head was spinning; it all felt unreal, plucked from an episode of *The Twilight Zone*, one in which she was the only person aware of the approaching danger, of the hideous monster perched on the wing of the aircraft, hell-bent on taking it down.

Disaster alert! Disaster alert!

"Obviously," Angel conceded, "the plan requires significant fine-tuning and rehearsal. But we are all clear on *why* we need to do this, right? This could be our *only* chance." The last word hung in the frangipani-scented air: Chance.

Lady Luck. A roll of the dice.

In an alternate universe, the treacherous Fates tittered and wrung their hands in gleeful anticipation, leaning in for a closer look at the mortals about to tempt their ire.

"Right," Lorelei said, "crystal clear."

"I—I don't know," Shivonne whispered, her face ashen grey. "It's so risky."

"It's batshit crazy," Luke repeated.

"Now is the time to back out," Angel said. "Up to this point, this has been nothing but a bunch of art nerds playing a game of 'Would you? Could you? Should you?' But this is no game; there is an urgency here and we need to move fast if we are going to do this. There is much at stake. We are facing serious legal consequences if we fail." It needed to be said; art theft from a major museum was a felony. "We would forever be branded as criminals. Cast out from society," Angel said.

"Pfff," Luke scoffed, no stranger to being an outcast.

They huddled in silence under the gravity of it all. Just like Atlas, bearing the weight of the world on his shoulders.

Lorelei, the go-getter, was the first to commit. "I'm in. I want to do this ... hell, I *need* to do it," she said. "Angel is right, we won't be suspects. People think of art educators as dull and risk-averse."

"Um, hello? Speak for yourself." Luke rolled his eyes. "There is nothing dull about me." He gestured from his gelled-back pompadour past the oversized rose

135

print blooming on his shirt and down the strip of sparkly trim on his skinny jeans. "As for risk? That's a whole different enchilada. I have a whole life of risk behind me. Not sure I want more of it." He fingered the vintage Hermes kerchief tied to his belt loop while speaking. "I guess that makes me a coward."

"I think it was George Bernard Shaw who said one cannot be a hero *without* being a coward," Lorelei said glumly.

"Yeah? Well, cowards sleep well at night," he rebutted, "and *not* in a cold prison cell on a scratchy mattress."

"Luke," Angel soothed in her sage Athena voice, "don't forget what we learned from Sunday's book discussion, that art crime seldom carries a long sentence. I will take the blame if we are caught; it's my brain baby, after all." She pointed to her chest, and then to him. "You? If we get caught—and we won't, because we have unique skills plus the element of surprise on our side—you would spend a year or less in jail as an accessory. The experience would provide enough fodder for a Harvard-worthy thesis on the psychological repercussions of being an art thief." She nudged Lorelei for support.

"Yes," Lorelei said with a conspiratorial smile, "I can see it already ..." She fanned her hands out to mime theatrical lights sparkling on a marquee: "'How a year in prison for art theft taught my small-town, gay-conversion-failed ass the *true* meaning of life.'"

Luke, who had always relied on the wisdom of strong women—fairy godmothers—sighed with an exaggerated shiver. "Okay, what the hell ... I'm in. Can't believe I'm saying this. Holy shitballs." He shoved his glasses higher up the bridge of his nose.

They all looked at Shivonne, whose lips were still pressed against the apple gripped in her hand. Her headscarf had slipped down, and her reddish-gold hair burned an inferno of flames in the afternoon glow.

"It's up to you now, Shivvy," Angel said.

Shivonne fought the urge to throw up. Around her, the gardens were morphing into a Salvador Dali-esque surrealist painting: the trees were melting, the birds were flying upside down, and the poisoned apple in her hand was teeming with worms. In her ears, tortured violin strings squealed a high-pitched pizzicato, urging her to bolt with giant ballet leaps.

Sauté. Sauté. Grand jeté!

She wobbled to her feet, a look of shame preceding the words before they tumbled from her mouth.

"I'm so sorry ... I can't be a part of this. I will lose Riley if we fail. Joe—" She wrung her hands together, begging for understanding.

And then, without another word, she pivoted on her heels and stumbled away. On the grass, her Red Delicious apple glistened in the afternoon sunlight. A black crow saw its chance and swooped in to skewer the forbidden fruit, scaring the remaining Olympians out of their stupor. Angel looked at the crow and then at Lorelei, her eyes flared like an owl's. Was a crow not the harbinger of death and doom?

But Lorelei just smiled, taking comfort in the ancient belief of the Indigenous tribes of her Nova Scotian heritage—that a black crow was a spiritual symbol of creativity and magic.

But above all, it was the herald of transformation.

CHAPTER 13

THE BIRTH of ARTEMIS

O n her way home following the disastrous meeting with its proposal of doom, Shivonne could think of nothing else. Art theft from their place of work? Luke's indignant, "Batshit crazy!" still echoed in her ears. She was in shock, and ashamed for turning arseways on the people she loved fiercely. And why?

Because you're a coward, Shivonne.

"You cannot be a hero without being a coward," Lorelei had said in the Pallas Garden. Shivonne disagreed. She lacked the courage to be a hero. Fearful of staying with Joe, fearful of leaving Joe. Fear of escape, fear of change. All day, every day, day after day. Controlled by fear to the point of submission.

Sit, Shiv. Stay, Shiv. Roll over and beg, Shiv. Good bitch!

She clutched the steering wheel as if it were a lap bar on a rollercoaster, preventing her from falling out, and when she pulled into her driveway after commuting through the narrow canyon and tricky twists of her conscience, she could not recall how she got there.

The second she unlocked the front door, she knew something was wrong—very wrong. It was not the default clench of anxiety she experienced every time she walked through her front door; it was different—a sense of immense dread—and the smell of it … It was faint, but she swore she could smell death.

She dropped her bag on the foyer tiles and called out her daughter's name, her voice helium-thin. "Rileeeeeey!"

Initial relief surged through her when the little girl burst from the kitchen and threw her body against her mother's thighs. But, as always, relief was but a fleeting tease—gone before she could relish its comfort—because Riley was seizing with heart-wrenching sobs, soaking her mother's pants with her despair.

"Oh, Mummy. Mummeeee!"

Shivonne sank to her knees. "What is it? What happened, my pet?"

Riley was bawling so hard, she couldn't get a word out. Over her daughter's mop of curls, Shivonne saw Joe lurking in the hallway, his hip against the wall in a nonchalant slouch, his arms crossed in front of his chest. She knew he was drunk by how he leaned against the wall for support.

"What have you done to her?" she barked at the stiff mask of apathy on his face, her hands fluttering over Riley's neck and arms, searching for bruises but finding none. "Tell Mummy what happened, love."

"Mummy, F-f-f- ..."

"Calm down, Riley. Deep breaths."

The little girl's chest heaved up and down as she fought for composure.

"It's F-Fitzi, he—" At the mention of her beloved Pomeranian fur-baby, Shivonne froze, and when Riley's body shuddered against her chest, she knew. "Daddy hurt Fitzi."

"No," Shivonne managed. It was no more than a whisper, still wrapped in a protective layer of disbelief and self-preservation.

Riley pulled out of her arms and looked up at her mom's face, with eyes swimming in tears. "Fitzi and I were playing. He was barking and doing the z-z-zoomies, but Daddy was watching football. I t-t-tried ... I tried so hard to keep him quiet, Mummy, I really did." She grabbed hold of her mother's knees again and melted into them with renewed sobs. "Daddy kicked Fitzi and now he won't get up."

Joe was still leaning against the wall, a few yards away from her, not offering a word in his defense. His aura, however, spoke volumes, dripping with defiance. *So what?* he demanded with raised eyebrows, daring her to confront him.

What are you going to do about it, Shiv?

With a sharp intake of breath, she barged forward past her husband and fell to her knees next to the lifeless clump of golden-red fur on the floor behind him, its tiny neck twisted at an awkward angle against the wall. A thin trickle of blood had congealed at the corner of Fitzi's mouth; a little piece of pink tongue was peeking through. His golden eyes were ajar.

Shivonne scooped the limp pup into her arms and threw her head back in an aphonic scream that came with years of requisite practice; it lasted several seconds before any sound escaped—an animalistic gargle that originated from her gut.

"Nooooo! No-no-no-no!"

Fitzi had been a gift from Joe—a "love bomb"—right after the miscarriage he had caused by shoving his wife down the stairs when she was sixteen weeks pregnant with their second child, a boy she was planning to name after her deceased father, Fitzgerald. Now this Fitzi was gone, too; six pounds of unadulterated, unconditional puppy love, crushed under the foot of a 190-pound man.

Her guttural roar snapped Joe from his zonked-out state; he lurched from the wall and pounded a hole in it with his fist. Plaster and paint rained down on the floor. "I just wanted some goddamn peace in my own goddamn house! That animal ..." He pointed at Fitzi's broken body on the floor.

"There is only *one* animal here, Joe," Shivonne spat at him through gritted teeth, "and it's *not* Fitzi."

Immediately after those impudent words flew from her mouth, she flinched and turned her cheek, anticipating a blow. When it did not come, she rose from the floor with Fitzi's body cradled in the crook of her arm, grabbed Riley's hand, and shoved past Joe up the sweeping staircase. She was very calm—fearless, almost.

The only animal here ... Did she actually say that aloud?

Upstairs, she locked the bedroom door from the inside. With Riley's help, she pulled the pillowcase—cornflower-blue roses in watercolor swirls—from Joe's pillow and swaddled Fitzi's body like a stillborn baby. Joe never allowed Fitzi on their bed— "It's a filthy animal, Shiv"—so it was bittersweet to see the pup cocooned inside *his* pillowcase.

A silent act of defiance.

They lay that way, crying and hugging the little papoose between them on the bedcovers until darkness wrapped her shroud over the house. Outside the room, Joe was pacing the hallway, howling like a wolf exiled from his pack. "Shiv?" he called through the keyhole in his sinister, Outlook Hotel voice. "Open this door, you hear me?" Riley shuddered in her arms, and Shivonne hugged her a little tighter.

"Mummy," the little girl asked, her cheeks wet with tears, "why did Daddy kill Fitzi?"

Shivonne looked at her daughter, who had so recently lied to her preschool principal to cover for her father's actions, and who had just used the words "Daddy" and "kill" in the same sentence. This would be where she usually lied to Riley, making excuses for her father's erratic behavior to help him preserve dignity in her eyes.

But not tonight.

She wiped through the tracks of tears on Riley's face with both her thumbs and cradled her cheeks between her palms. "Daddy was angry at Fitzi, so he kicked him. He was so wrong to do that. Your father does bad things sometimes when he's angry."

"But Mummy," Riley sniffed, "Daddy is *always* angry."

Shivonne's heart clenched; this was the first time Riley had openly called out her father's aggression. To deny it would be a grave disservice to the astute child.

"Yes, love. Yes, he is."

Riley fell silent, her mouth pulled inwards as if sucking a pacifier. "Does that mean he will kill *us,* too ... if we make him angry?"

A solitary violin trilled a high-pitched tremolo in Shivonne's head, and every muscle in her body contracted reflexively. She resisted the impulse to leap, to pirouette like a swan trapped in her death thrall.

"No, hun, I will *never* let that happen. I promise you."

What's one more lie for peace of mind?

"Okay," Riley bit her lip, "but—"

"We will bury Fitzi tomorrow, you and I," Shivonne deflected, "under his favorite tree in the backyard. He would love that."

"The mongolia tree?"

Her daughter's sweet mispronunciation recalled happier times, of Fitzi and Riley—both young pups then—playing under the tree, with Fitzi barking at the oversized white Magnolia blossoms. "Yes, my love," she answered, "the Magnolia tree."

Riley smiled with the far-away look of near-sleep in her eyes. Shivonne slid off the bed, tucked the comforter around Riley and Fitzi, and kissed them both on the head. Life and Death, side by side. In the bathroom, she closed the door behind her and filled the porcelain sink with cold water.

No time to cry, Shivonne.

She gripped the sides of the sink and stared at her reflection in the mirror, hating what she saw: a broken, scared wisp of a woman. Just like pathetic Persephone.

She submerged her head in the water and screamed as loud as she could, making bubbles boil up to the surface. When her breath ran out, she pulled her face out and looked in the mirror. The face of a stranger was staring back at her—it was not Persephone and not Lucretia. She felt a tectonic shift in her body that made all her hair stand on end.

Pleased to meet you, the stranger said with a grin.

Standing there, face to face with her new alter ego while her heartbroken daughter cradled Fitzi outside the connecting door, Shivonne pulled her phone from her skirt pocket and texted her fellow Olympians.

Athena, Demeter, and Hermes,
I was weak earlier, but I've had an epiphany.
It made me reconsider Athena's plan. I'm in. I'm 100% in.
PS: Persephone is dead. Call me Artemis:
The goddess of the hunt.

CHAPTER 14

A TALE of TWO JACKETS

T ransformation ... Redemption.

Luke pondered the overarching themes of his favorite novel, the one he had absconded with fourteen years earlier, wrapped up in Ms. Latsky's gown. It was ironic how appropriate Dickens' tale was for his current situation: it was the best of times—and, also, the worst.

How can something feel so wrong and yet so right at the same time? he wondered.

The two weeks since they had all committed to Athena's plan had flown by at supersonic speed, yet he was trapped in amber, somehow, along with that very unfortunate—if well-preserved—mosquito. They were planning a heist at one of Los Angeles's most respectable art institutions, and he was a crucial cog in the wheel. He, the sweet and harmless farm boy from Wisconsin ... an art thief.

Well-pleasing Luke? Unequivocally not—in more ways than one.

His role in the heist would require him to impersonate that which he had reviled most of his life: a scoundrel, a macho man. To achieve such a feat, he would need the incognito mantle of his mischievous alter ego, Hermes. God of thievery.

He mulled over this dichotomy while mixing a late-night cocktail in a tall glass. Unlike his father—who had stared deep down into the neck of the closest seductive bottle with the same devout fervor he had while thumping his Bible—Luke preferred to drink only in celebration of a special occasion, and only light, floral concoctions that were sweet on the lips and tart on the tongue. Just like him. Tonight, however, he needed something with a little more kick. A Bourbon sweet tea would do nicely, a throwback to his mama's sweet tea, but with the added kick of holy firewater. It seemed fitting for the occasion.

The old Luke versus the new.

He lifted a jug of ice-cold sweet tea from his fridge. The recipe was the only thing from his childhood he had *not* cast off; it reminded him of the saccharine sweetness that had clung to his mother when she was not drunk on God or his father's headship. He measured one-and-a-half ounces of Bourbon, added half an ounce of limoncello, and topped his Collins glass with the sweet tea. A handful of novelty ice "cubes" shaped like tiny, frozen penises—a gag gift from a classmate for his most-recent birthday—and a single, long-stemmed Maraschino cherry provided the finishing touches.

"Cheers, Hermes, you handsome devil, you," he toasted his reflection on his oven door, and took a long sip, letting the dose of liquid courage slip down his throat long enough to catch the cherry between his teeth. He rolled it around in his mouth before pulverizing the flesh, and then—with intense concentration—tied the stem into a pretzel-shaped knot with his tongue; it was a party trick he learned while moonlighting at the go-go bar in New York. He spat it out into his palm and stared at it, painfully aware that he was stalling.

Shit, Luke, what kind of cluster knot have you gotten yourself into?

The Olympians had all received personalized instructions for Athena's plan. But what was it Mama always used to say to discourage his youthful ambitions? "When Man makes a plan, God laughs." Or something along those lines.

"Enough already, Hermes," he said to the oven door. "Get to it." He had a masterful disguise to orchestrate.

Already a touch tipsy, he flung open his closet doors and pulled an armful of jackets from their coat hangers, fanning them out on his quilted bedspread. The first one that caught his eye was the solemn black blazer he had worn to his father's funeral two years earlier. It was stiff and formal, smelling of mothballs and regret, with none of the color and pizzazz he was known for. He wondered why he had kept it; he never guessed he would ever wear it again. How wrong he had been; it was perfect for a federal crime.

Next to it lay a suede jacket he had found at a vintage store on Melrose and nipped in the waist to fit his tall, slender frame. Its perky fringe trim had a jive of its own whenever he danced in it. When worn with skinny jeans and a large, silver-buckled belt, he resembled the randy cowboy from the Village People. It would, most definitely, *not* do.

The only other option on his bed covers was his favorite cream-and-navy seersucker blazer, the one he was wearing the day he met his Apollo in the sculpture gallery. It was lightweight, but a little too "barbershop-quartet" for the job. It also lacked the requisite bling factor.

"You know what to do, Luke," Angel had said. "Bring the vogue."

"As you command, divine goddess of wisdom."

He hung the suede and the seersucker back in the closet and when he pulled his arm out, something scraped the back of his hand. Theatrically splitting the coat hangers like a young, flamboyant Moses parting the Red Sea, he revealed the culprit: his "coming-out" jacket, a garment bursting with iridescent, Studio 54-like fabulousness. It was perfect for the job, light in weight but heavy in queer, with hundreds—if not thousands—of rainbow-colored sequins.

"Tada!" he exclaimed, lifting the chosen one out of the closet with an elaborate swoop, and taking it for a twirl à la Fred Astaire on the braided rug. His late-night cocktail was showing its teeth, making him wobble a little on his feet.

"Vogue with a capital 'V' for va-va-voom, baby."

He draped the technicolor jacket on his bed next to the funeral black. The former evoked happy memories: balmy Palm Springs, euphoric nights under a rotating disco ball, pool parties with pastel paper umbrellas in cocktails, and freedom.

The latter evoked nothing but death—and pain.

He remembered feeling like an imposter in that black jacket at the funeral, standing in the back of the church filled with the racist and homophobic congregation, while the pastor exalted his old man's reputation as a "jewel among pastors, a leader of God's flock." His mother had passed away years earlier from advanced metastatic lung cancer. She had never smoked a day in her life, but his father was a Marlboro Reds, pack-a-day kinda guy. It was another ironic example of how his father had driven his loved ones from his life—in one way or another.

With both his parents gone, all that had remained for Luke at the funeral was the reproachful look his estranged older sister had flashed him when filing out past him, pushing her MAGA hat-twiddling sons in front of her corpulent body.

"What are you doing here, Luke?" she had hissed, not even turning to face him. "He would not have wanted you here."

"I'm not here for him," Luke had said. "I'm here for *me*. For closure."

"Well," she'd drawled in her nasally upper-Midwestern twang, "don't let God's door hit you on your way out, ya?"

His sister's scorn had re-awakened his childhood anxiety, and, fighting the sting of familiar rejection while the Greyhound bus coughed up black dust over his hometown, Luke had vowed never to return.

He looked down at the two jackets lying side-by-side on his bed, their sleeves touching as if holding hands. Together, they represented his Before and After, his Pain and Pleasure. He pulled his trusty old Viking sewing machine from its white coffin under his bed, plugged it in, and sat down behind it at his work desk. The desk stood against the only window in his studio that did not face someone else's brick wall, so he cranked it open to allow fresh air—and the smell of a neighbor's Chinese takeout—to waft in. Outside, someone was dragging their garbage bins out onto the street.

It was here where the well-pleasing magic happened. Here, he spent his non-museum days behind his laptop, slogging away toward a perfect 4.0 GPA for his Art History and Psychology undergraduate classes. Here, behind his sewing machine, he created Instagram-worthy outfits for spoiled celebrity brats as a side gig. He thought it ironic that his sewing machine was a Viking. His father would have spurted beer through his nose had he known that the closest his Nordic-blooded son would *ever* get to anything Viking ... would be in the form of a girly sewing machine.

"At least *this* Viking stitches straight, Father," Luke giggled and glanced at Ms. Latsky's silk gown glistening in the buttery glow of the flea market chandelier suspended above it. He imagined her face above the neckline, watching him with a quizzical look. "It's batshit crazy," he said to her ghost.

"I know," the ghost in the silk gown replied in that soothing voice from his past. *"But with me by your side ... "*

"I fear no longer," Luke said. Emboldened by the buzz of alcohol coursing through his veins and Barbra Streisand sending in the clowns, he picked up the two jackets by their collars, hoisting them high like naughty puppies that had piddled on the carpet, studying their construction, and turning them this way and that. "A tale of two jackets," he said, laying them on either side of the sewing machine—his dark past on the left, and his sparkly present on the right. It was now up to him to create his future.

He picked up his heavy fabric shears and wrapped his fingers around the icy cold metal of the handle, which matched the frost in his heart as he made the first cut into the seam of his funeral black.

CHAPTER 15

THE HEALER and the DEALER

"*H*oo-*hoo!*"

The melancholic call of the great horned owl rang out in the black night. Lorelei scanned the canopy of the California oak leaning over their fence from the neighbor's yard. She squinted and tried to summon her Nova Scotian ancestral homing beacon to locate the exact perch of the nocturnal bird, but she came up short. The owl had burrowed deep in the foliage overhead, from where it could pinpoint its prey with the acoustically reflective feathers cupped around its eyes.

"*Hoo-hoo,*" it taunted again, and she shivered; not because it was cold outside, but because of the eerie premonition she experienced every time an owl voiced its lament. She loved owls—they embodied the spirit of her beloved homeland—but in the dead of night, their call was a harbinger of bad news. Wasn't there an old wives' tale about hearing an owl hoot three times in a row?

Almost immediately, she regretted thinking about the stupid superstition, but still, she glanced toward the house where Grace was tossing and turning through fitful sleep, her brow damp with a low-grade fever. Both girls were sick with a cold, but Grace—with her ravaged immune system—teetered on the edge of a secondary bronchial infection. If Lorelei's herbal remedies did not bring relief by morning, she would have to take Grace to a doctor, and she knew how the appointment would go: he would frown at her daughter's thick medical folder, shrug an apology, and slide a prescription for some broad-spectrum antibiotic across the desk to the exasperated mother on the other side, his eyes downcast like a dog with its tail between its legs. Peeing on a forest fire to put it out.

"Thank you," she would say. *Thanks for nothing.*

She ducked back into her shed, where she kept a variety of medicinal plants and herbs in opaque glass jars on a shelf. Benjamin had built the lean-to for her shortly after their move into the smaller ranch-style house, but it could not compete with her barn back in Nova Scotia. How she missed its Dutch gambrel roof and red shingled walls; the days spent inside its warm embrace while the rain played percussion overhead and the woodsy smell of wet ferns and muddled pine needles wafted in from the forest floor outside. The nights hosting traditional kitchen parties inside, with Benjamin on the drum box, matching his percussion to her heartbeat, his brother on the fiddle, and a lobster boiling in a 12-quart stockpot set directly on the coals.

Inside her Los Angeles shed, the only percussion she heard was the *click-click-click* of squirrels scurrying on the roof. The shed was nothing more than two rough-planked walls supporting the tin roof and an etched metal Moroccan lantern suspended from the center beam, scattering mellow crochet shadow patterns as it twisted in the summer breeze. The rear of the lean-to was the exterior stucco wall of the girls' bathroom. Lorelei had left the light on inside for extra illumination and its small window open to listen for sounds of distress.

Meanwhile, her own distress was broiling red-hot like that lobster in the pot. She had an important task to complete, but she struggled with inner conflict because, at her core, she considered herself a giver, not a taker. And *taking* was what they were planning to do.

"I need you now, Demeter. Help a sister out," she said to herself.

From underneath a lidded container full of hallucinogenic Liberty Cap 'shrooms, she pulled her well-thumbed companion of herbal medicine and paged through it, sliding her finger down the list of medicinal plants, fungi, barks, and flowers hailed since ancient times for their healing properties. She sang them aloud to the concealed owl: "Alder, bayberry, and bloodroot," continuing down the chronological list of remedies, "chokecherry, dogwood, echinacea, fennel ..."

A little further down the list, her finger froze over the word "hemlock"—the evil huntsman who could kill with a single kiss on the lips. The deadly cousin of innocent parsley belonged to the Class B noxious weed category. Every part—from the purple-spotted stem to the delicate, white flowers—contained an egregious poison of lore that caused paralysis of various body systems, toppling them one after the other like a deadly game of dominoes. It almost always culminated in the shut-down of the respiratory system, leaving the victim lucid throughout the ordeal—a particularly cruel way of dying.

But Lorelei McAllister was a healer—not a killer—so she forced her finger to slide past the hemlock to "Indian hemp" and "labrador tea." Smiling, her mind drifted to their senior labrador mix, Smokey, who was curled up at the foot of their bed where Benjamin was sleeping, matching him snore for snore.

When her hand reached the bottom, she could not make herself turn the page. As if manipulated by the powerful force of a Ouija board, her finger slid back up, a pulsing *planchette* hovering over the evil huntsman. When measured correctly and prepared carefully, she recalled, hemlock could also be a powerful sedative.

Nah, it's too risky, Lorelei.

Every ounce of her healing nature rejected the idea of using such a toxic substance, yet wholesome herbal sedatives like valerian root and chamomile were not potent enough for the requisite knock-out effect she needed. And stocking up on pseudoephedrine products from a drugstore was out of the question. It would require her to provide identification, as required by law, the kind of indelible and damning evidence that would implicate her in a court of law.

But she feared miscalculating a dose of hemlock, as well she should; the huntsman was a nasty adversary. It was one thing to risk a short prison sentence for a nonviolent act like stealing a piece of art ... it was quite another to risk life in prison for calculated, cold-blooded murder. Or *mis*calculated, as would be the case with unstable hemlock.

"Shit."

She scanned the jars and containers on the shelves. Everything she had ever needed was right there: snipped, dried, shredded, or emulsified. Among her stash, it so happened, was a burlap pouch with twelve ounces of the deadly *herb du jour*, hemlock. Balancing on her tippy toes on a rattan chair, she retrieved it from its secret hiding place—inside a weather-beaten, hollowed-out copy of *Grey's Anatomy*—in the furthest corner of the top shelf. The skull-and-bones symbol on the pouch shone in the dark with glow-in-the-dark urgency: "*Danger – Peligro,*" it warned.

Stay away.

It had been an impromptu, novelty purchase from a fellow medicinal-plant enthusiast at a convention—a risky move, akin to eating Fugu blowfish in Japan. She contemplated the securely wrapped pouch in her hand. Was she skilled enough to manipulate it into a powerful sedative *without* killing the target with an accidental slip of the hand?

"Darn it, Demeter, think," she lamented, smacking her forehead with her palm as if doing so would dislodge the answer.

"Lorelei, darling?" Benjamin's sleepy voice startled her from behind. She spun around to see his face—reddened from sleep and sporting a pillow-seam imprint on one cheek—peeking through the girls' tiny bathroom window. She laughed at the comical sight of his disembodied head floating against the white stucco wall. He squinted. "What time is it? What are you doing out there?"

She stepped closer to pat the top of his head through the window; it was warm and comforting. When she buried her nose in his hair, she smelled blissful sleep and sweet dreams. "Go back to bed, babe. I'll be there soon. I'm just experimenting with cough tinctures out here."

"Okey-dokey," Benjamin said from the window and, when he pursed his lips, followed with a sweet, sleepy, "Kiss?" she was happy to oblige. As soon as their lips touched, a spasm of intense love—that quickly morphed into a jolt of guilt—pierced her chest. How devastated would he be if his beloved wife were branded an art thief? Would he continue to love her the way he did, so unconditionally? Did "unconditionally" count when the condition was felony grand larceny?

God forbid.

"I'll be in soon," she repeated, ruffling the matted mop of hair in the window. She did not know it then, but that was a falsehood as well. Lorelei McAllister had a long night ahead of her.

Benjamin grumbled something indecipherable and pulled his head back inside. In his half-asleep state, he switched off the bathroom light, dumping her in near-darkness outside in the shed, but for the diffused embers of light streaming through the punched-out etchings of the lantern overhead. She searched for the pouch of hemlock she had dropped on the floor with her phone's flashlight app.

"*Hoo-hoo!*"

That's it, she thought, the flashlight beam dancing a jittery shadow-dance on the cement floor, *a clear sign from the Great Beyond not to proceed with the huntsman.*

Once the hemlock was back in its secure spot, she plopped down in the rattan chair to gather her thoughts. She considered calling Angel and admitting defeat, but the anecdote of the mouse churning cream into stiff butter played on her mind's movie screen, on repeat.

Kicking and screaming, Lorelei. Kick-ass mouse, that's you.

She pitched her ears for another hoot from the resident owl. But it was quiet.

"Dammit Demeter, help me!" she moaned.

And Demeter, the goddess who presided over the cycle of life and death, did just that, delivering to Lorelei's mind an abhorrent alternative.

Uh-uh, not that. "Nope. It's illegal," she objected.

But Demeter was insistent, and Lorelei knew she had no choice. She bent over, hanging her head between her knees. The telltale signs of panic flitted in her chest and gathered momentum until it threatened to pull her ribs apart and outwards, like a Viking blood eagle.

"*Deep breaths, Gazelle.*"

This time, it was not her goddess alter ego but her mother's voice addressing her from the Great Beyond. She was fifteen years old again, lurched forward in the starting blocks at a track-and-field meet, her eyes fixed on the infinite white lanes stretching out in front of her on the brick-red tartan, ears pitched for the starter's gun.

"On your marks ..." *Breathe, Gazelle.*

"Get set ..." *Raise your knee, lift your butt.*

"Go!"

The starter's pistol would go off with a puff of chalky smoke, and her mother's words would ring in her ears and propel her forward.

"Run like the wind, Gazelle." Her mom's pet name for her—because of her speed and agility—had always bolstered her during the most stressful times. *"The 400-meter is the toughest race,"* her mom would say. *"It requires speed and endurance. And you, my Gazelle, you've got spades of both."*

In the backyard shed, forty-eight-year-old Lorelei lifted her head from between her knees; she knew what she had to do. Stepping into the pitch-black nothingness, out of earshot of the open bathroom window, she swiped through the contacts on her mobile phone, dialed a number, and waited. If the owl hooted again, it would be her signal to hang up the phone.

But it was still deathly quiet from the treetops. The only sound was her breath fluttering against the mouthpiece and the ringtone in her ear. On the screen, his name flashed in menacing acid green: "Ace." A dubious "healer" she had met online in a Holistic Healing Meetup group years earlier, who purchased cannabis from her before it was officially legalized in California. He had praised her cannabidiol and THC for their potent, medicinal properties, and swore he *only* sold it in cases of drug-resistant epilepsy or chronic pain.

But a mutual acquaintance had alerted her to one of Ace's posts on a different forum, mentioning he had a dealer with a homegrown THC stash which he labeled a "high-class, tight-ass party drug." Lorelei had balked at being called a "dealer" and cut off all business with him. He was nothing more than a low-life masquerading as an herbalist. Tonight, however, she needed his help; she would need to swallow her pride and grovel. Tail between her "tight-ass" legs.

The ringtone continued to buzz in her ear. Was he still scorned after her blatant rejection? She pulled the phone away from her ear, on the verge of disconnecting it, when he answered, not bothering with formalities.

"Yo, who dis?"

His real name was a mystery, so she used his "dealer" name and her username from the holistic healing group they had both frequented back then.

"Ace, it's Gazelle." Hip-hop music thumped in the background; a heck of a party was raging wherever he was. It was 3 a.m., prime time for a scumbag like Ace.

"Gaaah-zelle," he crowed, pulling the syllables of the name apart like sticky taffy. He sounded high as a kite. "Ghost from the past, whoa." The background music was so deafening, she had to step further away from her slumbering house and cup her free hand around the microphone. "What can I do you for?" Ace asked.

She was tempted to say, "Nothing, I butt-dialed you," and take her chances with the evil huntsman, Hemlock. But then she remembered she had run out of time and more wholesome alternatives.

"I need your help, Ace," she said. "A trade, if you're game."

"Uh-huh?" he mumbled, sounding distracted. She imagined him with his phone pinched between his ear and shoulder while separating cocaine into parallel lines with a platinum credit card.

"I had a good yield from my specialty Bomb Chron cannabis this past season," she said, priming the trap. "Powerful stuff, high-grade cerebral. I can offer you a quarter pound."

Ace did not respond—she hoped he was mulling it over and not passed out on a bathroom floor, foaming at the mouth. The pounding music continued to assault her ears. It took no stretch of imagination to picture the scene: silicone-enhanced babes with Brazilian butt lifts, tattooed eyebrows, and tarantula lashes, twerking to Cardi B's "WAP" on white linen tables.

"A quart?" he finally asked. "That's dealin' low, Shawty. What am I gonna do wit dat? I got me a large clientele."

"I'm not asking for much in return. Plus, it's my high-class, tight-ass stuff, Ace," she reminded him.

C'mon, sucker, take the bait.

There was a shuffling sound from his end and when he spoke again, the background noise sounded muffled, suggesting he had stepped away from the cacophony into a quieter room of whatever party mansion he was renting for the bacchanals.

"Cool, whaddya need?" he asked in measured, slurred sloops.

"Something for—uh, for a project I'm working on," she lied, on the odd chance he figured out her identity later and decided to dangle their little transaction over her head for a hefty ransom.

"I'm all ears," he slurred. "Name yo poison. Blow? Blues? Rock? My Apache is super dope."

She shuddered at the veritable list of doom he had rolled out so casually. "I need some Ro—Rohypnol ... roofies." She tried to sound nonchalant, but her tongue stumbled over the word. "About three adult doses will do for my um ... project."

Ace was too intoxicated to notice her voice faltering or how unusual it was for a woman to buy benzos from him. His usual roofies client was the clean-cut frat boy with dirty intentions, who slipped him dough under the table at a nightclub. Or the bloated Hollywood honcho who sent an intern in a black sedan to meet him off Sunset for a handover of his best "Mexican Valium."

"Cool," he answered, "but it will cost ya more, Gah-zelle. Imma be breakin' my balls to score that shit ... let's say one pound of your kryptonite for my healing work."

She almost scoffed out loud. Ace offered no "healing" of any kind other than the intoxicating, hallucinatory kind. But he was a rat, and rats could smell the earliest hints of decay and desperation a mile away.

Fine, let's play, creep.

"Half a pound of my stuff for yours. Final offer. Take it or leave it," she said. It was highway robbery; her high-class cannabis was worth much more than his three tablets, but she was desperate. "You're not the only 'candy man' on my contact list, Ace." She was bluffing, of course; he was most definitely the *only* "candy man" in her contacts.

Please don't make me use hemlock.

His reply was rapid, coated in the stink of greed. "Chill, chill, chill, Gah-zelle ... you win. Jeez, you a badass."

Lorelei did not feel "badass," just ... bad. It was a means to an end. "Cool," she said, "let's do it."

"Imma be texting you my twenty. Be there in thirty," he slurred and hung up.

She had no clue what that meant, but she lifted her phone away from her ear and waited for his text. Within seconds, her screen pinged with his "twenty" and she Google-mapped it: a swanky Bel Air address, most likely a rented party house behind security gates at the end of a very long driveway.

"Nice digs, Ace-hole," she muttered in her best badass accent.

Back inside her shed, she unscrewed an orange bucket and scooped a heap of dried cannabis onto the electronic scale. The needle jumped past the half-pound measure, so she scraped a little back into the container until the needle hovered on its mark. He would not weigh it, she wagered; he would either roll a joint and toke it on the spot or sell it to the partygoers. She brushed the cannabis into a Ziploc bag and tucked it into the waist of her jeans underneath her T-shirt.

Sounding too close for comfort, the resident owl-harbinger who had just witnessed sweet Lorelei negotiate a hardcore drug deal called out to her in its most reproachful tone yet. This time it was unequivocally not a *"Hoo!"* The owl had asked, *"Who?"*

"Who are you?"

"Badass," she replied.

She tiptoed into the house to grab her purse, car keys, and Ben's black zip-up hoodie from the hat stand by the front door. Inside her car, she flipped the hood up to cover her white-blond hair and added an old surgical face mask dangling from the gear shifter. Backing her secondhand Prius into the street, she was grateful for a silent, electric vehicle that cruised away stealthily from her home where her sleeping husband and twins lay wrapped in layers of safety and ignorance. Unable to dissuade her as she set off to rendezvous with a drug dealer.

One block from home, she cruised past two coyotes jogging on the sidewalk, scanning front yards for late-night snacks taken for potty runs on bejeweled leashes by little old insomniac ladies. They did not even look up when she drove past, unfazed by their fellow night hunter. It added another layer to her surreal night: two coyotes on the prowl, one drug-dealing rat, and one accusatory owl that had not just hooted at random but had confronted her three times that night. Demanding self-reflection.

"Who?" it had asked, *"Who-who?* Who is the *real* drug dealer?"

159

"Not me, I'm not a dealer," she told Demeter in the rear-view mirror. "I'm a *healer*."

Once again, her mother's words rang out with a requisite dose of confidence as Lorelei drove to a drug swap in the topiary-lined driveway of a Bel Air party mansion.

"You, my Gazelle, you've got spades of both."

CHAPTER 16
THE NAUGHTY COP

S hivonne paced the foyer at her front door, counting her steps across the eight-by-eight encaustic tiles with their Moorish designs, interlocking spades and stars that made her head spin the way an M. C. Escher lithograph puzzle did. One where fish morphed into birds and staircases twisted upward and tumbled down simultaneously, without logic.

It reminded her of the recurring Sigmund Freud-styled nightmare she frequently startled awake from; the heroine—a tiny, ginger-haired ballerina in a tulle skirt—running from a fire-breathing dragon, perpetually just out of reach of his savage claws, its acid drool dripping on the back of her heels. Spiraling up and up on a twisty flight of marble stairs just to find herself, inexplicably, at the bottom again. Shivonne would bolt upright in bed with a bloodcurdling scream and pinch herself to make sure she was awake, only to have the moment of relief shattered by the sight of the real-life monster beside her, under the bedcovers.

For the umpteenth time that evening, she pulled apart the brocade drapes at the front window to look for Joe's car. The evening stretched out in front of her like the deserted highway in a David Lynch noir film, yellow divider lines zooming by on the blacktop under her at a dizzying pace. There were only five days left before their heist, and tonight she had to do her part. Her scheming had started earlier that Friday morning by arranging a sleepover for Riley. Joe usually forbade sleepovers, but she had twisted his arm with an intriguing proposition; something she knew he could not refuse. She had dropped the first hint while laying out his outfit for the day on their bed—as a dutiful wife did—alongside a special surprise for him. It spelled out the message in no uncertain terms: a fetishistic, Sexy Cop costume he had ordered from a dominatrix mail-order catalog, years earlier. It comprised a lace-trimmed mini skirt, a pair of fishnet stockings with suspenders, and a vinyl corset laced up so tight that her breasts spilled over the top like hot cross buns rising on a baking tray. Joe *loved* that part; anything that constricted, contorted, or distorted parts of her body was a huge turn-on for him.

The outfit came de rigeur with an authentic-looking police hat sporting a silver star badge flashing the rank of "Officer Naughty." It was the cheap plastic star, she guessed, that sealed the deal for Joe. As the one who usually delivered punishment in the name of the law, he had a penchant for bondage on the flip side. She had discovered it the hard way. Sex and power were Joe's two currencies of choice.

So, it was no surprise to see Joe's eyes widen with lust when he saw the raunchy costume displayed on the bed next to his.

"I need you *alone* tonight. Be home at six sharp or Officer Naughty will have to punish you," she had whispered in his ear with a little slip of the tongue and considerable effort to hide her disgust. A cringe-worthy moment, it was, but necessary to ensure he was cooperative and non-combative later while she finished her task ... without having to cower in a tub behind a locked door.

Joe had shivered in anticipation that morning, bending her over the bed for a playful spanking. The smacks had fallen hard on her buttocks—covered only by a thin layer of silk pajamas—and brought tears to her eyes. But the tease had achieved its purpose: Riley could sleep over at her friend Beatrice's house.

No pain, no gain, Shivonne.

The game was on. Artemis had set her trap.

Her feet were hurting in the plastic stripper heels where she waited at the window, so she kicked them off. The ball of her right foot subconsciously brushed the floor in a series of brisk *battement frappés,* beating against the lower calf of her supporting leg. Forward, sideways, backward, sideways: rapid foot flutters that matched the frantic contracture of her heart chambers.

Frappé, frappé, frappé. Switch to the other foot. *Frappé, frappé, frappé.*

She heard the roar of his pickup truck pulling into the driveway, stepped back into the heels, and skittered across the hallway to set the plan in motion. And when Joe walked into the kitchen, she was waiting at the marble island. On it stood two coupe glasses spitting champagne bubbles into the air, next to a tray of fresh oysters from the fish market. Her strategy was to stall with the oysters and bubbly, wooing him into submission. Two tapered candles flickered a warm glow across the counter; she hoped the muted light would accentuate her sultry red lipstick and distract from the look of deceit on her face. Barry White was oozing testosterone from the recessed ceiling speakers. She preferred Bublé for romantic occasions, but Joe loved the raw masculinity of the "Walrus of Love," and it was *all* about pleasing Joseph O'Roydon that evening.

He took in the spread and dropped his keys on the counter. She flinched.

Relax, Shivonne. Make this look good, Artemis coached.

One hip jutting out seductively, she pulled a plastic police baton from its holster clipped to her black belt and whacked it with theatrical clout in her palm.

"You're late, O'Roydon," she growled. "Freeze right there and show me your hands." He froze and raised his hands, grinning from ear to ear. "Now, turn around and place your hands behind your back," Shivonne said.

Joe obeyed—eager to "sit" and "stay" for a treat—turning his back to her and bending over the counter with his head near the oyster tray.

"Good boy," she said.

So far, she had him eating out of her hand, but she needed to proceed with caution lest the situation got out of hand before she could follow through with the next phase.

Easy does it, Artemis cautioned.

"Spread 'em, buster." She forced his legs apart with her knee and ran the baton up on the inside of each thigh, stopping against the underside of his crotch with a sharp tap. He groaned. "Any concealed weapons I need to be aware of?"

It was a loaded question, of course.

"Why y-y-yes, officer," he sputtered, "as it happens, I have a loaded pistol right *here.*" Grabbing his crotch, he turned to face her, his free hand sliding under the lace trim of her skirt. His breath quickened when his fingers brushed bare skin; she almost gagged from the alcohol fumes he breathed into her face.

A dragon's fiery breath.

It was rare that Shivonne O'Roydon had the upper hand during an interaction with her husband, so she leaned into it.

"Not so fast, lad. First, you need to eat and drink something before undergoing a full-body strip search. This is going to be a long night." She dragged out the word, "long" for dramatic effect while using the baton to smack his hands away from her body. He persisted with the fondling; she persisted with the baton.

Grope. *Smack.* Grope. *Smack.*

After a few thwarted tries, Joe dropped his hands, disappointed. She could sense his excitement bordering on impatience. It was time for Artemis to move to the next stage of the night's hunt. She picked up an oyster from its bed of crushed ice, garnished it with a squirt of lemon and Tabasco sauce, and held the scalloped shell to his lips. She hoped the sharp flavors would throw off the bitterness receptors at the back of his tongue. He slurped it hungrily, his eyes rolling back with ecstasy. Next, she lifted his glass of champagne—the one she had marked with a tiny splotch of red nail polish on the crystal foot—and handed it to him. Then she picked up her own.

"Cheers," she toasted, proud for resisting the "bastard" she was dying to add. Their glasses butted heads in mid-air.

"Cheers to *you*, Officer Naughty," he said, fully engrossed in the role-play. She watched him like a hawk as he downed the entire glass of bubbly in one fell swoop.

Yes!

"Blech." He scrunched up his face, and she worried he tasted traces of the bitter sedative she had mixed into his champagne.

"It's the oyster," she lied, remembering the time he had blamed the bathtub for her black eye. Now it was *her* turn. At the bottom of the trash can behind the counter lay the evidence of her deceit—a glass vial emptied of the three Rohypnol tablets Lorelei had crushed into a little water and slipped into her palm at the museum the previous day.

"Pour all of it into his first drink," Lorelei had instructed, "every last drop."

"What is this stuff?" Shivonne had asked, "Valium?"

"Better you don't know," Lorelei had grimaced. "All I will say is that it's ten times *stronger* than Valium. It should kick in within minutes, though it is a bit of a shot in the dark with a man as large as Joe." Six feet two of muscle and brawn. It was hard to estimate how long it would take for him to go down.

Shivonne thought of Lorelei's instructions while gauging the expression on her husband's face. "Want another?" she asked, filling up his glass before he could answer. He was already primed, but this was a case of more is better. Down the hatch, it went. The champagne was a crisp Brut that would help disguise the sedative she had poured into his glass while wearing a pair of latex gloves, catching herself on the verge of licking her finger after wiping a couple of errant drops from the side of the vial.

What a disaster that would have been.

Next to her, Joe slammed his empty glass on the counter. She was ready for him, dipping another chilled oyster seductively toward his lips. Anything to delay his inevitable grab for action.

"Eat up, bad boy. You will need stamina for the *special* interrogation I've got planned for you," she teased. "I don't want you passing out on me tonight." In her head, Artemis was giggling; Shivonne was surprised by how calm she felt. It was *so* much easier to relax when you knew your abuser would soon pass out cold.

"You look so hot, Shiv," Joe moaned, dribbling oyster juice and Tabasco down his chin, his hands fumbling with the lace-up ribbons on her corseted bodice. She resented the suggestion that looking like a streetwalker was "hot." It disgusted her.

"Hands off," she ordered, whacking his knuckles with the baton. "And it's *Officer* Naughty to you."

"Yes, Ossifer," he slurred, giggling like a naughty schoolboy with a crush on his teacher. His slurring of the word "Officer" did not go unnoticed. Her shoulders dropped a little; she did not realize they had been hovering around her ears.

"More champagne before the pain?"

How much longer is this going to take, Demeter?

"Expect the unexpected and prepare for the worst," Lorelei had warned. With the words "unexpected," and "worst," Shivonne understood her friend had meant "violence." She glanced at her wristwatch while pouring Joe his third glass. Almost half an hour—and half a dozen oysters—had slipped by since his first spiked drink. She had barely wet her lips from her champagne glass because she needed to stay clear-headed for the proceedings that lay ahead.

Just as she started worrying that the dosage was not strong enough, Joe's hands became limp and heavy on her bodice. He tried—and miserably failed—to untie the bow at the top of her corset. It would have taken a determined, sober man only a gentle tug at the two satin ribbons to unravel it and release the entrapped breasts. Joe, however, was too far gone to achieve even the simplest of tasks, so she bit her lip and endured his fumbling at her cleavage, red-faced, and perspiring. It made her nervous; a frustrated Joe was a lion with a thorn in its paw—unpredictable at best. It was time to relocate him to a more convenient spot.

A *safer* spot.

She pushed him away playfully. "Keep those hands where I can see them, mister."

He obeyed, but she noticed how his eyes were drooping, and how his hands—normally so strong—now hung flaccid from his raised arms. With one limp arm twisted behind his back, she perp-marched him into the living room, where she shoved him onto the sofa. From the belt around her waist, she unclipped a set of handcuffs—the regulation pair he kept in his sock drawer for sexually charged "games"—and dangled them in front of him.

"Ooohhh," he drooled, like Pavlov's dog, proffering his wrists willingly.

Oh, okay then, Joe. Since you asked so nicely ...

Seconds later, he was tethered to the stainless steel and glass coffee table. He flopped back onto the sofa, without resistance, his handcuffed arm dragging the coffee table a foot or so across the flocked carpet. At last, Shivonne could breathe easily; it was the first time she experienced relief that night. *Genuine* relief. She climbed on top of him, straddling his body to assess his reaction. His eyelids were straining to stay open, his body akimbo.

"Shifff—" he tried, but it was clear his lips were refusing to cooperate. "I don't feel so good, Shifff ..."

The way he said her name sounded like air escaping from a balloon—a comical, farting sound. Stifling a giggle, she gave him a moment to see if he would finish the sentence. He did not.

"Joe?" She slapped his cheek—a tentative Persephone kind of slap. No reaction. Perhaps using his much-hated little-boy name would evoke a reaction? "Joey?"

It did not.

She slapped him again, much harder—an Artemis wallop that left her angry, red handprint on his cheek—and still, nothing. Lastly, she used her knuckles to rub hard across Joe's sternum, the way EMTs did when checking for pain stimulus.

No reaction whatsoever. He was unconscious.

"Finally, *yer fecker*," she chastised limp Joe. "*Póg mo thóin.*"

Kiss my Irish ass.

There was no time to waste. She rolled off his body, kicked off the stripper heels underneath the coffee table, and rushed upstairs to change out of the rest of the ridiculous costume. While mounting the stairs, she ripped the fishnets from her legs and dropped them in the bathroom trashcan. The naughty-cop outfit followed; she would never wear it again.

When she descended minutes later, she wore practical joggers with large pockets she had stocked with tools for the task ahead. Her hair was in a high ponytail to keep the annoying ringlets out of her face, which she had scrubbed bare save for the red lipstick. She liked the way it looked—that smear of blood-red lipstick underneath a look of pure determination.

It was time for Artemis to hunt.

She approached her unconscious husband and tried to tilt his body to access his back pockets. The act of lifting his butt was akin to hoisting a frozen beef carcass, but she huffed with puffed cheeks and managed to tilt him just enough to free the bundle of keys in his rear pocket. Prize in hand, she hustled over to his study—the "off-limits" room—which he locked with demonstrative compunction every morning before he left the house, rattling the handle while glaring over his shoulder with a look of "don't you dare."

In front of the forbidden door, Shivonne pulled a pair of latex gloves from her pants pocket, and slipped her delicate fingers into them, snapping them over her wrist bones with surgical precision. It was crucial she left zero evidence behind; Joe was a detective, after all.

She tried key after key in the lock. When Joe snored loudly from the sofa, her hand froze mid-air; the evil house entity blew its frosty breath on her neck. She waited, not daring to turn around. But no one came, no strike from behind. No coarse hands around her neck. She blinked and tried another key in the lock.

Click.

The door swung open, creaking spookily on dry hinges, as she stepped into the musty darkness of Joe's disturbed mind.

CHAPTER 17
THE EAGLE and the RATTLESNAKE

H e smoked in there; the dank odor of tobacco and sweat clung to her skin. She felt sick to her stomach.

It's just nerves, Artemis coached. *Mind over matter.*

Shivonne slid into Joe's oversized office chair and flicked on the desk lamp. His laptop was charging on a navy leather desk pad; it flashed a warning at her when she flipped it open.

"Enter Password."

"*Feck* it," she cursed aloud to the cigar-scented room, feeling naïve to have hoped for easy access to Joe's electronic bunker. She should have known it would not take a single key to crack a conundrum like him—he was a complicated man, even on his best behavior.

Just like Hades, god of the Underworld.

She started by pulling open his desk drawers in search of clues, but the drawers yielded nothing more than a few case files—some with grisly crime scene photos of bodies eviscerated by high-velocity bullets—blank legal notepads and other innocuous office supplies. She huffed her disappointment with each drawer's yield, ready to abandon the search when she discovered a much smaller drawer recessed into the back of the bottom one. A lockbox of sorts. It resisted when she tried to pull it out; she frowned. A locked drawer inside another drawer, inside a locked room?

"What are you hiding from the world, Joseph Cillian O'Roydon?"

His chunky keyring held one key tiny enough and with the right type of notched tip to unlock the secret drawer. Upon opening it, something heavy rolled around inside with a clatter. She crouched to reach it and when she pulled her hand back from the lockbox, it held an impressive dagger. Its steel blade made a *schwing!* sound as she pulled it from the throat of the scabbard. An intricately crafted weapon with a Damascus blade that tapered to a sharp point at the business end. Where the slanted amber grip met the blade, a formidable, embossed eagle spread its metal wings across the crossguard. The eagle's head faced left and between its claws, overlapping the base of the blade, it clutched a wreath. And, in its center ... was an embossed swastika.

Shivonne gasped and dropped the dagger onto the desk as if it had burned her palm. She could see an inscription acid-etched along the length of the blade:

"SS. MEINE EHRE HEISST TREUE."

No translation was necessary to understand the universal hate symbolism of the swastika and those two cursed initials. It was explicit and unambiguous. She shoved the dagger back into its leather sheath and dropped it with an accusatory *clang* back into the hidden drawer.

Something else rattled in the back of the lockbox. Hooking it with her nail, she pulled it from the shadows. A cigar box bearing the insignia of a new generation's misogynistic hatred: a black rattlesnake against a bile-yellow background, its head also facing left, the fangs exposed, and its diamond-backed body coiled into three spring-loaded loops. Ready to strike. Underneath it, the words "DONT TREAD ON ME" threatened the reader with misplaced—misspelled—bravado.

Shivonne held it in her palm and lifted the lid. Inside were three pill pouches filled with green tablets bearing the letters "OP" etched into one side, and "80" into the other. She had recently watched a TV show about the Sackler family and Perdue Pharma, so she knew what they were.

"*Jaysus,* Joe."

Joe had no injury or pain that required such heavy opioids. It explained a lot—further evidence of his recent decline along with binge drinking, political extremism, and escalating abuse. The rattlesnake box also held a USB stick and the Allen hex key that would unlock her padlock necklace. Her fingers hovered over it, ready to pluck it out and free herself from Joe's bondage. But she resisted the urge and closed the lid of the box, shoving it back into the secret drawer, and locking it with a trembling hand. A look back at the laptop screen on the desk reminded her it was still, much to her disappointment, waiting for a password.

"*Shite.*"

She typed in Riley's birthday.

"Password denied."

She paused and tried to think like the Joe she had glimpsed in the secret lockbox of his mind. She typed in the motto underneath the threatening rattlesnake, but the laptop did not like that either.

"Ugh."

She suspected she had one chance left before the computer would lock her out. Hovering her hand over the keyboard, she was on the verge of typing the German inscription on Joe's dagger blade, when she noticed an animated "eye" on the screen, blinking, scanning the perimeter for its owner's gaze.

Of course, Artemis tsk-tsked. *Why didn't you think of this earlier, Shivonne?*

She unplugged the device and hurried to the living room, where Joe was still passed-out on the sofa. His face was slack, drool glistening on his chin. Circling behind the sofa's roll arm, she tried to pull him up into a half-seated position. The dead weight of his body made it an impossible task, so she stacked a throw pillow under the back of his head to lift his face. It kept dropping forward onto his chest.

The clock was ticking, and she was starting to panic.

And then she had a vision of another of Artemisia Gentileschi's famous revenge paintings, *Judith Slaying Holofernes*, where the Israelite heroine, Judith, after having seduced Holofernes, an Assyrian general about to invade her hometown, plied him with wine, drugged him … and then beheaded him. With one hand gripping his head by the hair, the other brandishing a sword.

Grab him by the hair, Artemisia whispered in her ear. Or was it their shared alter ego, Artemis?

Shivonne did not hesitate; she pulled Joe's face up to the laptop screen with a death grip on his hair. His head weighed a ton; her biceps were screaming in protest, but she held on as long as she could. The stupid laptop "eye" took its sweet time to search Joe's face.

"Please dismiss the sign-in screen and try again," it taunted.

"*Feck* it!" she cried out, the Irish lass coming through strong. It was not working. The annoying "eye" on the sign-in screen needed to make *actual,* open-eye contact with Joe, she guessed. She released her grip on Joe's head, causing his chin to smack down hard onto the laptop lying on his chest. It would leave a bruise, she knew.

Good.

She stood back with her hands on her hips to assess her options. His eyes needed to be wide open. But how? With what?

Help me, Artemis, send me another sign.

Quick as Zeus' lightning bolt, an idea popped into her head. She hurried into the kitchen, rummaged through the catch-all drawer next to the sink, and pulled out the travel sewing kit she used for repairing Joe's shirts and socks. She would sew his top eyelids to his brows to force his eyes open.

But the idea fell flat as fast as it had risen.

Too gross, Artemis. Besides, it would leave puncture marks on his eyelids.

When Shivonne put the sewing kit back in the drawer, it jostled a small box behind it, announcing a solution with its rattling sound. With a wide grin, she picked up the box and marched back to Joe with a spring in her step.

"I'm afraid this is going to hurt a wee bit, Joe," she announced, the way a demented dentist always told his unfortunate patient before revving up the drill in a horror movie. She opened the flaps of the box and shook out two cocktail toothpicks—the kind used for skewering olives or cubes of cheese—a little thicker and blunter on the ends than those used to dig between teeth.

"No sharp points, eh? Lucky you, Joe."

Joe startled her with a deflating "Pfffttt ..." from his lips.

But the cocktail picks were too long for the task, so she snapped them in half and held the splintered pieces to his face for measurement.

"Oh dear, now the edges are a wee bit jagged again ... bad luck, Joe."

She giggled, followed by an unladylike snort that surprised her. It felt liberating to let the unfettered melody of laughter bounce between the walls of the haunted house on Lavender Lane. After a few tries, she managed to position the toothpicks between Joe's lower and upper eyelids—one on each side of his irises—so his eyes were forced open between drooping lids.

Shivonne was still smiling when, quick as a spring-loaded Jack-in-the-box, Joe jackknifed upright, staring dead ahead with those crudely propped open eyes. Right at her. She almost peed her pants. She held her breath and waited, her face frozen inches from his.

This is where he kills me.

But just as unexpectedly, he collapsed backward again with an ungodly growl. She waited for eight counts to be sure he did not repeat the maneuver, then grabbed him by the hair once more while positioning the laptop screen in front of his face. The daft Artificially Intelligent "eye" searched the flaccid face in front of it.

"Making sure it's you, Joe."

"Oh, for the love of God, it's him, damn you. It's Joe!" she cried out, a sheen of perspiration forming on her lip. "His *feckin'* head weighs a ton, dammit. It's him, okay?"

The spiteful eye weighed its options, and then two micro-lights flashed green on either side of the camera at the top center of the screen. The machinery whirred into action.

"Welcome back, Joe," it announced.

"Woo-hoo!" Shivonne cheered, performing a few nifty pirouettes, but the rush of exhilaration was brief; she had a task to complete, and time was running out.

Joe had a fast metabolism.

She pulled the cocktail toothpicks from his eyelids, dropped his head back onto the pillows, and retreated to his study with the laptop under her arm. At his desk, she initiated the Google search engine. Confident, thanks to Luke's strategic tutoring sessions, she typed in a flurry of keywords: "Famous art heists," "Art theft," and "Pallas Museum blueprints"—anything she could think of to get the most comprehensive result. She opened a new browser window for each relevant result, performing a cursory scan of the contents. Next, she searched the web, focusing on the black market for art and known criminals with links to stolen masterpieces. To pull off a successful art heist, the thieves needed a buyer to take the tainted loot off their hands. Professional criminals often took an interest in masterpieces, not for their aesthetic purposes per se, but to use as currency in drug deals or other shady business. She clicked through the articles detailing the usual suspects and their links to the art world.

Once she had completed her dive into the dark net, she searched for "offshore banks" and "ways to covertly transfer money out of the country." Scrolling past well-known tax havens like Switzerland, Luxembourg, and Panama, she settled on Bermuda—a British island territory known for its pink sand beaches and maritime history. She had always wanted to visit Bermuda, but Joe had no interest in leaving the great US of A, where people spoke his language and he held superior status and privilege as a white, middle-class man. From a list of banks, she selected a recent upstart in Hamilton, with a name that warmed the cockles of her heart: "Lighthouse Limited Bank." The idea of a lighthouse appealed to her sensibilities.

Protection from the storm.

"Welcome to Lighthouse Ltd. Bank of Bermuda. Guiding your way to a brighter financial future," the bank promised. The word "brighter" shone inside a lighthouse cupola, casting a halo of light that shadowed the rest of the phrase.

From one of her pockets, Shivonne pulled a bank card for Riley's account-in-trust, for which she, alone, was the custodial steward. Joe had been told the money bequeathed to Riley by her grandfather was tied up in a generation-skipping, irrevocable trust. He had tried, several times, to get his hands on the funds—to buy a speedboat his buddy, Eddie, was selling—but Shivonne had held firm and played dumb. The truth was, it was *her* inheritance from her father, which she had hidden from Joe in a custodial account for Riley. As if she had known back then that they would one day need money independently of Joe.

Did you know I can sometimes predict the future? The irony of the question she had asked her school group in the chandelier gallery was chilling.

As far as Joe knew, Lord Fitzgerald Claddagh III, Esq. had bequeathed his daughter nothing but a cabinet full of shiny, monogrammed family silver, which meant nothing to him. "What good is a pot," he often lamented, holding up one of the Sterling Silver serving dishes engraved with the family crest, "if you can't eat from it or piss in it?"

Since her father's passing—until recently—she had only dipped into the trust money on rare occasions, and only to help her friends: Luke's community college fees when he was younger and broke, and a sizeable donation to Lorelei's GoFundMe account for Grace's staggering medical bills. Recently, however, she noticed that Joe's income had dwindled. True to character, he refused to talk about it whenever she brought it up. So, she had to dip into her inheritance a few times, surreptitiously, to pay Riley's tuition and ensure their health insurance stayed active. Besides those instances, she kept a tight lock on the secret account. It was a golden parachute for sunnier days ahead, she hoped. A contingency plan, should it all go to hell in a handbag.

The account balance fell just over $215,000—all that remained from the £220,000 lump sum she had received from her father's estate. Upon his deathbed, Fitzgerald had bequeathed her ancestral home in Ireland, Claddagh House, to his second wife—a Brazilian ex-model named Isadora—who was five years younger than Shivonne, and whom he had married mere months after his wife's death, much to the distaste of the rest of the clan.

Shivonne considered all this as she typed the custodial account number into a new checking account at Lighthouse Limited Bank of Bermuda. She pondered the amount to wire transfer, then typed it into the space provided: $205,000.00. She had to hold back a contingency to cover emergencies in the interim.

Ogling the zeros, she hesitated; it was a lot of money. But it was essential to her plan, so she confirmed the transfer amount with a gulp and finished the last of the required information and digital signatures on the form. She remembered the social security number from memory and typed it into the required box. When prompted to enter an email address, she started inputting her own ... and paused.

Don't be an eejit, *Shivonne, focus.*

From Joe's Gmail tab, she followed the prompts to create a new email account with a name matching the one on the new banking account. Any subsequent notifications or communications regarding the Bermuda account would go straight to the new email address. She waited for the bank's authentication request to pop up in the new inbox, and when it did, she confirmed. It was now up and running.

Done and dusted.

The last item on her extensive to-do list was to purchase two airline tickets from Los Angeles to Bermuda—LAX-BDA, one-way, business class—departing in two weeks. She bit back the tears when she entered Riley's details in the "Passenger #2" section; she could not believe she was doing this.

From the living room, she heard Joe snort—a crude, animalistic sound resembling a bear about to wake from hibernation. A chill of pressure nipped at her neck; she leaned forward with intent. "Delete, delete, delete," Angel had commanded, and Shivonne complied, clearing the browser as Luke had taught her. She snapped the laptop shut, flicked off the desk lamp, and walked to the door, only to whip back around to plug the laptop back into its charger, exactly the way she had found it. After a final scan of the room, she locked the door of the study and approached the couch where Joe lay, limp and harmless, a crust of congealed drool at the corner of his mouth.

Time was running out; her temporary semblance of power was draining fast, like sand in an hourglass. She mounted his body again, straddling his torso with her face inches from his. When she leaned forward to pull a black, disposable face mask from her back pocket, her padlock necklace—used to mark her as his chattel—dangled over Joe's nose, swinging like one of Lorelei's pendulums. His jaw was slack, and his mouth hung open, his tongue a speckled pink blob lolling through fleshy lips.

"Not quite so handsome now, huh, Joe?"

She smacked his face again, with an open hand; the prolonged burning sensation felt gratifying on her palm. Still no pain reflex from Joe. The way he lay there resembled poor Fitzi, dead in the hallway after Joe had kicked him.

How appropriate, she thought, *that the man who had killed Fitzi lay splayed out in such a similar manner.*

She thought of the wee pup's death and the look of horror in Riley's eyes as she shoved the black face mask over Joe's nose and mouth, pushing down with both palms. From her mind's stage, a requiem piped in, a *Danse Macabre*—Man's dance with Death. But this scene was not the vulnerable swan's death at the hands of the dark prince ... this time, the script was flipped: incapacitated Joe was the puppet, and *she* was the handler for once.

The one in control.

Doubting she would ever get another chance, she applied more, and still more, pressure to the mask suffocating her husband. Joe lay motionless at first, his reflexes disabled by the Rohypnol, but soon he started squirming underneath her—an insect trapped in a black widow's web—powerless ... breathless.

"Your turn to dance now, Joe," she said through gritted teeth. His body seized and his hand flexed against its restraint, causing the metal to clang and scrape against the table leg, holding it in place. "How does it feel to fight for your life, *motherfecker?*"

Resolute, she maintained her grip on the mask and briefly considered switching it for one of the throw pillows. It would require no more than a steady continuance of pressure to end her suffering, to shove the dragon from the top of the incessant, spiral staircase onto the concrete below.

To break the curse.

Joe sputtered. She averted her eyes and settled her gaze on a silver-framed photo on the buffet table behind the sofa: Riley on her first day of preschool, posing on the front steps of the home on Lavender Lane, her arms wrapped around Fitzi. It was her daughter's eyes—those piercing green searchlights above the gap-toothed smile—that stirred Shivonne's maternal instincts enough to make her loosen her grip on the mask over Joe's face. Riley would be an orphan if she followed through, with her father dead, and her mother on death row, for making it so. So, she withdrew her hands with reluctance, allowing Joe to sputter for air. His face was red and covered in spittle, but he was alive, sucking deep dragon breaths once more.

Begorrah, Shivonne, that was close ...

Joe uttered a deep-chested groan; his close call with death had fast-tracked his awakening, and he was emerging through the veil of catalepsy. She slid off his body and raced against the clock to clean the scene. The mask that had almost killed Joe O'Roydon went into a Ziploc bag, stashed inside her docent bag. In the kitchen, she pulled off the latex gloves with her teeth and dropped them in the outgoing trash. She double-checked that she had locked Joe's office door, jiggling the door handle a few times, and then—with considerable effort—shoved the keyring back into his rear pants pocket.

While fiddling with his pocket, she had the idea to unbuckle his belt and unzip his pants, pulling them halfway down his thighs. He would wake up believing he got lucky the night before. She ripped open his shirt as well, flinging buttons—that she would have to sew back on later with the sewing kit from the catch-all drawer—to the floor, exposing tufts of hairy chest. As a parting gift, she leaned forward and dug her nails into the soft pectoral flesh above his nipples, scratching hard and deep as she drew her nails downward, drawing blood like a feral cat. Scouring faux ecstasy tracks for him to show off to his colleagues in the locker room the next day.

"You had fun tonight, Joe. It was wild."

He stirred, so she freed his hand from the handcuffs and dropped them on the floor. The dragon was untethered now, free to inflict harm when it came out of hibernation. She did a parting sweep of the room: two empty champagne glasses on the counter, her stripper heels under the coffee table next to the handcuffs, his unzipped pants, the bloody scratch marks ... It all looked authentic, she hoped, evidence of a night of uninhibited ruckus with the naughty cop. Her years spent as a performer had served her well that night; the dress rehearsal was complete, and the scene was set. Only one more thing remained for her to take care of before Joe awoke with a killer hangover ... and a monstrous mood to match.

Leaving the waking dragon behind, she hoisted herself up the stairs by the wrought-iron handrail; her legs were heavy as lead, her head pounding. In the bathroom, she pulled her hairdryer from the under-sink cabinet—not her new, lightweight Dyson, but the older, bulkier one she's had for years. It was heavy in her hand. It would do nicely.

In the mirror, she noticed that her eyes—despite the dark hollows underneath—were sparkling with the glow of achievement, a *fait accompli*. Artemis after a triumphant hunt. From downstairs, she heard another groan and the evil enmity wafted up in an icy breeze to warn her.

He's waking up, Shivonne. It's now or never.

With a final, determined gaze into the eyes of Artemis, and with the courage of the Olympian goddess, she swung the heavy hairdryer upward and whacked herself in the face, on the underside of her jawbone. The pain was searing; her knees buckled and for a moment she saw nothing but stars. Dazed, bent over the sink, she waited for her vision to return. It had to look real to Joe—as if he had wild fun with her tonight—his *special* kind of fun. Perhaps, she hoped with her fingers crossed, he would see her bruises and resist the urge to cause more harm when he woke up.

Perhaps.

But "perhaps" was not good enough. So, Shivonne looked back at Artemis nodding encouragement from the reflecting glass ... and swung the hairdryer a second time.

CHAPTER 18
PANDORA'S BOX

*P*erhaps *it's not too late to cancel the whole shebang.*

Angel was sitting at her kitchen island with her chin on her palm, her elbow on the counter, and her feet curled under and propped on the crossbars of a stool. It was a pose reminiscent of Auguste Rodin's *The Thinker,* which was precisely what she was doing as she stared ahead into the dusk, serenading her from the bay window above her farm-style sink. Thinking and strategizing ... fretting.

What grave idiocy have I set in motion, Athena?

With only four days before the heist, the deadline was no longer creeping up on her; it had leaped upon her back with its claws dug into her neck. She marveled at how far they had all stepped out of their comfort zones—a crew of unassuming underdogs going against the grain of all reason, with almost superhuman resilience, to achieve their tasks. Simple tasks, in keeping with the idea that simplicity seemed to be the winning recipe for a successful art heist.

"Simplicity is the ultimate sophistication," the original peacock-owl, Leonardo da Vinci, had once said. And he was a genius many times over. Angel took immense comfort in that.

To her relief, she had been receiving coded text messages from her fellow Olympians' burner phones, confirming that they had completed their tasks.

Luke had been the first, texting an image of a bronze Hermes sculpture, his *caduceus* staff with its twin snakes gripped in one hand and the other gesturing skyward. On his head, the adolescent god wore his winged cap of invisibility with matching winged sandals on his feet. Below the image, Luke had typed a coded message:

Hermes is dressed to impress and ready to fly.

Lorelei's confirmation had followed the next day, featuring the image of a marble Demeter as she reigned over the verdant Boboli Gardens in Florence, a sheaf of wheat held aloft, and a cornucopia filled to the brim with harvest in the crook of her other arm. Superimposed over Demeter's bare, marble midriff, Lorelei's message read:

Demeter's harvest has been bountiful and is ready for the feast.

Lorelei had been successful in securing the sedative.

Angel was most nervous about Shivonne's confirmation, in part because of the combustible nature of her situation at home and the monumental courage required to complete her task, assuming she had been able to pull it off.

She rose from her pensive perch at the kitchen island to pour herself a glass of wine and sat down again to refresh the Messenger app on her burner phone. If Shivonne were unsuccessful the night before, there would be no need for Angel to waste any more time. The heist would be dead in the water. They all knew it and secretly hoped for it. Stealing art from a world-famous museum was a daunting endeavor.

As if concurring, the burner phone buzzed in her hand, hours later than expected, but there it was: an image of Augustus Saint-Gaudens's sculpture of the goddess Diana—Artemis's Roman equivalent—reigning victorious from her exalted position in the central hall of the Metropolitan Museum in New York. Poised on her tippy toes like a golden ballerina atop a gilt cupola, the goddess was drawing back an arrow from a taut hunting bow. Invisible fingers tickled the back of Angel's neck as she read Shivonne's poetic message:

Artemis drew her bow and released the arrow.

The moon was full, and the hunt was successful.

It conjured up fierce Artemis hunting by moonlight, unafraid of the dangers lurking in the woods, undeterred by the threat of night.

Brava, Artemis.

With all three of her co-conspirators' pre-heist tasks completed it was time for Athena to spearhead the rest of the effort. Angel had rehearsed the moving parts of the plan over and over, memorizing each segment as if it were a movie reel screened in her mind. Sometimes she scrolled the reel backward, looking for flaws that could lead to failure of Olympian proportions. Only one thing was certain—stealing art was an *un*certain business.

Courage. Hope. Tentative words; uncertain words.

Her mind drifted to Deacon, and how she imagined he would react if her plan failed. How he would describe his wife's secret alter ego to the reporters camping out in their front yard, detailing how he had noticed her gradual unraveling. Her downward spiral into a psychotic break. He would omit, of course, that he had not been around much to witness said decline. He might tell them about the assault in Memphis and how her near-brush with gang rape—and the years of depression and therapy that ensued—must have caused the fissure that had finally cracked her mind wide open.

"Always a bit of a peacock, that one," he might tell the reporters with a disapproving shake of his head. He would likely visit her once or twice behind bars, bringing her art books or candy before gradually retreating, his visits dwindling until a process server delivered his divorce petition. A busy lawyer at the peak of his career did not deserve to be dragged down by a deadweight wife who taught art appreciation to fellow inmates at the Central California Women's Facility in Lynwood.

Despite his would-be desertion, the thought of her husband made her pine for him. She started dialing his number, then realized she was still holding her burner phone. What a disaster that would have been. She imagined Deacon querying her about the strange number; the lies she would have to fabricate to cover for it. She switched to her mobile phone, stroking his thumbnail photo when it popped up on her screen. It reminded her of happier times.

"Hey, you," he answered in a gravelly voice. It was daybreak wherever he was; he sounded half asleep.

"Hi Deke," she said with superficial cheer. "I thought I'd jump the gun and call you before you called me. I know how busy you are."

"Uh, was I supposed to call you today?" He sounded surprised.

Her face dropped, and she gripped the phone so hard, she inadvertently took a photo of the dark cavern of her inner ear.

"No, not really," she said. *Not unless you meant to wish me happy birthday, no.*

She withheld that information to give him the benefit of the doubt. He was on the opposite end of the world; his body's circadian rhythm was mixed up. He would figure it out later and call her back.

Hope ...

"How have you been?" he asked, and she could hear water running on his end of the line. He was shaving or brushing his teeth while talking to her. "A man can walk and chew gum at the same time," he would always say to her when she demanded his undivided attention. "Ange, can you hear me? How are things?"

You don't want to know.

"Oh, fine. Not much going on." *Just planning a major art heist from a global institution.* "You?"

"The usual, putting out fires left, right, and center. International entertainment law is a bitch. I'm either in a conference room or alone in a hotel room."

She thought she heard someone cough or clear their throat; it did not sound like Deacon.

"Who's that?" she asked. "Is someone with you?"

"What do you mean?" he asked.

"I thought I heard someone cough."

"Nah, there's no one else here. I've got the TV on. BBC News."

"Oh."

Trust ... Doubt ...

"When will you be home?" A surge of pain was radiating in her chest. She didn't know if it was the burn of suspicion or the mother of all hot flashes.

"I'm flying to Dubai tomorrow for the final stretch. Should be home in a week or so."

Good, he will be home to buffer the blow for the kids if their mother is arrested.

"Okay," she said. "I miss you. We don't talk enough."

Among other things.

"Yeah," he said, "I can't wait to come home and sleep in my own bed."

It was a gut punch; she wished he had said, "I can't wait to come home to sleep with *you*," instead. "Me too," she said, thinking of the hollowed-out dip in the mattress. She heard rustling from his end of the line and pictured him pulling on a suit jacket or running a comb through his hair.

"Sorry Angel, I'm meeting the team for a breakfast pow-wow downstairs in ten." He said her name like it was her name—which it was, of course—but lacking the fuzzy term-of-endearment tone of an "angel-honey" or "angel-darling" she craved from her husband. "I'm glad you called. Let's talk again, later."

"Sure," she said. *As soon as you realize you've forgotten your wife's 53rd revolution around the sun.*

"Bye, Ange."

"Bye, Deke. I lo—" He hung up before she could get the second word out—the most important one.

Seated at her kitchen island, she wanted to cry but no tears materialized. Athena never cried; it was a sign of weakness, right up there with politeness. In retrospect, she should have used the burner phone to call Deacon after all. Made him worry about *her* for a change.

To boost her mood, she selected Vivaldi's *The Four Seasons* from her playlist and soon the effervescent sounds of "Spring" piped into the kitchen. Her attention shifted to the large UPS box on the counter. Now that the other Olympians were prepped, she could proceed. She scored the packing tape, folded the flaps open, and lifted a rectangular box from the bubble wrap. It was more beautiful than she remembered from the antique store's website. An authentic painter's box, constructed from reddish mahogany flaunting its age with swoops of concentric woodgrain, a brass handle on each side, and a lift-top lid with an old-fashioned tumbler lock. Before opening it, she emptied her docent bag and lowered the box into the yawning bag. The specifications for the box had stipulated that it measured twenty inches long, fourteen inches wide, and eight inches deep, but online measurements were a spin of the roulette wheel. Luckily, it easily slid in with a few inches of space to spare on each side. She would be able to hinge the lid open inside her bag.

Luck ... And good, old-fashioned planning.

"Thank goodness." She lifted the box back out. A tiny brass key on a gold tassel protruded from the keyhole; she twisted it and lifted the lid with a shiver of suspense.

"Oh, wow ... look at *you*."

Wedged into its underside was an oil painting on wood paneling, executed by the hand of an anonymous artist in an unidentified 19th-century *atelier*. A portrait of a reclining nude reminiscent of Titian's *Venus of Urbino,* a confident woman flaunting explicit sensuality and basking in the adoration of the male gaze. Dabs of cream and pink formed her luminous skin, with the occasional spot of white where the painter wanted to reflect a light source. In true Impressionist style, her features looked unfinished—devoid of detail—no more than a blur that suggested the model was in motion. Or squirming in ecstasy, perhaps, reclined against lush drapery in muted Van Dyke brown, burnt umber, and vermilion red.

Inside the wood box was a painter's palette stained with confetti-like splotches of dried oil paint, its wooden edges smoothed by centuries of paint-stained finger grips. Angel lifted it to reveal three metal paint tubes and a variety of flat, hog hair paintbrushes stored underneath. She handled the white paint tube with caution; traditionally, whites and yellows had contained substantial amounts of toxic lead. It was rumored that Vincent Van Gogh, he of the self-mutilated ear, ate some of his yellow paint during those asylum years—the universal color associated with what had so famously eluded the tortured artist: happiness. As if he could ingest happiness that way, poor soul. Instead, ironically, the lead he had consumed that way must have contributed to his madness and untimely death by his own hand.

Carefully inserting the blade of the paring knife into the groove at the bottom right of the nude portrait, she leveraged it toward her to unseat it from inside the lid. It dislodged with a *plop* and pivoted forward into her waiting palm. Up close, she recognized much of herself trapped in the blurry nude—the suggestion of an identity crisis, the wanting of plump flesh, the sensuality oozing forth from the oiled skin.

"Pandora," she christened her, caressing the painted skin that must have been much adored. "Lucky lady."

May you be my Lady Luck.

With Pandora removed from the lid, the depth of the mahogany box had increased by about two inches, which is what she had hoped for. To be sure, she constructed a rough mock-up from the empty UPS box and packing tape, cutting, and folding it to the exact dimensions of the object it would hold, assuming all went according to plan. After constructing the mock-up, it was time for another acid test.

She held her breath and, squinting with one eye, lowered her homemade package into the empty painter's box. If any of her neighbors had passed by at that exact moment and happened to glance into Angel Hendridge's kitchen window at 7:45 p.m. on that ordinary Saturday evening, they would have thought they were witnessing a curvy, middle-aged woman in a faded Oxford University sweat-shirt and elastic-waisted yoga pants, defusing a parcel bomb with a nitroglycerin payload ... and a very short fuse.

Her rudimentary package nestled inside the mahogany box with millimeters to spare on the long sides.

"Phew."

She was not a backup-plan kind of goddess. Nothing would be left to chance—Athena would have it no other way. Everything was painstakingly planned, to the millimeter, down to the minute. She had extensively researched how museums protected their treasures during visiting hours, and at night when the galleries were dark. Apart from the requisite security guards, most employed vibration sensors and motion detection lights as part of their theft-deterrent arsenal. But, as her research revealed, art institutions could only afford to tag their most expensive objects with sensors, which were costly and risked damaging the delicate artwork. In most cases, sensors were active only at night when the galleries were empty ... apart from the odd opportunistic thief, according to art crime lore.

A ladder. An unguarded window. Happenstance.

She had considered all those factors and had planned accordingly, measuring the risk-to-reward ratio. It was impossible to know in advance if the painting they aimed to steal was armed with sensors, without setting off alarm bells of a different kind. All they could do was hope that luck was on their side that day.

There was that word again: *Hope.* The only thing that remained in Pandora's jar after she had released every worldly evil upon humankind. Pandora. Eve. Primal women who broke the rules and invited misery upon mankind. Angel's hope was no more than a calculated guess, a shot in the dark based on an incident she had witnessed once while leading a tour in the Decorative Arts Gallery. A young boy, aged four or five, had come barreling ahead of his father and, without missing a beat, lifted a rare Qing dynasty vase from a credenza, hoisting it like a trophy to show his dad. The father had looked on, unperturbed, his hands clutched behind his back. It had only taken seconds, but Angel would never forget the panic she had experienced.

To her surprise, no alarms pierced the solemnity of the gallery after the boy had lifted the hard-paste porcelain vase. No blinding lights had flashed, nor gates dropped down to seal the hallways. She understood a child's compulsion to touch something igniting their imagination—an absentminded stroke of fingertips over the shimmery gilt surface of a Renaissance painting, or a poke into the glass eye of a polychrome sculpture. But the fact that the fragile vase had not been secured with museum putty or wires to guard against a bump or an earthquake, had surprised her.

The system was flawed, especially in a new museum like the Pallas, where things often went awry. Consider an elevator glitching amid a brushfire ... with people trapped inside. How lucky they had been that day. It could all come down to nothing else on Thursday when they would discover firsthand whether their targeted masterpiece fell into the well-secured category ... or not.

Hope. Luck. Chance.

She lifted her mock-up from the painter's box and replaced it with a stack of coloring sheets featuring the outline of Medusa's face. They would come in handy during her Greek-themed activities on Thursday. Then, from in between two books on her library shelf—Homer's *The Odyssey* and Dante's *Divine Comedy*—she pulled a square of folded vellum and spread it open on the counter: a schematic blueprint of the Pallas Museum's interior floor plan. With a mental one-finger salute to the Feds who considered her past her prime, she studied the planned route: past royal-court sculptures, a dandy King in his red-heeled shoes, woven tapestries, and a priceless still life of a silver tea set. On to the Dutch masters. She walked the route with her fingers, forward and backward. Back and forth. Again, and again.

"Planning to rob the museum, Ma?"

"Fuuu—!" She jumped a good six inches from the stool, her skin chilling in a flash. She had not heard her son enter the kitchen above the frivolous strings of Vivaldi. "Ha-ha, hilarious," she grinned, attempting to denounce the absurdity with sarcasm. But her "ha-ha" emerged sounding rather feeble and defeatist, drained of its intended punch. She elected to change the topic instead. "Your T-shirt is growling at me."

Distraction is key.

Roman looked down at his chest and rolled his eyes. He was wearing one of City Morgue's—his favorite band—concert T-shirts, featuring a monstrous logo reminiscent of Cerberus, the three-headed dog guarding the Underworld. In Roman's heavy-metal world, Cerberus was a snarling Rottweiler; it reminded Angel of Walter's description of ruthless lawyers. She wondered whether seeing Cerberus right before the heist was akin to a groom seeing his bride in her wedding dress before the actual day. Bad luck for a pseudo-goddess.

Roman rummaged noisily for a pot in the drawer under the stove and flung open the pantry door. "Do we have any pinto beans?"

She watched him, pining for the sweet little towhead he used to be before he morphed into a strapping eighteen-year-old on the verge of deserting her. She hoped he would be okay if his mother went to jail for the crime he had so accurately guessed.

In the kitchen, Vivaldi's "Spring" and "Summer" had segued to "Autumn" during her painter's box prep. Now "Winter" was blowing in gales and dripping icy stalactites from the kitchen ceiling. Since childhood, Angel had always experienced music with her whole being, interpreting it as colorful *tableaux* in her mind. It was a type of synesthesia: an involuntary perception of sound as colors or images. Sometimes, she could even *taste* the sound, or feel its texture on her skin. Pop music felt squishy and elastic, in shades of bubblegum pink and turquoise. But classical music had gravitas: deep swills of mauve and rich, velvety royal blues.

It flowed in silky waves, rising and falling, and folding in upon itself until it was a stack of patchwork quilts. And she was the princess on top, feeling every *sonata* and every *scherzo* vibrating through her body.

Whenever Vivaldi's "Winter" played, she experienced the scent of pine needles and the sensation of icicles striking painfully at her core, reminding her of pain ... but also love. And of love lost.

"So ..." Roman interrupted her daydream with his eyebrows raised, his chef's knife gesturing to the blueprint map, "*are* you?"

An iron fist grabbed her insides and twisted them counterclockwise.

"Don't be silly. I'm mapping my route for next week's tours, that's all." Her face went numb, so she hoped she was lying without the telltale twitch at the corners of her mouth.

"Ah," he said, "cuz you look all *Ocean's Eleven* and shit here."

Meticulously folding the large schematic map back into a square, she feigned calm. "Your pathetic old peacock mom an art thief? Wouldn't *that* be something ..."

Roman's gest was a little too close for comfort, even though she knew he would never suspect his mother capable of something so *owl*-like. Peacocks did not have what it took to pull off such a feat.

At the butcher block, he went to task, dicing an onion with the same knife she had used to score her UPS box. She noticed with pride how his left-hand fingers curled under, his knuckles resting against the onion, the other hand chopping with the edge of the knife, close to the heel. He was making one of his legendary pots of chili that would deposit a mess of legendary proportions all over her stovetop. She would let it slide tonight.

Watching him duck in and out of the pantry reminded her she had one more important task before the night's end, at her neighbor's house across the street.

"I'm heading to Lisbeth's," she announced, grabbing the spare key for the sage-green home across the tree-lined street. When she brushed past Roman on her way to the back door, he held out one of the ear pads of his headphone set. It smelled like raw onion.

"You've got to listen to this, first, Ma," he said, his voice sounding young and sweet. "I think you'll dig it."

She accepted the earpad; for an instant, the electrical cord dangling between her and Roman reminded her of the umbilical cord severed eighteen years earlier. She was in a hurry to get to her neighbor's house, but the rare chance to connect with her son was staring her in the face and she could not pass it up. They shared a passion for music; he had inherited her musical synesthesia, but not the same genre. He liked polyrhythmic jazz, rap, and metal so heavy it should come with a Geiger counter; she loved classical music and 1980s rock anthems. There was one genre, however, that they *both* appreciated, albeit in different manifestations: opera. His version was a Scandinavian construct called symphonic metal, where the artists took their inspiration from opera and incorporated it to spine-tingling effect into their tracks. The inclusion of ethereal interludes among the corrosive deathcore growls allowed her the patience and reprieve to bear through the rest of the nails-on-chalkboard screeching. In those moments, she felt their bond, the urge to hug Roman to her chest.

So, when he asked her to listen, she jumped at the chance.

There, in a suburban kitchen with the evidence of a would-be heist scattered around them, Angel cupped one of her son's earpads to her ear—while he rotated the other to his—and listened, a finger plugged into her other ear to avoid an unwelcome Vivaldi mash-up. The melodic, mauve segments washed away her doubt; even the spiky, lime-yellow discordant parts had a cathartic, sandblasting effect on her troubled psyche. It was exactly what she needed.

With her eyes closed, she showed her son the goosebumps popping up on her arms when the soprano's divine aria morphed into an unholy growl, blending genres, and overlapping generations. Roman smiled—a bright, warm smile that diffused his usual scowl and revealed the little boy again, the one who used to hold her hand even when they were not crossing a busy road.

"Right?" he asked, excited by her enthusiasm.

"Right," she agreed. "Chills ..."

She handed the earpad back to him and wiped the corner of her eye. Angel Hendridge hardly ever cried, but it seemed Athena had a weakness for tender moments between a mother and her son, never having borne one of her own.

Or maybe it was just the onion.

Roman beamed and touched her shoulder with the softest hand; she leaned into the fleeting touch with her whole being. But then, with the release of a handful of raw onions into the pan, he was back in his solitary world—the brief interaction with his mom having drained his quota of social energy for the day. The headset glued back over both ears; his back turned.

"Winter" was gnawing on her bones again.

CHAPTER 19
THE NEIGHBOR'S PANTRY

The gnawing sensation lingered while Angel crossed the street to feed her neighbor's cat. Lisbeth was out of town—gallivanting somewhere in the tropics with her latest Bumble-boyfriend. Neighbors and friends for more than a decade, Lisbeth knew her well—but she did *not* know that her neighbor across the street was about to become a criminal. When interviewed by the FBI or the press after the fact, she would most likely say, "I did not know she had it in her. She was so sweet. So ... harmless. I mean, she had the keys to my house."

As soon as Angel disarmed Lisbeth's alarm and stepped over the threshold, the Bengal cat sidled up to her and wrapped its lithe body around her shins.

"Hi Tiger," she cooed, "who's a handsome boy?"

She flung open Lisbeth's Shaker-paneled pantry doors to reveal an impressive array of delicacies: tuna-stuffed cherry peppers from Italy, black rice from Persia, and rooibos tea from South Africa. Truffled this and fortified that. Lisbeth liked the finer things in life; even her cat was a designer breed that cost a small fortune. Everything was impeccable, organized into wicker baskets that rolled in and out on silent, wheeled shelves. Next to the canisters of farro and amaranth, two regimented rows of spice bottles stood at attention in perfect formation and predictable alphabetical order.

"I knew it," Angel said, laughing; there was most likely a Marie Kondo book stashed on Lisbeth's color-coded bookshelf in the den. She was envious, suddenly, that her neighbor was somewhere far away in an over-water bungalow, enjoying rum-and-grenadine cocktails and coconut oil massages, while *she* was cleaning up cat poop and planning to rob a prominent museum. She hesitated for a few seconds ... then switched around a couple of Lisbeth's spice jars to mess with her *feng shui*. Thus, "sage" got to stand to the left of "saffron."

The horror.

From the bottom shelf, she selected a tin of chicken liver pâté for Tiger, scraped it into his bowl, topped up his water, and cleaned out his litter box in the laundry room. Satiated, Tiger resumed weaving through her legs in a figure-eight sequence. His marbled fur beckoned; she bent down to stroke the soft rosettes and feed his long tail through her fingers. It was getting late, and she was not done in Lisbeth's kitchen.

She selected a shiny dinner spoon from her neighbor's cutlery drawer and stepped back into her bespoke pantry. Behind the lemon rind *marmellata* from Sorrento and the spicy dandelion honey from New Zealand, she found what she was looking for. True to character, Lisbeth had the fancy-schmancy version, bearing a designer label and a blue ribbon of excellence. Angel lifted the glass jar and read the label aloud. "'Dreamy & Creamy. Organic Valencia Peanut Cream.'" The price tag of $24.99 was still stuck on the back. Scoffing, she unscrewed the lid and stuck the spoon deep into the golden deliciousness to scoop out a generous dollop. Holding the spoon aloft, she wrapped it in two sheets of aluminum foil from a drawer where plastic bags, paper towels, and cling wrap stood with Tetris-like accuracy. It would be a special treat ... for much later.

Her phone rang, and she almost dropped the spoon.

Deacon?

She pinched the phone between her cheek and shoulder and bumped the pantry doors shut with her bottom.

"Hey!" Her voice was smiling.

"Ange, it's Lorelei."

"Oh. Hi, Lore." She hoped she didn't sound too dejected.

"Just saw Shivvy's text," Lorelei said, "Gah, that girl! Does that mean the Olympians are a go?"

"Um, don't forget, Lorelei ... this is my *private* number," Angel cautioned. They were only supposed to discuss the heist on their burner phones.

"Oops, right you are," Lorelei chattered on, cleverly pivoting. "I just called to say happy birthday!" She sang a sped-up version of the "Happy Birthday" song.

"Awww, thank you for remembering," Angel said when Lorelei finished her off-key version. "That makes me so happy!"

It really did.

"Oh, also … I wanted to double-check that the *birthday party* we are planning for next Thursday is still on," Lorelei said conspiratorially.

And just like that, Angel felt the happy feeling fade as the black dog jumped on her back again. She thought of the injustice of Walter's looted painting, of Shivonne's treacherous situation, Lorelei's financial distress, and Luke's childhood trauma. Of her own sinking self-worth. The FBI's rejection, Deacon's neglect …

"Oh, it's most definitely still on," she said.

"Holy shit," Lorelei answered, "that's nuts!"

"Yes," Angel acknowledged, eyeing the large spoon of peanut butter hoisted in front of her face. "Yes, it is."

With the phone call done and her petty act of theft from her neighbor's pantry completed, Angel was about to head out but stopped short at the front door. Lisbeth had been a good friend; she did not deserve bad karma. So, she went back to the pantry and reinstated sage and saffron to their rightful places.

After reactivating Lisbeth's security alarm—her mind on much bigger thefts and much tougher alarms—she slipped back out into the dark street and trudged up her driveway with the spoon of liberated peanut butter shoved under the elastic band of her sweatpants. At home, she found her kitchen quiet and deserted but for a half-eaten bowl of chili Roman had left on the butcher-block counter atop a greasy, brown smudge. She glared at the brown smear, thinking it an apt metaphor for her life: rather shitty looking from where she stood. She hoped the heist would change that, perhaps color her life in brighter shades. Mellifluous, jewel-toned symphony shades.

Eager to put the stress of the evening behind her, she propped the oil portrait of Pandora against the open lid of the painter's box on the kitchen counter and arranged the paint-splattered palette and paint tubes around it. Squinting, she scattered down a few of the hog hair paintbrushes as well, letting them fall where they may like pick-up sticks. She stood back, hands on her hips, to assess her arrangement. The composition called to mind a classic, Renaissance-era still-life painting, perfectly asymmetrical and adhering to the rule of thirds. The only items missing, she thought, were a couple of peaches and a dead pheasant or two.

She snapped a photo on her burner phone and attached the image in an outgoing text to her crew of pseudo-Olympians:

Behold Pandora's Box.

Open me to release the misery and evil of man.

Henceforth, inside me, only HOPE will prevail.

PART THREE

THE HEIST

CHAPTER 20

THE SECRET NOTE

O n the morning of the heist, Shivonne woke up with a faint glimmer of hope anchored in the pit of her stomach. Deep sleep had evaded her the night before, leaving her twisting and turning in bed next to Joe, his arms flung overhead as if falling in slow motion. More than once, she had startled awake, drenched in a cold sweat, fearful for the little ballerina with nothing but a frayed tutu between her and the dragon's ripper claws. Up and up those never-ending stairs she ran, toward a web of darkening sky overhead. And certain death below.

Once, she had slid out of bed and tiptoed into Riley's room to tuck her in a little tighter and whisper "Mummy's here," into the soft outer shell of her ear, followed by a muffled sob when she remembered she might not be there after the Olympian task that towered above her like that twisted Freudian stairway.

If disaster ensued, she could not risk leaving Riley in Joe's care—not after the trauma and abuse they had suffered. So, she had crafted a safety plan, starting with a detailed recollection of the abuse. It had not been easy; ripping off old memory scabs revealed fresh trauma still festering underneath. She shared the records with her three cohorts, agreeing that the last person arrested would send it to the FBI and media if necessary. With the help of Angel's acquaintance, a family law attorney, she had drawn up documents challenging Joe's fitness as a resident-custodial parent, in the light of forthcoming evidence branding him unfit. Instead, Riley would be placed in the custody of her godparents, Shivonne's cousin Maeve and her husband, Billy, in Dublin. Far enough away from her father ... and her imprisoned mom.

While struggling under the dead weight of such hefty concerns, she sat in front of her dresser mirror, applying her makeup on the very day that could

199

make her worst nightmares become reality. The bruises on her jawbone shone a greenish-purplish hue, and when she pressed her fingers into them and pulled them away, pale-white ghost prints lingered. The cruel mirror reflected a frail woman in the early morning light—the petite dancer running for her life.

Where are you, Artemis? I need you today.

She bent forward to search for courage in the emerald pools of her eyes, willing her fierce alter ego to appear. But the huntress failed to show herself. Trying not to panic, Shivonne squeezed her eyes shut and conjured the horrors they had endured under Joe's hair-trigger iron fist: his hands clamped down on Riley's shoulders, his gun to her head, Fitzi ... And when she opened her eyes, Artemis was there, armed with a defiant glare.

You never need to call for me, Shivonne, the goddess scolded. *You* are *me.*

Reassured, she sponged a thick dab of concealer over the bruises and absent-mindedly smeared a deathly pale streak of it across her lips. A *kabuki* artist getting into character; a ritualistic rite of passage.

Joe was in the bathroom—she could hear the shower running—so she laid out his outfit for the day: denim jeans, a white button-down shirt, and his black business casual blazer. She set his black Converse sneakers on the floor; he favored comfort over killer Oxfords when on active duty.

After completing that crucial task, she changed into her Artemis costume: an accordion-pleated khaki skirt and a white tank top, with a faux animal skin—resembling a wolf's hide—across one shoulder. The faux pelt, usually draped across the ottoman at the foot of the bed, overpowered her slender frame, so she cinched it around her waist with one of Joe's leather belts.

For the finishing touch, she strapped on her tan gladiator sandals—goddesses were female gladiators, after all—crisscrossing the long leather straps up and around her calves and tying them in a neat bow in the hollow behind each knee. The whole ritual of becoming Artemis had a therapeutic rhythm to it: the smearing of war paint, the winding of straps round and round, the tying of knots. When she stepped in front of the floor-length mirror, she looked like a character plucked from *Game of Thrones*.

The dragon-slaying huntress.

Defiant Artemis stared back at her from the full-length mirror on the back of the bedroom door, running her fingers through the soft grey-and-white pelt of the fur. The rain shower slowed to a drip and Joe appeared behind her, dripping wet and naked. When he smoothed his hair back, Shivonne felt a pang of nostalgia for the handsome man she used to know before bits of him started eroding, chipping away to reveal a crude, troglodyte truth.

The wistful moment did not last long.

"What do we have here?" he smirked, groping at her faux-fur vest, his pelvis grinding into her back. "Another treat for me like Officer Naughty the other night?" He tilted his head back and howled like a wolf, grotesquely reminiscent of his werewolf howl the night he killed Fitzi. The sound of it made her shudder.

"No, not today." She had to be careful not to encourage him or, worse, vex him. She was walking a tightrope between the two. "There's a special theme at the museum today: Greek gods and goddesses. The staff and docents are allowed to be in costume, so I'm going as Artemis, goddess of the moon and the hunt." As she said "moon" and "hunt," she realized she had said it in that order on purpose—a subconscious attempt to make her seem less assertive in front of the head of the household. She turned to face him.

"Well, *hello* there, Artemis," he sang, trying to pull her closer by the thick brown belt. She managed to twist from his grasp—a fox sidestepping a steel trap.

"I'm running late, Joe. I have an important date—uh, I meant *day*, today." Despite her quick correction, she noticed a micro-twitch next to his eye. "I'll make it up to you later." She left him standing there, dripping naked disappointment onto the rug. On her way down the stairs, she called out to her daughter, "Riley, love, let's go. Don't forget your violin."

She waited by the front door, at the half-moon table where she left her car keys and sunglasses every evening. The tessellated floor tiles spun their dizzying patterns underneath her sandals; her feet were cold. Ice, ice cold.

Be quick, Shivonne, a nervous Artemis urged inside her head.

"Riley!" she called again, with more urgency. The little girl came bounding down the stairs, her coppery hair tossing about as she skipped, her unicorn backpack on her back and her violin case clutched to her belly as if protecting her vital organs behind it.

"You look so pretty, Mummy," she cooed, stroking Artemis's fur vest with a tiny, flat palm—the same way she had stroked Fitzi's fur on that tragic day. Shivonne noticed a fleeting comet of pain zip across Riley's eyes. She was remembering it, too.

"Hmm, I don't see anyone's Mummy here," she teased, pretending to look around. And then, in a deeper voice, "I am Artemis, Greek Goddess of the Hunt and the Moon."

This time, the words were back in the correct order: "Hunt" and *then* "Moon," for Riley's benefit.

Shivonne assumed the heroic pose of the Saint-Gaudens sculpture, one hand pulling back an invisible bowstring up to her cheek, preparing to release the arrow. The dark shroud lifted from Riley's face, and she giggled, burying her face in her mother's wolf pelt. It warmed Shivonne's heart to hear that foreign sound—the sweet bells of little-girl giggles. She had noticed a marked shift in Riley's demeanor since their conversation about Joe's cruelty, as if giving voice to it had smoothed the jagged edges of her anguish. Or maybe it had been the mother's empty promise to her child, vowing to never let anything happen to her.

Crouching down, she pulled the little wisp of a girl into an embrace; Artemis with her sacred deer, the protectress of children. "I love you so much, Riley Bear. *Never* forget that ... no matter what happens. Promise *yer* Ma." Her words rang with urgency and desperation. Fighting back tears, she kissed Riley on the head and tucked one of her daughter's baby-soft curls behind her ear, for good measure. For luck.

"I promise, Armetis," Riley said.

The adorable distortion of her alter ego name made her smile and, with a soft hand to her daughter's back, she guided Riley out the front door, pausing for a final look back over her shoulder into the ice-cold interior of the house on Lavender Lane. There was a chance she might never see it again.

She would not miss a thing—not the ugly, nightmarish tiles, not the cursed hallway where Fitzi's ghost still lay crumpled against the wall, not the bathroom

202

mirror that had shown her so many battered faces. Above all, she would not miss the dragon who had chained her by the neck, branded her with his claws, and scorched her soul with every fiery breath. Everything she needed, she had right there, the little hand wrapped up in her own, holding on for dear life.

The heavy front door slammed shut behind them and it was quiet in the house for a moment or two before Joe plodded downstairs, dressed in his black blazer and black sneakers.

"Shiv? ... Riley?" he called out to the empty house, "Hellooooo?"

He searched the downstairs rooms with a scowl. They had left without saying goodbye—a firm "no-no" in Joe O'Roydon's rulebook. What had been their rush this morning? He jiggled his study door and was about to exit the front door when he saw something on the floor underneath the fluted legs of the cherry-wood *demi-lune* table. He bent down to scoop it up with a quizzical look. It was Shivonne's laminated keycard, the one she needed to bypass security at the museum entrance.

Silly, absent-minded Shiv.

With a cluck of his tongue, he pulled out his phone to call her, when something else on the floor caught his eye. At first, it looked like a crumpled piece of trash, so he picked it up and drew his arm back to slam-dunk it into the empty umbrella receptacle by the door. But his arm froze when a faint whiff of aftershave skimmed past his nose. Not perfume. Aftershave.

The scent of a man.

Joe dropped his arm to examine the piece of paper. It was a note scribbled on artisanal paper in the palest blue hue, with a thin band of silver leaf edged around its distressed edge. He straightened it out with his fist on top of the little table to read the boxy, free-hand script.

The handwriting of a man.

With deep dragon breaths, Joe read the note aloud to the evil house entity:

"*SHIVVY, DARLING,*

SEE YOU AT 11:30 A.M. ON THURSDAY.

OUR USUAL SPOT.

XOX, A."

It was the word *"DARLING"* and those three capitalized letters, *"XOX"* that blew the final fuse in Joe O'Roydon's brain.

"You ... two-timing ... bitch!" he spat through clenched teeth, the note fluttering in his hand like a bird with an injured wing. He ripped it into tatters with a stream of expletives and pounded the remnants onto the console table with his fist. The dainty table resisted the violent assault at first, but then it caved in with a creak and a groan and splintered onto the black-and-white tiles. Joe glared at the detritus of his wife's betrayal and bent down to pick up a fragment of the note—for evidence—a small sliver of the puzzle that read: *"XOX, A."*

While Shivonne and Riley were on their way to school, singing along with Elmo—about being a happy family—and glancing at each other with happy eyes, Joe was nursing his injured fist under running tap water in the kitchen, glaring at the shreds of blue paper churning in the sinkhole. Plotting his revenge. "That fucking c—"

The garbage disposal sputtered and spat out its twisted encouragement in his ear.

"Make her pay, Joe."

"Damn right," he nodded at the hole in the sink. He would do just that. He had her museum key card, her rendezvous time, and her exact location pinging on his phone—a flashing red dot moving away from Lavender Lane, about to turn left on Palm Avenue. The bitch and her lover, this mysterious 'A,' would be sitting ducks for a seasoned hunter like him. For the second time that morning, Joe O'Roydon hurled his voice at the ceiling. But instead of a cocky wolf's howl, it was the roar of a maimed dragon, fraught with centuries of cuckolded spite.

With the spittle still moist on his chin, he patted down his jacket pockets and pulled out a small screw-top vial filled with white powder. Trembling with rage, he shook out a bump onto the sink counter and, too impatient to roll a straw, snorted it directly from the stainless-steel surface while pinching one nostril shut with his forefinger. He chipped one of his front teeth in the process but did not register the pain—the cocaine had fast-tracked euphoria straight into his bloodstream, causing his pupils to dilate and his eyes to roll back in rapture. Not a man to waste, he mopped up the residue with a fingertip and massaged it into his gums.

"*What are you waiting for, Joe?*" the sinkhole taunted. He scowled at it with black pupils and, with his cheating wife's ID chain wound so tightly around his wrist that it threatened to cut off the circulation to his fingers, stomped toward the front door, crunching over the splintered detritus of the late *demi-lune* table scattered across the tessellated tiles.

Those cursed tiles, where fish morphed into birds, and grown men turned into monsters.

CHAPTER 21
THE HEIST of the OLYMPIANS

It was a day like any other at the Pallas Museum, its metallic, convex panels morphing into Pangolin scales and glistening in the early-morning sunlight where it crouched atop Mount Olympus. For the four would-be art thieves—a motley crew in cobbled-together Greek costumes, like paper dolls in flimsy paper outfits that clung on by thin tabs—it was a day that would forever alter the trajectory of their lives, in one way or another. Like the lone traveler in Robert Frost's poem, they were about to take the road far less traveled, hoping it could make a difference.

They stood at the foot of the Pallas fountain, bathed in the musky perfume of a nearby blooming wisteria canopy. The expansive view of Los Angeles shimmered in the distance behind a veil of early-morning marine fog. Each one had woken up at dark o'clock with hope in their hearts and trepidation buried shallow in their eyes. The early bird ... and all such useless bravado. The truth was they were petrified, feeling unprepared and oh-so-mortal on the precipice of an Olympian task.

Sensing their doubt, Angel turned to face her friends and cleared her throat. Athena had something to say.

"Today is the day we have been preparing for. This is your last chance to back out if you're having second thoughts. Last chance before gravely risking the integrity of the group. Speak now, or forever hold your peace."

They all stayed silent. Pallas murmured her accord from the center of the fountain.

"Last chance, Luke," Angel prodded. He bristled but stayed mum. "Good," she said, "let's all stay on task and remember *why* we are doing this today." They nodded solemnly. "Then so be it. We are ready."

She did not ask them; she told them. They needed to hear it from their Athena as they did that day in the sweltering elevator cab, six years earlier, when *she* was the one who kept them calm.

Hope. Trust.

Nothing else needed to be said; no more needed to be done. It would all come down to fifteen minutes of finely orchestrated strategy. Angel tapped her Apple watch, and the rest of the Olympians lifted their left arms to synchronize. There would be four alerts at five-minute intervals, culminating in a grand finale.

The first alert would be fifteen minutes before—*Get in position.*

Then ten minutes before—*Initiate the distraction.*

Five minutes before—*Unleash full chaos.*

And finally, at 11:30 a.m.—*The moment of truth.*

Four levels of descent into the dark chasm of immeasurable consequence, not unlike the nine concentric circles of hell described in Dante's *Inferno*—each one more horrifying than the preceding.

When they had all synched their alarms, they embraced in a group hug, clinging to each other longer than usual. A history of blood friendship and unconditional support zapped between them like neurons firing up an electrical storm. They had supported each other through the best of times and the worst. This time could be the last.

Angel was the first to pull back and extend her hand into the void in front of them, her palm facing down as if summoning energy and wisdom from the sun-warmed, ancient stone.

"Athena," she said, manifesting her alter ego's strength and wisdom.

Lorelei added hers on top, "Demeter." There was much to be harvested that day.

Then Luke. "Hermes," he said, channeling the skills of the fleet-footed god.

208

"Artemis," Shivonne said, thinking of her sacred deer at school, and drawing courage from her feisty alter ego's protective nature. Her pale, freckled hand was the last one to join the overlapping quilt of comfort and strength.

"Olympians," Angel said, deputizing them. Knighting them with the requisite courage for the day's agenda.

Their hands dipped down as a unit, and then flew up in an exuberant swoop to the skies. On its descent, Luke's middle finger pushed his glasses higher up the bridge of his nose and Lorelei made the *signum crucis,* kissing her fingertips to cement the blessing. Shivonne tucked a lock of resplendent coppery hair behind her ear.

"May the wind be at our backs," she said.

Whichever way it would go that day, Shivonne's luck-o'-the-Irish blessing freed the catapult torsion suspending them and dispersed them—North, South, East, West—to start their momentous day. There was no telling when they would all gather again and whether it would all have been worth it when they did.

Only time will tell, Angel thought. But Father Time, as they all knew, was an old bastard thief himself.

THE GOD of THIEVES

On the heels of their Olympian salutation, Luke spent the earlier part of his morning with a group of annoying seventh graders, going through the motions of *See, Think, and Wonder* ... but with none of his usual flair. He found the thirteen-year-olds a hard sell, immune to his attempts at charm. But to be fair, perhaps it was *him*, not them. Luke Lorenson had a lot on his mind that Thursday morning.

The first three stops of the tour had passed in a blur, but in the final gallery, he became more invigorated. How could one not feel a burst of energy in front of one of Vincent van Gogh's dazzling sunflower paintings? With younger students, Luke would have them pretend to *be* those flowers. They would start as germinating seeds from a crouched position on the parquet floor and pretend to grow, pushing their eager tendril-arms through the dirt, then spreading out green finger-leaves that rustled in the wind.

"How does this painting make you feel?" he would ask and smile when they inevitably said, "Happy!" while secretly cringing. For Vincent's melancholic demise and for all unfortunate souls cast aside by society, as young Luke Lorenson had been. That morning, however, on the verge of taking the biggest risk of his life, he bypassed any notion of happiness in front of the sunflowers and told his seventh graders the infamous, morose anecdote of Van Gogh's ear instead. How, in a moment of mania, the artist had cut off his ear and gifted it, wrapped in newspaper, to a local girl rumored to be a brothel worker.

Immediately after telling them the shocking tale, Luke regretted corrupting the wide-eyed group, so he made up for it by handing out paper and pencils for a sketching activity. While he stood by, fiddling with his Danish *farfar*'s Hermes handkerchief, and thinking of Ms. Latsky's gown, a few diligent students produced beautiful, charcoal-hatched sunflowers and leaves. The rest sketched a severed, bloody ear. Luke hoped his task ahead would be more of a sunflower ... and less of a gory ear.

Following his lackluster tour, he sleepwalked through the Renaissance galleries and descended the main staircase's Fibonacci spiral to the lobby. Sunlight poured in from the mullioned windows on his way down. Outside, it was not yet full summer, when the desert sun and hot Santa Ana winds would scorch the Southern California hills into a mustard-yellow *gouache* and ignite thousands of acres of centenarian forests. In the botanical gardens, the late winter pollarded trees were spouting their finest greenery, and sprays of blooms erupted with intoxicating fragrance.

What a beautiful day to commit a crime, Luke thought, stroking the multi-colored sequins scattered across his jacket. He was wearing the flamboyant one—in all its glitz and glory. With each step, the sunlight ricocheted off the sequins and scattered a spray of chromatic shimmer against the stark, white lobby walls. It

210

made him happy; for a fleeting moment, he forgot about the stupendous task ahead.

Shortly after 11 a.m., he strolled into the museum store, past art supplies for budding artists, bespoke leather-bound journals, and cheap replicas of jewelry once worn by Egyptian mummies. Jerome was in the back, on his haunches, stacking art books onto shelves from a pile at his feet. He had rolled the cuffs of his gingham shirt, exposing part of a tattoo that ran down the length of his inner arm—a sinus heartbeat intersected by a G-clef music symbol. It cemented Luke's image of Jerome as Apollo, the handsome god strumming his lyre, making mortals swoon with his music.

Jerome looked up from his pile of books, squinting at the glare of a thousand sequins. "And who do we have here? Joseph and his amazing technicolor dreamcoat?"

"If only," Luke said, a little shiver tickling the hollow between his shoulders. The sight of his new friend hunkered down in an alcove dwarfed by shelves of books transported him back to Ms. Latsky's library, where he had once checked in a broken soul and checked out a vault of knowledge bubble-wrapped in empathy.

Jerome shielded his eyes from the disco glare of the sequins and chuckled. "I swear I could hear 'Stayin' Alive' playing when you sashayed in."

"Hermes, fleet-footed god of mischief, at your service." Luke winked, followed by his trademark Louis XIV bow, allowing his jacket to project a kaleidoscopic light show across the glossy covers of the shelved books surrounding them. "Look ..." He pointed to two, foot-long wings he had crafted from sturdy white felt, sprinkled with glitter, and attached with double-stick Velcro onto the sides of his black sneakers. His "wings" extended backward like tail fins on a pink 1959 Cadillac Eldorado.

"A very *queer* Hermes, without a doubt," Jerome laughed.

When Luke's hand flew to his mouth to feign taking offense, he glanced at his watch. "11:11." A high-vibration number, a sign of luck from the universe, as Lorelei would say.

Quick Luke, make a wish.

He wished everything would go according to plan for the next thirty minutes. By then, he would know whether wishes did come true. Next to him, Jerome was chatting excitedly, but Luke did not hear a thing. He was too busy psyching himself up for his performance as a well-pleasing, fleet-footed god.

Ready, Luke? his alter ego, Hermes, prompted. *And ... Action!*

"Ooofff." He clutched his stomach and bent sharply at the waist. The frown on his face was not an act; he was queasy, but he needed to exaggerate it for the sake of his alibi.

"Are you okay?" Jerome's hand on his back flooded Luke's heart with a rush of warmth that quickly morphed into sickening guilt—for having to deceive his friend.

"Leftover Kung Pao chicken from two nights ago," he lied. "I feel sick to my stomach."

Truth.

Against Luke's wrist—the one with the cutting scars—his watch alarm vibrated a nerve-jangling tune and an ice-cold bolt sliced through the warm mush in his stomach.

11:15. Get into position.

The rest of the Olympians would have received the same alarm. It was official now; the gears of Fate were turning. In the next fifteen minutes, he would pull off his part—if not the *most* crucial part—of the heist. The urge to empty his bowels was real this time.

"Gotta run to the powder room," he told Jerome. "I'll be back soon." Without waiting to see if Jerome had bought his excuse, he rushed out into the lobby, his winged sneakers flying over the honed tile floor.

Fly, Hermes, fly on the breath of Boreas.

The men's room closest to the entrance lobby was too busy this time of day, so he bolted for another one closer to the galleries. It was in a quieter hallway where a group of headless Greek sculptures stood in line as if waiting to use the restroom. Luke cut in front of the muscular torso of Hercules, its shoulders draped in the skin of the Nemean lion. Brave demigod Hercules, abandoned by a ruthless father—just like him—who had faced twelve monstrous tasks, emerging victorious every time. Luke considered it a good omen.

It was empty inside the restroom, as he had hoped it would be. He ducked into the largest stall in the back, slid the bolt across, and flipped the toilet lid down to serve as a pedestal for his docent bag.

Time for a little fleet-footed mischief.

The first thing he did was slip out of his sparkly jacket, hanging it on the hook behind the door. His hands were shaking, so he pinched them in the hollows of his clammy armpits to calm their flutter.

Pull it together, the god of thieves coached, *Chronos waits for no one.*

Four deep breaths later and with renewed focus, he rifled through his bag and produced two cork insoles—purchased from a website for Napoleon-statured men—which he slipped inside his high-top sneakers. His feet were clamped as if in a vice, but he had practiced walking—ignoring the pain—in the vaulted sneakers up and down the four flights of his apartment building's stairs. If a drag queen could master dancing in six-inch platforms, then Luke Lorenson could manage fifteen minutes in two-inch padded insoles. Not only did the cork boost his height, but it corrected his tendency to strut like RuPaul down a runway, which was prudent considering the solemn occasion.

Next, he pulled the two felt wings from the sides of his sneakers with an audible *r-r-rip*, folded each in half with their Velcroed parts facing out, and repositioned them as shoulder pads inside his white shirt. They bulked out his scrawny chest into a swimmer's "V."

The jacket was the most transformational part; it had been Luke's brainchild, sealed with the approval of Athena. He unhooked the razzle-dazzle garment from the back of the stall door and started turning it inside out to reveal his father's dull funeral black, sewn with precision on the flip side. Thanks to his experience in theatrical costuming, he had crafted the perfect reversible garment: scintillating showstopper on one side; somber funeral on the other.

Yin and yang.

He held his breath, slipped his arms into the inside-out jacket, and then stepped outside the stall to face critique from the bank of mirrors. The result was praiseworthy if he had to say so himself. Gone was goofy Luke. Gone was his glitzy alter ego, Hermes.

The man in the mirror looked like a more respectable, generic adult. Tall and seemingly buff. Someone with a professional job, who drank beer and ate surf-and-turf while watching the game in a pub. This man looked nothing like a late-bloomer student with a penchant for glitter ... and penis ice cubes. There was not so much as a hint of sparkle or a trace of color in sight. The psychedelic sequins were now facing inward, hiding their splendor under a dark shroud. Exactly like Luke had been forced to do when he was still the son of a preacher man.

This new man looked ready for business—the thieving business.

Luke removed his signature Buddy Holly glasses and bent toward the mirrors to slip contact lenses over his irises, fighting the burn as they settled in. When he blinked, the face of the new man flickered into focus. This man would never wear his hair in a gelled-back quiff like Luke's, so he wet his fingers under the faucet and smoothed his dark hair down with a sideways part. The final accessory was a black N95 face mask from the pocket of his black jacket. It would provide another layer of anonymity—a lucky break afforded the thief thanks to the recent pandemic and the paranoia it stoked. Nobody would glance sideways at someone still wearing a mask, post-Covid.

Just as he pinched the metal strip over the bridge of his nose, his watch buzzed again.

Ten minutes to "Go Time."

He needed to make haste; Chronos, the grim reaper, was cutting away vast swaths of time with his scythe. Luke stashed his docent bag behind the large 30-gallon trash container in the corner of the men's room and glanced at the mirror one last time. Three parallel frown lines stacked above the black mask when he confronted the new man and understood that the once bullied sissy-boy—named after a Bible verse "delivered" by a mangy pigeon—had just stepped into the guise of the very thing he had vowed never to emulate: a macho man, a man without scruples ... a criminal.

"It's only fifteen minutes," Ms. Latsky's ghost assured him. *"You can do this, Luke."*

"Yes, ma'am," he said, and then, in the deeper voice of the man in the somber, black jacket, "you betcha."

The tall, buff stranger in the black jacket adjusted his crotch, pushed open the restroom door—no, *flung* open the door—and strode out. His hands were shaking, but he walked with a well-rehearsed, manly stride, manifesting The Four Seasons' "Walk Like a Man" in his head, and taking utmost care not to swivel his hips.

O FORTUNA!

Lorelei heard the phone ring for the umpteenth time.

But the ringtone emitting from the bottom of her docent bag was not her own—hers sounded like dogs barking—it was Shivonne's, chiming away with bells tinkling. Something by Tchaikovsky, Lorelei thought, sugarplum fairies or such. It was a soothing tune, bound to calm the listener's nerves unless, of course, said listener was planning grand larceny at their place of work. Played on repeat, even tinkling bells sawed at the nerves of such a listener.

As planned, Lorelei had borrowed Shivonne's phone during their briefing that morning. Shivvy's iTunes library brimmed with a selection of classical ballet and opera music, including a track Lorelei would use for her next gallery activity—a song that played a critical role in the heist. Athena had choreographed the whole shebang to music.

However, since taking possession of Shivonne's phone, it had rung consistently in Lorelei's bag. Obsessively so. She searched the depths of her bag with her fingertips and pulled out the culprit. Shivvy's home screen announced several missed calls from Joe—twenty-seven so far.

Hell's bells!

A man who called twenty-seven times—and counting—was angry. Furious. There was nothing she could do; she had a group of fourth graders to entertain, and mere minutes left before all hell would break loose in the next gallery on her tour. An inferno she would orchestrate like a demented conductor.

She would deal with Joe later.

With the students trailing her through the hallways, Lorelei was quite the remarkable sight: a blonde goddess in a white eyelet lace dress with a diaphanous chiffon scarf draped diagonally across her chest like a toga. Braided into her spun-gold hair, she wore a crown of faux poppies and wildflowers—among Demeter's identifying symbols. She looked the part: soft and luminous, a wood sprite guiding a chirpy group of Guinea fowl chicks to their roost.

When they traversed the Baroque gallery next to her assigned Romance gallery, she shot a knowing glance at Angel, who sat on the parquet floor surrounded by a group of students. Without making eye contact or smiling, Angel acknowledged Lorelei by flexing the fingers of her hands to flash "ten," followed by the five fingers of her right hand.

Fifteen minutes to go.

Lorelei's watch vibrated in confirmation, and she nodded at Angel.

Message received, loud and clear.

In the gallery next door, she sat her students down in front of one of Joseph Mallord William Turner's seascapes. On the canvas, large, slanting brushstrokes depicted turbulent storm waters with high waves crashing up and over the bow of a tilted ship in the foreground, its sails billowing in the wind. Turner had used the scumbling technique to wondrous effect, slathering white paint in critical areas to highlight the explosion of sea foam from the crashing waves. The viewer could almost taste the saltiness on their lips.

After a few minutes of *See, Think, and Wonder*, Lorelei initiated the conversation: "What do you see? ... How does it make you feel? ... What do you wonder about?"

The students wondered about the waves, the flags on the mast of the ship, and the darkening skies on the horizon. But, above all, they were concerned about the precipitous way the ship tilted in the storm. Their docent was operating on autopilot, drifting in an out-of-body daze, looking down upon a calmer version of herself. Engulfed in the seascape drama while a tempest of a different caliber

216

was brewing in the back of her mind. So engrossed was she that when her watch vibrated its ten-minute alert against her wrist, it jolted her like the prod of a stun gun.

Holy Mother of God.

Lorelei tried to swallow down the hard lump in her throat, but it refused to budge. It was time to launch her part of the distraction, to create a timed sound-track for the chaos, to coincide with the climax of the heist of the Olympians.

Here we go, Demeter ...

"Who has ever sailed on a boat?" she asked the ten-year-olds, her voice quivering. A few hands hoisted high like boat sails. "Was it a calm ocean or stormy, like in this painting?"

"Calm," a young girl volunteered. "We went whale watching with my cousins."

"That sounds lovely," Lorelei said, but the truth was the student could have recalled a vicious shark attack, and she would have responded the same way. "Anyone else?"

"My *abba* took me and my brothers fishing once," a boy volunteered, "but I barfed the whole time."

Her heart was racing like an F1 super car. "Cool," she said, shifting on her bottom—one of her butt cheeks had gone numb. It matched how she felt inside. Paralyzed. Drowning in those brown waves. She pushed on, explaining how the artist had requested to be tied to the top of a ship's mast to experience the motion of being tossed by unrelenting waves.

"That's crazy!" someone exclaimed.

"Isn't it?" she agreed, not about the reckless whim of the painter but about her *own* folly—her part in a risky art heist. Luke was right; it was batshit crazy.

Her watch buzzed its pre-ultimate warning.

Five minutes, Demeter warned. *Time to release the Kraken.*

"Let's all pretend we are on that ship in the painting," Lorelei instructed, "tied to the very tippy top of that mast." A murmur of excitement rolled over the group; their eyes shone with glee. "I'm going to play some music and I want you to listen to it while looking at the painting. Show me how it would be, tied to the mast of that ship, tossed by those waves. Just promise me you won't get seasick, okay?"

217

She winked at the boy who had mentioned throwing up over the starboard of his father's fishing boat. He nodded excitedly. Lorelei could not make the same promise.

She toggled to the chosen track on Shivonne's playlist: *O Fortuna,* a 13th-century poem of the *Carmina Burana* song cycle by the composer Carl Orff. It was the perfect musical accompaniment for the scene of an epic storm—the one depicted on the canvas, *and* the one about to be unleashed in the galleries. It had the requisite instrumental drama to emulate crashing waves. The pace of the *cantata* would escalate to a crescendo worthy of a shipwreck in a turbulent ocean. Chaos, at the crux of the heist.

Athena had strategized well.

Seconds after Lorelei pressed "play," without even so much as a gentle overture, the grandiose opening chants boomed through the gallery in the haunting key of D-minor and hung in the atmosphere like an existential question.

"Oooh For-tunaaahhh!"

A call to attention. A chorus of plaintive voices imploring Fortuna—the Roman goddess of Luck and Fate—and admonishing her for her cruel puppetry, begging her for her blessing. The students perked up; one by one, they started responding to the rhythm of rolling waves—hesitant at first—their upper bodies swaying and settling into meditative, figure-eight swoons, the way a pendulum did if suspended long enough. Their eyelids drooped in response to the trancelike vibration of the operatic harmonies. The woodwinds sighed, and the strings emoted, bathing the gallery in a medieval aura.

Percussion was holding her breath ...

Lorelei glanced at her watch and toggled her phone volume to its max in anticipation of the approaching crescendo. The music surged, increasing its tempo twofold; on the painted canvas in front of them, the ocean seemed to burst into life. Tempestuous waves were swelling and dropping with each clash of the orchestral gong. Poseidon's wrath flooded the room and spilled over into Angel's Baroque gallery next door.

A crowd of bystanders heeded the hypnotic call and gathered in the doorways, watching with wonderment as the students were swept away on an imaginary, doomed ship. The resonant orchestra gong exploded then, setting in motion the imminent climax.

Bhwaaahhh!

Lorelei started the count, anticipating the lightning-strike cymbal clashes with her hands held aloft—like a conductor elevating his baton for a pregnant pause—capturing the expectant gazes of the students. She held them suspended thus for a few breathless seconds before clapping her hands together as if they held large alloy cymbals. Four wet, explosive crashes in sync with the orchestra, intersected halfway by beats of symphonic *fortissimo*.

Crash! ... two, three, four ...*Crash!* ... two, three, four ...

Fortuna tensed up her chords and arched her back.

Lorelei was so engrossed in the shipwreck activity that she almost forgot about Angel in the gallery next door, preparing for her *own* catastrophic crash, timed to the bombastic crescendo of the cymbals.

When at last the final alarm vibrated against her clammy wrist, the salty cacophony swirling around her like a cyclone's vortex drowned it out.

Here it comes ... Crash! ... two, three, four ... *Crash!* ... two, three, four ...

She closed her eyes and let the storm she had curated wash over her in deafening waves. She was Demeter, scorching the earth with her torch of vengeance.

THE CURSED GORGON

Fifteen minutes to go ...

Angel locked eyes with Lorelei and flashed an inconspicuous "fifteen" with her fingers splayed wide, her eyebrows raised for emphasis.

In contrast to Lorelei's peaceful Demeter, Angel's Athena was dressed for battle: a 21st-century warrior in black jeans tucked into leather riding boots, a silver spandex top to suggest chainmail, and her shock-white strip of hair gelled back into a glossy helmet. Athena's omnipresent symbol—a plush toy owl from the museum store—sat pinned to her shoulder.

This would *not* be a peacock kind of day.

That had been her mantra since early morning; the milky eye of her back-alley savior staring into the depths of her soul, preparing her for the events of the day.

And here she was now, seated with her students at her feet in her favorite gallery, filled to the brim with evocative creations of *chiaroscuro* and high drama by Baroque masters like Bernini, Caravaggio, Rubens, and Rembrandt. Light versus darkness. Right versus wrong. A most appropriate venue for the drama about to go down.

She picked up her Aegis—Athena's formidable shield—which she had constructed at home from sturdy poster board and laminated with sheets of tinfoil burnished to a glint with the back of a spoon. In its center, she had glued the frightening image of Caravaggio's Medusa, Athena's evil-averting amulet.

There was much evil to be averted in the world.

And today was the day. They had planned and rehearsed it, ad nauseam. With the museum overflowing with jostling visitors—many still wearing their pandemic face masks in an abundance of caution—and staff in costume, the stage was set for the grand finale.

The heist of the Olympians.

Angel smiled at the fourth graders facing the wall behind her, where Gian Lorenzo Bernini's marble bust of Medusa commanded their attention. It was on loan from Rome, the perfect object for a myth-themed day. Bernini's gorgon was mid-transformation, her face frozen in surprise, her hair transforming into a nest of poisonous vipers. What better mythical monster could a docent ask for? And who better to tell the story than Medusa's creator, Athena? The students were chattering with suspense, but when Angel raised her shield, they fell silent.

Oh, what power a goddess has. Especially one with a badass, evil-repelling shield. Ancient superhero.

"Has everyone looked closely at the sculpture behind me?" she asked.

No Greek hero was more feared than the viper-haired Gorgon, but in Bernini's version, she still resembled the cherubic maiden, freshly cursed for an indiscretion beyond her control. Her head was still very much attached to her shoulders.

"I'm going to tell you the story of Medusa," Angel began, "but I need your help." Wide-eyed, the children hung on her lips. "Every time I say her name, 'Medusa,' I want you to mimic her, like this ..." Both of her hands flew up to her head, her fingers waving about like a nest of coiling vipers. "Got it?"

The students squirmed with anticipation. It was story time.

"Now remember, my friends ... the story of Medusa is just make-believe. She was not real," Angel announced to the group; they responded with a communal sigh. It was an important disclaimer considering the horror of the tale, and the additional terror she knew the students would experience shortly in that very gallery.

"Like the headless horseman?" a boy asked.

"Exactly," she said, "or Disney's Ursula, or Maleficent."

That seemed to further appease the little ones.

"Ok, here we go," Angel said. "There once was a young Gorgon who worked in Athena's temple. Her name was Medusa ..."

She waited for serpent-fingers to emerge from mops of hair.

"She was beautiful and innocent—"

"Huh?" Surprise registered on the children's faces; Medusa's reputation pegged her as a stone-cold monster and *not* the beautiful young ingenue their docent was describing. They scrutinized the sculpture: the frown knitted between the young woman's brows, her eyes registering shock, perchance sadness, her petal lips slightly parted as if to object.

"She was so beautiful," Angel said, "the god of the seas, Poseidon, wanted her to be his girlfriend—"

A gale of laughter erupted from the group; the suggestion of a powerful, trident-wielding god of the seas being someone else's boyfriend was ludicrous. Angel grinned. Greek mythology was like a telenovela—on steroids. Tales of cheating husbands and desperate housewives of Olympus were interwoven with drama, gossip, and betrayal. Oh, so much betrayal—the kind that demanded revenge. And then some ...

Her watch vibrated then; it wiped the grin clean off her face.

Ten minutes to chaos, her alter ego warned. *Pick up the pace, mortal.*

"Yes, friends, Poseidon dared to anger the most powerful goddess of all—Athena—by kissing Medusa inside Athena's temple ..." She waited for the finger-snakes to emerge from their dens. "Now, the goddess Athena was so jealous of Medusa's beauty, and angry that Poseidon had used *her* temple, she cursed poor Medusa ... by turning her into a man-repelling monster with snakes for hair. She swore that any man who dared to look upon her face would turn to stone."

Eyes agog, they were rapt.

"But ... but ..." a young girl protested, "that's not fair. It was not Medusa's fault."

"No, it wasn't, was it?" Angel regarded the young student with pity. The poor girl had much to learn about being female in a world ruled by men.

She had deliberately withheld the adult version of the Greek myth, the one in which Poseidon—in top chauvinist pig form, like his brothers Zeus and Hades—had forced himself on the reluctant Medusa, after which she was slut-shamed and vilified by a jealous, jilted goddess. A classic and historic "Me Too" moment dating as far back as the 8th century BC. Angel wondered if Medusa, too, had been too polite to refuse Poseidon.

"But the other gods soon became tired of all the chaos the snake-haired gorgon caused and all the men she turned to stone," she continued the tale, "so Athena sent Perseus to kill Medusa ..." Squirmy snakes writhed on little heads. "But even *after* he chopped off her head ..." Angel mimicked a fell swoop with an invisible sword, accompanied by a chorus of gasps, "... it continued its curse of turning men to stone."

The ensuing silence was tangible. Angel stood up from the floor, picked up her makeshift shield, and held it to her chest. She motioned to the group to rise to their feet. It was time to kick it into high gear.

"Who can remind me," she asked, "what happens when you look Medusa in the eyes?" She raised her eyebrows into a frightening stare for emphasis. A dozen hands shot skyward, but she let them blurt it out in unison.

"You turn to stone!"

"Exactly. We are going to play a game of freeze with Medusa's face."

She explained the rules; they would walk in a slow circle—calm and controlled, and far enough from the sculpture podium or the art on the walls—while she attempted to sneak up on them with the image of Medusa on her shield. If she caught them looking, they had to turn to stone until she called "game over."

"Everyone ready?" she asked.

Oh, but are you *ready, Angel?* Athena asked her.

While the students strolled in "Ring Around the Rosie" fashion, Angel ambled into the corner by the doorway leading into Lorelei's gallery and quickly placed her bag in the same position where Walter had stood on the day of their tea party in the French gallery ... directly underneath the security camera, but out of its recording range. A tiny Bermuda triangle of sorts where, she was told, things can disappear. She opened the 19th-century painter's box inside her bag on the pretext of retrieving the stack of Medusa coloring-in sheets, making sure to leave the mahogany box wide open. She stacked the sheets in a pile on the floor, a few feet in towards the center of the room, and cast a final glance at the yawning box inside the bag.

Ready, Pandora?

The box flashed an open-mouthed, toothless grin back at her. It was ready. Angel, far less so; she could hardly believe what she was about to do.

She snuck up on the slow churn of children in the middle of the gallery and flashed her shield, capturing many of them in a frozen pose. They played along with gusto; some purposefully seeking the malicious glower of the Gorgon in a show of bravery, holding their poses like good, little stone pillars. A few boys, as she had anticipated, shielded their eyes when she confronted them with the Gorgon's visage. There were always a few critical thinkers who would not run off a cliff with the rest of the lemmings.

"Good job," she praised, high-fiving the artful dodgers—palm to palm—one after the other. After the third or fourth high-five, the vibration of the five-minute alarm buzzed like a death knell against her wrist. The tingle made her skin crawl; it was a chilling foreboding.

It's now or never, Angel, Athena prompted with an internal shove to her gut. *Hurry, before you lose courage.*

While freezing a few more hapless victims with Medusa's petrifying gaze in her left hand, she surreptitiously inserted the other into the back pocket of her jeans until her index finger touched the sticky, dime-sized glob of Lisbeth's designer peanut butter shoved into the corner. She had deposited it there that morning, scraping a dollop from Lisbeth's spoon while wearing latex gloves. The simple act of handling the spoon with its deadly load had given her chills. But at that crucial moment in the Baroque gallery, Athena's resolve descended upon her, and she was as calm as one could be when surrounded by a group of rambunctious Gorgon evaders ... while staring death *itself* in the face.

She pulled her finger from the pocket, coated with a smidge of creamy peanut butter, casually rubbed it onto her bottom lip, and licked it off. It was an innocuous, covert gesture that drew no more attention than it would have had she rubbed her nose or applied lip balm.

Deadly lip balm.

It won't be long now.

From the neighboring gallery, she heard the opening chorus of *Carmina Burana*—the mortals' beseeching call to Lady Luck.

"O Fortuna," they cried.

The haunting tune spilled into her gallery and the synesthete in her *saw* it, vividly, in hues of deepest-ocean teal and navy, flooding the gallery and making the floor vibrate under her feet. Or it could have been her legs trembling; she could not tell. The music would keep building and surging until it reached a crescendo of epic proportions. The four Olympians had memorized the track and rehearsed their actions, anticipating the climax of the cymbals. That part was up to Lorelei; Angel's task was to create a second distraction of Olympian proportions, as only the Goddess of Wisdom and Strategy could do.

Help me, Athena. Help me stay strong and alert as long as I can.

And then she felt it—that telltale warning tickle around her lips. The sticky sweetness of the peanut butter was assaulting her tongue, triggering a cascade of histamines that flooded her system. Her face froze as if she, too, had stared into the stony eyes of the cursed Medusa.

O, Fortuna!

A student stopped short in front of her and gawked, no longer concerned about the wrath of Medusa, the smile on her young face dissolving.

"Miss, are you okay, miss?"

No, I'm not. Every ounce of her wanted to yell it, to beg for immediate intervention. But she said nothing; she needed to stall and wait for the climax of the crashing waves from next door. Around her, the gallery was abuzz with visitors drawn by the thunderous music and the "freeze" activity.

"How fun!" she heard a bystander remark.

Near the doorway, she saw her favorite guard, Walter Friedlander, inspecting the age spots on the backs of his hands. It was ironic that *he* would be the one guarding her gallery that day, she thought, glancing from him to her docent bag in the opposite corner. Walter's Narcissus pin featured prominently on its exterior flap, the mahogany box inside it empty and open, awaiting its treat.

Help! her bottom lip pulsed in silent morse code against her teeth; her airway was tightening like a paper straw chewed to a pulp on one end. The Aegis shield slipped from her grip and dropped to the floor; she followed, down to her knees. She was the Pallas Athene in the center of the fountain: mortally wounded.

"Miss ... Miss!" she heard again, and her head pivoted slowly, as if through molasses, toward several pairs of headlight eyes pinned on her ashen face.

"Your face is all puffy, miss."

The teacher, whose name Angel would have remembered under normal circumstances, pushed through the crowd of students, and grabbed her by the shoulders.

"Ms. Hendridge," the woman stammered, her voice sounding distant, "are you okay? You don't look good."

No shit, Sherlock, was what she wanted to say, but a sputtering cough burst from her lips. The teacher recoiled; Angel wanted to laugh and cry at the same time.

It's not contagious, for God's sake. Call 911.

As Fortune would have it, no sooner had the thought formed in Angel's head than the teacher voiced it to the rubberneckers leaning over the squirming woman. "Somebody, call 911! Guard!"

Finally ... took your sweet ti—

Angel slid forward from her knees and collapsed onto the cool floorboards, settling prostrate on the floor like a novice nun's first profession of vows. Her hands were flailing, grabbing at the phantom breaths evading her just as the nimble boys had dodged Medusa's curse moments earlier. At eye level, she noticed many pairs of shoes facing inward—toward her—and away from the walls.

Good.

Through the joint doorway, Lorelei's thunderous chorus bellowed; the parquet vibrated under her cheek. She squinted, relieved to see the four wheels of a gurney rolling toward her. Part of her preparation had been to research the median response time of paramedics for active callouts to the museum. It usually took them less than nine minutes; today, their punctuality was a matter of life and death.

Her life; *her* death.

Meanwhile, *O Fortuna*'s crescendo continued to crash into the gallery, pummeling her with monstrous tidal waves, lifting her, then dunking her, and slamming her down. Harder and harder. Filling her throat with its sponges and choking her with sand, squeezing every ounce of oxygen from her lungs.

Help me, I'm drowning, drown—

A cool hand breached the cacophony and grasped hers; through one swollen eyelid, she saw Walter's face filling up her vision.

"Angel, *mein Gott.*"

Her body was tilted to one side, a board slipped under her spine, and then a *whoosh!* A gust of cool air as two pairs of hands lifted her onto the gurney. It was the weirdest sensation: feeling as if she were falling while being hoisted upward. The music was still crashing over her, and her breath was fading, fading, fad—

…

She must have blacked out because when her eyes fluttered open again, a cool rush of oxygen was trying to flow through a tube into her nose. She gasped, fighting to suck it into her reluctant lungs. And then, suddenly, she saw it go down from the corner of one eye.

This is it, Athena.

The tall man in dark clothing entered the gallery, laser-focused on the wall opposite her—the wall with the pride of Holland on display: Hobbema, de Hooch, Van Ruysdael, and Honthorst. And, reigning in the center as he should, the master of Masters himself: Rembrandt Harmenszoon van Rijn.

Bhwaaahhh! Fortune's sonorous gong clanged, its hollow metal sound ricocheting inside her head and lingering there as if her skull were a crystal singing bowl struck with a padded mallet.

O Fortuna, it's happening.

For the briefest moment, before she continued dying, Angel felt nothing but euphoria. A contorted smile stretched at her lips. She had never been more alive, more essential. The cymbals crashed then, and her body arched on the gurney.

Crash! … two, three, four … Crash! … two, three, four …

The room was spinning, tumbling her around with coarse sand and salty foam. An epic storm was raging. Rolling and crashing over her. *Crush*ing her.

Crash! … two, three, four … Crash! … two, three, four …

And then, abruptly, with a culminating *force majeure,* the music died. The gurney wheels were rolling underneath her.

Am I on a boat? A ferry on the river Styx steered by Charon, hell's ferryman? She was not sure because her eyes were closed.

Charon? Why would I be going to hell?

A mental shove from her bossy alter ego refreshed her memory.

To hell in a handbasket, Athena said.

Angel's eyes flew open, straining against their swollen lids.

Hell? Handbag?

"My bag!" she shouted as the paramedics wheeled her away, pointing to it against the opposite wall. "Please bring my bag."

But no decipherable sound had escaped from her swollen airway other than an animalistic gurgle, and the arm she thought she had lifted still lay pinned to her side, tucked under a green sheet. Paramedics always took the patient's belongings in the ambulance, didn't they? That had been Athena's plan. But wherever gods and goddesses were present, so, too, were the Fates—those nasty bitches who interfered and schemed to cast a spanner into the spokes of the wheel of Fortune. To make it come to a grinding halt.

Wait! she tried to shout. But the paramedics continued wheeling her out of the gallery toward the elevator in the hallway. The last thing Angel Hendridge saw before she lost consciousness again was her docent bag left behind in the blind spot against the wall.

Fuck, she thought right before she sunk, dunked by a monster Hokusai wave of darkness. All in all, it was not an inappropriate final thought for one who was dying in the bowels of a beautiful museum, on the heels of a thundering operatic coda.

THE LAUGHING MAN

The havoc inside the Baroque gallery reminded Luke of a scene from an apocalyptic movie, at that climactic point where Good clashed with Evil in a showdown of epic proportions. Angel was on the floor, splayed out like Da Vinci's *Vitruvian Man,* surrounded by a crowd of onlookers and two paramedics in bright Day-Glo vests. One of the first responders was drawing liquid from an ampoule into a syringe, squinting and tapping the vial with his nail. Luke gagged and looked away. He had a fear of needles; sometimes he fainted without warning when confronted with the sight of one. It would be catastrophic if that happened now.

When he dared to look back, he saw that Angel's face had taken on the pallor and distention of a pufferfish.

Holy shitballs, Angel.

There was no turning back now.

He consulted his watch. The scene was ripening in front of him like a pomegranate on the verge of splitting open, but he had explicit instructions not to pick the forbidden fruit too early. It could spoil the whole harvest. So, he waited behind the door jamb—a bundle of jittery nerves—anticipating his cue. A sign from the gods, so to speak.

The gradual swell of the Orff *cantata* thundered through the gallery from the doorway opposite him. He counted the beats in his head. The music would continue to escalate from the angry, mezzo-staccato whispers of the chorus into full-throttled combustion, initiated by the first strike of the gong. It was a fitting soundtrack for their Olympian heist. Fortuna was one of the Fates, the capricious goddess that held Man's good luck—or misfortune—in the slippery palm of her hand. Gods and mortals, alike, were indentured by her folly. A flip of the coin. A roll of the dice. No guarantees; no sure bets.

And no shits given.

Art objects often depicted her crouching precariously on a large soap bubble, with one of her sandals discarded off to the side. How easy would it be for that bubble to burst and for Fortuna to come crashing down? How far would she get with only one sandal on her feet? Capricious Lady Luck.

Luke was at her mercy right then, desperate for her blessing on the brink of his gamble, obsessing over the fragility of that delicate soap bubble under his ass.

"Stop it, Luke," Ms. Latsky's voice reprimanded in his head, *"You've overcome so much worse than a fragile soap bubble. You've run farther than most with only one sandal."*

Obscured behind the doorway, he nodded to himself while lip-syncing along with the Latin chorus that thundered through the filtered gallery air. He knew it by heart; a magic mantra to infuse him with courage for the task ahead. As if summoned by his invocation, the first clang of the gong resonated from Lorelei's gallery.

Bhwaaahhh!

It burst his daydream like a soap bubble; his body jerked into action.

Now, Luke, do it now, Hermes urged.

He stepped forward from behind the doorjamb. *One, two, three.* He counted three manly strides into the center of the gallery where all hell had broken loose to the accompaniment of medieval incantations. At the opposite doorway leading into Lorelei's gallery, he clocked Angel's docent bag in the predetermined blind spot—its jowls gaping open as if shouting, *"Feed me!"* like Audrey, the carnivorous plant, in *The Little Shop of Horrors.* He stifled a nervous giggle with a gloved hand.

"Focus, Luke," Ms. Latsky's ghost chided.

After a quick glance over his shoulder, he inched—*one, two*—right up to the gallery wall studded with Netherlandish masterpieces. It was a litmus test; he was too close to the display wall now and the security guard should call him out. He waited, ready to abandon the heist and step back innocently with his hands raised, mumbling a perfunctory, "Oops, my bad." But the guard—and everyone else in the gallery—was preoccupied with the oxygen-deprived crisis unspooling on the floor behind him.

"O Fortuna!" the chorus lamented. The cymbals joined the cabal.

Crash! .... Crash! ...

The moment he heard the cymbals and the final alarm buzzed against his wrist, Luke reached forward with gloved hands cuffed by his father's funeral blazer and grabbed the beveled frame of the portrait in front of him. The second his fingers touched the wood frame, a bolt of electricity shot through them and struck his heart with such force it almost threw him off balance. But it was not an electrical current; it was the face of the oil-painted man in the painting, glowering at Luke with his father's lazy eye and sneering with his father's thin upper lip. As if the master painter of the Dutch Golden Era were in on the twisted joke, sending a harbinger from the past to distract the thief.

"You will never amount to anything, you little faggot," his father's cigarette-scarred voice taunted through those stained teeth, followed by a snort through the bulbous nose. The face of a farmer; the pockmarked skin and

sun-worn cheeks. In that chaotic gallery, under the disdainful gaze of Fortune, Rembrandt's self-portrait had morphed into the ghost of Luke Lorenson's abusive father.

Athena had chosen this painting because it packed a one-two punch; not only was it one of the more pedigreed paintings in the museum, but it was also one of the smallest, the size of a large postcard painted on a thin copper plate. The hefty, beveled frame added more bulk to it, but for a snatch-and-run, it made an excellent choice. It could easily fit under a coat flap or inside a large purse.

Luke had practiced the maneuver with a magician's sleight of hand. It was all in the wrists: lift and tuck. He could do it in his sleep. But what he had *not* expected was to be standing face to face with the ghost of his past. A lifetime of disdain and abandonment revisited: the gay conversion "therapy," the Bible, the belt, the countless hours locked in that basement closet.

Time ... grinding ... to a standstill.

It was that spiteful bitch, Fortuna, asserting her dominance, delivering an unexpected gut punch in the form of his father's ghost. Behind him, he heard someone exclaim in German, "Angel, *mein Gott.*" It yanked him back to the task at hand. The task *in* hand, his fingers locked around it, its subject continuing to taunt him mercilessly with his father's voice. The Fates did not give up so easily.

"Well, what are you waiting for, sodomite?"

His father's gravelly voice sandpapered at the raw patches on his heart, seeping through its cracks into his subconscious, willing him to fail. But his alter ego had no such trauma holding him back.

Gods be damned, Luke, do it now! the god of thieves urged.

Luke hardened his heart, tightened his grip, and yanked the painting from the wall.

Or ... so he thought.

Nothing happened. The painting stayed in place. Luke swore under his mask and pulled again but it did not budge. His father's ghost had unsettled him, and he wasn't thinking clearly. Panic crept her skeleton fingers up his neck.

Crash! ... Crash! ... the cymbals clashed again.

231

Fortune's bubble glistened and bulged beneath her. The laughing man sneered and taunted a familiar insult with his father's sour mouth. *"Lookit, homo-boy can't even lift a painting with those limp noodles he calls wrists. Sissy-b— "*

"Nope," Luke insisted to his father's face, "never again, you hear me? Never."

He shuddered; it was taking too long. Any second now, someone would turn from the scene of chaos and notice him doing the unthinkable in a museum gallery. When a mortal was in survival mode, Father Time liked to stand still and gape with morbid curiosity while sharpening his gleaming scythe.

Luke closed his eyes and imagined Ms. Latsky twirling in her silk robe, twirling faster and faster until one of the beautiful birds on her robe burst into life and took flight—up and away—into the sky like a phoenix. Upward, upward.

"Upward, Luke," his fairy godmother urged. *"Lift it upward!"*

With his back to the chaos behind him, and with slow, deliberate breaths timed to the philharmonic climax, he slid the Rembrandt up toward the ceiling and *then* pulled it toward his chest. The painting slipped from its stubborn hold and came away—free and clear—into his hands. No shrill alarm interrupted the death thralls of the *cantata*. No zig-zagging laser lights flashed across his body.

The fleet-footed thief wasted no more time. He swiveled on the balls of his feet, nimble as a tango dancer, and strode to the doorway connecting to Lorelei's gallery, the painting tucked nonchalantly under the flap of his jacket. In the blind spot by the corner—where Angel had assured him the camera's limited peripheral range glitched—he dipped at the knees and slid the painting stealthily into the mahogany box inside her docent bag. He glared at the sneering face disappearing into darkness.

"Go to hell, old man."

The lock snapped shut with a satisfying *click* that reverberated back through time to his pre-dawn escape from his father's pious, pitiless farmhouse; the soft *click* of the screen door that had shuttered that part of his life.

Closure.

The whole affair had taken mere seconds, though it felt to Luke as if he had stood wrestling with the painting for an insufferable hour, held hostage by the ghost of his past. Once he stepped back into the camera's field of vision, he slid his absent eyeglasses higher in a habitual, subconscious gesture and strode out with one hand tucked under the flap of his jacket as if still concealing a stolen painting there. From the gallery next door, Orff's tempest was dying down, and, with a lustrous carillon of tubular bells, culminated in a final, extended major key chord.

A happy resolution.

In the space where the Rembrandt had hung, sneering in Luke's face mere seconds earlier, a faded rectangle of flocked velvet wallpaper glared into the chaos.

The laughing man was gone.

CHAPTER 22

THE ILL-FATED LOVERS

*D*on't go. Stay.

The nymph, Eucharis, did not want to let him go. She was leaning into his shoulder with both arms wrapped around him, her fingers dovetailed behind his neck. *Don't leave me,* her posture projected—the post-coital flush on her cheeks and those downturned rosebud lips pressing against his skin. Telemachus was resting his golden curls affectionately against her forehead, but his eyes stared straight ahead into those of the viewer, imploring for resolve.

What do I do? he seemed to ask, one hand still resting on the nymph's thigh. *Do I stay with the woman I love, or continue my quest to find my father, Odysseus?*

Shivonne's group of high schoolers had been enrapt with Jacques-Louis David's painting during the last stop of her only tour, earlier that day. She could not fault them; it was by far her favorite painting. David had been a master Neoclassical painter and his impeccable skill with a fine-haired brush was evident. The skin of the two young lovers looked photo real: flushed and plump, as if supported from beneath with bone and muscle and plumbed with delicate veins. Perfectly smooth with not a brush stroke in sight. Youth in its prime.

Teenagers were often familiar with this scenario—an obsessive puppy love—so the emotions on the canvas in front of them rang true. Shivonne loved playing devil's advocate with this age group, so she had instructed them to consider the clues on the canvas; then she polled them.

"Who thinks Telemachus wants to *stay* with Eucharis?" A few hands, mostly female, rooted for the lovesick damsel. "And who thinks he wants to *leave* Eucharis?" More hands—mostly from the boys this time. Telemachus had had his fun, right? It was time to move on to the next conquest. Finally, she had polled the group again, "Who thinks he *wants* to stay with Eucharis, but that he *has* to leave for some reason?"

Hmmm ...

They had considered the clues again, studying the expressions and the body language of the young lovers with intent. One by one, they came to agree with the latter option. Yes, it was clear that Telemachus was torn between *wanting* to stay and *having* to leave. Poor fellow, on a mission implored by his mother, Penelope, to search for his father, Odysseus, who had disappeared from his kingdom of Ithaca twenty years earlier. But, while shipwrecked on the enchanted island of Calypso, Telemachus had been sidetracked, falling madly in love with a local beauty, the nymph Eucharis. Distracted, just as his father had been years earlier. Torn between familial love and the carnal kind.

Stay or go? That was the burning question.

Mere minutes before the tidal wave of unconsciousness would sweep over Angel in the Baroque gallery, Shivonne was thinking of Telemachus' dilemma and of the heartbreak that awaited Eucharis. The same question rang true for her: stay or go?

She looked up from the paper coffee cup she was mutilating with her nails to the handsome man next to her on the wooden bench at the edge of the lily pond. Overhead, native sycamores cast a canopy of shade and, alongside them, a chorus line of foliage skirted the pathway. They had been meeting this way, twice a week, during his lunch break, since that day when Lorelei's love quartz had passed its magic between their fingers.

Just friends. At least, that was what Shivonne told herself each time she stared into his eyes and felt a disconcerting jolt of electricity. But the buzzing came from her watch, the first alert—*fifteen minutes to go.* Cristian had felt it, too; he lifted her wrist.

"Got something more important to do, Cinderella?" he asked. The innocence of his question flustered her.

If only you knew ...

"Not at all. I'm happy right here," she said.

It was partially true; she had no role in the active stage of the heist other than to stay out of the galleries until it was over. Instead, she would remotely experience the countdown of those fifteen tense minutes in the calming presence of her Telemachus, while all hell broke loose in the galleries nearby. She thought of her fellow Olympians braving the thick of the storm while stirring an eternity pattern with her finger through the leftover cappuccino foam in her cup. She licked it off at the exact moment Angel licked the deadly dose of peanut cream from hers. Cristian's eyes tracked the bit of foam as it disappeared into Shivonne's mouth. The scent of the late spring garden's lavender, sage, and gardenia wafted up into their nostrils. Intoxicating them. They watched the koi fish swim lazily in the pond.

Shivonne realized that his hand was still resting on her watch arm; blushing, she thought of Telemachus' hand on Eucharis' thigh. Cristian was in his chef's uniform, but he had added a laurel wreath over his dark curls in honor of the Greek Gods and Goddesses theme. It was sitting askew, drooping down a little lower over one eyebrow, so she reached out to adjust it. When her fingers touched his hair, his eyelids fluttered shut.

"Shivvy—"

She pulled her arm from under his fingertips and rested it in her lap.

"Cristian, I ..."

"I know," he said, crestfallen. "You're married."

The dimple in his cheek deepened; she swooned over it, tempted to touch it, to feel the divot under her fingertip. The slanted laurel wreath made him look like Cupid, woken up from a nap.

"There is something you *don't* know," she said, shifting until their knees touched kneecap to kneecap. A spark of static sizzled between them. She cast a furtive look over her shoulder to where visitors were ambling from the museum patio into the gardens.

If Joe had to see us like this ...

There was no uncomplicated way to say it, so she simply blurted out the words—dangerous words—words dipped in poison that could doom the very lips that uttered them.

"I don't love him, Cristian. He—" She flinched.

The act of acknowledging abuse did not come easy to its victim. The shame and disabling fear of it often silenced the bearer, dooming her or him to carry the burden alone. But on this momentous day, emboldened by the fierceness of her friends, Shivonne found the courage to push past the fear.

"He is cruel ... abusive to me and our daughter," she said, her index finger tugging at the padlock pressing against her throat. "He has threatened to take Riley away from me if I dare to leave him. And worse ..." She could not give voice to Joe's ultimate threat.

Cristian did not recoil or pale in response to her revelation, as she thought he would; he simply blinked and waited for her to continue. When she did not, he tenderly grazed the bruise on the underside of her jaw with a whisper-touch.

"I was going to ask you about this. Did he do this to you? I'll kill the *malparido*." His eyes hardened, and the hands that gripped hers were soft, yet insistent. Protector's hands.

"I ..." She hesitated; it would be an outright lie to confirm his suspicion about the fresh bruise under her jaw. It had been her own doing, the *only* bruise without Joe's fingerprints embedded in it. But how would she even begin to explain injuring herself with a hair dryer? The truth wasn't an option because it was too convoluted.

Cristian mistook her silence for confirmation and wrapped his arms around her shoulders so that her head rested against his chest, the way Eucharis leaned against Telemachus in the painting. The faint whiff of rosemary and garlic clinging to his chef's jacket evoked comfort and safety. When her watch vibrated again, she had a vision of Artemis dipping her weighted arrow in hellebore and pulling back the plaited-horsehair bowstring to her cheek, straining to hold it taut. Waiting ... waiting ...

Five minutes to go.

She shifted on the wooden bench, overcome with guilt for sitting in a garden of paradise sipping cappuccino, while her fellow Olympians were drowning in chaos in the galleries.

I should be there, too.

But Artemis had set her traps in advance. A good huntress knew when to strike ... and when to lie in wait.

An errant copper curl fell onto her cheek when she unwrapped herself from Cristian's hold. His eyes followed the curl as she tucked it behind her ear.

"You look beautiful, Artemis," he said dreamily. "I'm entirely under your spell."

His words triggered a spasm of euphoria in her throat—a spasm much briefer and less constrictive than the one that held Angel in its death grip, a stone's throw away.

"What can I do to help?" he asked, as a gentleman would. A protector.

She thought of Telemachus and Eucharis, of Orpheus and Eurydice. Adam and Eve, and Romeo and Juliet, too. Things did not end well for ill-fated lovers. Lovers were fools and fools made mistakes—deadly mistakes.

"It's complicated," she sighed, "but I hope to figure it out ... soon." *If all goes well.* She rose from the bench just as her watch vibrated its final alert.

Begorrah, it's happening!

Cristian extended his hand to help her up, his face mirroring the melancholy on Telemachus' in the painting.

"Don't go," he implored. "Stay."

At precisely the moment when Angel was clawing at her throat, and Luke confronted the ghost of his father, Shivonne rose to her tiptoes and kissed Cristian on the lips. A forbidden kiss. Around them, dozens of pollen-drunk bees dive-bombed the stamen of colorful spring petals, and the birds-of-paradise tangoed and dipped underneath the azure skies.

Had he looked down from the courtyard parapet into the lush gardens below, the livid husband would have seen the couple embrace amid the birds and the bees. But Fortune seemed to favor the "ill-fated lovers," for Joe did not slow down or divert his gaze. He had an agenda—and myopic focus—to catch his wife red-handed with the mysterious "A." He barreled across the fountain plaza with his fists balled and a hive full of murder hornets swarming inside his head, buzzing schizophrenic missives in his ears, and sharpening their stingers against his taut nerves.

"She's cheating on you, Joe, humiliating you."

Disoriented, he shook his head to scatter the hornets, even though he knew they were speaking the truth. *The lying, cheating bitch!* He had called her cell phone a gazillion times with no answer. She was avoiding him, and he knew why; the words on the lover's note were seared into his memory.

"Cuckold. Fool," the murder hornets whispered in his ear.

"Shut up!" he screamed, whacking his head with the heel of his palm, desperate to dislodge the interlopers. A group of tourists by the fountain whipped around to stare at the lunatic, but Joe stormed past them, unaware that just yonder, beyond the wall bordering the courtyard, his wife was in the embrace of a handsome stranger at that exact moment.

Brandishing his mobile phone like a water diviner's dowsing rod, he locked onto the flashing red dot pinpointing her phone's location; it appeared to be inside a gallery to his left. He quickened his step; it was almost 11:30 a.m.—her agreed-upon rendezvous time with "A"—and he intended to crash that fateful meeting. God knows what he would do when he saw them. His hands itched for his service weapon, which he had left behind in the car's trunk for fear of tripping the metal detectors by the entrance.

Consumed by rage, he barged through the doors and forcefully shoved a mother with two young children aside at the stairs. The stunned woman stumbled to the floor, her hands still clutching those of her two toddlers.

"Asshole," she whimpered, but recoiled as soon as she saw the murderous look in Joe's dilated pupils. Alarmed, she pulled her children close to her bosom, shielding them with her body as Joe sprinted past them up the stairs.

"Those Columbine eyes," she told a guard later, "that's what a mass shooter looks like."

CHAPTER 23
THE AFTERMATH

F or a moment, time stood still in the Baroque gallery, the empty space against the wall a black hole between the past and the future. It was imperceptible to the occupants of the gallery who merely felt a subtle electrical spark tickling up their arms like a daddy longlegs spider, oblivious that, in Greek mythology, the aftermath of a dramatic event often bore consequences significantly more unpleasant than the actual event.

The Trojan War was a prime example, where every participant lost everything that they held dear. Achilles, the greatest Greek warrior, succumbed to an arrow in his vulnerable heel, where his mother had held him as a baby to dip him into the river Styx for immortality. The Trojans were slaughtered, and their beloved city was sacked to ruins. Odysseus, the conqueror of Troy, suffered a ten-year-long, arduous journey back to his kingdom and family in Ithaca after Poseidon had cursed him. Even Helen of Troy, whose beauty had launched those thousand ships that triggered the infamous war, died by revenge-hanging years later.

Yes, those fickle Fates who spun their web and unspooled thread from the spindle of life, wrung their hands with glee, and put their heads together to scheme and interfere. To cast a spanner into the spokes of the Wheel of Fortune ... and make it come to a grinding halt.

So it was, too, on the day of the heist of the Olympians, in the aftermath of their ostensible triumph.

THE DOCENT BAG

No sooner had the dying throngs of Orff's symphony faded away than the brouhaha spilled in from next door: strained voices in pinched octaves, unsettling sighs, and cries of anguish. Lorelei said a silent prayer, hoping everything had proceeded as planned next door.

"Everyone, please get up slowly and follow me," she instructed her student group. There was urgency in her voice and the children heeded it. Clinging to her scarf as if it were a life raft, they shuffled into the Baroque gallery next door.

The sudden absence of thunderous music had left a hollow echo in its wake and a persistent ringing in their ears. Lorelei noticed the glaring gap against the wall immediately upon entering, but a quick scan around the room confirmed that no one else had seen it yet. It was *her* responsibility to delay them further.

Strapped to the gurney, Angel looked like death defrosted; Lorelei made the sign of the cross. Her friend could use a dose of divine intervention, even if she did not believe in it. One of the first responders was fitting a plastic cannula into her nose while the other released a yellow lever to unlock the gurney's wheels. Any minute now, Angel would ask for her docent bag—using the EpiPen inside it as a ploy—and Lorelei, as her proxy, would make sure the bag went with her in the ambulance. To be spirited away under the guise of life or death.

That was the plan.

The docent bag was leaning against the wall in the predetermined blind spot, near the doorway where she stood. While the students were preoccupied with the gurgling noises coming from the lady with the grotesque, puffer-fish face, she took the opportunity and deliberately stumbled into the stack of photocopies Angel had left on the floor, causing them to scatter through the gallery. She was the sweeper, the one who swooped in after the fact to ensure all went as planned, without a hitch. And sweeping is what she did with that sneaky shoe, distributing a backup load of distraction across the gallery floor. Sheets of Medusa's face fluttered through the air like autumn leaves caught in a sudden squall.

"Oops," she exclaimed, "my bad."

The small Baroque gallery was chock-a-block with rubbernecking visitors and panicked school students who now had to dodge slippery sheets of paper. It was Chaos, with a capital "C." The security guard on duty had a look of panic on his face as he directed visitors toward the doorways.

"Out, everyone! *Raus!*" he croaked.

He reminded Lorelei of airport runway agents guiding planes into landing bays with their orange ping-pong-like paddles.

"Excuse me, ma'am," she alerted her school group's chaperone, "you should probably take the kids outside, right now." The teacher nodded with flared eyes and began rounding up the group. Lorelei turned and saw that the paramedics were about to roll Angel out of the gallery.

"Hey," she called to them, over the heads of a small crowd of rubberneckers, "don't forget to take her—"

But before she could finish the sentence, a high-pitched squeal—akin to a submarine's dive alarm—drowned out her voice. She clapped her hands over her ears; it was so loud that she thought someone must have noticed the missing painting and triggered the museum alarm. But she realized quickly that the sound was not emanating from the speakers overhead; it was coming from her bag. Someone had activated the device-pinging alert on one of the two mobile phones at the bottom of her bag.

"What the heck?"

She drew out Shivvy's phone first, assuming it was another desperate attempt by Joe to reach his wife. But the alarm was pinging from her *own* phone, which could only mean one thing: something was wrong. A notification from Benjamin on her home screen hit her like a sledgehammer:

URGENT. Call me!

Holy shit. Grace.

All the blood drained from her face and everything else faded into a blur. The Fates were playing dirty, producing their trump card. The *only* thing that could derail Lorelei McAllister from her crucial task: her daughter, Grace. Hyperventilating, she turned her back to Angel on the gurney and dialed Benjamin's number. He answered on the first ring.

"Lorelei, I've been calling and calling. Why didn't you answer your phone?"

His accusatory tone hurt her feelings, but she shoved it aside. There was a hint of panic in his voice, and that was far more concerning.

"What happened, Ben? Is it Grace?"

He mumbled something indecipherable; she had to step out into the hallway where a lull had followed Poseidon's storm. Her heart was trying to burst through her chest, so she pressed one hand against her ribcage to hold it inside.

"Ben, talk to me. Is Grace okay?"

"She's fine, don't worry. It's not one of her bleeds. She fell during recess. The school nurse called me about twenty minutes ago. They tried calling you first, but it went to voicemail," Benjamin said. "I'm in the car; they took her to Providence."

"Oh no. How bad is it?"

"Not sure. A bracing fracture of the wrist, the school nurse suspects. She said it is very swollen. Grace was asking for you."

Lorelei cast her eyes heavenward. A broken arm was not life-threatening, thank God. Grace would be okay ... this time.

"So sorry I didn't respond, babe. I was teaching in the galleries ... with loud music. I'll meet you there as soon as I can, I promise." When she said "promise," she remembered her Olympian task, her promise to Angel. "There is a—um, a situation unfolding here right now. I'll explain later. Got to run."

She disconnected the call without saying goodbye and was about to step back into the Baroque gallery to make sure the paramedics had taken Angel's bag when she heard the gurney wheels clattering noisily behind her, traveling down the hallway toward the elevators. Farther and farther away with each beat of her heart. She whipped her head around.

"Wait!" she called out to the paramedics at the far end of the long hallway. "Did you guys take her bag?" They either did not hear her ... or were ignoring her. *Crap.* She was going to have to run after them. "Stop!" she shouted, bolting forward as if a starter's pistol had fired overhead. But her mad dash came to an abrupt halt right outside the gallery doorway when she crashed into the chest of a large man dressed in a white shirt and black jacket.

Luke? she thought at first with a jolt. *What is he still doing here, at the scene of the crime? He should be long gone by now.*

But it was not Luke.

"Oh, it's you. Hi, Joe," she said with superficial cheer to hide her shock. Over his shoulder, down the hallway, she could no longer see the gurney. *Shit.*

Charming and cool, Demeter coached, *charming and cool.*

Ignoring her, Joe craned his neck to scan the interior of the gallery behind her. She noticed he was tracking two dots on his phone—one blue and one red—overlapped like a Venn diagram on a map, blinking ... pulsating.

"Where is she?" he growled with flared nostrils.

"Where's w-who?" Lorelei asked, though she knew very well. Joe's googly eyes made the hair rise on the back of her neck.

"My wife, who else?"

"Oh, you just missed her," she lied. "She left about fifteen minutes ago before all hell broke loose in here." His brow furrowed, and she noticed beads of sweat along his hairline. "Could you—?" She fumbled through her bag and brought out Shivonne's phone, easily identified in its Degas hard case: a bronze figurine of an adolescent ballerina, posed in fourth position, her arms clutched behind her tutu, a silk hair ribbon dangling down her back. "Could you please give this back to her when you see her?"

Joe's eyes shifted from the surroundings to the phone in Lorelei's hand—the way an eagle's eyes locked onto a rabbit it was tracking from the sky. With a bewildered look, he yanked it from her hand and held it up next to his own. The two flashing dots were now copulating, one on top of the other.

"Why the fuck do *you* have Shiv's phone?" he growled, his eyes drilling into hers.

If looks could kill ...

"Um," she shifted on her feet. *Stay calm,* Demeter reminded her. "I borrowed it from her this morning for my tour. She has a classical music playlist with the perfect track to accompany Turner's seascape. It's called *O For—*"

"Don't ... you ... ever ... shut ... up!?" Joe screamed in her face, causing her to recoil as if slapped. Around them, heads swiveled in their direction.

245

Good. Make a scene, Joe. Make them look.

Lorelei wiped his spittle from her cheek and watched him stagger back into the hallway to stare over the staircase balustrade. She was ashamed to admit later that week, while in the confessional booth at church, that she had experienced a brief impulse right then to give Joe O'Roydon a little shove—to *help* him down the stairs.

"Bless me, Father, for I have sinned. I was tempted to kill someone ..."

She wondered how many penances it would take to earn absolution for *that* level of sin.

"Where *is* she?" Joe hissed, his voice lowered for the benefit of the by-standers. When he leaned in, she got an up-close view of his pitch-black pupils. They looked wrong, like dead, taxidermized animal eyes. It gave her the briefest glimpse into what Shivonne had to deal with in the privacy of their home, alone, with no bystanders to deter her volatile husband.

"I t-t-told you," her tongue belied her forced calm, "she left about fifteen, twenty minutes ago. She was supposed to meet Angel here at 11:30 a.m., but there was a medical emergency. Did you not see the paramedics wheeling Angel away, just now?" She pointed through the windows where they could both see the Day-Glo yellow vests rushing a gurney across the courtyard outside. "If you'll excuse me, I've got to go after them to check on my friend," she said, and without waiting for his reply, scurried down the double-wide staircase.

Near the bottom, she glanced back to see if Joe was still standing there, and tripped over her long scarf, smacking both knees on the stone floor. Ignoring the shooting pain, she sprung back up and half-ran, half-limped outside to catch up with the gurney.

Go Gazelle, go!

Bolstered by the adrenaline rush—the chaos, Benjamin's call, Joe's fury—Lorelei sprinted across the courtyard. She caught up with the paramedics just as they were wheeling Angel into the elevator that descended into the underground parking lot. It was the same elevator car that once trapped the group of friends inside, where it had all started that memorable, miserable day. Their deep-rooted friendship. Her panic attacks. The elevator was closing its heavy jaws as she ran up to it, her knees throbbing.

"Wait, please!" she begged, shoving her hand into the gap between the doors; one of the paramedics looked out at her with an annoyed expression.

"Ma'am, we have an emergency here. Please release the doors."

But she persisted, puffing her cheeks to resist the pressure from the doors. There was no longer any sign of the serene Demeter; her whimsical flower crown had detached, and a string of plastic daisies was dangling down one cheek. Her once-virginal white dress was bloodstained at the knees, like religious stigmata. A hint of rusty coin lingered in her mouth; she must have bitten her tongue during her tumble.

"Yes-I-know-so-sorry-I'm-her-friend," she sputtered, out of breath. "You need to know that she's allergic to peanuts. I don't know if that's what this is …" she gestured to Angel, "but she's highly allergic. Her EpiPen is in her bag." Lorelei scanned the gurney for the docent bag. Perhaps it was underneath it, on a rack, she hoped. "You took her bag, right? It was in the gallery by the door. It *must* go with her."

Angel had instructed the Olympians not to touch the bag after Luke made the drop. It had to be she herself or the paramedics, according to Athena's plan. But what was that old Yiddish adage? When Man plans, God laughs.

Well, God was having a good old, knee-slapping chuckle right then.

The paramedic scoffed. "Ma'am, we didn't have time to search for a purse. We have her identity right here." He pointed to the key card around Angel's neck. "And we have already administered the first dose of epinephrine for anaphylaxis. We got this."

Oh, shit.

"You d-d-don't have her bag? Her EpiPen, her wallet?"

Her stolen Rembrandt?

"We are taking her to Cedars. On Beverly. You can meet her there or come with us now." The paramedic beckoned her inside; Lorelei stared into the metallic interior of the cabin and shook her head.

Nope, no way.

She has avoided elevators—*all* tight spaces, for that matter—since those horrific hours trapped in a steel box, years earlier. Her heart was pounding so hard she thought it would break its restraints and gallop away.

"Ma'am," the paramedic barked, no longer holding back his acute annoyance, "your friend's well-being is literally and figuratively in your hands right now." He gestured with a lift of one eyebrow at her hands bracing against the elevator doors.

"Oh, sorry. Yes, okay then ..."

Dejected, she pulled her hands free to release the elevator and send it down to the parking lot, where the ambulance was waiting with flashing lights. When the doors closed and the elevator started dropping, Lorelei's heart sank with it—into the depths of despair.

The bag!

They were doomed. And it was her fault; the sweeper had failed. The stolen painting was supposed to be on that ambulance with Angel, whisked past security before the alarm sounded and before access to a clean getaway was barred. She recalled Angel's words that day on the grassy knoll outside the galleries, "No one else touches that bag, got it? If it fails, I promise to take the blame—me, alone."

It took Lorelei five seconds of robust hesitation before she decided to defy that directive like the feisty little kick-ass mouse she was. If the bag stayed behind, she knew, their goose would be cooked. And there was no way in hell she would let Angel take the fall if there was something—anything—she could do about it.

"O Fortuna, you traitor, what have you done?" she lamented while sprinting like a gazelle back to the scene of the crime, racing against the impending alarm.

At the top of the staircase outside the Baroque gallery, Joe pushed back from the balustrade and smirked. He had watched the crazy dingbat bolt down the stairs and splat, ass-over-tit, onto the stone floor. Shiv's friends were intolerable to him, especially this Lorelei character with her boho, coochie-coo witchery and shit. He did not trust her—they burned bitches like her during the good ol' Salem trials of the 1600s.

He peered into the gallery one last time to double-check that his wife was not hiding there with her secret lover. All he saw were visitors slip-sliding on sheets of paper and a security guard doing his darndest to clear them out. Shivonne's fiery witch's hair was glaring in its absence.

"*You were duped, Joe,*" the hornets sniggered.

He growled and swung back into the hallway, slamming his shoulder into another security guard on his way in. The young guard whipped his head around and glared at Joe. "Watch it, buddy," he snapped. But Joe was already lumbering down the staircase, double fisting his and his wife's phones. He would deal with the bitch at home. The murder hornets egged him on to the nerve-wracking accompaniment of Rimsky-Korsakov's frantic *Flight of the Bumblebee*—a distorted, garbage-disposal version.

THE ROOKIE'S ALARM

Mario, the security guard, was experiencing a particularly bland day at work. He had only been a security guard at the museum for three weeks and was still called "Rookie" by the more experienced crew. As a result, his scheduler always assigned him the odd shifts in the quieter, more remote parts of the museum where a guard could stand for hours on tingling legs, staring at some unpronounceable Scandinavian artist's boring, grey-toned shit. On an average day, his job involved nothing more thrilling than reminding the odd student or grumpy older broad to stay behind the appropriate viewing distance line on the floor. He had concluded that blue-haired pensioners were worse than kindergartners. Both age groups tended to lean in too close, but at least the little snot noses respected authority. Entitled old Boomers didn't give a damn.

Not surprisingly, when he strolled past the Baroque gallery at 11:35 a.m., already late for his shift in the "boring" gallery, Mario perked up at the first sound of discord—the promise of a little excitement. As soon as he stepped through the doorway, a tall man in jeans, a white shirt, and a black jacket rammed him hard in the shoulder.

"Watch it, buddy," Mario grunted, suppressing a more authentic—if unprofessional— *"hijo de puta"* under his breath. Son of a bitch.

The man flashed him a hairy eyeball and bolted down the stairs. Mario stared after him, rubbing his shoulder where his collarbone burned like a ghost pepper. Still rubbing, he turned to face the chaos inside the gallery. It looked as if a tornado had twisted its serpentine cone through the small space, leaving a pile of debris—sheets of paper featuring a snake-haired monster, a trampled cardboard placard shedding tinfoil dandruff, an empty glass ampoule—in its wake. A few stragglers were piling out through both doorways and soon the gallery was empty except for the other security guard. The older guard looked flabbergasted, surveilling the mess from the center of the gallery with both hands clutching at his silver-gray hair.

Mario approached just as the guard lowered himself to the floor with a groan to scoop up armfuls of the papers scattered around his shoes, mumbling to himself in German. But Mario was not listening because, as soon as Walter bent down, Mario's eyes had nowhere else to focus but on the wall directly behind where the older guard's head had been seconds before. He stopped dead in his tracks.

"Dios mío."

There was an unmistakable, empty rectangular space between two gold-framed baroque paintings, where earlier there had hung a priceless masterpiece. Mario blinked, shook his head, and blinked again, hoping it was just a mirage. He had attended his niece's *quinceañera* rehearsal the night before and was still suffering the brain fog that followed the requisite tequila shots. He pinched his eyes shut, willing them to show him an alternate view. But the space on the wall remained empty, the blatant void mocking him. He groaned.

It's supposed to be right there.

Mario, as was apparent to him right then, was one of those unfortunate souls who froze in an emergency. His *mami* had been right about him not being cut out to be a firefighter or police officer. That painful realization dawned on him as his mind took another spin around its loop of incredulity.

It's not there, Mario.

Sí, but they could have taken it for cleaning. Or whatever they do with the paintings in the museum's basement workshops.

Maybe ... but then they would have hung a plaque in its place, no? Alerted the guards?

Sí.

It's gone, isn't it Mario?

Dios mío, sí.

His bladder let go a little—just a trickle, but enough to make him look down to see if a wet patch had formed at his crotch.

Do something, he thought, *say something.*

He lunged into action, scrambling for the panel that held the operational controls by the doorway. "Alarm," he whimpered in a helium-balloon voice while fumbling with the tubular key that opened the metal panel. "Thief!"

Puzzled, Walter turned around to face the glaring void on the wall. His hands went limp, releasing a pile of scary Gorgon faces to the floor. "*Scheisse!*" he exclaimed. And then, for the second time that day, "*O, mein Gott.*"

By then, Mario had managed to unlock the control panel, scraping an angry red welt across his cheek as it flung open. He grappled with the red internal phone and dialed the extension of the Security Head Office. It was only three digits, but it took him a few tries before he could get the sequence right.

"Thief!" he shouted into the mouthpiece. "Activate the alarm ... Yes, you heard right the first time. Theft in the uh, the Baroque gallery, room number—*mierda*, I don't know ... There is a missing painting ... Yes ... Uh-huh ... What? No, I don't know which one is missing, *estúpido*, I'm no art specialist!" He slammed the receiver down and five seconds later an ear-splitting alarm pierced the hallowed hallways of the museum.

Whoop-whoop-whoop! ... Whoop-whoop-whoop! ... Whoop-whoop-whoop!

Walter stood frozen in the middle of the gallery, like one of Medusa's petrified victims, staring at the violated wall. Mario, in contrast, started prancing like Mick Jagger at the doorway, high on the fumes of excitement. His initial panic was a distant memory; he was overjoyed to be the guard who had called foul. It would look good on his record.

"*Vámos, amigo.* Let's go." He tapped Walter on the shoulder to snap him out of his daze, and they stood back-to-back—each one facing a doorway—to secure the scene.

From the built-in speakers in the ceiling, an automated female voice spoke calmly over the whooping alarm: "Attention all visitors, please evacuate the museum and proceed calmly to the nearest exit. This is not a drill. I repeat, this is not a drill. Please proceed calmly to the nearest exit."

Elsewhere in the museum, panic-laden instructions rang out over bull horns and via walkie-talkies: "Attention all staff: There has been a breach in the Baroque gallery. Prepare for search protocol."

Downstairs, by each exit door, security officers were facilitating the thorough searching of visitors and employees alike, inspecting bags and backpacks, and patting down bulky coats and jackets for any sign of a concealed painting. There was confusion among the staff: what were they supposed to look for? Nobody knew. Some visitors panicked, whispering "bomb" or "fire" to anyone within earshot, and a low hum—hovering somewhere between discontent and panic—resonated through the entrance hall. Impatient and scared, people started shoving each other in the bottleneck areas.

"Attention visitors, this is a security matter and there is no immediate danger. Please exit the museum calmly and proceed to the parking lot after you have been cleared," someone announced over a megaphone. "Security will conduct a quick vehicle search upon exiting. Please see the attendants in the red vests outside for ride-share or special-needs assistance. Thank you for your patience." A communal groan rose from the congregated masses.

Minutes earlier, in the underground employee parking lot, the ambulance with Angel secured in the back had evaded the impending shutdown with minutes to spare before the alarm rang out and the parking booms were lowered to spar an easy exit route for all vehicles. Now, it was speeding away, its high-pitched siren harmonizing discordantly with the deeper-toned bleating of the museum alarm. Had Angel's docent bag been with her on that rig, its acquired treasure would have been whisked away safely, without detection or deterrence. It was a brilliant plan.

But those cunning Fates were no pushovers.

Inside the eye of the storm, Mario and Walter were still standing back-to-back—like cowboys preparing for a shoot-out—when Mario stiffened suddenly, his gaze fixated on the spot next to the doorway leading into the Romance gallery, where a lone docent bag leaned against the wall.

"*Qué—?*"

He broke away from his anchoring position and strode toward it with purpose. With suspicion. Somewhere in the ether of Mount Olympus, the mischievous Fates were wringing their hands in eager anticipation. *O Fortuna!* they cried when Mario narrowed his eyes and reached out to open the flaps of the bag.

"Wait," he heard and spun around to see Walter approaching. "I know this bag." Walter pointed to a miniature painting of a single flower in a crystal vase pinned to its exterior. "It belongs to my friend, the docent who collapsed. I'll take it for her."

The Fates must have held their immortal breaths while Mario hesitated, weighing his options, his hand hovering over the bag. *I saw it first,* he thought, wanting to lay claim to the find, but then he considered the consequences of giving up his foothold in the center of the brazen daytime heist. It was just a stupid docent's bag. Sometimes, after a school tour, a spacey educator or two would leave behind their bag or art supplies in the galleries, and then a lackey like himself would have to run it down to the security desk to be reclaimed. There was no way Mario wanted to leave the excitement of the violated gallery for any reason. It was *his* scene, and he would stand his ground. Security Guard of the Month, guaranteed. His Mami would be so proud.

"*You* take it," he ordered Walter, his tone dismissive. "I'll stay here until the authorities arrive." He returned to his coveted spot in the middle of the floor, hands on his hips, legs spread wide in a "don't-mess-with-the-sheriff" grandstand. He wished more than anything he had a gun holster strapped to his inner thigh.

Walter lifted the bag by its leather straps and carried it out of the gallery, pressed to his chest as if guarding precious cargo. In the hallway, he hesitated, not sure what to do next. He was an old-school gentleman, raised to respect the privacy and the property of others—a hard-won trait shaped by the indelible, intergenerational trauma suffered by his Jewish forebears. So, he stood pondering for a moment, not knowing which way to turn. The repetitive *whoop-whoop-whoop!* of the alarm was wreaking havoc with his blood pressure, and the bag weighed unusually heavy in his arms.

If only he knew, the Fates chortled.

From its wooden coffin inside the docent bag, against the chest of an old German security guard, Rembrandt's laughing man flashed his forty-million-dollar grin in the dark.

By the time Lorelei reached the gallery, she was wheezing, her forty-eight-year-old joints rebelling. She leaned her hand against the door frame just as the first alarm obliterated the silence, piercing the soap bubble under Fortuna, and shredding the last remnants of Hope.

Oh, no ...

She watched anxiously as Walter picked up the straps of Angel's bag and lifted it from the floor.

God help us.

It was too late; Demeter, the protectress, had failed.

Moments later, when Walter stepped out of the violated gallery with the treasure hugged to his chest, the hallway was empty save for the ghostly breath of disappointment lingering on the doorjamb.

THE FLEET-FOOTED GOD

I am Hermes, the fleet-footed god, Luke thought with disbelief while making his way through the museum's lower levels, moments after officially joining the ranks of world-class art thieves.

It would be a matter of minutes before the museum erupted with deafening sirens, so he sped up his walk—as fast as the two-inch cork inserts would allow—one hand still tucked inside his jacket for show. Cameras were present in the hallways, so he walked confidently with his head down, cheeks flushed under the mask. It surprised him how calm he felt despite what he had just pulled off, despite his frightening brush with the ghost from his past. He guessed it was because he had no incriminating evidence on his person—no multi-million-dollar masterpiece that had graced the wall of the gallery moments earlier.

Outdoors, he took a deep breath of fresh air through his mask. The courtyard was buzzing with activity and conversation. All was calm.

Not for very much longer, he thought with a nervous giggle, channeling Magenta from *The Rocky Horror Picture Show.* Even while committing a crime, Luke Lorenson experienced the world through Broadway lyrics.

A crew of siblings in matching T-shirts stood in line by the snack cart tucked under the shade of the crepe myrtles. He watched the youngest, a boy of about five years old, reach up impatiently for a soft serve cone from his mother's hand.

Eat up, buddy boy, he beamed telepathically to the unsuspecting youngster. Soon, shrill alarms would shatter the Rockwellian moment, and splatter the sweet, vanilla stickiness all over the little one's T-shirt.

Scanning his surroundings, he spotted the ideal opportunity to blend into obscurity at the Pallas fountain, where a public tour group of more than a dozen adults had gathered. Their docent was pointing at the marble statue, regaling the group with the heart-wrenching tale of a childhood friendship cut short by an overzealous father.

Stealthy as a cat burglar, Luke snuck into their midst and slipped out of his black jacket while pretending to tie a shoelace. When he stood erect again, the jacket was inside out again, its colorful, sequined side draped over his arm. The black face mask and latex gloves he had worn during the heist were stashed in his back pocket. Anyone who might have seen the man in the black jacket rush across the courtyard would have lost sight of him in the crowd, as if he had disappeared into thin air. The god of thieves, Hermes, ducked under his cloak of invisibility.

He lingered with the group a little longer, feigning interest in the lecture, but when they moved on in the direction of the now-deflowered galleries, he broke away and walked with an exaggerated swagger toward the restroom. The same one he had entered earlier as Luke Lorenson ... and exited a fleet-footed, light-fingered god.

However, before re-entering the museum from the courtyard, he pulled a different black face mask—*not* the one he had worn during the heist—from a Ziploc bag in his jacket pocket, pinching it by its elastic straps to avoid touching the three-ply fabric. He dropped it into a large trash receptacle by the door. Back indoors, the restroom guarded by the headless sculpture of Hercules was no longer empty. A trio of teenage boys were jostling each other at the urinal.

"Don't, you'll piss on me," one said, followed by gales of laughter. "Seriously, bruh."

Their tomfoolery triggered painful high school memories for Luke—his face pressed against a toilet rim in a locker room, the countless jokes about bending over for the bar of soap, and the non-stop taunts:

"Tick-tock, tick-tock, the pastor's son sucks c—"

"Ahem," Luke said to clear away the intrusive thoughts and hurry the boys along. These were not the ghosts of his youth, he reminded himself; they were harmless, half-formed mortals. No match for a god of thieves who had just pulled off a Herculean feat.

Nobody messes with Luke Lorenson anymore. *Never again.*

Like typical self-absorbed teenagers, the three stooges at the urinal did not even look up when Luke walked in or cleared his throat. He discreetly retrieved his docent bag from behind the large trash can in the corner while their backs were turned and ducked into the largest stall again. Soon, he heard them shuffle out, dragging their feet as teen boys did. The door sucked shut on its seal and it was quiet again, but for the deafening heartbeat in his ear.

Tick-tock, Luke. Time flies.

He jumped into action and slipped his arms back into his sparkly jacket. His body eased into the seams, and he felt safe again. Joseph in his technicolor dreamcoat. He fished the black mask he had worn for the heist from his back pocket, tore it into thin strips, and dumped the shreds into the toilet bowl. When he depressed the handle, the toilet gurgled once ... and went on strike. The water was rising fast, and strips of mask churned in the blue-tinted water like a shiver of sharks in a feeding frenzy.

"Shitballs," Luke swore, stepping back to avoid the potential deluge threatening to besmirch his sneakers. The toilet sputtered, burped, and filled right to the rim, the sharks circling ominously. Worried, he jiggled the handle and then depressed it again. This time, the toilet surrendered and swallowed the load with a loud *burp*.

He resumed his reverse-change activity, first pulling the cork inserts out of his shoes, and then the Hermes wings from under his shirt. They were not as perky as before, but he smoothed them between his palms and Velcroed them back to the sides of his sneakers. In front of the washbasins, he removed the contact lenses and flushed them down the drain. He had seen scary things through those lenses—the ghost of his father—as if they were 3D goggles that allowed the wearer to see a different reality. An upside-down of sorts where monsters lurked. He had no intention of looking through them again.

With wet fingers and a bit of spit, he sculpted his hair back up into its elevated "Luke scoop," as Lorelei called it, and slipped his thick-rimmed eyeglasses back on. As soon as he executed the habitual slide of the frame higher along the crest of his nose, the opportunistic Fates played a dirty trick on him and let loose the first wails of the alarm.

Whoop-whoop-whoop! ... Whoop-whoop-whoop! ... Whoop-whoop-whoop!

Luke almost soiled his pants. "Holy shitballs!"

He scrambled to gather his belongings and burst from the restroom. Two security officers were approaching at a trot from the far end of the corridor. To grab him and cuff him, he was sure. Resigned to the inevitable, he stiffened and waited for them to close in while contemplating a witty comeback he would use when they did. "Call me Lupin," he thought he might say, "Arsène Lupin, gentleman thief. At your service." Garnished with one of his elaborate Louis XIV bows, of course.

Play it cool, Hermes. It was Athena's voice this time.

With his bag slung over his shoulder, he started walking toward the guards.

"Luke, over here!" he heard, and turned to see Jerome approaching from a bank of windows to his right, behind Hercules' back, both hands clamped over his ears to muffle the deafening alarm.

"Hey," Luke said back over the din, "how long have you been standing there?" He hoped Jerome had not witnessed him dashing into the restroom minutes earlier.

"Got here seconds before the alarm sounded. I was worried about you," Jerome shouted. "Are you okay?"

The two burly guards were upon them. "Clear out, everyone. Clear out," they barked before continuing down the hallway to smoke out lagging visitors. Jerome grabbed Luke's hand and pulled him toward the exit door. For a moment amid the chaos, time stood still, and Luke Lorenson swore he could hear bells and whistles above the squall of the alarms.

"Attention all visitors, please evacuate the museum and proceed to the nearest exit," an automated female voice broadcasted an urgent message from the ceiling.

"What happened?" Luke asked close to Jerome's ear, his cheeks still flushed from the bells and whistles.

"No clue, I hope it's not an active shooter," Jerome shouted over the din.

"Or a brush fire," Luke said, remembering the time he was pressed up against his fellow Olympians, sealed like sardines in an aluminum can.

They caught up with a throng of evacuees pushing toward the main hall entrance, where guards searched their bags and frisked their torsos. When it was his turn, Luke stood with his legs spread, and arms raised for the pat down, looking out through the exit doors, and trying hard not to project the guilt he carried inside. He could feel his face redden.

Easy, Hermes. Easy, boy. Deep breaths.

Once outside, he thirstily sucked in deep breaths of cool freedom. When he closed his eyes, the image of his favorite sculpture flooded in—the young boy asleep at the feet of his goddess mother, a dagger in his hand. But now he imagined the young boy wide awake and playing outside in the garden, catching tadpoles in the lily pond. Without conflict or threat.

Safe.

"I fear no longer," he said out loud, hoping it was the truth.

"Say what?" Jerome asked.

"Hmm? Oh, ... nothing important," Luke answered, even though it was the most important thing in his life thus far. He felt stronger, no longer traumatized by memories of neglect or silly, misguided refrains. No longer craving the protective canopy of a mother's cape. The smile on his face persisted while they joined the throng of visitors marching to the parking lot. Above the shrieking museum alarm behind them, he could hear the coyote-like wailing of an ambulance siren, its pitch decreasing in a Doppler dip as it sped away. He crossed his fingers and hoped Angel was in that ambulance.

Angel and the Rembrandt portrait with his father's face.

The freeway rushed below them, its thick stream of traffic winding up and over the hill like the river Styx. The bleating of alarms and sirens grew louder and louder in Luke's head. He turned to Jerome, still holding his hand.

"Apollo," he said, and then his fleet-footed legs wobbled under the weight of the new him, and he sank to the stone path that led away from the museum, perched like a jewel atop the apex of Mount Olympus.

CHAPTER 24
THE INTERROGATION

T he car engine was idling the low growl of a cornered feral cat. Parked in the driveway outside her beautiful home, Shivonne was trying to summon the courage to step out and walk to her front door. She had left the museum minutes before the pandemonium and driven aimlessly through neighboring streets before coming in for a pit stop at a strip mall near Riley's school. There, she waited on tenterhooks for more than an hour, sipping her second or third coffee and chewing her nails down to the quick. Without her phone, she was clueless about the aftermath of their heist. More worrisome, however, was that Joe had been unable to reach her all day.

That was *far* more frightening.

After picking up Riley from preschool and dropping her off at violin practice, she made her way home and sat outside, clinging to the safety of her car. Desperate to pee but petrified of what awaited her inside. She closed her eyes and recalled the sweet moments on the bench with Cristian.

That kiss…

The memory of his soft lips on hers boosted her courage, so she stepped out of the car and walked the plank into the house. The sliver of bravado dissipated the second her goddess sandals crunched over the splintered remnants of her once crescent-shaped console table in the entryway. The foreboding *crunch-crunch* of antique wood under her shoes announced her arrival to the dormant house; she could sense evil lying in ambush, in the shadows ahead.

Did you know I can sometimes predict the future?

The kitchen was dark—he must have lowered the Roman blinds—so she reached for the light switch by the doorway. But before she could flip it, the ceiling lights flickered on overhead, shining like searchlights on her pale face. Joe was standing at the far end of the kitchen island, his expression chilling her to the bone. It spoke of unfathomable depths, of lava bubbling underneath the earth's crust, of a rattlesnake coiled underneath a rock. There was no way around it; she had to lift that rock.

"Hi, you startled me," she said, placing her bag on the counter. All forty-three microscopic muscles in his face contorted simultaneously, as if maggots were squirming underneath the epidermis. The sight of it dried the spit in her mouth. "Y-you won't believe what happened at the museum today."

But her husband was in no mood for small talk.

"Who is 'A'?" he asked with a forced-calm, deadpan face, forming air quotes around the scarlet letter.

"'A'? What do you mean?" *Shite, here we go* ... Her hand fumbled with the padlock at her throat. It was cold and slick between her fingers.

He advanced toward her, his hip in line with the marble countertop, his hand a hairy tarantula crawling across its mottled surface. Slowly. Menacingly. She circled away from him to the opposite side of the large island. A twisted game of cat and mouse.

"Seriously, Joe, I don't know who you're—"

The tarantula spasmed and slammed down on the cold slab—the same type of marble slab where *other* mothers in *other* homes popped cans of pressurized pastry dough and rolled sweet cinnamon rolls with their giddy, carefree daughters.

"Don't fuck with me, Shiv! Who ... is ... 'A'?"

He shoved the incriminating sliver of blue notepaper so hard against her nose that a dribble of something—snot or blood—trickled down the groove above her lip. Triggered by the pain, her mind's red velvet curtains cranked apart to reveal a bare stage, dimly lit by a single bare light bulb swinging across it on a long chord. The fragile ballerina was warming up: *rond de jambe* to the left, *rond de jambe* to the right, brushing tentative half-circles with her feet skimming the floor.

Cross-eyed, Shivonne pretended to read the strip of paper in his hand, though she knew full well what it said. And what it meant.

"'A' for Anakin Skywalker, perhaps," Joe drilled, "or Captain America? No, don't tell me. I know ... 'A' for Anonymous, right?" Each word out of his mouth was more ominous than the previous. His eyes were veiled behind a filmy glaze. He was finally coming undone, she was certain. A psychotic break.

"Joey, plea—"

She realized her mistake immediately after his little-boy name left her mouth, but it was too late. He yanked her head back by the hair so that she had no choice but to stare straight up into the glare of the light fixtures over the island—three stainless steel cages with frosted globes suspended within like frozen tears. The pain propelled her back onto that imaginary stage—not gracefully, but with a floundering leap as if shoved from behind. An arrow released from a bow. And she danced there in the spotlight, twirling, twirling like the tiny, plastic ballerina inside a child's music box after someone had cranked it with the windup key. And cranking was Joe's specialty. He cranked it so hard, the imaginary music ringing in her ears became distorted: the eerie, creepy-doll soundtrack of a carnival haunted house.

Or a tomato-red egg timer, on repeat.

Fouetté ... fouetté ... fouetté.

An endless series of sharp, whipping ballet turns on tippy toes till blisters broke open on her feet and Charley horses agonized her calves. Spinning and whirling; her anchoring leg bending and twisting to create torque at each turn, the other whipping to the side to gather momentum. Spinning faster and faster by drawing in her arms, her slippers stirring up puffs of dust that twirled like Tasmanian Devils around her, faster and faster ... She was the black swan now, Odile the sorceress, her eyes fixed on a single focal point to maintain her center of gravity.

Riley. Whip around. *Riley.* Whip around. *Riley.*

Far away from her sanctuary stage, she heard herself cry out, "Joe, you're hurting me! 'A' is for Angel ... my best friend, Ang—"

"Lying bitch!" Spittle sprayed over her face; it reeked of alcohol. He raised his fist above her.

"Please," she whimpered, maintaining eye contact despite the hammer hovering above, "I can prove it." She pointed toward her docent bag on the counter.

"Look for yourself. Angel borrowed my Rubens folder two days ago. She wanted to return it, y-y-yesterday. She left me a note ... Look in my bag, Joe, look at the—"

He lowered his fist and released her hair, causing her to fold down like a rag doll. He upturned her bag, spilling its contents across the countertop: a box of colored pastels, her wallet, a granola bar, and a single, apple-green folder labeled "PETER PAUL RUBENS" in thick Sharpie. Mumbling incomprehensible nothings to himself, he tore through the folder, flinging loose pages onto the floor—a bio of the Flemish artist, activity notes, and glossy photo prints of two of Peter-Paul Rubens's most evocative paintings: *The Descent from the Cross* and *The Entombment*.

The latter was the sort of painting a warm-blooded human could not tear their eyes away from—religious or not—but Joe was immune to its charms. It fluttered to the floor next to Shivonne, affording her an unobstructed view of Jesus, right after his crucifixion, his body limp and tinged blue with lividity, his face cradled in the hand of his distraught mother, Mary. Shivonne stared into that persecuted face and wept.

"Huh," she heard Joe mumble.

It was hardly a sound, but the quiet, acquiescent muttering suggested that he had found it, paperclipped to the inside of the green folder: a second note on the identical blue paper with its silver-leafed edge. He yanked it out, skimmed it past his nose, and held it up to the light. Written on it, in the same all-caps handwriting as the note he had discovered that morning, it read:

"SHIVVY DARLING,

THANKS SO MUCH FOR SHARING

YOUR RUBENS NOTES!

LUNCH IS ON ME.

XOX"

But this time, the mysterious anonymous "A" had bothered to spell out their name. The note was signed: *"ANGEL."*

His cheeks flushed with defeat, Joe let the note slip from his hand.

Oh no.

Shivonne knew from experience that defeat emasculated her husband. And an emasculated psychopath was akin to a hand grenade with the pin pulled. She flinched, anticipating a blow. When there was none, she dared to look up at him.

"I'm so tired of having to check up on you all the time, Shiv," he said with a distorted Joker smile. "You made me hunt you like a ... like a desperate fool today." He pointed at her where she lay, puddled on the floor. "It's your attitude. That's what it is. Always sneaking around behind my back like a dirty little rat. Why do you do this to me?" He buried his face in his hands, his meaty fingers clawing at his scalp.

For an instant, he resembled the pitiful young boy he must have been once, his dark hair disheveled like that, his eyes glistening with pain. A harmless little boy who would grow up disappointing his WASP-y, republican East-coast family by achieving nothing more than mediocrity in life. The scion who had chosen not to—or, worse, *failed* to—follow in his father's shady footsteps defrauding pensioners from a high rise on Wall Street, who had failed the LSAT three times before abandoning the idea of law school and become a police officer, instead. In liberal La-La land, of all godforsaken places. A ball-buster still, but with much less status: no penthouse apartment in NYC or summer house in the Hamptons, no exclusive golf club membership, no Stepford wife, and—his worst offense by far—no male progeny. Shivonne pitied him in that moment of apparent humility.

"Joe," she soothed, grabbing onto his legs for support while staggering to her knees. But his humility was short-lived; she should have known better. Self-pity never stuck long to the slippery skin of a shapeshifter.

"There's a good wifey," he smirked, the little-boy-blue façade evaporating in the blink of her eye. "Look at you, on your knees, begging to make it up to me."

She froze, her mind racing through a series of frantic dance paces as he unzipped his jeans with one hand and forced her head to his crotch with the other. The ballerina spun on the deserted stage, faster and faster, shedding feathers and clumps of down in a bluster of panic.

"Please, Joe," she begged, "it's been a horrible day. There was a theft at the museum. I had to—" He pulled her face into his groin, muffling her voice.

"There you go again, Shiv, always thinking about yourself. Now, be a good bitch ..."

Gasping for breath, she thought of Angel, breathless on that cold, hard gallery floor. Fighting for her life.

What would Athena do? her alter ego, Artemis, asked with a lilting Irish accent.

And Shivonne knew the answer: the dragon with the thorn in its claw needed to be appeased, or it would rip her head off. When she understood that truth, she allowed her body to go limp when he scooped her up—his rough hands clamping her buttocks—and slapped her down onto the marble slab like a raw steak.

But her soul was not inside her body while he violated it. It was dancing a passionate *pas de deux* on her mind's theatrical stage, no longer under the spell of an evil sorcerer. This time, the hands that lifted her high and made her swoon, belonged to the protector, Cristian.

Sway, sway, lift, and hold ... hold ... hold ...

Vaulted high above the ground on a golden cupola, she aimed her arrow at the heavens. And the Olympians cheered them on and rained flowers down on them from the gilded balcony seats of the gods.

Bravo, they shouted. *Encore!*

On the marble countertop, Shivonne turned her head away from Joe's contorted face ... and smiled.

CHAPTER 25
THE SPECIAL AGENT

N ight reluctantly wrapped her azure cloak around the museum perched above the city expanse, its hollow insides still vibrating with the echoes of shrill sirens and slapping footsteps. The perimeter was sealed off from the public, with police vehicles blocking both access roads and officers guarding the shuttered doors and gates. The buildings were dark, but for a handful of lighted cubes inside; high above them, news helicopters were *thup-thup-thup*-ing, their taillights flickering like fireflies mating in the crisp night air.

FBI Special Agent Colton Jamisson surveyed the horizon from a second-story balcony, the night's static electricity making the hair rise at the back of his neck. From his vantage point, the sun dipped its crown under the horizon over the Pacific Ocean and hemorrhaged in pinkish-red streaks.

This is what chaos looks like when it goes to sleep at night, he thought.

Eight hours earlier, a brazen daylight robbery had taken place in the Baroque gallery, not far from where he stood pondering the darkening sky. This was his first serious art heist case since his transfer to the Los Angeles branch, a few years earlier, right before the Covid pandemic had turned him into a miserable desk jockey, shuffling cold cases around while walking mile after mile on his treadmill desk. Turns out global pandemics were bad for the thieving business.

In his mid-thirties, Colt was champing at the bit like a saddle-bronc horse, rearing up to make a name for himself. He had qualified near the top of his class at Quantico after graduating with a degree in art and archeology. But, because of an old rodeo injury that made him walk with a limp and had benched him during active field training, the Bureau handpicked him to work in the Art Crime department instead. That was fine by him. He had always been interested in cases of plunder, albeit theft of masterpieces from secured safes or looting from sacred archeological sites.

Everybody tended to raise their eyebrows when they met the cowboy from Wyoming with the Art and Archeology degree—an incongruous concept if ever there were one. But he did not mind their surprise; it gave him an edge, and he milked it for what it was worth—at work, and with the wannabe Hollywood starlets he wooed on Tinder.

Since childhood, young Colton had idolized Indiana Jones, dressing like his hero in a weathered leather jacket and carrying his rancher father's bullwhip. He wanted to *be* the witty archeologist, hunting for lost treasure in dusty, old warehouses and digging for clues in exotic excavation sites. But that kind of excitement had evaded him up to that point. He was nothing more than a young steed, far from his Wyoming homestead, hobbled in his stable—a musty apartment in North Hollywood, overlooking the Los Angeles River. Calling it a river, he had decided, was an insult to rivers. A lifetime of cantering the family steeds across Jackson Hole grasslands framed by snow-dusted mountain peaks and intersected by rushing rivers worthy of the title made Colt a de facto expert on what constituted a river.

"No, siree Bob." He bent over the railing and spat down into the dark hillside below. In his heart, he was still a cowboy, albeit one without a horse ... and a river. An art crime special agent without a headlining case. What good was that?

But the Pallas heist excited him; it could be his breakthrough case. He could feel it in his bones, especially the femoral one with the compression lag screw and titanium plate held in place by six bone screws. It spoke to him in fiery overtones while he limped back inside the museum, past the violated gallery sealed off with yellow police tape, where forensics agents in white bunny suits and booties were dusting for fingerprints around the faded rectangle of wallpaper on the wall.

Downstairs, in the belly of the sleeping whale, he knocked twice on the door of the Security Control Room and flashed his FBI badge. The room was crowded with Bureau colleagues, insurance company representatives, Pallas Security's head, and the Chief of the Los Angeles Police Department. A palpable stench of tension and urgency permeated the room. When he entered, everyone rose to greet the man who would captain their efforts.

"Please, everyone, as you were." Colt slipped out of his leather jacket, rolled up his shirt sleeves, and gestured to the bank of computer monitors against the front wall. "Before we watch the security recordings, I'd like for us to get the 4-1-1 on the missing art object." He aimed a digital remote at one of the monitors, summoning the image of Rembrandt's self-portrait, and beckoned forward a tall woman from the back of the room. "I'm told you are the curator of the gallery in question. Ms. van Trummel?"

"*Doctor* van Trummel, Ph.D.," she corrected him with a hint of a Dutch accent. "Yes, I am the curator who oversaw the loan of the Rembrandt. Highly embarrassing that we should lose it on our watch." Her face showed the level of devastation one would expect from a pet sitter who had lost the family's dog while they were vacationing in Aruba. A beloved dog that had *not* been microchipped.

"Tell us about the painting," he said. "Why *this* one in particular?"

The curator wiped a slick of perspiration from her neck. Her spiral curls hung flaccid from the humidity in the room. "It's an early self-portrait by the master ... priceless. It's a *Rembrandt* after all." She delivered the artist's name with an insinuated sarcastic "duh!" aimed at Colt.

He did not flinch. "Yes, one of his earlier *tronies,* a study in character with the artist's typical exaggerated facial expressions done in *chiaroscuro,*" he countered, making good use of the surprise factor of his years of art education. "What do you estimate it's worth?"

"Well," she hesitated, befuddled by the Fed cop's knowledge of art terminology, "I would guess approximately forty million, potentially more ..." She glanced at the insurance guys, who either nodded or made "more-or-less" hand wobbles. "Today's art market is volati—"

"Thank you, Dr. van Trummel. That's all we need from you."

"What we *need*, Agent Jamisson," she implored, "is to find this painting. I'm inclined to stay and give my input—"

"Unnecessary," Colt bristled, "we will reach out if we have additional questions." He waved her toward the door and the curator's face dropped into a pout.

269

She gathered her belongings and slunk out past the collection of crime fighters in the room. At the door, she cast a wistful look back into the think tank, a flush of rejection on her face.

"Good luck, then," she said, dejected. "Let me know if—"

Colt closed the door, eager to get on with it. He had a bull to rope; a prize to win. "Let it roll please, Chief," he instructed the museum's head of security, Feliciano Rodriguez.

Rodriguez nodded to the young officer seated in a wheelchair by the monitors, who started scrolling through the day's recordings using a joystick and trackpad. On the main screen, the interior of the Baroque gallery blinked to life, with public visitors and school groups streaming in and out in two-point-five, fast-forwarded motion. It reminded Colt of countless childhood hours spent watching red harvester ants burrowing through blue tunneling sand against the Perspex viewing panel of his ant farm. In the top right corner of the recording, a digital clock was indicating the passage of time, down to the millisecond.

"Are the galleries always so crowded?" he asked.

"No, sir, not always," the security head replied. "We had a special Greek mythology theme today, and that gallery has one of the museum's most popular objects depicting Medusa." He mimicked vipers writhing in his hair, mirroring the group of students, play-acting it on the screen in front of them. "You know the one? She's a fan favorite." Acutely aware of the amused stares from the occupants of the control room, he dropped his hands.

Colt had not diverted his eyes from the screens while Rodriguez was babbling. "Stop right there," he instructed, then rolled his index and middle fingers backward in a "rewind" motion. The young man behind the monitors obeyed. "Slowly, slowly ... there."

The control room hub fell silent, all eyes locked on the screen. Even the insurance agents against the back wall leaned forward, their fingers hovering over their laptops. The recording rolled in agonizing slow motion, its time code ticking over: "11:28:13, 11:28:14, 11:28:15, 11:28:16 ... "

On the screen, a group of looky-loos crowded around the docent on the floor, and two paramedics in Day-Glo vests were kneeling next to her. The recording

270

had no sound, so the room full of crime solvers was not privy to Orff's stunning *cantata* building to a climax, or the ingenious timing of the heist to *O Fortuna*.

A tall man in a dark face mask and blazer strolled in through the doorway, heading straight for the Rembrandt wall. He glanced back at the unconscious docent, hesitated briefly, then seized the Rembrandt firmly with gloved hands.

"Sonofabitch," Rodriguez muttered, reaching out to brace himself on the back of his junior officer's wheelchair. The brazen burglar briefly grappled with the painting on the screen before managing to lift it away from the wall. Turning back to the doorway, he lifted his jacket flap and tucked the painting under his armpit.

A communal groan rolled through the room.

That, right there, is the reason he chose that painting, Colt thought. It was the only one in the gallery that could fit under a jacket despite its thick frame. He was about to ask the security chief why the painting did not have a trigger alarm when he saw a flicker on the screen just as the thief dropped his jacket flap. A purplish-greenish metallic shimmer, akin to the sheen of petrol on a puddle of water.

"Whoa," he exclaimed, the way a cowboy halted his horse, "did you all see that?" He motioned the "roll it back" signal again and pointed to the suspect's jacket. "There." A gleam of refracted light shimmered for a split second as the man lifted his jacket, and again when he dropped it over his white button-down. "What was that?"

"Specular reflection, sir," a junior FBI agent said from the back of the room.

"Please elaborate," Colt said.

The agent stepped forward wearing the aura of a gold-star West Point Academy graduate, her back stiff, her hair pulled back into a tight, glossy bun.

"It's a mirror-ball halo effect, like the glint of Chroma Flair car paint," she elaborated.

"Uh, in plain English, please?" the police chief asked.

"Something reflective under his jacket, sir."

Colt scanned the ID badge around her neck. "Sharp observation, Agent Solis. Look into it for me, STAT."

"Sir, yes, sir," Agent Solis said, and stepped back again.

The tape rolled on. Sticking close to the wall, the thief, with the painting now obscured under his jacket, circled toward the opposite doorway. In the corner by the doorway, he briefly disappeared out of frame, but it was so brief that it registered as a mere blink of an eye to the viewers of the recording. They simply saw the perp walk through the doorway ... and then he was gone.

"Follow that man," Rodriguez ordered, slapping his employee on the back. "Follow that sticky-fingered sonofabitch."

The digital playback jittered as the officer scrolled and zoomed, alternating between cameras to track the exit route of the man in the black jacket. They observed him making his way through the internal connections between the galleries: from the Baroque gallery to the Romance gallery, and from there through Neoclassical, where it was more crowded. He blended into the crowd briefly before they spotted him again outside. Somewhere in the museum courtyard—amid the summer crowd of visitors—the surveillance cameras lost their hold on the mysterious man in black.

He was there one minute and ... *poof!* ... gone the next.

"*Mierda,*" Rodriguez emoted, smacking the desk next to the younger officer's keyboard. Colt was sorry for the portly security chief; the museum's safety and security were his responsibility, and his system had failed that day. Miserably so. Heads would roll.

"Based on the recordings," he summarized, "from the moment the suspect walked into the gallery to the moment he exited, it took him less than a minute to steal the painting." Rodriguez groaned off to the side. "On the surface, it appears to be an impromptu grab-and-dash by an opportunist, taking advantage of the chaos ..." Colt stared at the screen with steely eyes, "but I have a gut feeling there might be more to it than that." A twinge in that rodeo hip.

He turned to face the group, his back to the bank of monitors. "Chief Barnham, I need the LAPD to hold the perimeter tight and keep the media crazies out. Chief Rodriguez, assemble a team to comb through your internal recordings. Cross-reference the data. I need an accurate timeline. We saw the suspect enter the gallery and leave with the painting under his jacket. Find out how he arrived and left the museum." Rodriguez nodded while scribbling old-school notes in a small notebook.

Colt eyed his FBI colleagues next, pointing at two junior agents. "You, Clark, and you, Samboya, supervise the gathering of physical evidence in the gallery upstairs. Go over every inch and I mean *fine-tooth* comb the whole enchilada. Fingerprint the doorways, the walls, the floorboards ..."

"Sir, that is a near-impossible task," one of the agents said, forlorn.

"Yes, Agent Clark, I know it's going to be a shit show fingerprinting this well-frequented joint," Colt acknowledged. "I don't care. Just find me something to run through IAFIS to help identify the perp. *Capiche?*" Both junior agents nodded vigorously; the Don Corleone reference helped provide a little extra motivation.

Colt turned to Agent Solis again, having been impressed with her acute eye for detail. "Solis, you will be with me." She stiffened her pose. "We'll interview eyewitnesses—anyone who saw this man before, during, or after the heist." She nodded, and he continued, "Alert Interpol, as well as the international Geneva Freeport, to be on the lookout for suspicious activity. We need all eyes on this."

"Yes, sir, on the double," she said.

Next, Colt shifted his attention to the insurance agents who had remained mum throughout the debrief, typing like maniacs on their laptops. "Gentlemen, we need to prepare for a ransom situation. Art theft is a short-sighted crime—the stolen painting will be hot property once it hits the news, and they will be unable to sell it on any legal market. Unless it goes underground as drug collateral, chances are they will approach the museum to get rid of the hot potato for a quick buck as fast as they can."

Had she still been in the room, senior curator of Netherlandish Art, Dr. Saskia van Trummel, would have balked at the priceless Rembrandt being referred to as a "hot potato." The agents bopped their heads like identical, grey-suited bobbleheads lined up in the back window of a station wagon.

"Also," Colt held his finger aloft while taking a swig of water from a plastic water cooler cup, "we must keep in mind that only a small percentage of stolen art is *ever* recovered. I'm afraid that is a real possibility." He scrunched up the plastic cup in his fist; the insurance suits winced. "Is there a conference room where we can set up for an extortion call?" he asked Rodriguez. "I need insurance reps and a few of my guys stationed there around the clock to intercept incoming calls."

"On it," Rodriguez said.

"Good," Colt nodded, "keep me in the loop."

Special Agent Colt Jamisson was on a roll, pivoting like the shadow around a sundial. From the panel of monitors and hard drives behind him, the young security guard who had continued scrolling through the recordings was trying to catch his attention.

"Um, hello? Commander?" But Colt's rapid-fire instructions drowned out the young man's voice, so he tried again, louder this time, waving his hand for more impact, "Sir, over here ... I found something."

The conversation stopped abruptly; one by one, heads turned until all eyes were pinned on the young man. He blanched under the pressure.

"Yes? What is it, Daughtry?" Rodriguez demanded, sounding annoyed.

Daughtry popped a wheelie in his chair and rolled backward to reveal the full expanse of his monitors to the occupants of the cramped office. The timestamp on the screen read "11:39:57"—minutes *after* the heist, but before the alarms went off. The screen showed the outdoor platform above the main parking lot, where visitors were waiting for an elevator. A tall man in a dark blazer, jeans, and white shirt stood in the group, clutching a purple key card which would allow him to bypass the parking lot pay station and exit the structure faster.

"I'm not sure, sir, but this could be our guy," Daughtry announced. "Dude did not realize we have cameras outdoors as well. He forgot to keep his mask on, the bonehead."

"Show us," Colt instructed, clearing his throat to suppress his excitement, "zoom in on that face."

Officer Daughtry perked up, overjoyed to be an essential cog in the machine that would crack this case. He went to work, manipulating the recording with nimble fingers at warp speed, the kind of high-APM skill—Actions per Minute—acquired from a decade's worth of all-night eSports tournaments from his mother's basement. Spooling the recording forward, and then back until he found the clearest angle. Zoomed in, the perpetrator's face was blurry, but his basic features were clear: tall, male, athletic build, dark hair, and clean-shaven.

"Print me a screenshot of that, ASAP. Can you get a clearer image of the ID badge he's holding?" Colt asked, knowing it was a long shot. Daughtry complied, zooming in until the purple rectangle had enlarged to a pixelated, indecipherable blur on the screen.

"He's one of ours," Rodriguez mumbled. "Educators from the museum's teaching corps use those purple ID badges. He could be a docent for school groups or a public tour guide."

"It's not his ID," Colt said.

"Huh? How can you tell?" LAPD chief Barnham asked, squinting at the monitor. "We can't even see the suspect's face clearly, never mind a tiny thumbnail photo on the blurry ID badge. Do you have X-ray vision or something?" He sounded exasperated, a little sarcastic.

"No X-ray vision, just common sense," Colt said. "I wasn't referring to the photo on the ID badge. I was referring to the lanyard it is hanging from." All eyes in the room swiveled back to the zoomed-in image on Daughtry's monitors.

"Oh," Barnham mumbled.

The lanyard attached to the ID badge appeared to be a string of pearls or beads.

"Sir, pearls or not, it could still belong to a male staff member," Agent Solis reminded him. "Nowadays, with gender fluidity and such ..."

"Yes, of course," Colt said, caught off guard. "We need to consider *all* the clues."

On the screen, the man in the tailored black jacket stepped forward amid the group of departing visitors to enter the elevator. Just for a moment, he glanced up at the fisheye camera positioned above the elevator. It looked as if the thief were taunting him, challenging him through the lens.

Catch me if you can, that scowl conveyed.

"It looks like he made a clean getaway," LAPD chief Barnham said, his mouth turned down at the corners, his shoulders slumped.

"Yup, this timestamp and that access key card mean he had ample time to exit the museum parking lot *before* we mobilized the checkpoints," Rodriguez said.

"Shit," Colt said. It was obvious that the painting had left the premises. Now he had to focus on identifying the thief before the trail went cold. Before the painting changed hands and disappeared into thin air. "We have a blurry face and a blurry ID card. It looks like he came in without a mask, then used one for the heist, and left again without it. He might have discarded it on the premises. We need to find that mask for a DNA match. Chief Barnham, a job for your guys. Black or navy blue."

"Black," Agent Solis said. Colt pointed at her and nodded.

He turned his attention to the officer manning the controls. "Daughtry, was it?" The junior officer beamed. "Give me a split screen of the guy waiting at the elevator next to one from inside the gallery, please."

Officer Daughtry did his magic and soon, side-by-side images of the suspect filled the screen: one indoors in a black face mask; the other outside, without.

The room sighed.

"It's the same guy," Rodriquez said.

Colt squinted at the screen. He was 90% sure it was.

"Fine work, young man," he addressed Daughtry. "One of my agents will collaborate with you to sharpen the pixels on these low-res images, using the FBI's Photo-Enhancing Super-Resolution software. Bring me a clear money shot of this man's face."

"Yessir!" Daughtry said, his eyes blinking with pride. He had a hell of a "Big Fish" story to tell his Dungeons & Dragons crew later.

"Everyone, thank you for your insight. Let's reconvene in fifteen minutes to hammer out the next steps," Colt said, before stepping outside the stuffy room for a breather. The empty hallways stretched out before him like gopher tunnels in the dark. Suspicion was nibbling at his amygdala—a sixth sense, so to speak.

Why would an employee of the museum use his key card if he planned to steal from it? Perhaps it was just an opportunistic grab-and-dash by a disgruntled employee, after all.

The thought did not please Colt. He did not want this to be a half-assed act by a desperate person. He needed it to be *big*—a criminal underworld type of heist with multiple, complex levels of intrigue. Indiana Jones never had the treasure delivered to him on a silver tray. No, he had to risk his life for every clue, tangled in roots and bugs, and dodging boulders and poisonous blowpipe arrows to recover the stolen artifact. And why?

"Fortune and glory, kid. Fortune and glory," Special Agent Colt Jamisson muttered the famous words of his icon, Indiana Jones, into the cavernous hallway of the museum.

CHAPTER 26
LUCKY LOCKER #13

*W*ake *up, Angel. Wake up, now!* the old man urged, his one milky eye a torch piercing the darkness surrounding her. Angel tried to move, but she couldn't. She was trapped in a dense forest of cattails and bald cypress trees, entangled in their ropey roots with Spanish moss drooping from branches that grabbed and prodded her with gnarled, bayou-boy fingers. A rabble of bizarre steampunk critters skittered on metallic tarsi across her body, emitting a cacophony of beeps and chirps. It made her skin crawl.

Where am I? Am I dead?

Her eyes fluttered open, slow to adjust to a flood of blinding light from above. Through a window in her peripheral view, a resplendent Jacaranda tree was shaking off a flurry of hazy purple blossoms and sprinkling them down against a deep-blue sky. Fuzzy colors and bright white light?

Yup, I'm dead.

She wondered whether she should walk into the white light—as you were supposed to do when you were dead—or wait for it to envelop her and whisk her soul upward in a puff of purple haze. But then the chittering of critters in her ears morphed into more recognizable sounds: the static *bzzzzz* of fluorescent tubes, the shuffling of footsteps, and an incessant *beep ... beep ... beep.*

She turned her head gingerly toward the source of the beeping ... and gasped. Inches from her face, a grotesque creature squatted on the bedside table. Shocked, she scampered backward on her bottom until her head banged against the metal headboard.

"Ow!"

The hirsute creature watched her, stalking her every move with all six eyes tightened into slits, its three heads bobbing up and down with jaws snarling and drool dripping. Two brothers and a cousin, perhaps?

"Hollywuuuud!" it howled.

Her heart monitor increased its tempo to a foxtrot: *Beep-beep. Beep-beep. Beep-beep.* She lay still until the confusion drained away to make space for clearer thoughts. And then ... *bam!* ... it all came rushing at her—a dizzying deluge of memory fragments of the minutes preceding her dance with death: snakes in her hair, gasping for breath, a tall man wrestling with the Rembrandt, the paramedics wheeling her away, her bag leaning against the wall ...

Shit, my bag.

She had no recollection of what had happened following her loss of consciousness. Was Luke successful in his attempt to steal the painting? Did he drop it in Pandora's box, as rehearsed? And, most importantly, did the bag make it into the ambulance?

Was it all just a bad dream?

With considerable trepidation, she lifted her head, then one arm, expecting to have it yanked back by handcuffs shackling her to the bed. But there were no metal cuffs or even rubber restraints. The only thing tethered to her was an intravenous line inserted into the top of her hand, secured by a piece of transparent medical tape. She couldn't recall how it got there. Mesmerized, she watched cool saline dripping into her vein, counting five drips before her arm dropped back down onto the crisp white sheets. She was in a hospital, not dead or under arrest.

Not yet.

Dizzy, she sank deeper into the pillows to counter the vertigo. The door creaked open, followed by the soft shuffle of shoes entering the room.

Is that them? The Feds?

When she dared to open her eyes, she was relieved to see a group of innocuous white coats instead.

"Good morning, Ms. Hendridge," the man in the long white coat said, "I am Doctor Henry Richards, the attending physician, and this here is my team of minions. How are we feeling today?"

"I don't know about you, doctor," she croaked from a bone-dry throat, each word delivering a sharp sting, "but I'm feeling pretty crappy."

He smiled and picked up her wrist with two fingers pressed to her radial artery. "Do you know where you are?" Hovering about four feet behind him, in a half-circle of shorter white coats, the student doctors leaned in, bright-eyed and bushy-tailed.

"In heaven?" she joked, bolstered by the overwhelming relief that the fingers gripping her wrist were gentle. "I was seeing bright lights and hearing angels sing."

Doctor Richards released her wrist back to her. "You came *this* close to meeting those angels, Ms. Hendridge," he said, making the pinching sign in front of a squinted eye. The tiny space between his forefinger and thumb showed how close she came to that blinding white light of permanency. He produced a penlight from his pocket and instructed her to follow its beam—left, right, up, and down. "Pupils equal, round, and reactive to light," he announced to the room; behind him, one of the students typed "PERRL" on a tablet.

"Do you remember what happened?" Dr. Richards asked, pushing the penlight back into his breast pocket. She feigned ignorance with a little shrug. "You suffered a life-threatening anaphylactic reaction yesterday morning at the Pallas Museum. Are you aware of any severe allergies?"

She flared her eyes. "Oh yes, I've had a severe peanut allergy since childhood. I always carry an EpiPen with me in my bag. I guess I couldn't get to it in time ..." Her voice trailed off as she recalled those panicked moments on the floor of the Baroque gallery. "But how—? How could this have happened? I had nothing to eat before my tour; I avoid all nuts and I don't keep anything containing peanuts *anywhere* in my home."

Truth.

The panic in her voice was genuine enough. She had not intended to get quite that close to death when she orchestrated her part in the distraction. The thought of how it could have ended nauseated her. Nothing was worth dying for.

Well, *almost* nothing.

The doctor sat down on the edge of the bed and patted her ankle. "We're not sure how it happened. People with peanut allergies are sometimes acutely sensitive to even the tiniest micro-particles of the nut—whether through inhalation of its dust or contact with trace amounts. Can you remember touching anything out of the ordinary at the museum? In the lunchroom, perhaps?"

Angel pretended to think; her mind was clear now, and she had to be cautious. "No, nothing unusual. I'm very careful, especially in the cafeteria. Perhaps ... oh, I'm not sure if that could have been the cause, but I *did* high-five a few young boys during a game we played in the gallery. I was pretending to be Medusa, and they were supposed to turn to stone."

The medical students smiled knowingly behind Dr. Richards's back. Angel pictured them as the kind of high achievers who would have soaked up Greek mythology in school. She continued spinning her intricate web of lies.

"A few boys were smart enough to avert their eyes, so I high-fived them for their initiative ..." She let those last few words hang in the air, holding her hand up high to demonstrate. Her palm was still flushed from the histamine rush.

Doctor Richards arched his eyebrows and stared at the hand floating in front of him. "That must be it," he said. "One of the students must have had PB&J remnants on his or her hand, causing it to come into direct contact with your skin. And then from there, to your mouth or nose. You're lucky the paramedics were on the scene so expediently. Severe reactions like yours could be fatal if not treated within fifteen minutes."

Wincing, she looked up at the buzzing tube lights, as if gazing heavenward.

Lucky? *Perhaps*. Well-strategized? *You betcha*.

"How long have I been here?" she asked the physician.

He unhooked a clipboard chart from the foot of her bed and skimmed its contents before handing the patient monitoring sheet to a minion behind him. A baby-faced student doctor scrambled to grab the clipboard before it clattered to the floor.

"Can you tell us about the patient, Chiang?"

"Patient Angelique Hendridge, female, 53 years old," the student read, "admitted at 11:47 a.m. on Thursday. The patient presented with advanced anaphylaxis; severe hypotension at 84 over 57. Patient experienced hypoxia and was intubated at 12:13 p.m. Additional epi was administered," he gestured around his throat for her benefit, "for the swelling. Patient was stabilized and extubated at 06:04 p.m. Patient is receiving IV fluids and electrolytes. Blood pressure has stabilized to 109 over 72. Normal pulse-ox of 98 percent." Chiang handed the clipboard back to Dr. Richards, who rose from his perch on her bedsheets.

"It means you are going to be just fine, Ms. Hendridge," he said. "Do you have any questions for me?"

Yes. Where is my bag? Have the cops been here asking questions? Is the FBI waiting outside with an arrest order?

She shook her head no.

"I recommend keeping you here for another 24 hours to guard against biphasic anaphylaxis—that's a second attack that could occur anywhere from one hour to 72 hours after the initial one," Dr. Richards said. "If everything goes smoothly, I will come and sign your discharge papers tomorrow. Deal?"

"Deal." She proffered her hand up high for a tongue-in-cheek high-five. The doctor regarded the hoisted hand and smirked.

"Ha, good one." He started toward the door with his students on his heels. "You have a gaggle of persistent friends waiting outside. Shall I send them in?"

She nodded and shut her eyes for a quick reprieve from the glaring lights and the strain of her Oscar-worthy performance. Keeping up a lie was stressful, especially after almost dying because of it.

The heavy door squished open again and her team of Olympians trickled in—Luke on his tiptoes, as if not wanting to disturb the dead. All three wore the telltale dark hollows of sleepless nights below their eyes. Solemn and restrained, they took turns stepping forward to hug her, careful not to disturb the web of tubes and cables plugged into their friend.

"Well, you guys look like shit," Angel joked to diffuse the tension. "I thought gods and goddesses never aged."

"Not funny, Angel," Lorelei chided, "you almost *died*. My God, why the hell did you let it go that far?" It was typical of Lorelei to use the words "God," and "hell," in the same sentence.

Angel, always on guard, gestured with her finger to her lips: *shush, they might be listening.* Luke's eyes widened and darted around the ceiling, searching for cameras or microphones.

"The doctor suspects I might have unwittingly been exposed to trace amounts of peanut butter," she said for the benefit of any listening devices. "I'm glad to be alive. It could have gone the other way." Her thumb dove toward the floor.

Shivonne wiped at a tear welling in her eye and grabbed Angel's hand, squeezing it twice. "Angel, I'm so sorry. I—"

"Shivvy, look at me. I'm fine," Angel reassured her.

"Yes, but we almost lost you. I don't know how to say—"

Angel shot her a grave "say-no-more" look. "I'm just relieved to see all of you. Does my family know about this? My phone was in my docent bag, so I can't call them." When she mentioned the bag, she felt a subtle change in the atmosphere, a tightening of ozone.

"I called Deacon yesterday, right after the uh ... the incident," Lorelei said. "He's on his way back from Dubai as we speak. He was very worried about you; said he would come straight to the hospital from the airport tomorrow morning. Clio drove from San Diego as soon as she heard. She was here this morning, but she went to your house to clean up and eat something. As for Roman ..." Lorelei shrugged, "I left a few messages, but I haven't heard from him."

Angel glanced back at the three-headed creature that had terrorized her earlier from its perch on the bedside table. "That's okay," she said, smiling. "Roman was here, I know it." The squatting creature turned out to be a harmless bobblehead toy—Cerberus, the three-headed hybrid dog of Hades—and *not* the monstrous embodiment of her worst nightmare. Her son must have left it there for her, to watch over her.

To guard the guardian angel.

"Regardless," Luke said, grabbing her hand, his eyes welling up, "you've always got us ... your Olympian family. We've got each other's backs."

The four of them regarded each other and linked hands to form a circle like the Greek *ouroboros:* the snake swallowing its own tail.

A symbol of eternity.

Lorelei broke the connection to pull a folded newspaper from her purse and held it up for Angel to see. The headline—in fat, newspaper font—pulsed in sync with the heart monitor flanking the bed:

"PALLAS MUSEUM ROBBED IN DARING DAYTIME HEIST."

The photo underneath the headline was an archival image depicting Rembrandt's self-portrait with its curator-in-charge, Dr. Saskia van Trummel, pointing to it with red fingernails. Angel could swear the heart monitor had increased its tempo, skipping erratically.

Beep-beep ... beep ... beep-beep-beep-beep-beep ... beep.

Cerberus was bobbing its heads to the frantic disco beat.

"Apparently," Shivonne said, "someone used your medical emergency in the gallery as an opportunity to grab the painting and run off with it."

"You mean, while I was in there? That's nuts." Angel said. She was tempted to add "pun intended" but caught it in her mouth before it slipped out. "Did you guys see it happen?"

"No," Luke said, a little too hastily, "I was downstairs in the bookstore, and Shivvy had already left."

"And I was next door with the Turner," Lorelei said.

"Do they have a suspect?" Angel asked. *Are we off the hook?*

They shook their heads in unison.

Her empty stomach churned as she recalled the last thing she saw before losing consciousness: her docent bag leaning against the wall, and *not* on the gurney, with her, where it was supposed to be. She remembered trying to ask for it right before darkness overpowered her. Thankfully, Lorelei was there to ensure they took it.

The bag. Where is my docent bag?

Lorelei—besides being a sorceress of healing potions—seemed to read Angel's aura; she gripped her hand and shook her head, slowly, in a deliberate message to Angel. "The painting is missing. *Truly* missing."

Oh no.

We know, the others beamed back telepathically. When pseudo-gods and goddesses have walked over life's heated coals alongside each other for years, they developed a sixth sense of communication. Such mortal pseudo-gods could speak with their eyes, with slight gestures, and with their thoughts to fill in the blank spaces between spoken words.

"So, none of you saw my bag after I blacked out? All my stuff is in there. My keys, my wallet ..." Angel was looking at Lorelei; the trusty sweeper's hand went limp in her grasp.

"I'm so sorry," Lorelei said. "I called after the paramedics to take it, but I got an urgent ping from Benjamin right then. A family emergency. I swear," she held her hand to her heart, "I only stepped away for a minute to call him back. To check on Grace. And when I turned back ... it was too late."

"Too late?"

"Yeah, the paramedics had already left with you on the gurney. I ran after them ..."

"And then?"

"When I realized that they didn't have it," Lorelei said, "I ran back to the gallery as fast as I could, but all hell broke loose just as I got there. The alarms went off, and the guards started evacuating the galleries ... I saw one of them pick up your bag. That's when I hightailed it out of there." She took a deep breath to recover from her run-on sentences.

Angel shut her eyes and wished for the cool of that forest and the tiny critters crawling into her nose and ears. The *coup de grâce* of being swallowed by the blinding light.

"Christ, Angel. What were you thinking?" Deacon's voice echoed in her head, *"You should have been better prepared."*

He was right this time, she knew. The bag was gone. With a stolen painting inside. Oh, and with the culprit's identification inside the culprit's wallet. It was just a matter of time before the authorities were onto her—them. She opened her eyes to a flood of guilt on Lorelei's face and reached for her hand.

"It's okay, it will show up sooner or later," she said. Demeter had failed Athena, but all was forgiven.

"And Grace, is she okay?" Shivonne asked.

"She's fine, thank the Lord," Lorelei replied. "Fractured her arm at school. You guys know how brittle her bones are from the chemo meds. She's wallowing in the attention with her neon-pink cast. Her crush, Gerard, signed it with a heart."

Angel squeezed Lorelei's hand, acknowledging the unspoken rule: earthly family first, and *then* fellow gods and goddesses.

"What do we do now?" Luke asked. "I mean, what do *they* do now? The museum ... about the missing painting." He pushed his glasses higher up his nose and wrapped his arms around his torso as if fastening a straitjacket around it. Patience was not his forte—having spent a sizeable chunk of life living in limbo did that to a person.

"What they do now is *wait*," Lorelei announced, emphasizing the last word as if it were a command. With their Athena incapacitated, she was next in line to take the helm, by unspoken default. Her crystalline eyes broadcast the message, loud and clear:

We wait, and we stay calm.

His face ashen, Luke nodded. A heavy cloud of doom hung over the four of them. They were waiting for Athena to speak words of wisdom and comfort, just as she had done during those oppressive hours in the elevator car when they were still strangers. Angel felt the weight of their expectations.

"It's going to be okay," she obliged them. "Time will tell." In her mind, Father Time chuckled through his silver beard while flipping the hourglass carelessly between his palms. Relentlessly taunting her, tormenting her.

There was a loud rap on the door, and a nurse in pink scrubs popped her head around it.

"I'm sorry to ruin the party, Ms. Hendridge," she said, "but visitor's hour is almost over, and you have one more outside. Your daughter, Cleo. Lovely name, as in Cleopatra?"

"Nope, as in Clio, the Greek muse of history."

"Ah," the nurse frowned.

Shivonne, Lorelei, and Luke took turns hugging the patient and departed with a final glance back at Angel for reassurance. She flashed them her requisite thumbs-up ... and then they were gone. All was quiet for a blissful few seconds before Clio rushed inside, relief floating in the shallow end of her ocean-blue eyes.

"Mom, you're awake! We were so worried." She leaned down to kiss her mom.

Angel patted the space next to her, and Clio sat down. Her hair was still damp, and she smelled of shampoo and toothpaste—of innocence and purity, the inverse of what Angel was feeling right then. She ran her fingers through Clio's caramel tresses, recalling how she used to do that to comfort her daughter when she was younger. The feisty little girl had grown up and slipped through her fingers like those silky strands of hair—way too fast, way too easily. She mourned for that loss, for the bonding moments she had missed with her daughter while wrapped up in melancholy.

"I'm absolutely fine, Clio," she lied.

The truth was, she was sick with guilt and worry. Her docent bag was missing with a multi-million-dollar stolen treasure inside, and the odds were great that the FBI probably had it already. They would come with a warrant for her arrest soon; she imagined hearing "FBI, open up!" and then Miranda rights recited while her stunned husband and children looked on. The disgrace of it—the humiliation, the heartbreak. The inevitable schism in her family.

Clio interpreted the pained look on her mom's face as an emotional reaction to her near-death experience. "Mom, I know we don't see each other much any-more because of my job out of town," she said, "but what happened yesterday, almost losing you ... I cannot imagine my life without you." She wiped a tear from the outer corner of her eye.

Angel marveled at that single tear. Clio never cried; she was a tough cookie like her mom, stoic to a fault. Flushed with emotion, she stroked the hummingbird tattoo on her daughter's wrist—its wings spread wide in perpetual hover mode.

"I love you, too, Clio."

"I always tell my friends," Clio said, "I want to be just like my mom when I'm older."

"You want to be like *me*?" Angel replied, surprised. "I'm nothing but a dreamer, a poet without a pedestal, a ... a peacock."

Clio threw her head back in laughter, and her single streak of pink-dyed hair shimmered in the purple-tinged haze filtering in from the window. "Are you still hung up on that, Mom? It was just a silly game. Besides, peacocks are beautiful. Why would you *not* want to be one?"

Angel had never thought about it that way.

Until that moment, she had always considered her fun-loving, peacock side frivolous and reckless. A weakness. A liability. The flashy part of her personality that almost got her gang-raped in a filthy back alley; the part of her that had planned—not to mention executed—an insane act of desecration at a world-renowned museum. Was that not the *ultimate* peacock thing to do?

"Besides, you're only one-third peacock. The rest? Absolute badass owl," Clio said.

Inside Angel, Athena leaned back and blinked her steely-grey eyes.

"I'm not crying," her alter ego said to her, "you *are.*"

It was too much for Angel. Never had she felt so loved and yet so utterly ashamed. She did not deserve her daughter's admiration and respect. Not after the crime she had committed.

Oh, goddess Athena, what have you made me do?

In the hospital bed, where she had almost surrendered to the blinding white light, Angel was overcome with an overwhelming compulsion to confess her transgressions to Clio. She knew it would break her daughter's heart, but Clio deserved to hear it from her mother's lips before she saw it splattered across Headline News.

She cleared her throat. "Clio, there's something you need to know. Something that might ... that *will* change your opinion of m—"

But Fate—or perhaps it was Fortune—knocked on the door right then and interrupted Angel's confession. The nurse, again, eager to finish her rounds before punching out.

"So sorry to interrupt again, but visitor's hour is now officially over. We are changing shifts, and the patient needs her rest." She approached the bed, handed Angel a large white tablet with a plastic cup of water, and beckoned Clio to follow her outside.

"Please, can we have just a few more minutes? ... I need to tell her something important," Angel protested.

But Clio squeezed her hand and hopped down from the bed. "It's okay, Mom, you can tell me tomorrow. I can see you are very emotional—you've been through a lot. Take it from your daughter, the EMT: anaphylactic shock is no joke. I've had patients die in the back of my rig." At the door, she turned back, "I almost forgot ..." She pulled a small, padded envelope from her backpack and handed it to her mom.

"What's this?" Angel asked, frowning.

"Dunno." Clio shrugged. "An older man gave it to me this morning in the waiting room. The doctors would not allow him to see you, so he asked me to give it to you later."

"An older man?" Angel searched her fried brain for a clue.

"Grey hair ... spoke with an accent. Said he worked with you at the museum. Sorry, but I can't recall his name." The nurse popped her head back around the door. "Get some rest, Ma. Dad and I will pick you up tomorrow." Clio blew a kiss and then she was gone.

As heartwarming as the interaction with her daughter was, Angel shuddered from the harrowing emotional toll of visitor's hour—the anguish of the team of Olympians, the fear for the missing bag, followed by her near-confession of a momentous crime.

"Batshit-crazy" was how Luke would have described it.

Once the room was quiet again, save for the beeping and the buzzing of life-saving equipment, Angel tore open the flap of the padded envelope and dropped a plastic coiled bracelet into her palm. It was orange, resembling those spiral, rotary phone cords from the 1980s, with a brass Yale key linked to it. The number "13" was etched into an attached metal tag. Puzzled, she palpated the cryptic key, turning it over and over between her fingers.

What on earth?

She peered into the padded envelope and pulled out a card—from the Pallas gift shop—with *Still Life with Silver Teapot and Narcissus* depicted on the front. She immediately knew who had sent the envelope: her friend, the security guard.

With the orange coils pulled over her wrist so the key caressed her skin, she opened the card:

"Meine liebe Angel,
I am sorry you are ill. I pray you get better soon.
Tschüss, Walter"

The message warmed her heart, but it was the postscript that clenched it with an iron fist, spiking the heart rate monitor next to her bed.

"PS:
I found your bag in the gallery after you left in the ambulance.
I recognized it from the Narcissus pin I gave you.
I did not want someone else to take it, so I put it in a safe place for you.
Museum Lost & Found: Locker #13."

CHAPTER 27
THE GOOD TIDE

The breaking news jolted Luke like a stun gun on a lazy Sunday morning, ten days after the heist. He and Jerome were sipping peach mimosas on the sunbaked patio of a trendy café on Santa Monica Boulevard—the kind that served adaptogenic mushroom coffee and açaí bowls to the enlightened. The news of Lucky Locker #13 had brought a modicum of relief to the Olympians, but the treasure remained elusive. For all they knew, the Feds had searched every inch of the entire museum, found the bag, and were lying in wait. Lulling them with a false sense of security while preparing to strike. Luke was far from lulled; he had been soothing his frayed nerves with umbrella cocktails, late-night sewing marathons, and the occasional dose of sunlight from his Apollo.

They had stopped by the Pasadena Rose Bowl flea market early that morning where he wandered, zombie-like, among the trove of attic junk and vintage finds. But nothing had excited him—not even the bright orange, mid-century Saarinen womb chair an ignorant fool was trying to unload for only $250.

"Earth to Planet Luke, hello?" Jerome peered at him over Ray-Ban sunglasses.

"Hmm?" Luke was leaning so far back in his chair that he almost fell backward when he overheard part of the conversation from the table behind theirs.

"Oh wow, looks like the FBI just arrested someone for that art heist a couple of weeks ago. Do you remember the one? The Rembrandt painting. That was such a ballsy ..."

Stunned by the revelation, Luke overcorrected his precarious tilt and slammed forward, hitting his diaphragm against the rim of the table, and spraying his mouthful of mimosa all over the white linen tablecloth.

"Heyyy," Jerome protested, wiping droplets from his shirt with his napkin.

"S-sorry," Luke sputtered, dabbing at his mouth, and then at the puddle of peachy fizz in the breadbasket between them.

"You've been on edge all morning," Jerome said, "like a clock wound too tightly."

The FBI has arrested someone, Luke thought, *and it was not me!*

"Swallowed an air bubble," he said, clearing his throat. "I'll go grab us more napkins."

He scooped his cell phone from the tabletop and ducked around the corner, where a wall overgrown with ivy offered a modicum of privacy. As soon as his heartbeat settled, he scrolled through the "Breaking News" headlines on his news app—an update from the Mars rover ... the continued shortage of paper products post-Covid ... a brush fire threatening vineyards near Solvang. Then, there it was:

"FBI ARRESTS SUSPECT FOR PALLAS MUSEUM HEIST"

Trembling, he clicked on the accompanying video clip and watched a reporter deliver the breaking news in front of a suburban house wrapped in crime tape. Forensic investigators in white jumpsuits and gloves were entering and exiting the home, their arms loaded with boxes and computer terminals. Two FBI agents in tactical gear were perp-walking their suspect toward a white van with the intimidating triple initials emblazoned on its side. His hands were zip-tied behind his back, his head bowed, exposing only a tousled crown of hair.

"Holy shitballs."

A wave of dizziness overcame Luke, so he leaned back, letting the creeper ivy wrap around him as if pulling him away from the present and deeper into another realm. An upside-down of sorts, where a team of underdogs could pull off a major art heist ... and get away with it.

It's over.

He executed a series of subdued fist pumps, then composed himself to send a quick-fingered text to his fellow Olympians:

Attention all Olympians, Hermes has news from the gods:
The Fates have rolled their dice,
and Fortuna has been generous.
Hades has fallen.

He waited with bated breath; it did not take long. Lorelei, who was walking home from Sunday Mass with her family, clutching a Bible under one armpit and holding hands with Benjamin, texted one of her typical, paradoxical responses:

Holy shit, hallelujah!

Seconds later, Angel, who was listening to Samuel Barber's melancholic "Adagio for Strings" while studying her favorite painting, Jacques-Louis David's *The Intervention of the Sabine Women*, responded with a single affirmation:

Olympians!

It was no coincidence that she was staring at the brave Hersilia, identifying with the fearless Sabine woman who had flung herself into the center of a bloody battleground, her arms outstretched to plead for peace and shield the most vulnerable babes at her feet.

From Shivonne, not surprisingly, there was nothing but radio silence. Angel sent a follow-up message:

Olympus is still off-limits.

Let's rendezvous at the beach of the gods.

6pm sharp.

Luke replied with a thumbs-up emoji, pocketed his phone, and sauntered back to the table where Jerome was waiting behind two stacks of macadamia nut pancakes. There was an extra swagger in his step.

"No napkins?" Jerome asked as Luke settled back down in his chair.

"Hmm? Oh ... no," he said, "national paper product shortage, apparently."

"It's going to be all right now," Ms. Latsky's ghost told Luke as he hoisted his mimosa flute. In his mind's eye, she was twirling in her silk gown, looking happy and pink-cheeked with vitality. And those painted silk birds took to the skies in a flurry of color, rising from the ashes.

"To life, to luck ... and love," he toasted.

"I'll drink to that," Jerome said.

Above the table, the two flutes clinked together and there was no sweeter sound to Luke's ears. He picked up his fork and cut a deep, diagonal slice through three layers of fluffy comfort, watching intently as a dollop of melted butter slid down the crack and spread out in a pool of golden joy on his plate.

Underneath the table, his legs twitched and bounced uncontrollably.

The transcendental flow of Enya on full volume, as it should be, muffled the sound of gravel crunching under Lorelei's car tires down the path that led to their favorite beach—a hidden cove along the Malibu coastline—a couple of miles north of the Ventura County line. It was 6:08 p.m. and she was a little late, as usual.

Did we really pull it off without a hitch? she wondered.

Well, not entirely without a hitch, her alter ego, Demeter, reminded her: Angel dodged death by a hair's breadth, and they lost track of the painting for ten insufferable days. But no agents had pounded FBI search warrants on their front doors; no handcuffs shackled around their wrists. They could all breathe freely again, like that day six years ago when they had escaped the death-trap elevator—psychologically scarred but, otherwise, unscathed.

She dialed Shivonne's number. It rang several times before the voicemail delivered its message in Shivonne's usual skittish tone, sugarcoated in a superficial cheer that broke Lorelei's heart. "Shivvy, it's Lore," she said after the beep. "We've been trying to reach you all day. When you get this message, please call me. Or just meet us at our beach." She paused, then added, "You've got this, Artemis."

Lorelei pulled up behind Angel's car on the side of the road. There were no other cars in sight. Most visitors flocked to the more commercial, miles-long sandy stretches of Malibu beach along the Pacific Coast Highway, but the four of them favored the more remote beach—void of dental-floss bikinis, flying frisbees, and fat-wheeled coolers blasting music from built-in speakers.

A thick chain hung across the path under a sign warning, "No trespassing. Stay Out," blah-blah-blah, something about riptides and rockslides. But the four Olympians—as they had proven with their daring heist—were not averse to risk. They had jumped that chain many times over the weeks preceding the heist, to plot and practice with only the ocean to witness their duplicity.

Their cove nestled between two outcrops of rocks which, if one squinted, could be mistaken for a hidden Mediterranean coastal inlet, where gentle waves rolled in through a channel and crashed on a small crescent-shaped beach of golden Californian sand. Upon rounding the outcrop, rolling the cuffs of her linen overalls to avoid them getting soaked by the shoreline wash, she saw Angel and Luke under a rainbow-colored beach umbrella. It was no longer hot enough to warrant the umbrella, but the image of a rainbow arching over their heads was fitting.

"Olympians," she called upon approach, and they whooped in response, their exuberance echoing in the rocky bowl around them. She plopped down in the shade and withdrew a bottle of champagne from her legendary Mary Poppins bag. "To Victory!"

"Sure, but the *other* four Olympians deserve the praise," Luke joked, referring to Nike, the goddess of Victory. He was still a little giddy from his morning shot of good news.

"Has anyone heard from Shivvy?" Lorelei asked, plucking a stuffed olive from the smorgasbord of snacks laid out on the waxed beach blanket. The mood quieted down at the mention of their friend.

"Not me," Luke shrugged. "You?"

Angel shook her head, staring down at her lilac toenails burrowing in the sand like hermit crabs. "This must be incredibly difficult for her."

The ensuing silence was disturbed only by the rolling crescendo of waves crashing upon the wet sand. It reminded Lorelei of Turner's seascape and that nerve-racking day in the gallery. The storm and the aftermath. Today's ocean was the antithesis of that day's tempest; this was tranquility and serenity.

"Sometimes good things come at a steep price," she said, leaning forward to grab the Sunday Times spread out in front of them on the blanket. "Is this it?" The paper's "BREAKING NEWS!" headline glowed like a neon beacon against the black-and-white alphabet-soup newsprint.

"Let me," Angel said, her hand extended, and Lorelei acquiesced. The heist had been Athena's divine plan, so it made sense that she should announce the good tidings. Angel started reading:

"DISGRACED LAPD DETECTIVE ARRESTED FOR PALLAS MUSEUM REMBRANDT HEIST:
The FBI is confident they have the culprit, but the priceless painting is still at large.

By ANNA P. YOUNG
Times Staff Writer

LOS ANGELES, CALIFORNIA: *At 5:00 a.m. on Sunday, the LAPD, in conjunction with the FBI's Art Crime Division, executed a search warrant on a home in the San Fernando Valley of Los Angeles, and arrested a sole suspect for the recent heist at the Pallas Museum, during which one of Rembrandt's self-portraits was stolen in a brazen daytime heist.*

The suspect in custody has been identified as ex-detective Joseph "Joe" Cillian O'Roydon, previously of the LAPD's Gang and Narcotics Division. According to LAPD Chief Barnham, O'Roydon was suspended from active duty four months ago, in February of this year, on suspicion of police misconduct, including — but not limited to — dereliction of duties, intoxication while on duty, violations of police procedural policy, and the misappropriation of confiscated narcotics from a secure precinct evidence locker.

Ex-detective O'Roydon's spouse, Shivonne O'Roydon, claims to have had no knowledge of her husband's suspension and was under the impression he left for work, as usual, on weekdays. Mrs. O'Roydon's attorney stated his client will cooperate fully with the FBI investigation and has submitted aggravating evidence of ongoing and escalating spousal abuse perpetrated by her husband. The District Attorney has announced that ad-

298

ditional charges of Felony Domestic Violence will be leveraged against the accused, in addition to Felony Grand Larceny and Resisting Arrest, a misdemeanor.

FBI special agent in charge of Art Crime, Colton Jamisson, stated the evidence against the former detective is "staggering and conclusive," and includes museum security footage, witness reports, and a DNA match from spittle on a black face mask found in a trash receptacle on museum premises. O'Roydon had allegedly stolen the staff ID key card of his wife—an art educator at the museum—to gain insider-level access."

Angel paused and regarded the others with a half-smile that spoke volumes: relief and pride in a plan well-executed. Luke indicated for her to continue, rolling his finger like a movie director. "Go on, go on."

"An extensive search of the suspect's home yielded further incriminating evidence. A discarded vial with trace amounts of the date-rape drug, Rohypnol, was retrieved from the garbage container behind the suspect's home, which corroborates Mrs. O'Roydon's suspicion that her spouse had drugged her on multiple occasions for nefarious purposes.

In addition to the Schedule IV substance, a secret stash of cocaine and oxycodone was discovered in a concealed drawer. A team of FBI Cyber—"

"Wait," Luke interjected, "what 'secret stash of cocaine and oxycodone'? Was that something Shivvy planted, too? I don't remember it being part of the plan."

"Nope," Angel chuckled, equally surprised, "that was not part of the plan."

Athena's plan: Lorelei's procuring of a powerful sedative that enabled Shivonne to plant incriminating evidence on Joe's computer, then lure him to the museum with a fake lover's note on the assumption he would track her phone—safely diverted in the hands of Lorelei—directly to the Rembrandt gallery where several witnesses would place him around the time of the heist. All the while keeping his intended target safely out of harm's way. Luke's quick-switch disguise, Lorelei's orchestration of a cataclysmic storm, and Angel's death-defying distraction. Plus, of course, a hearty dose of Fortuna's blessing.

"The drugs were Joe's own doing—shooting himself in the foot like that," she continued. "It appears that he has been an addict for a while and was already in trouble at work prior to our, um, involvement. That's irony for you."

She resumed reading the article:

> *"During an initial, cursory search, a team of FBI Cyber experts were able to restore a trove of deleted computer searches and condemnatory information from the suspect's laptop. These included security blueprints for the museum, details of other major art heists, and criminal networks known for using stolen art as collateral in drug deals. It is assumed that O'Roydon planned to use the stolen Rembrandt as leverage in an illegal drug deal."*

"Way to go, Artemis," Lorelei pumped the air with her fist, "way to catch that salacious snake in your trap."

> *"Evidence overwhelmingly points to the fact that O'Roydon had planned the heist and intended to flee justice. Forensic investigators discovered a recent offshore bank account created in Joseph O'Roydon's name, allegedly funded with more than $200,000 he had illegally transferred from his daughter's trust account. Purchase records revealed two, one-way airline tickets*

to Bermuda—one in Joseph O'Roydon's name, and the other in his minor daughter's name—which further corroborate his intent to flee and abduct his child.

LAPD Chief Barnham has issued a statement expressing his shock and disappointment in the arrest of one of his former detectives, referring to him as "the one rotten apple in a bunch of good cops." Ex-colleagues of the accused testified to O'Roydon's downward spiral into erratic and aggressive behavior. Many were privy to the suspect's abuse of alcohol and narcotics and testified that he showed them "nudie pics" of Mrs. O'Roydon. FBI agents found these compromising photographs, among other pornographic imagery, on a USB flash drive in the suspect's secret lock-b—"

"Argh, that bastard!" Luke growled, shielding his face in his hands. "Poor Shivvy ..."

"Joe O'Roydon will *never* have the opportunity to harm her, or anyone else ... ever again," Angel said. "He's dug much of this grave for himself. All we did was give him a final little heave-ho."

Lorelei recalled her split-second of hotheaded impulse at the top of the staircase that day in the museum, her overwhelming compulsion to "help" Joe down the stairs. Any sliver of guilt she had felt for framing him rolled from her shoulders like the foamy white seahorses dipping backward from the tips of the waves. Eager to hear the rest, she took the paper from Angel's hands and continued reading:

"The FBI and LAPD will cooperate as the investigation continues. Mr. O'Roydon has been remanded to the Los Angeles County Men's Central Jail where he will remain pending further investigation. Due to his status as an ex-undercover officer, he will be isolated from the general population of inmates and remain in solitary confinement for the foreseeable future.

The accused's spouse has requested FBI protection for the duration of the trial, as well as post-trial witness protection for herself and her minor child, citing multiple death threats against them by her husband. Her attorney has filed for an emergency ex parte divorce, seeking sole custody on behalf of his client.

While a credible suspect is in custody, the whereabouts of the beloved masterpiece are still unknown. Baroque curator and Dutch Golden Age expert, Dr. Saskia van Trummel, Ph.D., has expressed urgent concern and testified to "sleepless nights," stating "the museum's loss is humanity's loss, too."

An initial trial date is scheduled for September. In the interim, anyone with knowledge of the location of the missing Rembrandt is encouraged to reach out to their local LAPD tipline or contact Special Agent Jamisson at the Los Angeles FBI branch. There is a $250,000 reward for its safe return.

No questions asked."

"Holy shit!" Lorelei lowered the newspaper and reached for a cheese-and-pickle cocktail skewer from the platter. "Two hundred and fifty thousand dollars? Man, I could plug a bunch of medical holes with that much green," she mused.

"And I could pay for grad school," Luke added wistfully.

Angel smiled at them, thinking of the risks they had all taken ... for no personal benefit. "I know," she said, "but we didn't do this for profit. We did it to save our friend and her child from a monster. In that regard, we all won the freaking lottery."

"Good riddance to bad rubbish," Lorelei said.

"Ay-men!" Luke cheered, both arms flung overhead, followed by one of his famous Anderson Cooper giggling fits. He did not even realize that it was the first "amen" to pass over his lips since his escape from the overzealous, toxic farmhouse of his youth.

Angel relished the sweet taste of justice.

Take that, Joe, she thought. *Take that, every man who ever dared to lay a hand on a defenseless woman or child. And take that, FBI Special Agent Colt Jamisson, for considering me past my prime.*

The heist of the Olympians had been a worthwhile risk with a charitable outcome. But it had done so much more for each of them. It forced them out of complacency to confront their darkest demons and stare them down, being the last to blink in the staring game of life. Angel tried to conjure up an image of her three-headed bayou monster in a darkened back alley, but try as she might, it had faded into blessed nothingness.

"I just hope Shivvy is okay," she said, "and that my docent bag is still in Locker #13 when the museum reopens tomorrow."

She hated dampening their mood, but it was her duty to keep the war helmet on until all the troops were safely back at the base. The missing painting was like the frayed end of a severed electrical line whipping around in an ice storm, threatening to electrocute anyone within reach.

"Why, thank you, Debbie Downer, for that generous dose of ice-cold reality," Luke grumbled. He watched intently while an olive slid over the newspaper—smudging its surface with oily globs of fat oozing from slices of sun-warmed salami—and came to rest underneath the words "a sole suspect."

But his was not the only pair of eyes on the runaway olive. Close by, a cocky seagull and its mate squawked and surreptitiously inched closer to the rainbow umbrella, their beady eyes zeroed in on the feast, their bodies primed to dive-bomb the snack platter at the slightest hint of inattentiveness.

"Can we forget about the painting in the locker for now and just celebrate our hard-earned victory?" Lorelei asked, hoisting the bottle of champagne. It was not chilled, but that was irrelevant; they would toast with plastic cups of seawater if that's what it came to. Not waiting for an answer, she angled the bottle away from her body and depressed the cork with both thumbs.

"Wait," Luke held up his hand, putting a temporary halt to the bacchanals, "we can't do this without Shivvy, Olympians. I wonder where she is ..."

Inside the austere, cold shell of the Los Angeles County Men's Central Jail, Shivonne felt an icy shiver blow over her shoulders. But it was not the frigid breath of an ill-meaning entity this time; it was just a harmless gust of air from the single-blade fan mounted above the table where she sat, waiting for an audience with her husband: Prisoner # 61316.

The clang of keys in the heavy metal door made her whip her head around. A guard accompanied Joe inside, unlocked one of his cuffs, and resecured it to a heavy-gauge steel screw-eye fastened to the surface of the metal table separating them. She noticed Joe had a chain shackling his ankles as well; it made her breathe a little easier.

His skin looked jaundiced in the orange jumpsuit, with white socks pushed into shapeless beige shower sandals. It was a far cry from Suave Joe, he of the argyle socks and sharp-pointed Oxfords. The unmistakable opening chords of opioid withdrawal lay shallow in his sunken and bloodshot eyes. They were staring right through her, biding their time until the guard left.

She braced herself.

"Ten minutes, inmate," the guard barked and—with a quizzical side-eye at the beautiful woman visiting the criminal—departed through the heavy door.

The second it clanged shut, Joe lunged forward over the table with such startling speed, he would have head-butted Shivonne had she not recoiled in time. His face stopped short inches from hers—so close she could smell his anger. Breathe its stench.

"*You* did this to me, didn't you, Shiv?" he hissed, stabbing her with his eyes for lack of an alternative. "You set me up!"

Behind Shivonne's flustered façade, Artemis stood her ground with her hands on her hips and her legs astride in a superhero pose. Confident and a little cocky.

You don't have to fear him anymore, Shivonne. Show him that.

"You did this to *yourself*, Joe. I had nothing to do with it. I didn't even know they suspended you from the police department. You must have been embroiled in serious *shite* for the LAPD to do that." She had rehearsed her response, tinting surprise and shock with underlying suspicion.

"I ... did ... *not* ... steal ... that ... goddamn ... painting!" he shouted, banging out the syllables on the metal table. "Yes, I took your key card and followed you to the museum. Yes, I bumped into some pussy-assed guard outside that gallery, but I was there to find *you*, Shiv. Okay?" He flopped back into his chair and ran his free hand through his greasy hair. "God knows, if I didn't know firsthand how fucking useless you are, I would be *convinced* you were behind this."

She flashed him a vacant, "good bitch" expression to solidify his impression of her as a helpless, hapless vessel.

If only you knew, Joe. If only you knew.

"You were extremely drunk that day," she said, "and we both know the horrible things you do when blustered, with no memory of it the next day. Fitzi in the hallway, me on the kitchen counter, your gun to my head ... Terrible things, Joe."

She sensed that Artemis's arrow had hit a sensitive spot. Despite his denial, Joe knew he was a blackout drunk, addict, and abuser. A hand grenade with its pin pulled, gripped inside a sweaty palm. The realization was all over his face; she could see the gears turning, the muscles contorting and releasing. What she could not see, however, was the swarm of murder hornets twitching inside his head.

"If it wasn't you, then who did this to me?" he questioned, his resolve wavering.

Shivonne shrugged. "How should I know, Joe? From the sound of it, you've made a ton of enemies—those 'powerful cartel honchos' you bragged about, remember? Or people you've been double-crossing or stealing drugs from?" She hesitated and then she said it, with a little shove from Artemis, "Perhaps it was 'A,' for Anonymous?"

That taunt was the final swing of the baseball bat against Joe's *piñata*, full of crazed stingers. Restless even before the hit, they exploded into a black swarm and propelled Joe forward once more. A bullet from a hot barrel. The grinding of handcuffs across metal reminded her of the night when she had cuffed him to the coffee table—the night she took the reins of her own destiny.

"Get out, you ungrateful bitch," he screamed. "Get the fuck out!"

It took every ounce of Artemis's courage for Shivonne not to flinch when he slammed the table, but she held her pose, unmoving and unblinking, on her chair.

"Oh, don't you worry, Joey," she replied, dangling his much-hated little-boy name in her heaviest Irish accent, "I *am* getting out ... for good, this time. But you?" She rose from her chair on steady legs, graceful as if choreographed by Balanchine—the swan once cursed by the evil sorcerer, resurrected from its death, and floating up in a cloud of white down above the dark lake of misery it had been drowning in. "You're *staying* ... behind a lock with no key."

Her hand slid forward on the table, and when she lifted it, a silver object gleamed on the cold surface. A padlock. From the necklace Joe had locked around her neck when he was still free to claim her and control her. The padlock's swing arm had been painstakingly sawn through with a metalsmith's micro-blade, in the skillful hands of a protector chef, with the beautiful woman's neck arched back in his lap like a swan's.

Joe stared at it with his head cocked, struggling at first to connect the dots. By the time he recognized the padlock for what it was, Shivonne had disappeared through the cell door, and out of his life. He exploded in a fresh wave of rage and swept the padlock from the table with a guttural roar, making such a racket that it took two burly guards to wrestle him down with his cheek to the linoleum. From that vantage point, he had an unobstructed view of the broken padlock lying on the floor of the visitation room, in a pile of grime and spit—exactly where it belonged.

"Shiv!" Joe screamed at the fortified door. "Shiv, you bitch," he screamed as he was hog-tied and dragged down the long, cold corridor to his solitary cell. "Shiv! Shiv! ... Shiiiiiivvv!"

Shivonne heard him scream from behind multiple layers of freedom, slamming shut between her and the dragon. "Shiv"—that cursed name that sounded and felt like a prison shank—a sharpened toothbrush, its handle wrapped in duct tape.

"*Aye,*" she said as she walked away, "be careful what you wish for in a notorious prison, Joe."

At the beach, Shivonne stepped out of her car and let the cool ocean breeze run its salty fingers through her hair. She inhaled it deeply, and her eyes scrunched up with pleasure. It smelled sweeter that day, somehow—the smell of liberation. She navigated the shallow rock pools, gripping smooth stones with her toes so as not to slip on patches of moss, one hand outstretched toward the sheer cliff face. Her footprints followed her through the wet sand by the water's edge.

Toe-heel, toe-heel, toe-heel.

They were lounging under a rainbow umbrella—her three rescuers—mortals deserving of godly status. Lorelei was hoisting a bottle of champagne the way Demeter proffered her sheaf of wheat in the Boboli Gardens of Florence. Luke was wrestling to restrain her; Angel's shoulders were shaking with laughter.

"Hey," Shivonne called out, "what about me?"

Beaming, she strolled toward them, looking like a goddess in a lacy sun-dress, her coppery-gold curls bouncing off her shoulders—untucked and unharnessed—her strappy Artemis sandals dangling from one hand.

"Shivvyyy!" they cried out, and it sounded like angels rejoicing to Shivonne—the perfect antidote to Joe's venomous version. Sprinting toward each other, they sprayed golden sand outward like sun rays. Not far from the crest of Mount Olympus where a stolen painting lay waiting in Lucky Locker #13, they piled on top of each other in a frenzy of unbridled joy, their laughter bouncing between the rocks and echoing through the canyon that dipped its cleavage behind the cove, deep into the Santa Monica mountains.

On the horizon, as the good tide rolled in over the azure blue of the late afternoon sea, Apollo stabled his golden chariot for the night, and dragged the remainder of the daylight behind his rowboat—in broad strokes of amber and rose over the platinum waves—just as Monet would have painted it.

And on the beach, behind the backs of the overjoyed mortals dancing like muses on the sand, the Bonnie and Clyde of seagulls swooped in under the rainbow umbrella and plucked feverishly at the bounty, ripping up large pieces of the newspaper with its breaking-news headline.

Up, up, and away, they carried their heist into the open skies, where Artemis would soon rise for another night of hunting under the crescent moon.

EPILOGUE

T wo years later ...

The muted light from an Emeralite banker's lamp cast a sickly green glow on Special Agent Colt Jamisson's face. It matched his frame of mind perfectly. It was 4 a.m. on another moonless, fruitless night and he was still hunched over his desk at the Federal Building on Wilshire Boulevard. His fingers danced a nervous jitterbug on a folder labeled "Pallas Heist," the case that had consumed him for the past two years. The bull was roped and subdued—castrated, for all intents and purposes—but the prize continued to elude him. The painting was still missing; O'Roydon refused to give up its whereabouts, insisting he was set up. O'Roydon was a scumbag, but Colt had a niggling clue he was missing something. He had felt it in his rodeo hip from the very first night when the ghost of Rembrandt's face was still burning against the gallery wall.

"X never marks the spot," he grumbled, quoting his idol, Indiana Jones.

For the umpteenth time, he started the crime scene recording on his laptop and watched the cocky thief stride into the gallery, grab the painting from the wall, and slip it under his jacket. A move so simple, yet so infuriatingly bold. He paused the recording, as he had done so many times since that day to scrutinize the elusive shimmer taunting him from underneath the thief's jacket. This time, as he did so, his reading spectacles slipped down his nose, prompting him to push them back up with his middle finger. It was an unremarkable, subconscious gesture were it not for the fact that—as the Fates would have it—the art thief on his computer

309

screen executed the *identical* maneuver at exactly the same time, sliding *his* middle finger up over his mask as if pushing non-existent eyeglasses higher. Colt froze.

Holy-shit-what-was-that?

He pressed "rewind," then "play," then again ... and again. Up and down, the finger slid. A middle finger, to add insult to injury.

"He's just flipping off the cameras, Colt. Deriding you," he muttered to himself. But his trusty old hip injury spoke otherwise, so he skipped the recording back to when Joe O'Roydon first entered the gallery and saw him repeat the gesture there, as well.

"You've got to be kidding me." Colt rubbed his aching hip the way a cowboy nuzzled his horse.

Perhaps he wore contacts on the day of the heist?

But Colt knew from the biometric stats in the manila folder that Joseph O'Roydon had 20/20 vision. This had to be it: the clue he had missed. Whoever stole the Rembrandt two years earlier must have been a wearer of corrective glasses ... with a habit of pushing them back up his nose. And even if it were merely a nervous tic, he had never seen Joe O'Roydon do it during the dozens of jailhouse interviews over the past two years. It meant there was a possibility that O'Roydon was *not* his art thief. It meant it was time for another round of ropin' and ridin'. And *this* time, Colt was certain, he would get his hands on the elusive painting. The ultimate prize of his career.

"Yee-haw!" he exclaimed exuberantly, slamming his fist so hard on his desk it scared the bejeezus out of the poor janitor who had chosen that unfortunate moment to enter the office, mop in hand.

Later that day, almost 6000 miles away in the Périgord region of France, the sun was about to dip behind an 18th-century *petit château* nestled among mature oaks and chestnut trees on the banks of the Dordogne River. Behind a wrought-iron gate cloaked in wisteria, Château La Chouette stood in all its splendor, its periwinkle-blue peacock shutters flung open against the golden native stone. The irony of its name—French for "female owl"—meant it was the perfect home for a goddess of wisdom.

Inside its Grand Salon, the four Olympians were gathered for the first time since their destinies had scattered them far and wide, a year or so earlier. Lorelei and her family had moved back to their quaint Victorian nestled behind the three churches in Mahone Bay, Nova Scotia. She was in her element there—as befell a goddess of nature—providing herbal remedies and hosting meditative sound baths for weary clients suspended in hammocks strung between balsam firs. Grace, too, was thriving in the slower pace and ocean air, regaining her strength through equine therapy and her mother's healing hands.

Shivonne and Riley were living *la Pura Vida* in Costa Rica with Cristian, in a cabin just a stroll from their beach-front champagne-and-oyster bar, FITZI'S. It was as far away as Shivonne could get from Joe, who still occasionally mailed her poison letters via her lawyer. She taught ballet classes for little swans and volunteered at a halfway house for battered women and children.

Luke was the only one who had stayed behind in the City of Angels to finish his master's degree in art therapy with a thesis titled, "Art as a Therapeutic Tool for the Treatment of Adolescent Trauma." He still led school tours at the Pallas Museum—for the love of art and teaching, but also drawn to the halo of light from his Apollo.

Angel had settled the farthest away, in the beautiful manor house near Sarlat-la-Canéda. She and Deacon had amicably separated a few months following the heist and, soon after, Walter invited her to meet him in the French gallery. She found him there, paying homage to the *Still Life with Silver Teapot and Narcissus,* alongside his very dashing—and very single—son, Jean-François, visiting from France. She had a sneaky suspicion Walter had engineered that first meeting as a blind date, setting up his favorite docent with his only son.

With the approval of the Fates, as it turned out.

Before year's end, they had fallen in love and she relocated to Jean's country home in France, leaving behind her black dog of depression in favor of the estate's two resident peacocks, Romulus, and Remus. There, she managed the property's four rental *gîtes* while Jean-François commuted to his art restoration shop in Paris. In her free time, she was writing a novel—a middle-aged woman, who had once stepped into the guise of a goddess of war to save a friend from the clutches of a dragon, had much to write about.

And so, at last, on that cool June evening, the four brave Olympians were reunited in the wood-paneled salon of Château La Chouette, huddled in front of a splendid stone fireplace. They had come to France to celebrate their Athena's 55th birthday and spend two glorious weeks exploring the Dordogne: land of 1001 castles. That was the plan ... or so they thought.

Athena had a different agenda.

"*Bienvenue,* Olympians," Angel said, welcoming them officially. All eyes in the room—including those of the stodgy ancestors against the powder-blue *boiserie*—watched with ceremonial awe as she uncorked a bottle of La Chouette's home-distilled pear brandy, her fingers caressing the label.

"What's that then?" Lorelei asked, craning her neck to gawk at the bottle label.

"Funny you should ask ..." Angel grinned, and passed the curvy bottle around for closer inspection.

On the label, against a background of deep crimson-red drapery, four silhouetted figures stood in a semi-circle around a gilt cup, each one bearing the mark of Greek divinity. One silhouette had an owl perched on her shoulder, another held a sheaf of wheat in the crook of her arm, and the third clutched a strung bow at her side, her hair fanning out like a halo over her shoulders. The only male silhouette sported two perky wings—like tail fins on a vintage Cadillac—sprouting from his bare feet.

"Holy shitballs," Luke exclaimed with a giggle, "it's us!" When he hoisted the bottle to the crystal chandelier for a better look, the diffused light danced across a tattoo of Hermes' *caduceus* staff inked on his inner wrist, the coiling of the twin snakes craftily disguising the horizontal cutting scars underneath. Amused, he passed the bottle to Shivonne.

"Wow," she said, using her favorite magic palindrome that evoked the unfurling of once-evasive freedom.

"It's an *eau de vie*," Angel said, passing out tulip flutes of golden nectar. "We call it *Ambrosia of the Gods*."

Olympus would have approved.

Lorelei raised her glass. "To Angel on her milestone birthday," she said.

"And to those four brave Olympians on the label," Shivonne added. "They were phenomenal."

"They still *are*," Luke corrected with a wink.

"And they will be ... *again*," Angel said without missing a beat.

The smile slowly melted from Luke's face. "Say what?" He swiveled his gaze to the other two.

Angel cleared her throat and Lorelei felt the hair rise on the back of her neck. *Uh-oh.* Whenever Angel did that, it meant Athena had something to say—something that would create a ripple of no uncertain consequence. Lorelei sank back into her overstuffed Bergère armchair. "Go on, spit it out," she sighed.

"Okay," Angel said. "I have another task for the Olympians ... another Robin Hood heist to right a terrible wrong."

Outside the château walls, a peacock honked as if on cue.

"You've got to be shitting us," Luke murmured, rising from the Lelièvre-smocked velvet sofa in a huff. "Is that why we're here? I can't believe you would d—"

"Sit down, Luke," Shivonne said with authority. Though they all shared the instant dreaded sense of déjà vu, she was no longer afraid. The last heist had changed her life; *saved* it, most certainly. "Tell us," she said to Angel.

"I will explain it all, tomorrow ... in detail," Angel said, wetting her finger and running it around the rim of her glass. Round and round, like the ouroboros. The most beautiful angelic sound rang from the crystal.

"My father always said, 'The devil is in the details,'" Luke said, mesmerized by the hypnotic tone.

"Your father *was* the devil, Luke," Lorelei reminded him. Angel stopped playing her glass harp.

Shivonne stared deep into the fire. "No devil stands a chance against an Angel and her team of Olympian gods," she whispered.

313

"And that's exactly what this next heist is all about," Angel said, touching the brooch pinned to her blazer—a Narcissus flower bent over in grief. "It's a devastating story ..."

A tiny seed, planted two years earlier in front of a painted tea set, had since germinated into a full-blown game plan. She thought of the silver-haired security guard holding an imaginary teacup with tears in his eyes. Of the Nazi-looted painting that was currently displayed in Paris, on the French leg of its exhibit tour. Time was running out for Walter, who was battling stage IV congestive heart failure, his broken heart finally, physically, breaking apart.

The house was momentarily quiet but for the creaking of centuries-old wood joints.

"What about the Rembrandt?" Lorelei asked. "I thought we were going to return it to the Pallas, somehow, once the charges against Joe stuck?"

"That's still the plan," Angel said, "but first, it might play a crucial part in our next heist."

"Where is he?" Luke asked. "Which bank vault do you have him locked up in?" The talk of devils had triggered his memory of facing the oil-painted man wearing his father's face.

Angel placed her glass on the fireplace mantel, where the framed oil portrait of a sultry nude leaned against the mercury glass mirror. Pandora had once graced the underside of an antique painter's box; now she occupied a place of honor in the Grand Salon of Château La Chouette. Angel gripped its beveled frame and, in one swift movement—a reversal trick not dissimilar from Luke's ingenious inside-out jacket—flipped the painting over so the back of it faced the room.

From its clandestine hiding place secured to the back of Pandora's nude, Rembrandt's self-portrait stared back at them. He had been there all along, eavesdropping on the conversation, waiting patiently to make a grand entrance.

Somewhere, in the depths of the manor house, a longcase musical clock chimed several times in steady, metronomic tintinnabulations, as if announcing the great reveal.

Lorelei made the sign of the cross; Luke—who did not see a single hint of his father's ghost in the face of the laughing man—grinned and pushed his eyeglasses higher up the bridge of his nose. And Shivonne tucked a lock of hair behind her ear with a serene smile. Angel regarded her team, her scalp tingling with excitement underneath Athena's silver-white helmet. Planning ... scheming. She picked up her glass and raised it.

"Olympians!"

"Olympians!" they toasted and clinked their glasses.

The log fire enthusiastically crackled its applause as the four friends threw back their heads and let the golden nectar trickle down their throats. From his perch above the fireplace, the laughing man gazed down at them.

"Nothing but ambrosia for hungry gods and goddesses," he seemed to say.

Firelight refracted from their crystal glasses and cast a golden halo around their faces. For a moment, they lit up like Grecian gods immortalized on a priceless amphora vase.

THE END

Afterword

Dear Reader,

As you close the final pages of this book, I want to thank you for embarking on this journey with my characters. I hope it provided not just entertainment but a glimpse into the resilience and strength of those navigating these difficulties. I want to extend a lifeline to anyone who resonated with the themes portrayed, whether it be domestic abuse, depression, PTSD, or LGBTQ+ concerns. Please know that you are not alone; there is help available. At the time of print, the following resources were live 24/7 and confidential:

National Hotlines (US only):

- **National Domestic Violence Hotline:** 1-800-799-SAFE (7233) or text START to 88788

- **The Trevor Project** (LGBTQ+ help and resources): 1-866-488-7386 or text START to 678678

- **Crisis Text Line** (any crisis/emotional distress): text HOME to 741741

For my international readers, local resources and hotlines may vary, but similar support networks are available worldwide.

With warmth and solidarity,
A. Young-Irving

ACKNOWLEDGEMENTS

The plot for *HEIST of the OLYMPIANS* first revealed itself to me during a lively docent book discussion on the topic of Art Crime. I vividly recall wondering: *How would a museum docent like me steal art?* And, more importantly, *Why would someone risk it all for such an audacious folly?*

"I think I might write a novel about this concept," I remember announcing at that meeting. And now, dear Reader, you hold the fruit grown from that tiny thought seed in your hands. Thank you for allowing me to take you on this rollercoaster ride with me.

I am deeply indebted to my loved ones who championed me on this personal Odyssey: my husband Robert, who was my sounding board on our long walks, brought me endless cups of coffee, and boldly offered to reduce swaths of my verbose writing with a single stroke of his red accountant's Sharpie. And to my beautiful, brilliant, and compassionate children, Annik and Richard, who graciously read several drafts, offering brilliant input from a younger reader's POV. I could not have done this without your support. This book is for you.

I am enormously grateful to my parents (in South Africa), Richard and Tokkie Young, both passionate, lifelong educators who instilled a love of learning and a yearning for global adventure in me from an early age. I owe my love for classical art to my mother, who exposed me to whichever theater production or art exhibit was in limited supply during the 1980s in South Africa, and my passion for opera and classical music to my father, whose angelic voice will resonate within me long after he earns his permanent wings. *Ek is oneindig lief vir julle!*

To my sister, Nicola T. in Luxembourg, thank you, from the bottom of my heart, for the much-needed praise and constant encouragement, your keen editing eye, and gut-checking feedback. *Mwah!*

Much appreciation and praise go out to my Ideal Reader/editor-par-excellence, Christy F., who edited earlier versions of my book, offered sound advice, and encouraged me to use profanity (when I hesitated) by emphatically stating, "I'm an adult; I want to read f@*#ing adult words!"

Many thanks, as well, to my list of fabulous beta readers (in alphabetical, first-name order): Anne-Rita T., Dominique M., Duane C., Gorman B., Hayden S., Heidi C., Kimberly S., Lara C., Liz S., Michael M., and Nicola C. Your stellar IQ and EQ are why I asked for your feedback; you did not disappoint.

I'm also grateful to Francesca W. for their keen editor's eye during the final proofreading of my novel, and to Brian B. and Todd S., for offering graphic design tips while I finetuned my cover design.

A special note of gratitude goes out to Simon Goodman—author of *The Orpheus Clock: The Search for My Family's Art Treasures Stolen by the Nazis*—for your mentorship, inspiring me with your incredible story, and allowing me to assist you in your ongoing fight for restitution.

Thank you to my "tribe" of fellow museum nerds and book-group clan, for the owl-like stimulation and knowledge I glean from you whenever I am in your company. I am deeply appreciative of the supportive community and friendship (not to forget the great coffee and Argentinian treats) at my office-away-from-home, Tortoni Caffe, in Sherman Oaks. And *muchos besos* to Claudia (and my dance crew) at Danzmundo, for the Latin dance therapy that keeps me on my toes ... literally and figuratively. *Olé!*

Last, but not least, to my beloved husky-malamute fur babies, Bowie, and Roxy, thank you for keeping my mind sane, my feet warm ... and my heart fuzzy. I *woof* you!

ABOUT THE AUTHOR

A. Young-Irving is an author, art nerd, world traveler, global dance enthusiast, and lover of all things classical, caffeinated, and canine. Born and raised in South Africa, she has lived in Amsterdam but calls Los Angeles home ... for now. She dreams of retiring to an 18th-century *petit château* in the French countryside.

Proficient in five languages, she has worked as a magazine journalist and editor, a crisis counselor, and a museum educator, guiding students in the art of *Look, See, and Wonder*. She also works as a freelance art researcher and translator to the heir of a Nazi-looted art fortune, assisting him in his ongoing fight for restitution.

She has incorporated her experience in Art Education and Art Crime into her debut novel, *Heist of the Olympians*.

A second, international art heist for the beloved team of pseudo-Olympians is currently pirouetting on her mind's stage.

To see what mischief she's up to, follow her at:
https://www.ayoungirvingauthor.com/

Made in the USA
Las Vegas, NV
29 January 2024

85084743R00194